The Punished
A Novel by
Peter Meredith

Peter Meredith

Copyright 2012 Peter Meredith
Kindle Edition
ISBN-13: 978-0983707226

Fictional works by Peter Meredith:

A Perfect America
The Sacrificial Daughter
The Horror of the Shade Trilogy of the Void 1
An Illusion of Hell Trilogy of the Void 2
Hell Blade Trilogy of the Void 3
The Punished
Sprite
The Feylands: A Hidden Lands Novel
The Sun King: A Hidden Lands Novel
The Sun Queen: A Hidden Lands Novel
The Apocalypse: The Undead World Novel 1
The Apocalypse Survivors: The Undead World Novel 2
The Apocalypse Outcasts: The Undead World Novel 3
The Apocalypse Fugitives: The Undead World Novel 4
Pen(Novella)
A Sliver of Perfection (Novella)
The Haunting At Red Feathers(Short Story)
The Haunting On Colonel's Row(Short Story)
The Drawer(Short Story)
The Eyes in the Storm(Short Story)

Chapter 1

The Thief

1

The home, from its tall red brick exterior with its great shading trees to the wonderful white walls and gleaming hardwood floors of the interior, could only be called beautiful or maybe elegant. However, the air had an odd, stiff feeling about it...a Nazi feel.

Books were aligned with precision on the shelves, pictures hung on the walls with an engineer's exactness, and even the furniture looked to have been arranged as if in preparation for a parade. Not a single mote of dust strayed upon any of the surfaces, and the glass of the windows showed not a streak, nor even a solitary fingerprint.

Everything looked far too clean, far too perfect, at least to twelve-year-old Curtis Regis, but not to Miss Gladys. Her large brown eyes took in the cleanliness and the order, seeing only an idealized suburban home, missing the truth.

Though generally quite astute, Curt missed the truth as well.

He was in too much of a state of shock and after a brief glance around at the home could only stare at the pristine, almost snow-colored square carpet that sat in the middle of the room. It looked practically brand new and before stepping off the hardwood floors Miss Gladys directed him to remove his shoes.

This he did, placing his stolen Converse sneakers neatly next to Miss Gladys' giant pink high heels. She stood as big as a house and like one she was trimmed around the edges. Her nails, her shoes, her lips, even the ribbon in her hair were all pink and a garish pink at that. The rest of her outfit, a great ballooning pantsuit, was a chocolate brown.

Curt didn't think that the brown went well with the pink, but it certainly matched her skin tone. She was a commanding black woman and filled the room with her presence. He felt like a mouse next to her, and though she hadn't been anything but nice, Curt was thoroughly intimidated by her.

This was the reason he had smoothed down his wild curly brown hair and had sat up as straight as he could during the car ride through the suburbs of Pittsburgh, to his new, but very temporary foster home.

"Curtis Regis," Miss Gladys announced in a big voice. "I would like you to meet Miss Feanor, your new foster mother."

Earlier that day, Curt had been punched twice, *where the bruises wouldn't show*, which turned out to be just above his left temple, and he had a doozy of a headache. Yet despite that, he still managed to smile up at the lady. Miss Feanor, on the other hand wasn't smiling at all. She wore a look of shock, which she laced heavily with revulsion.

He looked down to see what had her so worked up and noticed that his socks were dirty. At one point they probably had been white, but now they were such a dark grey as to rival his black converse. With the right one being the darker of the two, he timidly stuck it behind his left calf.

"Oh my! Is that your feet I smell?" Miss Gladys had her face wrinkled in resemblance of a prune. "Oh my!" She was quite loud. Everything about her was loud. Her volume seemed to make Miss Feanor cringe, and with his head thumping the way it was, Curt was right there with her.

"I...uh, haven't had time to get to the laundromat this week," he explained. Lying came second nature to him; he hadn't ever been to a laundromat to clean clothes, only to steal them. It was a fine place to pick up a spare outfit.

Miss Feanor acted as though she hadn't heard him and could seem to do little but stare at his feet. Her muddy brown eyes were huge and uncomprehending as if she had never seen dirty socks before. There was something else in those eyes that caught his attention.

Fear. She seemed actually afraid that he would make tracks on her perfect carpet.

Fear did not sit well on her features, even this silly fear of his dirty feet made her look older. With her hair a nearly equal proportion of grey and brown and her face lined with deep groves, he put her age at fifty-five. Normally he was quite accurate at this sort of thing, but he would be very surprised to find out later that he was off by fifteen years.

"Matt, go fetch a pair of clean socks," she ordered. Her voice sounded old as well, soft and quiet, dusty even, as if she wasn't use to speaking often.

Four teenagers, two boys and two girls, had been staring at him in tight-lipped silence and now the tallest of them, a boy with thin brown hair hurried off, disappearing down a hallway. They were not a very impressive or scary group; each was skinny and pale, and in Curt's opinion they wore the oddest outfits. Each had on blue jeans and white, white socks. This was ok he guessed, but their matching long sleeve, slate grey turtlenecks were downright strange.

He hoped they weren't expecting him to wear a turtleneck as well—they were ghastly.

Since he had entered the home Curt had snatched an occasional peek at the other kids and he really only expected trouble from Matt, who due to his size he suspected of being the eldest.

Matt had a look about him that made Curt think of the word Nazi again. Before he had been sent on his errand, Matt had stared at Curt's socks as well, and seemed just as appalled as Miss Feanor, though he hadn't shared in her fear. Rather, his look was tinged with haughty contempt, and in the brief few seconds that they were in the room together Curt had found himself judged. He didn't mind, however—whatever nasty thoughts Matt had about him were probably correct.

Finally pulling her eyes off of his socks, Miss Feanor looked him up and down. "Paul, have Matt fetch an entire change of clothes, please," she said, again in a low voice. Curt noted that the word *please* had a special quality to it. It was clear that it wasn't a word that frequented her lips; she even paused before using it as if to remember its definition.

Miss Gladys didn't notice this. Her eyes were on the two girls in the room. She beamed at them, purposely not paying attention to how Miss Feanor looked to have swallowed something nasty. Perhaps she was embarrassed at having brought Curt in such a condition.

He was secretly glad that she had. The chaos of Curt's life had made it a necessity that he assess people quickly, and many times he did this based on only the barest of information. His gut told him that Miss Feanor would be a hard one to hustle and coming to her door looking like an abused puppy was a happy accident.

He went with it.

Casting his face into a mold of sorrowful embarrassment, he said, "I'm sorry about my clothes. Ever since my mom left me all alone, I haven't been able to keep anything clean." He darted his eyes to her face every second or two as if he was used to being beaten; in truth he did this in order to check for the proper signs of concern.

Her face registered none of these signs. Her mouth didn't come open and her eyes failed to widen. Her hands didn't reach out to touch the wretched child in front of her, and worst of all she didn't say, "Ooh, poor thing."

Instead, her lips, already set together, tightened so that he could see many tiny lines emanating from them. Worse were her eyes. It didn't appear that she had seen through his charade; instead it looked as if she couldn't care in the least.

This wasn't a new thing for Curt. As a seasoned panhandler he had seen it before, many times. In fact, for every dollar he stuck in his pocket from the gullible, he had to endure a dozen or more of such looks. Normally, he would go on to the next person as quickly as possible, knowing that begging was a numbers game. However, in this situation he couldn't move on so easily, nor did he want to.

The home, despite its Nazi-like perfection, was a very nice one and he felt this would be a good place to rest up for a bit before he got back to his life. He'd allow Miss Feanor to fatten him up somewhat, to clothe him, and get him new school supplies since all of his stolen ones had been confiscated. Only then would he leave.

"Do you have anything I can eat?" he asked. "I don't remember the last time I had a proper meal." He placed his hands on his stomach for emphasis. This move was a guarantee with women; it had never once failed to elicit a motherly reaction.

Except for now.

Miss Feanor's eyes narrowed and he saw that within them were innumerable calculations. Instinctually, he knew she wanted to tell him no, but instead she gave him a wintry smile.

"Let's get you dressed properly first." She held him with her eyes and he decided she would be even harder to hustle than he first thought. Just then Matt and Paul came back into the living room. Without a word to anyone they handed the clothes, socks, jeans and a vile grey turtleneck to Miss Feanor, and she handed the socks to Curt.

When he had slipped them on Miss Gladys' eyes went to squints, "Wow, those stink to high heaven. Here, let me put them outside for now." She took the socks, holding them by their very ends, and moved to the door but couldn't open it.

"Does this lock on its own?" she asked Miss Feanor, who hurried forward.

"No, but it does get stuck sometimes," the older woman responded and with ease opened the door. "You just have to know how to work the knob correctly."

Turning back to Curt, she handed him the bundle of clothes and jerked her head toward the hallway. He was about to ask where exactly he should change, but a hand turned him around and Paul nodded his blonde head toward the hallway as well.

Curt paused in confusion; Paul gave him another tug and it was clear that Curt was to follow the boy, which he did walking past the two girls.

The taller of the two looked like nothing more than a five and half foot tall mouse. Her brown eyes were small and protruded slightly from her narrow face. She wore her thin brown hair parted in the middle and hanging straight down. Her stick thin body, she held stiff and nothing about her moved except her eyes. These skimmed over him without pause for thought, or so it seemed to Curt.

The other girl, four inches shorter and roughly his own height, was easily the most colorless person he had ever seen.

Every part of her appeared to have been bleached, even her hair was so blonde that it was practically white. Her eyes had the greatest hint of color. They were a washed-out light blue, only he could barely see them as she kept her head down and her eyes half closed most of the time.

Albino probably, he thought as he passed her, misunderstanding the term. Curt understood little about science and less about math. He should have been in the seventh grade, but the last full grade he had completed had been the second. However, when it came to knowledge, what he lacked scholastically he made up in understanding human nature. For instance it was obvious to him that for some unknown rationale, Miss Feanor didn't want to feed him. At least not yet and that the only reason she had agreed to was that Miss Gladys was present. He made note of that, and as he followed Paul into a long hallway he wondered how he could best use it to his advantage.

However, he had trouble concentrating on this. Paul was clearly afraid of something. As Curt trailed along, he noticed that Paul turned to look back at him as much as he watched where he was going. Perhaps they had been warned about Curt's penchant for stealing, and Paul was just checking to make sure that he wasn't pocketing any of the nice bric-a-brac that sat upon many of the surfaces in the home.

Paul needn't have worried though. The porcelain figurines and fanciful vases were not the sorts of things that Curt would ever likely steal. He had no idea of their value and what's more, they looked highly breakable. Nor would he steal on his first day in a new foster home; that was just stupid. However, if he were to steal anything his primary choice would be silverware and then jewelry or maybe a gaming system if they had one.

These things were portable and he generally knew their market value, or at least he knew what he could get for them. As he looked around he sadly realized there likely wasn't going to be a gaming system in this house and if he had to bet, he would guess they didn't have cable TV either.

The thought depressed him.

"Hey Paul..." he started to ask if there was a Nintendo or PlayStation in the home, but the rest of his sentence caught in his throat as Paul rounded on him with a frightfully angry look on his face. The boy snapped his fingers soundlessly and then held up his hand to his own mouth, making it clear that Curt should be quiet. Struck dumb by the surprising move, Curt just stood there until Paul took a hold of his shirt and dragged him on. A moment later the larger boy turned again giving him a quick look and winked at him.

It was the oddest thing, and so terribly perplexing that Curt barely paid attention to where they were going. The long hallway they were walking down had seven rooms leading off of it; the first had been the living room and catty-corner to that had been a family room. Further down on the left was a bedroom and judging by the size of it he guessed that this was the master bedroom.

The final three doors were at the end of the hall. Straight ahead, lay the kitchen, to the right a dining room, and to the left a small powder room. Paul pointed towards this last with one hand, while the other he kept up to his mouth, demonstrating that Curt still shouldn't speak.

Curt gave him a shoulder shrug and mouthed the word, why. At this Paul began gesticulating trying to tell him something with only his hands, but the movements were too quick, running into themselves, and Curt wasn't able to keep up. He shook his head.

Leaning in so close that his breath tickled Curt's ear, Paul whispered, "She will hear you." Or at least that what he thought Paul had said, the whisper had been just along the low range of his hearing. As the larger boy leaned back, he winked again at Curt.

Curt frowned at him, thinking the boy was either crazy or that he was pulling a prank on the new kid. But Paul missed the frown. He had turned into the bathroom and set the clothes down on the toilet. He then waved his arms again, this time telling Curt not to use the sink.

"Sure. Whatever," Curt said in his normal voice. This game Paul was playing at annoyed him, but since Paul stood a head taller than he, there wasn't much he could do about it. This time Paul didn't get angry at his words. He simply shook his head sadly, winked at him a third time and left the room.

2

The little powder room, like the rest of the house he had seen, looked to have been decorated by, and strictly for, women. There wasn't a thing about the place that could be considered masculine, not that Curt was the most masculine boy, in fact he was one of the least. He was very small for his age and rail thin. His features were somewhat delicate and when his mass of curly hair became wet, it wasn't at all obvious that he was a boy.

He did think it was strange for a house to be decorated in such a girlish manner. Everywhere he looked were figurines of kittens, little pink pillows, and odd containers of sweet smelling dried flowers. The pictures upon the pristine walls were of cherubs or babies or meadows full of flowers and the wallpaper—laced roses in a repeating pattern—was equally as feminine. It seemed over the top. He was starting to think there were a lot of odd things about this house and the people in it.

When he had changed clothes, he looked at himself in his new uniform and could only shake his head, feeling idiotic. For one the clothes were way too big for him and for two, he was wearing a stupid turtleneck! Still mortified at his pathetic attire he left the room and found the hallway happily deserted.

With no one about, Curt decided to see if this foster home was going to be a proper fit for him. On cat's feet, he slipped noiselessly into the kitchen and went straight for the refrigerator. Opening the door, a blast of stale air struck him, and with a single glance into the appliance he knew right away that he would need to find another foster home. The first thing he saw was a jar of prunes and right beside that was another jar holding pickles, and behind these, a glass container of oats or some such with the label reading: Wheat Germ. He had never heard of that before, but it certainly looked as unpalatable as its name. And perhaps the worst thing about the scene before him was the distressingly large amount of vegetables, most of which appeared limp and close to rotting.

The freezer was worse. It was practically empty, with only some ice trays and some ancient Tupperware containers filled with an unknown brown substance. He shook his head in disgust. There was no evidence that a frozen pizza had ever been in there, nor were there any of the TV dinners that he liked.

"Not even a microwave," he whispered, glancing about the room.

The kitchen, like the rest of the place was flawless. The cabinets were all of an oak hue, sporting intricate patterns and gleaming brass handles. The countertops appeared to be marble and fairly shined in brilliance, and the floor was constructed of large grey-blue tiles. And not a single crumb sat anywhere in the room.

There were three doorways in the kitchen. The one to the hall he had just entered through, one to his right that lead up some stairs, and another at the end of the room across from a little eating area. This last was the only one with an actual door and it sat partially open. He stared at this briefly, trying to remember if it had been open when he had first walked in; he hadn't thought it was.

To this, he gave a little snort of puzzlement, but just then his stomach rumbled, and he remembered his purpose to being in the room.

A line of cookbooks sat on the counter to his left and one had a place marked with a paperclip. When he opened the book to that page, Curt saw with a feeling of dread that it was a recipe for goulash, and the horrible picture that accompanied the title made his stomach turn upside down.

If this was the sort ghastly food that was served in the house, he had seen enough, and without checking any of the cabinets for chips, certain there wouldn't be any, he decided that it was time to move on.

3

"Miss Gladys?" he asked a moment later as he re-entered the living room. "May I speak to you in private, please?"

For a street urchin, he had surprisingly good manners; he viewed them as a tool. He found that a properly placed *please* or *excuse me* could work wonders. Of course, there was nothing that would beat a teary-eyed, *thank you* to elicit a second pull from a mark's wallet.

Miss Gladys, however, was not inexperienced at the game. "I'm pretty sure that you're safe to speak in front of your new family members."

"But it's kinda personal."

"We will leave you two alone," Miss Feanor said, and without another word, she and the children left, quietly.

Curt noted this as well and his sense of foreboding increased. He prided himself on his ability to move without making any extraneous noises. It was something that he practiced diligently, since it was life's wish to be a world-class thief. But they, as a group, had been as quiet as he was alone.

Where he had walked slowly, making sure to feel the floor as he did so, they glided. Each never lifted a foot, instead slid on their stockinged feet, however it wasn't a great obvious slide, just a quick movement. This was impressive, at least to him, but again also very odd.

The hushed and subdued nature of the house and its occupants worked on Curt's subconscious. He slipped over to the couch where Miss Gladys sat and said in a voice far lower than his usual quiet one, "I just don't think this will be a good fit. And you know, due to my history, I think it would be better if I was placed in a different home."

"No, I'm sorry," Miss Gladys replied quietly. At least for her it was quiet, but to Curt, who felt as if ears were listening in, the words were loud, they grated on him. She continued on in the same noisome manner, "This is going to be your new home, whether you like it or not."

"But," he floundered, looking for a workable argument. "Don't I have rights? Don't I have a say in any of this?"

Miss Gladys became roused and moved closer to him on the couch, her weight, demonstrating the force of gravity he had seen in science books at school, pulling him in to her.

"There are no other choices. You've burned all your bridges and no one will take you. Now if you would ever stop stealing and running away, that might change."

"Shouldn't you be worried that I'll run away from here..."

"No, I am most certainly not," she replied heatedly, interrupting him. "Miss Feanor is a good foster mom. She's been one for fourteen years and has had over a dozen kids come through here, and according to the paperwork, she has never had a runaway. And if you do run, it'll be Juvenile detention for you next."

Juvenile detention wasn't the terrific fear for him that Miss Gladys thought it to be, at the same time, he wanted to avoid it if at all possible. Like all foster children, he had heard the stories and rumors concerning juvie, fights and bullies, things of this nature, but these were hurdles he faced everyday on the streets. Where he roamed, danger was only a misstep away, yet he was adept at avoiding confrontations when he wished.

The thief in him, however, wanted to test his growing skills against the security of the juvie facility. Over the last year, he had begun attempting low-level B&E jobs on homes and downscale businesses. With his quick mind and even quicker hands, Curt was rapidly becoming an accomplished thief. He was always on the lookout for a good challenge, and when Miss Gladys used the words, *has never had a runaway*, she inadvertently ended any argument from Curt as to whether he'd stay or not.

He nodded his head sadly, disguising the eager machinations of his mind. He'd give Miss Feanor a lesson in running away that she would not soon forget.

Of course, if his caseworker was correct, running this time would certainly end the possibility of foster-care and without it as a winter fallback, he knew he would have to leave the vicinity of Pittsburgh.

He felt a pang of guilt or perhaps it was sorrow at the thought of leaving the city where his mom lived. Still it was only a slight pang, and he offered Miss Gladys a small shrug indicating he would prefer to stay in the foster home, rather than go to Juvie. She patted his knee and gave him a warm smile, happy that he came to the right decision. After struggling her bulk off the couch, she crossed to the doorway, her great weight sending vibrations throughout the room, and called down the hallway.

"Miss Feanor?" Her words were very loud; they disturbed the still air of the house, setting him further on edge. She continued, "I have some paperwork that needs signatures."

There was near silence from the hall, but now that Curt knew about the sliding, he cocked an ear for it, and sure enough there came a gentle swish from that direction. A second later, Miss Feanor and the other children slid into view. She gave Curt a long look, before she turned toward the social worker.

"I'm so sorry, but I'm getting a tremendous migraine," she said in a near whisper. "Can we get this over with so I can go lay down?"

Miss Gladys' eyebrows shot up, and finally pitching her voice low, she answered, "Of course. It's not more than five pages that need signing." The lady dug through her briefcase and very soon the paperwork was complete. "I'll get out of your hair and let you two get acquainted." She then turned to Curt and her face became stern, "You be good now."

Though he would never term it in such a way due to his limited education, Curt was a cynic of the highest order, an atheist, a non-believer when it came to the concept of good. His life and everyone in it were shadowed in varying shades of grey evil. This was true of every person he'd ever met and no matter how nice they might seem on the outside or how diligently they tried to hide it, their dark side would eventually show itself.

Miss Gladys was a fine example.

Though she had spoken only a few hundred words to him, there was no denying she was at the very least tainted with evil. He didn't need to look past her job to know this. The foster care system was a complete joke, adding to and extending the misery of all involved. It was rife with abuse and a haven for burned out and slovenly social workers and though Miss Gladys might have begun with good intentions, she was now an enabler of this.

And a conscious enabler at that.

She knew Curt would run at his first opportunity, taking with him anything he considered valuable, yet she had flat out lied to Miss Feanor, telling her that he was looking for a stable situation. Not only that, she had lied to him as well. She had told Curt that Miss Feanor ran a good home and that he would be happy there, when clearly no one was happy there, not even Miss Feanor as far as he could tell. The children were all wearing identical looks of sham contentment but beneath that, was an edge of nervousness, which was impossible to miss.

But despite all of this, Curt liked the big black lady; she had a motherly air to her. So he lied to her as she wished him to. "I'll be good," he promised.

"See that you are." Miss Gladys relaxed her face into a commiserating sad smile and turned to Miss Feanor. "Feel better."

When she left, the other children ghosted away and there was silence.

Not an awkward silence as one might expect, but a silence filled with anxious expectation. It lasted many seconds and during that time, he and Miss Feanor only looked at each other. Unlike her foster children, she at least dressed halfway decently, wearing a plain white button-down blouse tucked into a pair of navy blue slacks. Her face was stern, set in hard lines. She seemed to be appraising him, while he kept up his attempt at invoking sympathy by looking as if he were afraid of his surroundings.

It should've been mostly just an act on his part. This was his ninth foster-home placement, and he was too much of a veteran of the system to be afraid of a new home, or even of a foster mother as cranky-looking as this one was. He was sure that she would have a mean bark, but she was just five foot three inches tall and not very physically imposing.

All the same, he had a fear that he couldn't quite name. It felt as if it were in the air, or perhaps was the air. He hadn't noticed it at first, but once he was alone with Miss Feanor he became attuned to it immediately. It was as if the air had been gradually awaking since his arrival in the home and that with every word and sound, it had begun to take on a charge. He wouldn't have been surprised if the hairs on his arms stood straight out, but he didn't dare look.

After all the noise and movement generated by the mountainous Miss Gladys, the air hung about them heavy, thick with energy, like the moments before the grey-green clouds of a particularly nasty thunderstorm were about to break loose and Curt felt the need to remain absolutely still.

Miss Feanor acted as if she sensed it too.

When the social worker had left, she hadn't moved anything but her head, and this she only turned in the slightest. Curt suspected that she was warning him to keep still and quiet by the way she held her eyes on him, and so he did.

For seconds, they only stared at each other, until gradually the air seemed to lie back down, flattening like the surface of a pond after a rain. At length, he shook his head and blinked. The odd anxious sensation of a few seconds before was gone, and he wondered if it had all been in his head.

At his movement, Miss Feanor gave him an unusual smile; it showed too many of her teeth. With two simple gestures, she told him to follow her and be quiet about it. He watched as she slid down the hall and imitated her exactly. However, the action wasn't as effortless as it looked, and his slides invoked much creaking from the hardwood floors and more than once her shoulders tensed with irritation.

They made their way to the kitchen, and she directed him to sit before she leaned in close. "Would you like a spam sandwich?" she asked him with surprising sweetness. Her words were like a gentle summer breeze, a zephyr that carried only as far as his ear.

Curt found spam repulsive, and even though he had swallowed much, much worse during his time on the street, he felt it would be a good time to test his boundaries. His whole life, people had been saying that he was just testing his boundaries, so much so that now it became a conscious act on his part.

"I would like to have orange jelly on toast, instead...if you have any." He had seen the orange marmalade in the refrigerator on his first trip to the kitchen and it had been one of the few things in there that he cared for.

Miss Feanor pulled back from him, her eyes involuntarily narrowing before she realized it. Quickly she recast her features into her odd smile.

"Sure, that would be no problem."

Odd, but interesting. It was like she was two separate people. As he watched her, he wondered about her being a schizo. His ruminations only went so far, since his knowledge on the subject was limited to playground gossip. He thought it had something to do with having more than one person living in you, but he generally just assigned the label to anyone he thought of as weird.

She moved to a cupboard low and near to the nook, and pulled out a new jar of orange marmalade and a half a loaf of bread. He wanted to mention the opened jar in the refrigerator, but that would've required him to raise his voice and as well it would let on that he had been snooping, so he kept quiet instead.

As he waited on his toast, his head began to pound where the janitor earlier that day had hit him and he rubbed at the spot gently, feeling a slight swelling there.

4

Ten hours earlier, Curt's day had begun well enough.

Breakfast consisted of bagels and cream cheese, and this he ate in a relaxed manner, while doing a spot of light reading from a social studies textbook. He partook of his meal in the teacher's lounge at Benjamin Franklin Elementary, his home for the last six months. The teachers were generally big eaters and there was always something left in the fridge; he just had to make sure not to eat too much. Despite his precautions, however, they suspected a thief was in their midst, but he was certain they weren't looking at him as the culprit.

No one ever looked at him, if he could help it. The art of blending in, especially in a school setting was something Curt had mastered years previously. He had found that schools developed rhythms, and as long as he moved in accordance with them, he would be accepted as a student. Strolling the corridors, he was always a part of a crowd, never on its fringes and never in its center and certainly never alone.

If by necessity he ever had to move through the hallways between classes, he made sure to carry a bathroom pass, swinging it with the obvious boredom of a normal student, and he knew the locations of every bathroom in the school, as well as the name of every teacher in case he was ever questioned. However, this was a very rare thing. He was normally out during the day, roaming the streets, panhandling, stealing, and generally having fun. On occasion, usually when the weather was particularly nasty, he'd make appearances at lunch selling candy at a nice profit or bumming food from the social misfits who would do anything he asked as long as he stayed and chatted for a while.

Benjamin Franklin was a joy to him. On the whole, the children were sweet, it was in a nice neighborhood, and the clothes in the lost and found were generally of the highest quality. He could dress, if he so choose, in latest name brands. However, that day he had dressed for work. There seemed no explanation as to why, but Wednesday mornings were the best day of the week for begging, and he had dressed accordingly.

After six years on the streets he had discovered some fundamental truths to the art of begging, and dressing the part was of paramount importance. Many of his fellow street rats were oblivious to this truth and wore clothes in such a poor state that they were practically falling off them. Curt wore relatively nice clothes, but ones that were obviously stained and smelled a touch dirty.

He had found that if he looked too nasty, like many of his fellow beggars, people were far more apt to circle wide around him. But if he came across too clean he evoked little sympathy.

The proper look was for a child to appear new to his current sad station in life. A *mark* could then feel satisfied that the few dollars he had given would more likely go to feed the child as opposed to going to buy drugs. Interestingly, Curt had found that the number one reason people gave to beggars was that they wanted to feel good about themselves, still they would give far more freely if they didn't think their money was being wasted.

Curt became king of the street rats by combining his patented look with the true secret to begging, which was not to beg at all. When he spied a likely mark he would never actually ask for money. He'd open his mouth to beg, but then close it again as if the situation was just too humiliating. Frequently people would just offer him money at that point, and as always, he'd follow it up with a teary thank you; again a fine moneymaker when done right.

Now that morning, Curt had made an error in judgment. He had allowed himself to be lulled into complacency by too closely trusting in an established routine, not his own of course, but that of the schools. This routine had been so exact for the last six months that he was totally unprepared when it suddenly changed. None of the faculty had ever arrived earlier than six am before, however just as he was finishing his toasted bagels, somebody did.

He only heard the heavy footsteps outside the door to the lounge a bare two seconds before it opened, but this was plenty of time for someone as fast as Curt to dive under one of the long couches in the room.

"Hello?"

He recognized the voice as that of Mr. Gallarti, the school's janitor. The man was oddly protective of his school and always seemed to have an angry streak running through him. He was a vile tyrant who kept a bottle of whiskey in his desk that needed to be replenished every other day, yet everyone older than twelve respected him. For these reasons, Curt had kept his distance.

Lying there under the couch, he let the remains of his bagel dissolve in his mouth before swallowing. In the first few seconds, his heart beat so heavily in his ears that he feared that Mr. Gallarti would be able to hear it. However, it slowed quickly as the janitor turned and walked from the room.

"Hello...anybody here?" the man yelled from the hallway just beyond the door. Curt began to calm down. He figured that he'd relax for a while until Mr. Gallarti moved on to his quite literal broom closet of an office. At that point, Curt would speed over to the gym and slip into his lair until enough children showed up for him to become lost in the crowd.

Under the stage in the gym, in the most inaccessible spot possible, he had fashioned a lair with warm blankets and pillows. And save for the frequent visits by spiders and the occasional school play, it was a very comfortable setting.

But there was problem with his plan. Mr. Gallarti didn't leave, he walked back into the room, and Curt heard the unmistakable sound of sniffing. A moment later, the boy went stiff with fright as the janitor bent down and peered right into his eyes.

"Get the hell out of there!" he roared at Curt.

"Yes sir," the boy squeaked in a high-pitched terrified voice. Curt wasn't exactly scared; now that he had gotten over his initial shock, he calmed quickly and his brain kicked into high gear. Mr. Gallarti expected him to be frightened however, so he acted frightened and shied away from the man once he had pulled himself out from under the couch.

"What's your name, and what the hell are you doing here so damn early?" Mr. Gallarti seemed excessively irate—his eyes were red and his breath was of stale whiskey. Curt had seen enough bitter hangovers to know to tread carefully.

He wasn't careful enough.

"My name is Danny Stebbins and I was uh..." Curt started but was interrupted by Mr. Gallarti. Unbelievably, the janitor punched him in the side of the head, which sent him sprawling onto the couch. He had clearly chosen the wrong kid to impersonate.

There were three boys whose name he kept on the top of his mind just in case of such situation like this. Danny was his go-to name. Danny was quiet and shy, unassuming and tended to blend into whatever crowd he happened to be with, but more importantly, the two boys bore a passing resemblance to each other.

"You don't think I know all the children who go to my school? I've known Danny Stebbins since he was a kindergartener, so stop you're lying," Mr. Gallarti hissed. "Now tell me who you are."

The punch had been so unexpected that Curt almost blurted out his own name, but he had been in worse situations before and quickly collected himself.

"I'm a...I'm a..." he spluttered weakly. He felt a sudden wave of dizziness from the strike and decided to go with that. He swooned, playing up a head injury.

Mr. Gallarti wasn't buying it. "Oh look, you fell down a flight of stairs, running from the janitor," Mr. Gallarti said ominously, and with that, he picked Curt up and set him on his feet. "Now tell me who you are or you're gonna have another accident."

Curt felt a little chill go down his spine at this. Who would hit a student like this? If he'd been an actual student attending Ben Franklin Elementary, the janitor would've been skating on some thin ice, but as it was, Curt was doing the skating.

"I didn't mean it," he whined pitifully. "My name is Adam Malone. I'm in Mrs. Harpers class...I was out after my curfew and I got locked out. My dad would kill me if he knew I was out so late so...I came here. I didn't know where else to go and...and one of the doors was left open, so I just kinda slept here on the couch."

Curt used his fear and the whomping pain in his head to push out a few tears, and they dangled to nice affect from his eyelashes. The janitor's features softened slightly at this, and Curt knew he had told his well-rehearsed story perfectly. However, he wasn't going to rely on the story to get him out of trouble completely; that would be pushing his luck too far.

He suspected the janitor would take him down to the office and verify that he was indeed "Adam Malone". Curt would go along with him, acting the part of a sullen boy about to get in trouble, and when he saw an opening, he'd make a dash for it. It wouldn't take much of an opening.

Mr. Gallarti had a hundred extra pounds sitting on his waistline, and Curt knew he could escape with only a one-second head start.

But none of that happened.

"What were you doing out so late?" the janitor asked. The question, though unexpected, didn't faze the thief. There were only two reasons for a boy his age to be out so late: mischief and girls. For a sixth grader, mischief sounded more believable.

"Ron Harnet tee-peed our house and I was only settling the score," he lied so smoothly that he nearly convinced himself. However, the janitor responded in the most upsetting manner, he punched Curt again. It turned out that Mr. Gallarti lived down the street from the Harnet's and there hadn't been any toilet paper decorating their house that morning.

5

"You don't look so good," Miss Feanor watched him massaging his aching head and sidled up to him. "Do you have a headache? Would you like some Tylenol?" she asked, still with her sweet personality.

"Yes, please."

She was off again sliding back down the hall, and as soon as she left the doorway, he moved as well. His headache wasn't an act, but he was curious to a fault. He went to the cupboard, from which she had pulled the bread and jelly, hoping to find food there. Respectable food, proper food, chips or cookies, perhaps even soda. However, he found more of the same that he had already seen. The exact same. There were two more jars of pickles, two containers of wheat germ, one jar of marmalade and so forth. In the back of the cabinet, as if hidden away, were also a couple dozen cans of spam and carrots.

"Bizarre," he whispered, staring unhappily at the contents of the cupboard. It was then that he heard the whisper of feet, and he only just made it back to his seat before Miss Feanor re-entered.

"Here you go, these will fix you up," she handed him two very large white pills and a glass of warm tap water. To Curt, the pills seemed way too big to be Tylenol, and he looked at them skeptically.

"This is Tylenol?" he asked politely.

"They are extra strength. You'll see. Your headache will be gone in jiffy, though they may make you sleepy."

There was an impenetrable depth to Miss Feanor that kept him from reading her with any accuracy, but he could see no reason for her to lie to him. Therefore, he took the pills and found that she was right on both counts. His headache disappeared in minutes and by the time, he had finished his toast, he was already feeling groggy.

"Let me show you to your room," she said when he was done.

The house seemed extremely old, but despite that, it retained its original beauty and grandeur. Attention had been given to every inch of it as far as Curt could tell, and there wasn't a nick or scratch to be seen, anywhere. It might have been brand new, if it wasn't for the smell. It smelled very old. The smell, which he associated with a mental picture of a grandmother, was coupled with the perfection of the house in a way that he had trouble grasping.

"Miss Feanor? How old is this house?" he asked in a whisper. They were moving up a narrow backset of stairs, slowly and still quietly. She placed her feet just so and he followed suit, finding that if he didn't, he would cause the steps to *crreik* angrily at him. Before answering, she came to a complete stop and waited for him to catch up to her.

"One Hundred and forty-two," she whispered back, her smile was now gone from her face, likely due to what she considered an unnecessary question.

As she started up, he shook his head at her retreating rear end, deciding then that this place was just too weird, and that he'd leave the next day, or the next night to be more precise. This night, he would sneak out of his room and find the silverware, which a place as old as this one undoubtedly had by the truck loads.

Tomorrow, he would lay low, keeping quiet—what was clearly expected of him anyway and then he would take off around midnight. The plan was a good one and he even had a place to stay in mind: an abandoned theater he knew of, not more than six miles away.

The layout of the house though wasn't ideal for an escape. Its main problem was that Miss Feanor's room was almost dead center on the ground floor, and with the deathly quiet of the place, she might be able to monitor his comings and goings from her room. But there was a window overlooking the garage; he figured he would slip out of that one if needed.

The house was shaped as a two-story rectangle. The backstairs led directly from the kitchen and zigzagged on short flights to the second floor. It entered upon an uneven hallway, which jogged a few feet to the right at two intervals and then split at the main staircase. Each jog to the right came at a doorway to a bedroom. The first room that they passed was Matt's. Miss Feanor said his name quietly and pointed at the door. At the next door, she again pointed and said the name Beth. He didn't know which girl that was, but since he was planning on leaving, he didn't much care.

Now they came to the main stairs, and the hallway opened up and branched around it. There were five doors here and the first, just to their left was another bedroom. "Paul," she nodded in its direction. Miss Feanor then pointed further down the hall at a door catty-corner to them and said, "Amber."

The door across from hers didn't have a name associated with it and Miss Feanor didn't give it a second glance. The door just to their right and at the top of the stairs was a bathroom and finally, right next to the bathroom was to be his room. It was the most spartan room he had ever seen. It contained a single bed and a small three-drawer dresser.

That was it.

The walls were a bare, unblemished stark white, unadorned by a single picture, while the dresser held nothing more than a dull gleam of polish. A closet stood open and barren just to his left, and the only other feature to the room was a lone gloomy window, which was shuttered from the outside. Curt's eyes swept the room back and forth a few times as if he were unable to comprehend the emptiness of the space.

His grogginess had increased as they had walked from the kitchen, and now it was all he could do to keep his eyes open. Coming up the stairs, there had been a dozen questions on the tip of his tongue, but for the life of him, he couldn't remember even one now.

"You may nap until dinner if you wish. It might help with your headache," she whispered. The thought of dinner brought to mind one of his questions. He hadn't seen a clock anywhere in the house, not even in the kitchen. It felt to him very close to five o'clock and wanting to be sure, he began to ask Miss Feanor, only her eyes narrowed and he bit back the question.

Instead, he said simply, "A nap sounds nice." He gave her a smile of gratitude as if she had done him a favor when in truth, there didn't appear to be anything else to do. In fact, the house was so silent just then that he wondered if the other children were napping as well.

It may seem odd for a twelve-year-old boy to like naps, yet Curt liked them very much. They went along with his carefree life style. He stayed up as late as it pleased him and slept or napped when he grew tired. So it wasn't with a complaint that he laid himself down and slept through to morning.

Chapter 2

Once Bitten

1

"Curtis?"

Hands shook him, and then shook his some more.

"Curtis?" He heard his name and it was only slowly that he pulled himself from a very deep sleep. Immediately, he wished to go back. A tremendous headache started pounding the second his eyes fluttered open.

"Uhng," he groaned softly. Keeping his eyes open only made the pain in his head worse, but closing them made him fall back to sleep again. When that happened, the hands shook him and that little movement hurt terribly. His whole body ached as if he had been used as a punching bag.

"Curtis, wake up. We have to have a talk," the voice, a scant whisper belonged to Miss Feanor. Still it was a few moments before he was able to recognize her or his surroundings. He felt completely dazed; it was as if he were trying to think with someone else's brain.

"Miss Feanor? Where are we..." he started to ask, but her eyes went wide with alarm and she put soft fingers to his mouth.

"Shhh. Not so loud," she said. "Here take these. They'll help with the pain." In her palm sat two more pills—these seemed more appropriate in size.

"The pain?" Curt looked around confused slowly coming awake, the more he did the more he felt sick and out of sorts.

And confused.

"What time is it?" he asked in puzzlement. The light coming in from his window was all wrong. "Is it dinner time?"

The woman pushed the pills into Curt's hand and then held out a cup. She whispered, "You slept through dinner."

He swallowed the pills while his mind whirled—How had he missed dinner? And why did he hurt so bad? Every inch of him was alive with pain.

Curt tried to lay back down, but Miss Feanor pulled him up. "It's time to talk about the rules."

This came out so ominously that Curt pushed the pain aside and saw the queer look on her face. The lines running from her thin lips held fear, but her eyes were lit with danger. It was an odd and unsettling combination.

"Sure we can..." Curt started to say.

"Not here," Miss Feanor interrupted. She then waved for him to follow and then left the room. Because of the strange look on her face Curt didn't dally; he hurried to follow but it was then that his pain began to ramp up.

His legs and arms ached to the point he had to stifle groans as he moved, while navigating the stairs almost had him in tears. When he entered the kitchen, he stood swaying as his head went light and it was a moment before he realized that the other kids were in the nook, not twenty feet away. They were sitting as still and silent as the furniture under them. At length, in slow mechanical motions, they began to eat their toast with orange marmalade, and only their eyes demonstrated that they were truly alive.

They had expressive eyes.

All except the blonde girl, who hadn't looked up as the others, but sat staring at the remains of her toast, chewing slowly as if the taste of orange marmalade was a great thing and worth savoring.

But the other three had eyes that were very much alive.

Matt, the eldest, had small brown eyes that matched his hair and went well with the small features of his face. He would have been considered good-looking, except for the tinge of unkindness that marked his features. His eyes spoke to Curt, telling him in no uncertain terms that he was in charge and that Curt had better pay him respect.

Curt did so and nodded to him as a way of saying good morning. Oddly, Matt didn't seem pleased at this and looked at Curt as if he had done something wrong. Curt suspected there would be no pleasing this boy without plenty of butt kissing.

He looked next to Paul, who at five and half feet tall, was only an inch shorter than Matt, but where Matt was thin, Paul was downright scrawny. His arms were twigs and his face was narrow and haggard looking. He appeared unwell, like one of those boys with asthma or allergies, who seemed perpetually sick. Even his blonde hair hung limp and lifeless. His eyes were a dull grey and showed mostly sadness, but beneath that, Curt saw faint wisps of defiance, and he suspected that these wisps had been roaring flames at one point. Even as groggy as he was, the idea that the boy had been *broken* gave Curt the shivers.

Curt next took in the mouse of a girl. Her brown eyes were those of a butterfly in a tempest. They darted about with an unsettling speed, landing, seeming without control, all over Curt's body. He did pick out a pattern however. There was one area of his body that she seemed to take in more than the rest of him. His crotch. Her eyes would go from his hair to his crotch, and then to his arm...and then back to his crotch and so forth. It got so bad, that he was forced to look down, certain that he'd see his fly open.

It wasn't. Dully he blinked at the buttons until Miss Feanor took him by the arm; ignoring the other teenagers, she pulled Curt to the garage.

"Where are we..."

His mouth clamped hard as she turned on him with crazy looking eyes. "Hush!" The word came through lips that were stiff and brittle as tinder. She pointed at the passenger seat of the car and then climbed in as well, though she didn't start the engine—she only sat there gripping the steering wheel. She held herself tense as a spring, and again Curt's nerves overrode his pain.

She had to be one of those schizos for sure, he thought. One moment she was nice the next she's freaking. Just his luck. Though in truth it didn't matter too much to Curt as he wasn't planning on staying. Once he got his hands on her silver—if there was any—he'd be gone faster than Miss Feanor could switch from hot to cold.

She turned and looked at Curt, appraising him as she had the day before and just like then her eyes were cold and dark.

"You impressed me yesterday," she said, back to her customary whisper. "For your sake, I want you to impress me again. I need you to remain as still and quiet as you can, while I speak."

"I..."

"No talking. I'm going to tell you the rules of the house now, and you need to obey them to the very best of your ability. When you hear them, you may want to scream or maybe shout, and maybe even hit me...don't do these things, again for your sake. Nod your head if you understand."

He nodded, but he didn't really understand. The only thing he knew for sure was that he'd been likely right about her being a schizo. Just the way she was talking, told him that she was obviously a loon. Loons were like everyone else, they wished to be told exactly what they wanted to hear. The trick was knowing what that was. The wrong word could make them very dangerous.

With the way she was looking at him, Curt decided he'd be leaving that night, with or without silver. Even an eight dollars an ounce it wasn't worth it.

Miss Feanor had paused, perhaps knowing that he would need some time to come to grips with what she had said, and now she continued, "You're thinking that you'll run away tonight," she said.

His stomach took a sour turn, but then he realized everyone probably had those same thoughts. She shook her head gravely. "If you try you'll be punished. There's no escape from this house; smarter boys, bigger boys, luckier boys than you have all tried, and they have all failed, and they were all punished.

"When in the house do not talk or you'll be punished. Do not laugh, or cry, or scream, or make any noise that will draw attention to yourself, or you'll be punished.

"Do not sneak food, or attempt to cook or touch anything in the kitchen, or you'll be punished. The dining room, the living room, the powder-room, the basement and the attic are all off limits, stay out of these places, or you'll be punished.

"Do not scratch the walls, or the floor or break or mar anything in the house, or you'll be punished. Do not move any of the items in the house. If you do show the child in charge of that particular room. If you don't, you'll be punished.

"You'll want to test me, but for your sake, don't. Now, the first question everyone wants answered is what exactly is the punishment?" She looked at him grimly. "Take off your shirt."

"But..."

"Take off your shirt," she repeated coldly, raising her voice just the tiniest amount. Curt was still not especially frightened, unnerved was closer to his true emotion. Being punished was a part of childhood and some forms were worse than others, but since he could read people remarkably well and could sense their emotional state he usually avoided the worst of it.

That there would be a severe punishment for breaking her ridiculous rules went without question. The faces of the other children in the house had been enough to tell him this, but for him it was just a matter of avoiding it for as long as it took to make his escape.

So he obeyed and taking off his shirt he stared down at himself in dread fascination.

Terrific bruises covered his body. The bruises seemed to bloom like mottled flowers, erupting on his skin in shades of red and purple and black. They were horrible. He couldn't stop staring at himself and then he noticed an odd pattern in the discolorations.

Undeniably, within the bizarre and unnatural bruising there were bite marks on his flesh. Human bite marks. A wave of goose bumps swept across his bruised skin and he found that he now had trouble breathing. Miss Feanor had been right, he suddenly wanted to shriek in terror, the cry welled inside his chest, and it was a struggle not to let it out. It built greater and greater, the longer he stared.

"Huhh, huhh, huhh."

Noises began to slip from his mouth and he became terrified of himself that he would scream against his will. He looked up sharply at his foster mother expecting her to be looming over him with her mouth wide, but instead she only gazed at him with an ugly, pinched look on her face.

He snapped a hand over his mouth, stifling the noise.

"Last night I made sure you were out cold before your punishment...I won't do that again," she said this so quietly that he nearly leaned in to her to hear it. "You'll obey the simple rules of the house or you'll suffer. Is that clear?"

Around his fingers he said, "Yes..."

"Don't answer, just nod your head," she whispered viciously. He nodded, still with his hand clamped to his mouth. He hated being bitten. It wasn't only the sharp pain, it was the fact that struggling against it only seemed to make it worse.

"Yesterday, you were too loud," she continued in a low dangerous tone. "Don't try to deny it. I see in your eyes that you want to, but don't. You were loud and you were punished. And if you're loud again, you'll be punished again, am I clear?"

Still with his hand over his mouth, he nodded.

No longer did he feel the scream in him, instead he had a fantastic desire, an overwhelming need to make her happy with him, and he pulled his hand away and attempted a smile. He could tell that his eyes weren't part of the smile and he blinked heavily a few times trying to change his look. It didn't work. His eyes held only fear; still he hoped she would at least appreciate the attempt.

A corner of her mouth went up, but besides that she only looked upon him with her merciless gaze. Suddenly, she reached into the back seat of the car and brought forth a stack of pictures. They were snapshots of the downstairs hallway, the back staircase, and the powder room.

"These are your areas of responsibility. Every evening after dinner you'll make sure that they're clean, spotless, and looking exactly like these pictures. And I mean exactly, down to the smallest detail. You'll wax and polish the floors as needed, usually every two or three days. You understand what will happen if you don't?"

His mouth came open—at the last second he snapped it closed and nodded. She smiled at this.

"Good. So far every child coming into this house has wanted to test me. Don't. Please, please, don't," she said this last with fear in her eyes. It was a fear for him and this more than anything else, cemented the idea that she was insanely dangerous. To threaten him in such a way and then to pretend to worry for him...was simply crazy.

"You may go into the house now. The other children generally read or do puzzles, throughout the day, but I need to warn you again," she paused significantly. "Don't try to escape."

Of course he was going to try to escape.

Chapter 3

The second Day

1

Curt stepped out of the car and found himself two feet from a door that lead to the outside world. Through the small square window set in the door he could see the faded green of Miss Feanor's backyard and the trees that lined her large lot, but since the house was set so far back he couldn't see any of her distant neighbors. The view of the world beckoned to him and he felt a tremendous urge to run, to make a dash for it.

He held back.

It wasn't his way—it was daytime; he would run at night. The darkness had been his ally for as long as he could remember; it hid him and kept him safe and allowed him to do things that were impossible in the light.

So he turned away from the door and its false promise of freedom. Miss Feanor had been watching him with inquisitiveness and now as he looked over to her, she pointed at the door and gave a wave of her hand.

She wanted him to try to leave! He knew when he was being set up and so he gave her a strained smile and a small shake of his head. She snapped her fingers quietly and pointed at the door again. Her muddy brown eyes seemed black in the dim of the garage and they held more than a glint of annoyance at having to repeat her gestures. Therefore he turned toward the door— at first he couldn't bring himself to grab the knob.

It gleamed up at him and he could only stare at it, as he felt Miss Feanor's eyes burning into his back; he pictured her licking her lips in anticipation. It sent shivers up and down his body. Then he heard the snap of her fingers again, this time they seemed closer.

With a shaking hand, he made to give the cold knob a halfhearted turn, it wouldn't budge. It didn't even wiggle as many old doorknobs did, in fact it seemed welded in place. There would be no getting out this way.

He looked back over his shoulder and felt a touch of relief as he saw that she wasn't standing over him as he had imagined but had barely moved around the car. Seemingly satisfied, she nodded at him and then pointed toward the door that led to the mudroom. He was to go through it.

She waited next to it as he passed by and his muscles quivered as he turned his back on her, heading into the house. He hated the feeling of her behind him, knowing she could sink her teeth into the back of his neck like some horrible vampire. This thought sent the shivers down his spine again, and as much as he wished that he could stop himself, he couldn't. Just being so close to her made him feel vulnerable and his subconscious must have been envisioning terrible things. Stepping through the mudroom he entered the kitchen and saw that it was deserted; not knowing what to do with himself, he turned sideways and gave her a questioning look.

Her eyebrows came together in anger. 'Get out of the kitchen,' she motioned with her hands—these were quite capable at expressing what she wanted. He turned quickly and left the room. Feeling aimless and unsure of himself, he headed to the family room and was pleasantly surprised to see the four teenagers there. Now the room wasn't warm and inviting as the name would suggest. Like the rest of the house it clearly was for looking at, not for touching and the children sat on the floor instead of on the large expensive furniture.

The two boys were reading hard covered books, while the blonde girl doodled using an etch-o-sketch and the mouse worked at a puzzle. Since he was usually a loner, it seemed weird, but Curt felt an odd sort of camaraderie with them and he gave all a large, friendly smile.

They were not so happy to see him, however and didn't return his smile and each offered him varying looks. Matt's was a sharp look of anger. Paul wore a sympathetic look of sadness for the new kid. He then nicely gave Curt a friendly wink, but oddly he followed that with a second wink and then a third. Curt didn't know if the boy was trying to communicate with him in this way and if he were, Curt didn't know what he was trying to say.

Confused he glanced away, looking first at the mouse of a girl, and as before her eyes whipped up and down him. However now they bulged in their sockets as they moved and she shied back as if in fear. His smile froze on his face at this. Why would she be afraid of him? He nearly asked her, but just in time he recalled the warning about speaking and swallowed his question.

The pale blonde no longer appeared listless, like the mouse-girl, she was afraid of him and only glanced up at him as if scared to catch his eye.

Their fear was very real and within seconds of him entering the room, the two girls, followed by the boys left one by one, including Paul who had seemed the friendliest. They slipped up the stairs like soundless wraiths.

Now a sudden painful loneliness gripped Curt. He went to the bottom of the stairs and watched them go—none turned to look back. What was wrong with them? Why on earth would they be afraid of him? Questions came and went in his mind, but no answers and quickly he began to despair. Lonely tears came and Curt cried in honesty for the first time in years. These tears weren't part of a greater subterfuge as so many of his others were. These stemmed from a desperate overwhelming feeling that he had become enmeshed in something that would lead him to a horrendous ending.

Suddenly an answer to his question sprang up in his mind—perhaps the other children thought that he was about to be punished and wanted to be nowhere near him when it happened.

Curt began picturing teeth and his skin crawled in horror.

And now the shriek of terror that he had felt earlier, started to well up inside him again. Soon he worried it would burst right out of him and he pictured Miss Feanor charging into the room with her mouth open wide, blood already dripping from her fangs.

"Huhh, huhh, huhh," he began to cry louder at this image. In desperation he clamped his hands over his mouth. Those little noises travelled on the dead air and Curt worried they could carry into the kitchen—it was possible. Since he had entered the house, not a single sound had come to him. No whispers or footsteps, no ticking clocks...the place was absolutely still and his whimperings seemed vulgar in their volume.

He became louder still.

Curt found himself in a terrible loop. The more noise he made only caused him to become more afraid, which caused him to make more noise. He was moments away from shrieking in terror and running from the house. With his last remnants of control, he hurried out of the family room and after a quick look back down the hallway, he slipped to the foyer.

The old knob on the front door was just there and with a simple turn of the thing he could make a run for it. He'd show Miss Gladys his bite marks and she would almost certainly investigate that. All he had to do was get past that door. This didn't seem like much of an obstacle and that's what stopped him. It seemed too easy. This door wasn't welded shut like the one in the garage; he had seen it open a number of times already. His hand came up, yet an inch from the knob he held back as he suddenly pictured it hooked up to an electric current. With a sudden sweat on his brow he yanked his hand away quick.

The idea that the door was trapped flipped a switch in him. One moment he was practically on the verge of a meltdown and the next, he was bent over, peering in close as the thief in him came out in full force. He gave the door a thorough inspection, starting at the top, and working his way down; with his complete attention on the door, he calmed down without realizing it and his breathing relaxed to its normal state.

The first thing he noticed about the door was that it had not received the same attention as the rest of the house. Constructed of a dark heavy wood, the door had beveled edges on its panes and these held a light layer of dust. This was the first dust that Curt had seen in the house. The dust certainly wasn't years thick, but it probably hadn't been cleaned in quite a few weeks.

The knob of the door, he noted, seemed very old and there were intricate carvings and letters on it, but where the door hadn't been dusted in weeks, the knob looked to have never been cleaned. He would bet money that no child had touched that knob since the last time someone had attempted running away.

Now, he was heartily glad he hadn't touched the door and a sigh of relief escaped him. It wasn't loud yet still he cocked an ear, trying to listen for any sound from the house, but there was nothing and the feeling of being alone intensified. With the still air and the total lack of sound the house could've been deserted; it sure felt that way. Yet it wasn't. The children were there somewhere, probably sitting as motionless as statues, trying not to draw attention to themselves. So freaky, he thought and then bent again to the door.

This time he inspected the very large lock. It sat an inch below the knob and obviously was just as old. The key that fit it would undoubtedly be enormous compared to modern ones and Curt could only imagine the size of the tumblers within it. If the lock even had tumblers; he just didn't know enough about locks, especially ancient ones like this one, to know. Yet it hardly mattered, Curt wouldn't touch that lock even if he had the key.

Strike two, he thought to himself. The only doors out were impassable so he went back to the family room to check the windows.

The room boasted two tall shuttered windows on the eastern wall and after a quick glance around, he moved speedily to them, but before he even considered touching them, he went through an exaggerated ritual of inspection, inspecting every cranny and crevice. The sills were dust free, and the glass looked newly cleaned, even the little catch mechanisms were shiny as if freshly polished.

Clearly, someone had cleaned these recently, still Curt feared to touch the windows. Just as the front door, the window was too obvious an escape route. At least this one was. Within him he held out a slight hope that a second floor window wouldn't be considered a likely way out; after all they were quite high off the ground.

With that thought, he left the room and moved up the stairs, halfway up, the steps began to creak in harsh angry tones beneath him. He stopped with his heart in his throat and after a moment decided to go back down. However, his first step brought about another terribly loud squeal from the wood and this time he froze in place.

2

Curt stood paralyzed with fear at the thought of making any more noise and for minutes he sweated on the stairs, not knowing what to do.

"Sss," a barely perceptible sound came from above him, and when he looked up, he saw Paul peering down over the railing at him. Paul pointed at a spot on the next stair and then pointed at his right foot. Catching on, Curt put his own foot where the older boy had pointed and stepped up noiselessly. Paul then pointed at another spot further up— and in this way Curt soon made it to the top.

He smiled his thanks to the taller boy, who smiled back, but also winked at him. Paul's eye then winked twice more and as Curt rudely stared, it winked again. Only then did he realize that there was something wrong with the boy's eye. Curt looked away, quickly embarrassed for him, but Paul waved for him to look up at him again and by gesture he told Curt to follow.

Paul then proceeded to go up and down the stairs, pointing out areas that were safe and thus silent, and other areas that were loud and thus dangerous. Paul made not a whisper of a sound as he moved and Curt felt a touch of shame at this. Back on the streets, he would frequently look down his nose at many of the young would-be thieves that he hung out with, scoffing at how loud they were. He had thought of himself as a cat-like rogue and was proud of his ability to move noiselessly. Though compared to Paul, he was a complete amateur.

After he had moved up and down the stairs to Paul's standards, they then went and began to practice on the backstairs. At first Curt progressed well at these, but on his third trip down, he happened to look into the kitchen and saw Miss Feanor sitting at the kitchen table. His movement caught her attention and she eyed him with a malevolent stare.

Once again, he couldn't move. The thought of making even the smallest sound while she was so near at hand glued his feet to the stairs and it was all Paul could do to get him to budge again. Finally, they moved at a snail's pace up the stairs—Curt refused to go back down, he'd never been so afraid of one person in all his life.

He had associated with drug dealers, played pranks on escaped convicts and had carried on conversations with known killers, some of whom were terribly frightful, however none compared to this woman. Miss Feanor was only slightly bigger than he was, but his heart raced at the sight of her. In less than a day she had drugged him, beat him, chewed on him, and now held him as a virtual slave.

Paul pulled him bodily along until they came to the main staircase and then he forced Curt to follow him down again. They went to the family room and unexpectedly Paul left him. For a long while, Curt stood there alone not knowing what to do, and then the blonde girl came in. She stayed only long enough to grab a book.

[46]

Giving up on Paul, he turned to leave, but just then Matt appeared in the doorway blocking his exit. For whatever reason the older boy clearly didn't like him, and the look on Matt's face spelled trouble. Thankfully, Paul returned, pushing rudely past Matt and ignoring Curt altogether. He went to one of the bookshelves and put a book back in an empty spot. As he turned to leave, his eyebrows went up in the slightest way and his eye winked once, a slow deliberate wink, very much different than his others. Curt supposed there was some sort of secret significance to the wink, but he didn't know what it was.

At the doorway, the two older boys shared a look that left no room for doubt that there was animosity between them, then Paul pushed past and left. Curt had no idea what to do and only stood staring at Matt for a few long minutes before the older boy left as well.

Now Curt hoped that Paul would return, only he didn't and after about a half an hour, he became sleepy just standing there alone. Bored, he went to the shelves and after taking a quick peek at the dull book titles, groaned aloud. Immediately he regretted it and knelt there in desperate fear that somebody had heard. Like his earlier sigh, it seemed to go unnoticed and after a few minutes he relaxed and looked again at the books.

It was then that he noticed that one of the books stuck further out than the others. It jutted only by half an inch, but in that house of complete orderliness, it may as well have been half a mile. The book was Oliver Twist and it was very likely the one that Paul had put back only just then.

A sudden rush of keen excitement flooded through him, though he did have the presence of mind to keep his face a stony mask. Picking up the book, he gave it a long look, allowing his eyes to register sham contentment at the fine choice he had made. After a suitable period, he put the book under his arm and headed up to his room; using the quiet path on the stairs that Paul had shown him.

Curt had no idea if he was being spied upon by Miss Feanor, still he took no chances and shutting his door, he leaned against it. He then opened the book and slowly skimmed over it as if he found it a very interesting read. On the fourth page he stopped, seeing the note that he had desperately hoped he would find.

3

New kid,
My name is Paul Jenkins. i am 14 years old. Don't try to escape!!! The doors to the outside cant be opened and the windows are nailed shut. The glass in them isn't glass. i think it is some kind of really hard plastic. i think that it is unbrakable. My first day i tried using a chair to smash it and it didnt work. im sorry this is so short but you can't be too careful. There is a pen between the matresses of your bed you can leave me a note in this book. no one else reads it. Tell noone about this. Trust noone. At night stay under your covers. If you hear anything don't look!!! No matter what dont look!!!

This lay scrawled on a piece of toilet paper. Curt read it twice before he got up to use the bathroom. He flushed the message along with his urine and as calmly as possible, he took some toilet paper and made a show out of blowing his nose, while pocketing a few pieces. After that he went back to his room and sat on his bed in a silent state of shock.

There was no escape.

The idea left him empty inside. For the longest time he could only stare at his hands as a great depression settled about him. He wanted to lie down and sleep and maybe dream. He wanted to pretend none of this was happening to him and he wanted most of all, not to think about the punishment. That wasn't possible. His mind kept envisioning Miss Feanor biting him in his sleep and he had to force himself to think past it, and eventually he did, focusing on a new idea.

Paul had to be wrong.

Curt could escape. In his hard life, he had been in many rough spots before and there had always been a way out. He would just have to find a new route that Paul or Miss Feanor hadn't envisioned. This thought buoyed him and he scrambled off the bed and dug under the mattress, finding the pen right where Paul said it would be.

Just as he went to bring it out of its hiding place, his door opened and Miss Feanor stood there eyeing him. Making a clicking sound as he swallowed audibly, he froze with his right hand under his mattress. His heart began to beat with a great thumping noise in his ears and he felt certain that she knew everything about the note. However, she only pointed at him and then made the universal gesture for eating.

It was time to eat? That didn't seem right; it felt too early. Still there was no arguing with an insane person and so Curt nodded and then acted as if he were straitening the covers on his bed, before getting up. When he turned to the door she was gone. In a flash, he was back down on his knees and grabbing the pen from between the mattresses—worried that Miss Feanor now knew all about it—he stuck it on the lip underneath his box spring. This wasn't an ideal spot since it could roll off and drop to the floor if the bed were jolted, but it would have to do.

Using his new quiet technique, Curt moved down the stairs and made his way to the kitchen. He still couldn't slide soundlessly as the others, so he walked in his quiet fashion and found everyone waiting for him at the table in the nook. Taking the only remaining seat, he attempted to give each person a smile, but it was a waste of an effort.

Paul pretended not to see it and started eating immediately. The girls looked as if he were a bomb waiting to explode and dug into their food in a hurry as well, while Matt initiated the meal by sneering at him, but then progressed to a nasty hateful look that had Curt terribly perplexed. Miss Feanor ate with them too and he forced himself to give her a smile also. She ignored him completely and only sat eating and thinking, her eyes far away.

Without the benefit of clocks he had no idea if this was a very late lunch or a very early dinner. Either way it wasn't much of a meal. Steamed rice, spam, and uncooked carrots. Looking at his plate, his mind threatened to rebel at the prospect of putting any of it in his mouth. However, with Miss Feanor right there, he knew he would have to behave just like everyone else, so he took up his plastic fork and began eating.

He watched the blonde girl as he ate—the others were all too weird to look at for too long. Even with her pallor she had nice features. Small but pretty blue eyes, full lips and just a button of a nose; he considered her cute. Her plate was empty before he had barely begun to eat. After only a minute into the dinner she pointed at herself and then cocked a thumb at the door.

Miss Feanor nodded and the girl left.

A moment later the mouse did the same thing—Curt hadn't watched her. It was her buggy eyes. Even while she ate, they flitted about with a disconcerting speed and Curt hoped that she had a medical condition of some sort. If she didn't and he suspected that she didn't, it meant that she was going insane.

Paul had an odd eye problem as well and when Curt glanced his way, sure enough, the boy sat winking away at his food. It bothered Curt to see the wink and he wondered how long it would take before he started winking or acting strangely, or seeing things. At the thought, the muscles of his shoulders spasmed. It was only for a moment but still he quickly looked over at Miss Feanor to see if she had noticed. She had and for some reason she gave him a hard look. It was a look of warning and he went down the list of don'ts that she said would lead to punishment, only his little spasm wasn't on the list. But did it really matter? Her list was as crazy as she was and surely subject to change at any time.

Matt had seen his little shiver as well and he wore a look of spiteful glee. It seemed that the older boy considered the move a harbinger of something more and he watched Curt closely, with a fire of anticipation in his eyes. Curt disappointed him by going back to his carrots. These were very difficult to eat quietly and he kept making what seemed to him a very loud crunching noise that no one else had made.

After a minute, Matt didn't see what he had expected to see and went sullenly back to eating, at this Paul gave him the world's smallest smile. The corners of his mouth didn't move in the slightest, only the muscles near his eyes twitched in a little way. Curt relaxed a little at this, thinking he had passed some test. It made him wonder what they had been expecting.

When he finally swallowed the last of his carrots, he too asked permission to leave and went to his room. Shutting the door behind him, he grabbed his pen from its hiding place and hurriedly began to write a response. However, in his hurry he became careless and ripped the toilet paper.

"Shoot!" he whispered in anger and the word, like the smoke from a candle, hung in the air. He froze with the pen in his hand, listening for the near silent rumor of Miss Feanor's gliding feet. After a minute of listening for that dreadful sound and hearing nothing, he let his shoulders slump down. With far more care he returned to his note.

4

Dere Paul,
My name is Curtis Regis. i am 12 and going to be 13 next month. How long have you been here. How do we get out? There has to be a way. Have you tride the chimey? Why do we have to clean everyday? You say dont trust anyone but the blond girl looks ok, Is she beth or amber?

With the rip in the paper, there wasn't room for anything else, not even a signature and he was ok with that. What he wasn't ok with, was his handwriting. It looked like a five year old had written the note and he felt a keen sense of embarrassment over it, but there wasn't anything he could do about it, so he tucked the note into the book. He hid the pen again under the box spring and then slid the book under his pillow, thinking he would go to the family room and check to see if the coast was clear before taking it back, but just then the blonde girl came into his room, uninvited.

'Yes?' his eyebrows said to her.

She ignored him and from where she stood in the doorway, swept the room with her gaze. Her face gradually turned sour and eventually she held out her hands to him, palms up and touching. It looked as though she wanted him to put something in her hands. He didn't know what she meant by this, and said so with a shrug. She then opened and closed her hands rapidly giving him a look that told him just what a moron he was for not understanding. Curt considered himself a cut above the average when it came to brains, yet he was clueless as to what she was trying to tell him.

She sighed, and it was loud. Coming further into his room the girl began opening the drawers to his little dresser and he noticed for the first time that there were clothes in it. As she dug through them, inspiration struck him and he pulled the book, Oliver Twist from beneath his pillow and held it out to her. In exasperation she blew out heavily and snatched it out of his hands, before storming out of his room, it was a near silent storm however.

He watched her go, not knowing what to do concerning the note. He had less than a second to worry about it because Matt came into his room then, and ignoring the blonde girl, who had brushed right past him, beckoned for Curt to stand. When he did the older boy frisked him, checking his pockets, and even his socks. Matt then went to the dresser and rooted around in it and after that he checked Curt's bed, going so far as to lift up the mattress and peering beneath it. The pen sat just inches from his hand, but Matt didn't check beneath the box spring and by a miracle the pen stayed in place.

Unlike the blonde girl, Matt was absolutely noiseless. He was even quieter than Paul had been and despite Curt's natural dislike for the boy, he admired the way he moved. It was as if the air went undisturbed as he walked through it, and his feet seemed to pull the sound of his passing into them as he went.

After the search of his room Matt handed him the stack of pictures that he had inadvertently left in the car and then motioned Curt to follow. They went into the bathroom and in the closet were cleaning supplies of every possible nature. Curt groaned inwardly at the sight of them. He hated to clean. In his vision of the future, when he had developed his talents as a thief, he pictured himself living in the finest hotels where room service and maid service were only the touch of a button away. Not only did he hate cleaning; he wasn't good at it either. In one of his foster homes, after drawing on the walls in a fit of boredom, he was forced to clean up after himself. Only he had made the situation worse by scrubbing too hard and he accidently peeled the paint off the walls. After that he knocked over his bucket with an ill placed foot and stained the carpet.

For that reason he began sweating simply at the sight of the cleaning products. If he screwed this up he would have to face the punishment, and with that weighing down his mind, he watched Matt's every move and noted each detail. Matt went first to the back stairs and indicated that he should sweep it twice and then wash the walls, before moving down to wash the actual stairs and base boards.

The same attention was to be given to the main hallway, but there he also had to clean, dust and polish, two long running tables and the girlish nick-nacks that sat upon them. Next, they went to the powder room, which even though it was off limits to everyone, still had to be wiped down and polished to a gleaming white. Matt had Curt start there first, since the other children had to be able to move about the house in order to clean their own areas.

Even with the threat of a bizarre and horrible torture hanging over his head, he had trouble concentrating. Curt found himself, for the first time in years, missing his mother. Or to be more accurate, he missed a mother in a general sense. His own was a pathetic loser, a prostitute strung out on drugs.

Supposedly that hadn't always been the case and he liked to believe that to be true. According to her slurred ramblings there had been a time when she had been smart and beautiful, but a car accident shortly after he had been born had robbed her of this. Curt knew for a fact that she hadn't been lying about her looks, she had photos of herself that showed her as a fresh-faced, pretty girl.

That she had been intelligent was far harder to believe. But certainly if the car accident hadn't scrambled her brains completely, then the drugs had finished the job. His first memories were like flash pictures in his mind and even then she had been useless. He could picture himself standing on a chair, and so small was he, that there were two phone books beneath his feet as he put something in the microwave. Another memory from that distant time saw him spooning soup into his mother's mouth as she lolled in a stupor, and in a third he could picture himself laying an old towel over a fresh spew of her vomit. In each of these he couldn't have been more than three years old.

He had never known a time when he wasn't the one taking care of her, instead of the other way around. He could recall the day when it had all changed. It wasn't a great life-altering event complete with a vision from God, it was a sleepover.

Not long after his sixth birthday, he had been invited to his first sleepover and it opened his eyes to the reality of his situation. And once he had seen how others lived, he quickly became disillusioned with what could only laughably be called his home life. After that he began to spend more time away from home and whenever he returned it felt as if a grim weight would settle onto his slim shoulders. Duty to family slowly gave way to bitter resentment as more and more he noticed the love between his classmates and their mothers. His own mother seemed incapable of love and her emotions only seesawed along the thin space separating anger and wretched self-pity.

And so a full season of summer before his seventh birthday, Curt gradually stopped returning home altogether. It wasn't a heart breaking decision when he finally decided never to go back, it was a relief. That first summer was the most difficult on him and a few times he thought about going back to his illusion of safety. But even at the age of six years, he felt too much cheated anger to allow it.

He found spots around Pittsburgh where he built *lairs,* as he called them, though nests would be a more accurate term, and from these he made forays throughout the city. He learned quickly the arts of panhandling, pick pocketing, thievery and burglary. At first he acted strictly on opportunity; strolling through parking lots, checking for unlocked cars, or maybe rifling the pockets of an unconscious drunk that he would stumble upon outside a pool-hall. However, hunger and the approaching cold matured him well beyond his years and by necessity he not only worked hard to excel in his craft, but he became an adroit student of humanity.

Humans became his prey.

Though he knew nothing whatsoever about the concept of survival of the fittest, by his actions he demonstrated it to perfection. He preyed upon the weak. Not the weak physically, since he was always so small, but the weak mentally. The complacent, the unwary, the gullible, the foolish, and the greedy were his targets. But what paid the rent, so to speak, were the guilt-ridden. They made begging a breeze.

In Curt's kill or be killed world, there was absolutely no room for the concept of guilt. Even at a young age he understood that life was hard and you did the best you could with it, but he saw no need at all to apologize for any success one might have.

However, he did understand generosity. Giving from a position of generosity made a person feel good about themselves and that made more sense to him than giving from a position of guilt. The guilt-ridden gave in order to avoid feeling bad; this seemed quite backwards to him.

But backwards or not, they were the easiest marks and Curt used their guilt to his advantage. Not that he was immune to guilt himself, but he kept it well under control, living by his code: he never stole from anyone less fortunate than himself. Though he was a homeless rag-tag, the less fortunate encompassed more people than one would imagine, but still there were many, many people with wealth waiting to be taken advantage of.

There wasn't anything that he wouldn't use to his advantage. Every human trait could be worked to his benefit, one-way or the other; a push to his pull, a yin to his yang. It was only a matter of finding the right combination of words or expressions or the best circumstance, even if those circumstances had to be concocted.

The same could be said of his present situation. There had to be a way out and if anyone could find it, Curt could.

5

As he wiped away the streaks he had inadvertently put on to the mirror, he slowly pushed aside the little boy in him, the one that wanted to be pampered and coddled by a motherly figure and set his mind turning over ideas on how to get out.

With the doors impassable and the second floor windows likely so as well, the chimney and the garage door were clearly his easiest routes for escaping. For another child the chimney wouldn't have been an option, but Curt was small and slim and not only that he was fearless when it came to heights. He saw the chimney as the better of the two choices, since it would be an almost noiseless escape. Moreover, the garage door most certainly had an alarm hooked up to it, otherwise, someone would've used it by now.

Though he had checked, he hadn't seen an alarm on the front door, but in this crazy house, it was likely the alarms were on the outside, to keep the kids in, rather than to keep the bad guys out. He stood there stewing through different variables of his escape plans and with the combination of his mind being so preoccupied and Matt being so quiet, he didn't notice the bigger boy standing just behind him.

Matt punched him in the back of the head.

Thankfully, Curt was too stunned to even cry out. The room spun around sickeningly and for a moment he couldn't stand, but sagged against the sink. It was all he could do to hold himself up, but then the room spun again, this time in reality as Matt pulled him around. Despite his small size Curt was a very good fighter, yet there was no fight left in him after the sucker punch. Luckily Matt wasn't looking for a fight.

He yanked Curt to a standing position and then began to yell at him in a silent fashion, gesticulating madly—getting his point across all the same. Curt was being too slow with his chores.

With a final shove, Matt left in a silent huff. After that, Curt definitely began cleaning faster, and he would have been faster still if he didn't feel the need to look over his shoulder every few seconds.

Twenty minutes after the punch, he moved on to the main floor hall. Here, despite his head pounding away with a sharpness that kept him blinking, he set to work dusting with a will. He had barely begun when Matt showed up wearing a look of fresh anger. Curt followed him warily back to the powder room. Matt snatched up two of the pictures of the little room and began pointing at them with a face that suggested Curt was an imbecile. He had missed something.

Spotting the error in the first picture came easily, the hand towel lay an inch too far to the left, but he could see nothing wrong with the second picture of the floor-mat. He could only give the older boy an embarrassed shrug, thinking he was about to be hit again. Matt rolled his eyes and pulled Curt to his knees; there he ran his hands along the edge showing how the mat lay imperfectly aligned with the tile pattern of the floor.

Tugging it into place, Matt straightened and eyed the bathroom as if he were involved in a military inspection. The older boy then backed out, pulling Curt along with him and handed over the picture of the bathroom door, which showed it open about four inches wide. Curt adjusted the door, something he hadn't done before and looked to the older boy for approval. He didn't get it, but he also didn't get hit again, instead Matt turned without another look and slid away.

For a twelve-year-old, Curt possessed an amazing eye for detail, however Miss Feanor demanded a level that he worried was simply beyond him, and he went back to his dusting, doubting that he could avoid being punished for very long. It just didn't seem possible. He paused wondering how anyone, even a crazy person could find biting a proper punishment. Lifting his shirt, he looked again with revulsion at the bruises and bite marks.

With an inaudible groan, he lowered his shirt and returned to work.

The drudgery of his chores continued on for well over another hour with Matt making periodic inspections, but one punch seemed to have been enough for Curt. Making sure to eye the pictures from every angle, he strove in sweaty anxious silence to make his areas of responsibility perfect. He took the lack of hitting, coupled with the sour looks of disappointment that Matt gave him, as proof that he had somehow completed his chores properly.

Curt felt completely exhausted.

Without knowing exactly what he should be doing, he went to put away his cleaning supplies. But he had only just got to the top of the stairs when a stressed out looking Paul, winking as though he were sending a message in Morse code, pulled him into the bathroom. There the blonde boy handed him a new toothbrush and made it clear that Curt had to get ready for bed, fast. The little thief nodded in understanding, however in truth, he didn't. Judging by the light filtering in past the shuttered windows, and his own internal clock, he guessed the time to be somewhere around seven. Far too early for bed, but after everything he had been through he didn't bother to ask questions.

After he used the bathroom, he went to his room and in his small dresser, discovered a pair of lime-green pajamas that he slipped into. Even though he felt tired, Curt found it strange going to bed so early and he popped his head out of his bedroom door to see if the others were getting ready too.

Paul wasn't; he was cleaning the upstairs bathroom with a frantic speed. Wearing a hard look of determination, he wiped down surfaces and polished the chrome as if his life depended on it.

There was someone else cleaning as well. The blonde girl dressed in an ill-fitting pair of pajamas, washed the floor of the hallway on her hands and knees, backing toward him as she went. It was an intriguing sight.

She worked the brush in a circular fashion and as she did, her bottom shimmied in a small circular motion as well. With her pajamas fitting so poorly, being at least a size too small, Curt found himself gawking openly. Looking over her shoulder a minute later, the blonde found him gawking as well.

It was a few moments before he noticed her looking at him, and when he did his face went hot with embarrassment. Turning quickly to escape back into his room, he walked into his partially open door, hitting the side of his face sharply. Now the heat in his cheeks went straight to his ears like a wind driven fire. When he heard a snort of amusement come from her direction, he fled into his room.

Once in, he shut his door as quietly as he could and sagged back against it, shaking his head at how stupid he had been. Despite her being slightly smaller than him, the blonde girl seemed older than Curt, and on a certain level, a sexual level, he felt intimidated by her. There were only two groups of people that he ever had trouble speaking with: good-looking teenage girls and priests. The latter he suspected of possessing secret knowledge and he worried that they could see through his lies. He avoided priests like the plague.

It was quite the opposite situation when it came to teenage girls. An interesting thing about girls was that there had been a time when he could hustle them with relative ease. They fell for his patented, sad/cute/lost look, almost without effort on his part, however in the last year or so, even though his looks hadn't failed him, his tongue had begun to. Hustling them started to take on an extra challenge, one that he failed at with startling frequency. Still he tried, though many times he lost sight of what he was exactly trying for.

Picturing the blonde girl's bottom, shimmying in tight little circles, he sighed loudly and as if someone had been listening just for this, his door came open with a jerk. He jumped feeling guilty.

Paul stuck his head in to the room and glanced around. The older boy's face went from concerned/curious, to strictly concerned in a flash.

'Where are your pictures?' he asked by pantomiming operating a camera, coupled with a quick shrug.

Curt pulled the pictures from his dresser and was just handing them to Paul, when he caught sight of the shocked look on the boy's face. Paul stared at the open dresser drawer as if a dead body had been mixed in with the tangle of clothes. After snapping his head around at the darkening window, Paul quickly yanked out the drawers of the dresser and laid them on the bed. He then snatched the photos from Curt's hands, rifled through them, and found the pictures of the bedroom that Curt had overlooked.

'Make the drawers look just like this and hurry!' Paul said by way of hand gestures, pointing first at the pictures, then to the drawers and then tapping his wrist quickly.

The two boys worked speedily, folding clothes and laying them back in the drawers with an exactness not normally found in teenagers. Each article had to be folded just so, or Paul would point at it in a harsh manner. Curt discovered that his hands were beginning to shake with nervousness. Paul had a real fear coming off of him in waves and with his constant glances to the window, checking the progression of the advancing night; he had Curt feeling it as well.

Finally, they were finished to Paul's satisfaction and without further hesitation or explanation, the bigger boy said, 'Get in bed, now!' There wasn't much in the way of pantomiming this, just a good deal of shoving and with Paul's fear ratcheting up, Curt hastened to get in.

He wanted to know what all the rush was about, but Paul pushed him down onto the pillow and gave Curt a final warning. Pointing at his own eyes and shaking his head and then tugging on his ear, he motioned, 'Don't look. If you hear anything.'

With that, Paul covered Curt over with the blanket.

Chapter 4

Steps in the Night

1

Lying under his covers, Curt at first felt a great fear. Paul had been so frantic about the coming night that his fear had rubbed off on Curt, but after a while when nothing happened, the only thing that he felt was an intense stuffy heat.

He slowly pulled the covers back an inch at a time and found his room darker than he had expected. Paul must have turned off the light as he had left. With the setting sun and the shuttered window, the room was drenched in an unsettling gloom. Feeling a sudden and very rare nervousness about the dark, Curt sat up slowly, trying to see through the murk into the darker corners but there was nothing to see and the same was true with the closet.

He was alone.

And he felt loneliness. Just as his fear of the dark, this new feeling was quite unusual for him. Although he could be glib and gregarious, Curt in truth preferred being alone. People in general annoyed him, with their hypocritical selfishness, their tarnished self-righteousness, and above all their stupidity.

But now he missed people.

Wishing he were back in his lair at Ben Franklin elementary, he stared out at the crack of his door. It was dark in the hall as well, but not so dark that Curt couldn't see a little.

A shadow passed in front of his door.

Curt slipped under his covers, moving beneath them smoothly like the moon ducking behind a swift flowing cloud. Lying completely still, he breathed as lightly as he could, in attempt to hear the person in the hallway, but the person didn't remain there for long. Without hearing the slightest noise, Curt could sense that the air had shifted slightly in his room and he guessed that his door had been opened further.

Under the blanket he tensed, his muscled becoming tightened coils, ready to spring at the first sign of an attack. He felt Miss Feanor's presence. She seemed to be just over him and when she touched the blanket he thought he'd scream, however the noise caught in his throat. The blanket bunched in two places on either side of his head and he was sure that she would yank back the covers, but instead she moved them higher up, perhaps covering him better.

With that, her presence seemed to pull away from him and a moment later he felt the air shift again in that insignificant way, which made him suspect that she had left his room. Curt was desperate for air, but he feared that she had laid a trap for him and that she had only pretended to leave and was now standing in the dark near the door.

She was crazy after all.

His fear kept him paralyzed under the blanket, despite the fact that the air had become stiflingly hot. Minutes dragged slowly by and Curt decided he'd count as patiently as he could to a thousand and if he hadn't heard anything by then he would get some air.

He never made it to a thousand. Somewhere after two-hundred, his mind wandered and he found himself thinking of the blonde girl and her shimmying bottom again. Realizing this, he forced his thoughts back to counting, but a dreadful feeling of suffocation began to increase on him and just after six-hundred, he gave up.

Still he had the presence of mind to move with careful precision. He inched the blanket back at a snail's pace, but when the cool air of his room hit him, his presence of mind went out the window, and he gulped it in greedily, his chest heaving. Thankfully, the room was empty.

Maybe it hadn't been Miss Feanor creeping about, maybe it had been Paul.

Of everyone in the house, Paul had shown him the greatest kindness and it seemed like something the boy would have done. But the feeling remained that it had been Miss Feanor, and Curt considered it likely that it had been one of the nicer personalities that made up her schizophrenic mind. Thinking it possible that the crazy lady was still lurking about the house, Curt pulled the covers back over his head, and this time he fashioned a tunnel to breathe through. He could see a little as well, but only just the area near the top of his bed.

Now came the tough part. Waiting.

There was no way he could know the exact time, however he did know that it was still too early to reconnoiter the home as he had planned.

Patience was a hallmark of a top-level thief. There were four prime attributes that a successful thief must have: intelligence, patience, courage, and imagination.

Curt had far too little patience. It was a failing he recognized in himself but as yet had been unable to conquer it to a proper degree and now he found himself bored silly. To combat that, he thought about the layout of the house and tried to recall what the exterior of the place looked like.

All that he could remember was that it was three story red brick home with ornate shutters and a steeply slanted roof. If he had known that he would be forced to break out of the place, he would've paid closer attention. In his vague recollection of it, the chimney seemed regrettably small. He had been down a chimney before; it had been a sixteen inches on the side and almost too big. Miss Feanor's didn't seem nearly so big.

The other aspect of the house that he just couldn't recall was whether or not the home had eaves jutting from the roof. If it did it would making climbing down that much harder. His current plan had him climbing down the roof using the sheets that were currently on his bed. He'd attempt to rip them diagonally, wind them up, and tie them together.

This would give him approximately twenty-seven feet of homemade rope and that without eaves he'd still have to handle a nine-foot drop at a minimum. This he figured he could do. Anything more than that scared him. It would do no good to escape the house only to break his leg on its front lawn. If he had access to more sheets, this would be less of a fear, but so far he hadn't seen any.

And this was another reason that tonight would only be about research.

He smiled, realizing that he was acting on patience. Waiting until the situation was as perfect as it could be, before committing himself was the intelligent thing to do.

His smile was very brief and it disappeared beneath a huge yawn. Rolling over to get more comfortable, he began forming a list of the minimum required tools that he would need to escape. He became too comfortable and though he didn't think it was possible after what had happened the night before, he fell deeply asleep.

2

Crreik

The sound was quiet, yet the house quieter still.

Curt came awake with a strange but dreadful feeling that something was different.

Glancing around in growing fear, he saw that his room looked the same. Really the only thing that had changed was that his covers were tucked under his arms instead of over his head as they had been.

Crreik

Curt's eyes went wide in the dark. He knew that sound. He had made it himself trying his best to slip up the stairs that afternoon, before Paul had helped him out. It was the sound of someone trying to move slyly.

Crreik

Someone was coming up, and that someone brought with them a cloud of fear. The feeling preceded them up the stairs and it froze Curt in his bed. His only movement was to clutch the blanket closer to his thin chest.

Crreik

Now his blue eyes peeled back and he stared with fascination through the slim crack between the door and its frame waiting to see what horror it was that came up toward him. Was there someone else living in the house? Someone worse than Miss Feanor?

Crrrreik

There had to be, no one in the house made this sort of furtive noise, not even Miss Feanor. When she wished, she could be as quiet as the others and the only time she had been loud at all, had been that morning when she had woke him up. Even then, she had moved noiselessly.

Crreik

But maybe she didn't want to be quiet, perhaps she was just trying to scare him. Or worse, maybe the personality that was so weird for biting had come out and was hungry and was now coming for him. In the dark, she was coming for him.

Crreik

That thought took his breath away. He pictured her advancing up the stairs with her lips pulled back away from her overly large teeth, drooling in anticipation. In this vision of her, she had huge maniacal eyes and claws where her fingernails should have been.

Crreik

How long did he have? How many stairs were there? These questions came unbidden to his frightened mind and unbelievably he considered it. Picturing the staircase just outside his door, he figured the number thirteen to be close.

Crreik

That last footstep had been too loud. It was almost as if it had been purposely louder than the others, like a final warning. It jarred him into action and he pulled the covers over his head, for a moment he felt altogether stupid and childish.

Crreik

This one was sly again as the others and now Curt held his breath straining to hear, no longer feeling stupid, but rather feeling scared nearly to death. She was coming for him. In the dark house, she climbed the stairs, making sure he heard her coming, and her teeth were opening wider and wider...

Crreik, crreik

These last two steps had been quick as if she were trying to catch him in something and then he could feel her standing near his door waiting for his panic to engulf him completely, so that he would fly from his bed screaming. But Curt held back the panic with all that was left of his terror-stricken mind and lay as an absolutely motionless little ball under his covers.

He desperately wished he hadn't held his breath. Miss Feanor stood there for long agonizing seconds and soon his lungs burned with his need to breathe. There was no way he could do so now since just exhaling would be clearly audible. He laid there fighting against his natural urge and just when he didn't think he could last much longer...

Crreik

She turned away from his door and he could hear her footsteps moving slyly, but not slyly enough, down the hall toward the next room. He let out his breath as quietly as possible and fought the great demand of his body to begin hyperventilating. She was still too close.

After a half minute or so, Miss Feanor moved across the hall to the unnamed door and paused as she had done at the other doors, after this she moved on repeating the process, stopping at all the doors. Then no further sounds could be heard in the entire house and where she went to, he had no idea. Minutes ticked by and still he remained motionless, sweating through his pajamas with the stifling heat of the re-used air, waiting for some noise or sign of her. Eventually he felt himself go limp, feeling as though he had passed a great test.

He hadn't been punished again, so in one sense, he had passed a test. Presently he rolled over, away from the door and ever so slowly built himself a small tunnel to breathe through. The air was cool and wonderful.

The rest of the night passed with glacial slowness. Time stretched out in a way he had never experienced before and hoped he never would again. His adrenaline and his fear had him so wired that he couldn't go back to sleep and he only laid under his covers straining to hear the slightest noise.

If he had any clue of the time, he would've planned to wait a couple of hours before going to explore the house. But he hadn't the vaguest idea of how long he had slept for, nor was there any way to judge how long a couple of hours were, when a dark blanket and a beating heart were all he had to work with.

However, these were simply excuses. In truth, he was deathly afraid to leave the safety of his bed.

Chapter 5

A New Day. The Same Day

1

Eventually Curt felt a movement of the air in his room and his body went stiff and when a hand shook the blanket at his shoulder, he jumped beneath it. The touch had been light; still he was afraid to see who it was. A moment later the touch came again with more insistence and this time he felt his blanket being pulled down.

Miss Feanor stood over him, dressed in a soft looking, dark blue sweat suit. She looked at him closely and raised her eyebrows as if surprised.

'It's time to eat,' she motioned and then left the room.

Sunlight bounded through the slats of the shutters, making his dull room glow and for just a few seconds he lay back on his bed relaxing for the first time in hours. His exhaustion was such that he wanted to lie there longer, only he knew it wouldn't be wise to keep Miss Feanor waiting.

Despite that his first stop was to the bathroom. He had felt the need to go for the last three thousand heartbeats or so, but had held it without question. When he was done, he checked his reflection and saw what had so surprised Miss Feanor. Both of his eyes were shot through with red, he blinked at his reflection and felt the grit in them.

"Damn," he said quietly. The vibrations of the word bounced off the tile of the bathroom for a moment before being absorbed into the walls. Curt's muscles tensed at the sound...yet nothing happened.

Going down to the kitchen nook, he noted that little had changed in the other kid's demeanor towards him—except maybe their fear of him was more pronounced. He was too tired to care. They ate quickly and he ate slowly between huge yawns, some of which disturbed the air of the house. Miss Feanor would glare at him when he did this, and for that moment he'd remember to be quiet, but soon would forget again.

With breakfast done, he wanted to go check to see if Oliver Twist had been moved by Paul yet, however the moment he had begun sliding in that direction Miss Feanor stopped him.

'Take a shower. Brush your teeth. Get changed,' she said with her gestures. It was interesting to Curt how universal these signs were and he responded with the equally well-known sign for ok.

There was a short line for the bathroom, the blonde girl stood outside of it waiting with a towel in her hand. She purposely turned away from him so he wouldn't start any sort of conversation and that was fine with Curt. Breakfast hadn't perked him up at all and instead of bothering her with his presence, he decided to go wait on his bed. Though he didn't know it, he'd slept not even an entire hour the night before and so, relaxing on his bed, he was soon fast asleep.

As usual he had no idea how long he slept, though it had to have been a few hours judging by the position of the sun. And again it was Miss Feanor that woke him up. She didn't seem mad, but only jerked her thumb toward the shower. Quickly he washed up and changed and when he finished, he hurried down to the family room to check on the book. The sight that greeted him gave him such an intense feeling of déjà vu that he stopped in his tracks. Just as the day before he saw the blonde girl working the etch-o-sketch, the mouse was doing the very same puzzle and the two boys were reading. And again, just as the day before, they all left as soon as he walked in.

He shook his head in bewilderment, but this time he didn't cry.

Not even, close. Instead, he felt a fire of resentment burn in his belly—they were being unnecessarily mean, and acting like he was something to be feared was just stupid. He lingered there, looking about nonchalantly, giving the others enough time to make it back to their rooms, and only after a good five minutes did he go and check for Oliver Twist. It was gone and must have been the book that Paul had taken with him when he left.

Curt was terribly disappointed; he still had so many questions, almost all of them centered around how to escape. Sitting himself on the floor he decided to wait on his coming note before investigating a few possibilities that he'd been pondering. However, with his customary lack of patience, he was up minutes later, peeking up the stairs and down the main floor hallway. With no one about he slid toward the front door, but this time he veered away from the small foyer and went into one of the forbidden rooms: the living room.

He moved without hesitation to the fireplace and looking up into it, saw that the black metal flue was closed. With trepidation making his hands shake, he gave the handle a quick tug, it didn't budge. Glancing over his shoulder, he saw that the coast was still clear and so he turned back to the handle of the flue and gave it an even harder tug. Again, it didn't budge. A third attempt saw him straining at it in silence with all of his puny strength, but still nothing and he had to give up.

A curse almost escaped him. Instead, he quickly left the room heading for the bathroom to wash the black dust off his fingers before anyone noticed. Hurrying up the stairs he misjudged a step.

Crreik!

He had been too impatient and too quick and the noise had been very loud. He stopped for only a second, midway up the stairs; afraid that even then Miss Feanor was swishing down the hall to get him. The image of her in his mind was such that he fled in terror to the bathroom in a near silent rush. Desperate to get rid of the evidence of his crime he went straight away to the sink—the black dust came off easily, and Curt breathed a sigh of relief. What's more there wasn't even a hint that Miss Feanor had heard anything. Feeling a stupid relief he gave the room a casual glance and then did what came naturally, he snooped. There wasn't much to the room except a cabinet below the sink, which held little besides cleaning supplies, and a closet. This was where the extra bed sheets were kept; Curt gave them a grim smile.

2

Now if he could ever figure out how to get the flue open, he'd be in business. Unless...unless there was another way out. The boy went to his room to inspect the single window there; what he saw made his brow come down in consternation. The windowpane did indeed look very thick and was probably a hard plastic that hadn't been nailed shut, but more likely drilled down with screws—it appeared to be imbedded deep into the frame. Had it been a normal window, he'd be able to work the caulking loose and slide one of the panes out, but this was just one large sheet of heavy plexiglass. It wasn't going anywhere. Moreover, the shutters were thick and strongly built and Curt was very sure that these had been nailed shut as well.

To escape this way wasn't impossible, it was only impossible under the circumstances he found himself in.

A loud sigh escaped him, but in his anxiety the sound went unnoticed. His window wouldn't work as an escape route, however maybe the bathroom one would.

No such luck. The window there was unfortunately constructed in the same manner, but one thing that he did glean from his visit was that by peering through the slats of the shutters, he saw that the roof did indeed have eaves.

Unhappily, he sighed again. It was becoming a bad habit.

"Sss." The noise came from behind him; it was a little sound that sent his heart into his throat.

3

The blonde girl stood in the doorway eyeing him with a queer look of curiosity mixed with suspicious fright.

'What are you looking at?' She mouthed the word *what*, and then pointed at her own eyes and then out the window. Paul had told him not to trust any of them and so far he hadn't been wrong, so Curt pantomimed a bird.

This she didn't believe and advanced on him with a slightly unpleasant look on her face. He backed away from her, but she only wanted to see out the window. She ended up pushing him aside and looked up at what he'd been eyeing. Was she a snitch? Was that why Paul didn't trust her? If she was a snitch, then she was a snitch whose hair smelled of strawberries—as she looked up through the shutters, he breathed her in.

It was very nice, and for a moment he forgot his terrible predicament. She didn't let the moment last, instead she stepped back and gave him an odd look that he failed to grasp.

'Get out, I gotta go,' she motioned irritably as he only stood there.

Curt let his red ears speak for themselves and left, heading for the family room. Oliver Twist sat on the shelf, but this time it was pushed neatly into place. Without hesitation, he grabbed it and hurried to his room. There was a note right where the last one had been.

Hi Curt,

The blond girl is Amber and she gets punished a lot and you will too if you hang around her. Beth is crazy. Mat is crazy to and sometimes flies into a rage and gets punished. Hes neerly 18 and is afraid of what will happen then. Its making him try to be too perfect, like that will save him. i dont know why we have to clean, but we do. ive tried the chimney ive tried everything, the garage door, the back door the windows. Everything. i have been hear around three years, maybe four but i don't know for certen. i came when i was ten and half. What day is it?

This couldn't be.

Curt had thought that maybe Paul had been there for six months or so, but three and half years? All that time without finding anyway to escape? The idea seemed so impossible that Curt's mind reeled. Paul appeared to be an intelligent boy and if he hadn't been able to find a way out in all this time, there didn't seem a chance that Curt could.

Suddenly he had a great urge to scream.

He wanted to punch the door he was leaning against, he wanted to rage and stamp his feet, but the words written about Matt drained his anger and he found himself instead weeping, overwhelmed by helplessness. Feeling an urgent need to have a friend, he got up to jot down a return note to Paul but just as he left his room to get toilet paper to write on, he saw Matt coming up the stairs, heading right for him. Panic sent a bolt of pain into Curt's chest and for a moment he stopped in fright, but it was only for a second and then he turned to flee into the bathroom. He almost made it.

Matt must've ran to catch him, but catch him he did just in front of the bathroom. The older boy yanked Curt around, demanding the book that he still carried. The book was in Curt's right hand, while the note that quite clearly stated that Matt was crazy was in his left. Though this was his first time locked away in house full of crazy people, it might have been his millionth time dealing with a bully. Pretending that the book was of paramount importance, Curt pulled it back and to his right and when Matt lunged for it, Curt quickly stuffed the note into his mouth.

With great expectations Matt thumbed the pages, while Curt allowed his saliva to melt away the paper, swallowing it in little bits. When he got to the last page Matt let out a huff—and then went to frisk Curt, who tried his best to appear confused and innocent. Luckily, the pen still sat in its hiding spot beneath his bed and the search amounted to nothing.

When Matt was done with his pat down, he stared at Curt as if trying to read his mind. Curt offered a false shrug of non-understanding and then meekly backed into the bathroom. Right away he ran water into his mouth—he had a thing about germs and bathrooms in general and his mouth felt disgusting having eaten toilet paper.

Next he put his mind to finding a new method for passing notes, knowing they would be caught eventually if they kept using the book.

In truth, he didn't want to think about passing notes, instead he wanted to devise a plan to escape, yet after five minutes of sitting on the toilet staring at the tile pattern of the floor, he had to give up, depression robbing of him of any chance to come up with a serviceable plan. Therefore, he looked around the bathroom and in a flash, discovered that he didn't even have to get up to see how they could pass notes. The toilet paper dispenser sat just to his right. Popping it out of place, he opened it up and saw the perfect spot to hold both a pen and a note. He and Paul would just have to make sure that one of them changed out the roll when it got too low.

After waiting what he considered a proper amount of time, he got up and left, only to see that Matt had indeed inspected his room. He had also left it in a complete shambles with clothes and sheets strewn about. Curt didn't know what to do about this. Talking to Miss Feanor, a crazed, pit-bull of a woman didn't seem likely to help, nor did confronting Matt, who outweighed Curt by at least forty pounds.

So with no better idea, he folded his clothes and remade his bed. He worked slowly, wishing all the time that he was back in his lair under the stage at Ben Franklin. Sadly he realized that he'd have to find a new lair when he finally escaped from Miss Feanor's house of horrors. Probably he would have to move up to middle school; he was simply getting too big to pass as a sixth grader anymore.

Of course, he didn't have to stay at a school at all. But he was used to them and he liked the surroundings. Food and clothing were always plentiful, as was companionship when he wished for it. There was this as well, children belonged in schools, and he was rarely questioned, even when he was found lurking about after hours.

"I'm just waiting for my ride. My mom should be here any minute. She likes it when I stay indoors when it gets: fill in the blank- *dark or cold or rainy."* One time he had used cloudy as an excuse and it had worked.

Middle school was a little different. For many kids trouble begins in middle school and teachers and staff do their level best to stamp it out early. Suspicious activity is actively looked for and kids lingering at school are more likely than not to be questioned. Not only that, he would have to deal with more bullies. Bullies are uncommon in elementary school, but are a dime a dozen in middle school. Not that they were so scary to Curt, just annoying.

Still, there was a plus side to moving up, namely: ladies and lockers. Though he had a ways to go toward finding the correct rhythm when it came to talking to girls, he was still way ahead of his peers and he liked trying...it was fun. Lockers were fun as well. They were a snap to open and you never knew what would be inside, they were like a grab bag in that way.

There was one school that he had hung around for a few months where the lockers would open if you simply jiggled the handles enough. Curt smiled at that memory—then suddenly his mind strayed from lockers, as he remembered how easily Miss Feanor had opened the front door, while Miss Gladys had struggled with it. Curt hadn't really watched her closely, but now wished he had since there was likely some sort of trick to it.

That thought killed his daydreaming and he hurried through cleaning up the rest of the mess, wishing to get his note written to Paul. His lack of patience was on full display then. When he had finished with the clothes, he grabbed the pen, stuffed it in his pocket, and went to the bathroom. At the bottom of the stairs, Matt stood as if on guard duty. From his position, the boy could see the family room, the main floor hall, the living room, the stairs, Curt's door, and part of the bathroom.

Curt realized how foolish he had been about not checking out the area first, but this time it didn't get him in to trouble. Matt only eyed him sourly.

Once in the bathroom, Curt dashed off a note.

4

Dere Paul,

Its febuary 27 1997. Me and you have to be the only ones changing out the toilet paper or we will get caught. Put extra paper in the thing to keep the pen from ratling around. How does miss feenor do this? i was suppose to have a doctors apoitment, won't social services figure it out? Have you tried the garage door opener? How does she monitor us? Are there camras? Have you been in the basement or attic?

When finished, he took another sheet of toilet paper and wrote on it: *Toilet paper dispencer*. He tore away the extra paper so that only the three words were left on the tiny scrap. Carefully he folded it and put it in his front pocket. Next he rolled up the larger note and opening up the little silver tube, slid the note and the pen into it, adding a few extra sheets to dampen any noise. Now all he had to do was get the tiny three-word note to Paul. This should've been relatively easy, but clearly, Matt suspected them of passing messages and was on the lookout for it.

Holding onto the little note for a short while didn't seem all that dangerous since Matt's frisking had been amateurish, but Curt wasn't going to take chances; he wanted the note out of his possession as soon as possible. Unfortunately, when he stepped out of the bathroom Matt still stood in his same position and gave all the appearance that he could stay there for hours. Curt gave an inward groan at the sight of him and scurried to his bedroom, deciding to test the older boy's patience. Opening up Oliver Twist, which had been flung onto his dresser, he forced himself to read the first thirty pages. Unexpectedly, he found himself getting into the story, which was about an orphan raised in a terribly run orphanage and who is then shipped off to a workhouse where things aren't any better.

Though he was a slow reader, the thirty pages went by too quickly and he decided to read twenty more before getting up. When he did, he was surprised to see Matt still standing just as he had before. Again Curt was impressed. The boy's patience was as astounding as it was scary.

Scary or not, Curt wanted his note passed and so began a charade of misdirection. Tucking Oliver Twist closer to himself, he gave a purposeful pause just outside his door as if unsure whether to proceed or not, he then headed down the stairs. He kept far over away from Matt as he passed him and went into the family room. With quick guilty steps Curt went to the shelves to put the book back, but theatrically fumbled it into position, even taking a moment to cast a guilty look over his shoulder at Matt as he did.

The older boy watched him hungrily.

When the book was back where it belonged, he left the room in a hurry, and kept his face set in a fearful grimace, refusing to look up at Matt. Going up the stairs the grimace became a broad smile when he looked back over his shoulder and saw that the older boy had left his post to take the bait.

Figuring that he had at least twenty seconds while Matt searched the empty book, Curt hurried to Paul's room, which was as spartan as his own. In fact, the furnishings seemed identical and when he opened up the first dresser drawer, he saw the little stack of pictures that represented Paul's area to clean.

This was what he had fully expected to see and taking his three word note from his pocket, he placed it under the first picture and then left the room, going quietly to his own and lying down on the bed. Now he expected a visit from Matt, but that didn't occur, or if it did, he didn't know because within minutes he was fast asleep.

5

Later, Paul shook him to consciousness. As always Curt had no clue how much later it was, but he felt groggy and it took some time for him to come fully awake. When he did, he saw that Paul wasn't happy.

'Don't nap,' he gestured sternly. The boy actually gestured more than that, yet slow and sleepy as he was, Curt couldn't follow the rapid hand movements. Paul, seeing his slack jaw, gave up on what he had been trying to get across, and instead informed him it was time to eat.

Glancing toward the window, Curt guessed that it was dinnertime rather than lunch and he wondered briefly when that meal had been served. Shaking off the thought, he hopped up feeling suddenly famished and in his eagerness to eat, he nearly forgot to tell Paul about the note. Just as they were leaving his room, Curt pulled the older boy back for a second and motioned taking a picture and then nodded to Paul's room.

Paul's eyes narrowed for a moment as his mind worked through possible interpretations of this and then with a small nod, he turned on his heel and slid away on his white socked feet.

Curt didn't wait for him, thinking that would seem too suspicious. So he headed down the backstairs alone. He had not progressed very far in learning to navigate them quietly and after a good deal of near silent, but heart stopping creaking; he finally made it into the kitchen. There he had to take in the usual odd assortment of looks from the other children; mounting fear from the girls and nasty smugness from Matt. Miss Feanor looked hard and cruel, he saw punishment brewing behind her eyes.

The look gave him a sick feeling, which started to overcome his hunger so Curt crossed the rest of the floor to the nook as silently as he could. He took up his position at the table and what he saw there made the sick feeling grow into a stomach churning nausea. The dinner set out before him was once again, steamed rice, spam, and carrots. A sense of déjà vu struck him and it was so encompassing that he swayed in his chair. He gazed about him, trying to get a feel for the reality of his situation, but all he came up with was more bewilderment.

It was as though this exact moment had played out before and it was like a dream had been laid over reality, distorting them both. With his head rocking, tilting back and forth on his slim neck, he looked around at the others feeling strange, wondering if they were experiencing the sensation as well. He felt a keen need to know, and at that moment he knew a sudden desperate urge—one that was forbidden in the house.

Curt needed to speak.

It wasn't that he wanted to, he needed to, as a human, he *had* to. It was fast becoming a compulsion and he opened his mouth, staring at the faces around him, but they only registered a growing fear.

That little thing, seeing his drab plate set out before him, just as it had the day before had triggered a deep-seated need to communicate. It was like a switch had been turned on within him, and now that it was on, he didn't think there was any way for it to be turned off, at least not until he had spoken. Until he had his say. Until his many questions were answered. Until he could complain and whine and shout and yell.

He knew that he would be punished if he spoke.

It was quite obvious from the looks the others were giving him. Their eyes were all large and dry, as if they were watching someone who had just jumped from a building and they knew that something terrible would happen when he landed. Still they were unable to look away.

Nothing made sense.

Why? His mind screamed the word and it echoed throughout his being. Why did he have to be punished? It made no sense at all. What was wrong with talking, or laughing or singing? How would that hurt anyone? He looked to Miss Feanor, wanting to scream at her, WHY? But the look she gave him stopped the word from coming from his mouth. Her face was set in cold indifference and it was clear she didn't care at all if he screamed, or if he were to be punished, or if the teeth would hurt so bad that he would cry like a baby and maybe wet himself.

"But you should care," he said to her in astonishment. His amazement at her lack of feelings, fortunately for him, had taken away his breath, so that though the words had been clearly audible to those at the table, they hadn't been above a whisper. She only glared at him with hard dark eyes, and again her look quieted him, at least externally. Internally he raged. How could she not care what she was doing to all of them? That wasn't even human. Turning from her cold eyes, he looked at the two girls, his face pleading for understanding.

He didn't get that. Instead he looked into the crazy eyes of the mouse. He knew her name was Beth, but he could never think of her as anything other than mouse, and now her eyes spun with a greater madness than he had yet seen. He shrunk back away from her in horror, pointing, trying to get Miss Feanor to see those fantastic eyes. To recognize what she had done to the poor girl. Miss Feanor only ate her food quietly, sneering around her spam.

Curt stood up then and his entire body began trembling. From head to toe he shook, his insides feeling like sticks held together by string. This wasn't right! Nothing about the house was right—especially the mouse's eyes, they were definitely not right. He wanted to scream this at Miss Feanor, until she figured out that the mouse was insane.

He turned back toward the wild-eyed girl and saw that now she and Amber were shoveling food into their mouths as fast as they could. They expected him to blow sky high and he did as well. He had never felt so crazed and out of control in his life. Clearly Miss Feanor thought so too, or so at first he believed, because she slowly got up from the table.

Curt backed away from her with his small hands out but instead of heading at him with her teeth bared, she slid with dainty silent steps away toward her room.

Paul came in at that precise moment and his eyes went wide with fear for the newest member of the foster family. Coming up to the table, he shook his head imploringly and even mouthed the word, 'No' to Curt.

Curt was beyond pleading with. Even though the boy had been his only friend, he wanted to scream at the top of his lungs for Paul to go screw himself. He needed to vent. Although he had been in the house for just two days, the intense silence had worked its way into the crevices of his mind and now it felt as if he were simultaneously falling apart and about to explode.

Paul held his hands out to him and his face seemed desperate with fear for Curtis, still he ignored the blonde boy. The need to scream had now become a heavy ache in his chest that he could no longer stop from coming and with a feeling of letting go, he filled his lungs to shriek loud enough to wake the dead.

Only just then, Matt saved him.

Angered over Paul's involvement in the situation and without warning, the eldest boy in the house punched Paul full in the face. Curt was so shocked at this that the scream silently fled from his lungs and he only stood watching in amazement as the two boys began to fight in an eerie silence. They rolled around the floor, making the lightest grunting noises. Soon it was over and the house returned to its heavy stillness.

Paul got the worst of it, bleeding from both the nose and the mouth, and he seemed unsteady on his feet as he climbed back into his chair. Matt, on the other hand, looked perfectly fine, but disappointed as well. He obviously wanted to see Curt get punished. It was horrible thing to wish for and now Curt stared on the older boy with undisguised loathing. Matt simply snorted at him derisively and began to eat, as did Paul. This was the strangest sight. The two boys who had fought in a vicious silence only moments before were now sitting next to each other eating as if nothing had happened.

Curt rolled his eyes, perplexed and it was only then that he noted that the two girls had disappeared at some point, leaving behind empty plates. Staring at the plates, he felt defeated and deflated. His tremendous need to be heard, which had come from nowhere, left him completely, and at that point, he didn't care whether he ever spoke again or not. Glumly, he tried to eat and though he was able to force the rice and spam down, the carrots stuck in his throat.

He even gagged a little and seeing this, Paul, with the sigh of a martyr, ate the carrots for him.

With the end of dinner, the evening took on a miserable sameness. He was to clean again everything that he had just cleaned the day before. This should have been a breeze for him since he now knew what to do, but a will-sapping lethargy came over him and he moved lead-footed through his chores.

Still being slow did have one perk. When he went up to the bathroom, he again got to see that sweet shimmy of Amber's and it perked him up just a touch, but the note that he read from Paul a moment later had him straying deeper into the black waters of depression.

6

Hi Curt,

First, don't nap during the day. It'l make you go crazy, i mean it will mess up your sleep scedule and you will feel weird all the time. Second, Some how Miss F. fakes the doctors reports and reelly everything else. She has a computer and i guess she knows how to do that sort of stuff. Case workers come and go and they never seem to know what's been going on. All they care about is if they get the right paperwork from her. i've never been in the atic, its always locked, and ive never been to the basement, trust me, you don't want to go down there. i think Beth went there once and now look at her. i've never seen a garag door opener, i don't think we have one.

Curt stared long at the paper and forgot about Amber's little shimmy. After a while, he noticed the knob of the bathroom turning back and forth and he guessed he had been in there too long. Not wanting to upset Paul, he flushed the note without writing a response and left.

Paul was right about the social workers not caring. Not that he blamed them in any way. Their job seemed like the worst thing in the world to Curt. It was a wonder they didn't drown in the endless lines of broken families, the cases of abuse, drugs, alcoholism, sexual molestation, prison terms...on and on, they had to deal with the whole index of human misery. And any small triumph most certainly had to be swallowed up by the next ten cases of frightful inhuman behavior. It was no wonder they didn't bother Miss Feanor. As long as her paperwork was turned in on time and no one complained about her, Miss Gladys and the other case workers had hundreds of other problems to deal with. Because of this Curt couldn't expect any help from the outside world.

After leaving the bathroom, he went to his shuttered window, hoping to see someone on the lawn but the part of it that he could see, lay in deepening shadows and was deserted. He sighed. The sigh with its lack of energy and stale wind would've sounded more fitting coming from a hundred-year-old man on his deathbed than a twelve-year-old boy, still it was all Curt could muster.

With a casual glance about his room to see if it was in order, he shut his door the proper amount and climbed in bed covering himself as he had done the previous night and promptly fell asleep. He foolishly thought that he was too tired and too depressed to be afraid.

Chapter 6

His Insane Day

1

His door swung inward in complete silence and Curt went from deep sleep to instantly awake in a heartbeat. The house, at night was so perfectly still and silent that the tiny movement of air from the door's opening struck his blanket like a weighted breeze. His eyes shot open. It was so dark beneath the covers that they might as well not have been, however they still flicked about in a vain attempt to catch some light, while his ears strained for the smallest sound. Though it turned out that they needn't have strained at all.

"You were very close to losing it tonight."

The voice came from just above him and he jumped under the blanket. It was Miss Feanor, and with her voice pitched as low as it was, he knew that she couldn't have been more than an inch from the blanket that stretched across his face. When she spoke again, he could feel her breath through the light material.

"I thought you were going to be punished right there in the kitchen, and the way you talked to me, I hoped you would," she said still quietly. Now he felt her weight on the bed and he knew that she had put her hands palm down on either side of his skinny shoulders. The covers stretched tight across him—she had effectively pinned him there.

"You think I don't care about you and the others?" she asked in a dangerous tone. "Screw you, Curtis. I do care. I told you the rules; it's not my fault you wouldn't listen." She paused then, and though he didn't hear it, he felt her breathing heavily in anger. The heated air of her breath turned the covers warm over his face and he pictured her teeth, white in the dark and overly large. Curt's fear of her became a huge thing and with the constricting blankets, he felt trapped. He was only moments from panicking.

"If the teeth come for you tonight I want you think about how rude you were to me and maybe tomorrow you'll tell me if it was worth it."

The mattress creaked audibly and the blankets relaxed, unpinning him. In a second, the air in his room shifted again and he knew that he was alone.

Self-pitying tears came in a noiseless rush and he cried beneath his blanket, never feeling so small in his life. The words, 'The teeth may still come for you tonight,' began to replay themselves in his head and his silent tears became an audible blubber.

He was being stupid and loud again and he forced the blanket into his mouth to shut himself up, and after a while he began to suck on the blanket as a baby would. On a certain level he knew how pathetic he must have looked, however he was still only a boy, and no matter how self aware or composed he could be, there were times when he needed to be babied.

It took him a few minutes, and eventually he settled down, his chest slowly stopping its little kid hitching. Still he lay curled in a ball, sucking the blanket, it felt good to him. It soothed him. He deeply regretted having said anything to Miss Feanor and he wondered how he could make it up to her, perhaps by doing some extra chores around the house. Maybe he could wash the down stairs windows or...

Crreik

His heart stopped at the dread noise. It was the sound of Miss Feanor and her horrible teeth heading back up the stairs for him.

Crreik, crreik

Just as the night before the sounds were sly. They were insidious and with each slow step up, he felt more and more like throwing down his covers and begging Miss Feanor for forgiveness. She was coming for him...in the dark of the house.

Crreik, crrreik, crreik

It's not my fault! I didn't mean it! He wanted to scream this, but even more, he wanted to suck on his blanket and never hear those horrid steps again.

Crreik, crreik, crreik, crreik

The soft sound of approaching pain worked on Curt's mind so that soon he no longer thought about begging for forgiveness. Now he hoped a terrible hope. An unspeakable hope. He hoped the teeth would go and rip in to somebody else, and amazingly, the first person he thought of was Paul.

Crreik, crreik... Wwhhhhhh

This last noise wasn't a noise at all. It was the movement of air as his door swung open.

Bite Paul, please, he wished with all his heart.

Paul had been in a fight. Paul had written notes. Paul hates you! He thinks you're crazy. These insipid rationalizations came to Curt and he clung to them, needing a reason why the teeth should go and chew on the older boy. If she were to lift off his blankets and come at him with her teeth he'd tell Miss Feanor everything and not only would he tell her the truth, his mind quickly began to make up lies about Paul.

Miss Feanor walked slowly to his bed. She no longer slid silently, but instead walked in a poor attempt at being quiet, and now she stood over him.

Now Curt's mind no longer worked at making up lies about Paul. It seemed to shut down in terror. His breath caught in his throat and stuck there, and he froze in place with the blanket balled into his mouth. He became so still, that he felt as though he were becoming part of the bed itself, sinking into it.

For a very long time, he felt the presence of Miss Feanor hovering over him and then like magic—wwhhhhhh.

She left.

He thought he had gone limp with relief the night before, but it was nothing compared to how he felt then. It was as if he had no strength whatsoever and he didn't think that he could lift his arms, even if he tried.

After a moment, he spat out the blanket and listened as the near silent footsteps made their way down the right hand side of the hallway towards Amber's room. There they paused as they had the previous night, before continuing on, going around the U formed by the railing over the staircase, to what Curt thought likely to be the doorway to the attic. The same pause and then Miss Feanor went to Paul's room.

Here she didn't wait, but slipped into the room and Curt no longer heard the footsteps. His shameful wish for Paul to be attacked seemed about to occur and he knew that if it were to happen, he'd do nothing about it. He would only lay there, a disgraceful weakling. His fear of her was just too great.

Despite his exhaustion, he found he could still move his arms and he shoved the blanket back into his mouth and sucked on it like the baby he was.

A few seconds later, Miss Feanor left Paul's room without having punished him and the sound of her steps disappeared, heading down the hallway toward the mouse's room.

Sometime after that, twelve-year-old Curtis Regis fell asleep still sucking on his blanket.

2

For the third day in a row, Miss Feanor woke him up with a gentle shake. The diffused light making its bleary way through his covers told him that it was morning and that it was safer, but not altogether safe.

Though she was likely wearing her less evil personality, Curt still pulled the covers of his bed back timidly and only so far as to peek from beneath them. She eyed him briefly with a cold expression and then she reached out and pulled the covers further revealing his chest.

Oddly, she then lifted up his shirt. He allowed it. After his fear of the night, he worried that he would allow her to do anything to him. And if she were to bite him just then, he didn't think he'd be able to fight back. In fact, he knew that he would only lay there screaming as quietly as possible, perhaps begging her to stop, perhaps, telling her how he'd be good from then on.

No longer was it his life's wish to be a great thief. Now his only wish was not to be bitten and he trembled as she looked on his splotchy blue, green, and yellowed skin. She gave him a strange smile as if she were surprised at what she had seen and then told him it was time to eat.

With her right there, he dared not move, and it was only when she left did he slowly get up. Just how quickly he'd been cowed into submission surprised him. A few stressful days of painful silence and a couple of nights of intense fear had been all it took. As he dressed for breakfast, he felt a great deal of embarrassment at this.

Egotistically, he had always thought of himself as smarter, better, and definitely more courageous than any kid he'd ever known. Clearly he wasn't and at his current rate of mental decline, he would be a complete freak, just like the mouse, in months perhaps even weeks, instead of years.

That thought...the very idea of ending up like the mouse sent such a chill through him that he quite literally began to shake, and worrying that his shaking legs would collapse, he sat back down on the bed. It was some minutes before he was able to get a hold of himself enough to dress and it took even longer to summon the courage to go downstairs to face Miss Feanor and the other children.

As he entered the kitchen, he did not experience the same feeling of déjà vu as the night before. This was simply because he had taken so long to make it downstairs that four empty chairs sat before four empty bowls and just Miss Feanor was there to greet him. She didn't however; she only sat staring mindlessly at her coffee mug. He suddenly wanted very badly to skip breakfast that morning, but he didn't know if this was allowed so he made his way to his chair, giving Miss Feanor a wide birth.

Feeling an urgent need to be well away from her, he ate as quick as possible, however oatmeal, cold and thick wasn't easily swallowed and at one point he made a loud gulping noise. In his effort to get through the tense meal hurriedly, Curt didn't notice the sound and he took another larger bite, but movement caught his attention. Miss Feanor had pulled her eyes from the mug and looked at him coldly. They stared at each other and Curt was afraid to move a muscle but after a while, the thick glop of oatmeal that lay trapped in his mouth began to form a huge pool of saliva around it.

He had to swallow and when he did, the sound was even louder than the first. Her eyebrows went up at this for a moment, then she turned from him, looking back at her mug. Curt was so afraid of her, that his need to apologize, his need to make her happy overwhelmed his common sense and before he knew what he was doing he spoke.

"Sor..."

Too late did he remember that he wasn't supposed to speak and he sucked in his breath as if he could suck the word back into his mouth.

But he couldn't. The word had escaped from him and lolled about the still air of the kitchen.

It had an odd effect on Miss Feanor. He expected her to be angry, instead she leaned back from him, looking uneasy and a little sick. A moment later, she motioned for him to continue eating. As he ate, she eyed him closely. This only caused his throat to tighten, making the sound of swallowing more and more audible and with each successive spoonful, his blue eyes went wider in fear.

Though the oatmeal had the consistency of slow drying cement, he finally scraped the last of it from the bottom of his plastic bowl and presented it to Miss Feanor for inspection. At this she seemed relieved and pointed at the door for his dismissal. He was relieved as well and practically ran from the room in his desire to get away from her stare. All during his meal, he had relived the night before and he kept picturing her leaning over him in the dark gloom of his room, her teeth glinting as if lit from within.

When he pushed his way through the well-oiled kitchen door and stepped into the hallway, he felt another sudden rush of relief. He had fully expected Matt to be standing in the guard position he'd made for himself the day before, but the older boy was nowhere in sight.

Curt let out a loud sigh.

In alarm, he clamped his hand over his mouth. Just like the part of the word *sorry* that he had accidently let slip in front of Miss Feanor, this had simply popped out without him even thinking about it.

How much did it take to be punished? He had already made two stupid errors and it was only just after breakfast, there was still the whole day left to deal with. And worse, there was a need within him that was beginning to emerge.

It was a need to talk, to sing, and even to burp. The need was very similar to what he experienced the day before at dinner; however that had been a sudden thing, while this grew in him slowly. The silence of the house wasn't just oppressive, it was constricting in an unrelenting manner, and it felt like an invisible, but physical force that surrounded him, stunting his life. Holding him back from validating his own existence, not only with the sound of his own voice, but with all the normal sounds that accompanied a person's life.

It was as if he were being forced to become a ghost even before he had died. Both his mind and body rebelled against this, only that rebellion was for the moment, balanced by his fear of the horrific torture that would come if he were ever to succumb to the growing pressure to speak. That pressure was as physical as the silence. It was like a balloon swelling inside him and if his attention wandered for even a moment, as it had already twice that morning, it would slip out on its own.

Forming these concepts in his immature mind had the unfortunate consequence of bringing his awareness of the need to speak to the forefront of his thinking. It seemed to make the pressure greater and fearing that he would burst out screaming, he hurried to the family room, hoping to take his mind off his need.

The sight within the room and the alien feeling of déjà vu that accompanied it, nearly uncorked a loud exclamation from him. Luckily, he had slid down the hall still with his hand covering his mouth and only a quiet, "Mmff," trickled from between his fingers.

The family room seemed a part of a scene in a play that he kept walking in on. The four teenagers sat in the same poses, doing the same things they had done the two previous days. The boys read from hard cover books, Amber fiddled with an etch-o-sketch and the mouse worked on a puzzle.

As if he had arrived in the scene on cue, they all looked up at him at the same time, just as they had done before, and as before, they all wore the same expressions. Curt's mind boggled at what he saw in front of him and he questioned whether he was dead already and this was the house that he was doomed to haunt for an eternity.

He began blinking hard to clear away the feeling of déjà vu, but it wouldn't leave. It was like he had stepped into another day and he knew for certain how thing were going to progress. In a second, they would all get up and walk out of the room in silence, leaving him standing there alone. First, he'd cry—he could already feel the tears building in his eyes—then he would go to the front door where he'd contemplate the knob and think just how easy it would be to turn it and escape.

Yet he didn't think there would be much contemplating this time. If he went in that direction, he would try to make a break for it; he was sure he lacked the will to stop himself. But he knew deep inside that he wouldn't be able to escape, the door was locked somehow, and the teeth would come. The image of the teeth set his tears free to run down his face, they raced each other in an effort to get away.

Amber saw the tears and hopped up quick, as did the others and the déjà vu was fast becoming reality for him with its single grotesque ending.

But he changed that ending. "No."

The word, muffled by his left hand, still was as audible and as distinct as the sound of someone pulling the hammer back on a loaded gun. To the other children, it seemed as deadly as well and everyone froze in place.

This was suddenly new and different, and the feeling of déjà vu passed then, but Curt felt far from normal. Now he was looking at a room immobilized, stuck in time between heartbeats. No one budged, not even the mouse, who knelt on one knee with her head down and if her eyes spun madly in their sockets, then no one saw them. In those few seconds, it was a good thing for Curt that he didn't see them. He felt that his mind was close to breaking and every time he saw those eyes he wanted to scream.

In truth, he wanted to scream regardless, it had begun to form deep in his chest and it only needed a trigger to unshackle it. But the thought of a trigger made Curt remember that the scream was one as well; it would summon the foul teeth. One thing led to the next, day followed night, but what would follow the teeth?

Insanity.

The word fit the puzzle of the house.

Insanity, like the mouse with her mad eyes and empty mind, or insanity like Matt's: hate and anger filled, bordering on evil. This was the logical progression, and Curt felt a tremendous, yet very rational and sane fear of it.

Still panic wasn't exactly sane and as his fear slipped toward that mindless void, he backed out of the room before leaping up the stairs and racing in absolute silence for his bedroom as if the other teenagers were chasing after him, ready to drag him in front of Miss Feanor for sentencing and then punishment.

3

For a long while he leaned up against his door panting, using his slight form to bar entry into his room. No one had followed him up, and after a long span of time his breathing relaxed and his fear shriveled into a manageable knot in his stomach.

He went to his bed and sat upon it thinking about triggers. Need triggered sound, sound triggered Miss Feanor and she triggered insanity, and what came next was obvious.

For certain, death would come.

Dying as a raving lunatic frightened Curt badly, but the fact that he couldn't see any way to keep that from happening had his mind tipping. Even as quiet as he was he had to talk. It was part of his humanity and despite seeing the progression of the triggers he still felt the need to make noise, to be heard. To be someone. The contradictions that he wrestled with overwhelmed his twelve-year-old mind and without realizing it, he began sucking his thumb and rocking back and forth.

Sometime later Paul came up the stairs and stood looking sadly at him with his dull grey eyes. Eventually Curt became aware of the older boys presence and at the same time he realized what he was doing and quickly pulled his thumb from his mouth.

Before he could stop himself, he said, "I..." The explanation for his thumb sucking died on his lips as the word darted from between them. Paul stepped back in alarm as if he didn't want to be coated with the sound of the word, and he craned his head around listening, not to Curt of course but for Miss Feanor.

She must not have heard.

Paul grimaced at his new friend and between winks, he flicked his eyes toward the bathroom, where a note undoubtedly awaited Curt. With that he left, only Curt did not immediately head for the bathroom. He was afraid of the note. Writing notes had not been expressly forbidden, still Paul's secretive ways suggested that it too was a path toward punishment and just then Curt feared the punishment far too much.

So instead of going to read the note, he wrapped himself in his blanket and purposely ignored Paul's warning against sleeping in the daytime. Napping seemed the best way to follow the rules as well as a good way to pass the time and he cuddled up with the corner of the blanket in his mouth, falling quickly asleep.

It was a dreamless sleep and later, minutes or hours, he couldn't tell, there came a nasty sharp pain at the back of his neck, which woke him in a hurry. He pulled himself blearily into a sitting position. Rubbing the sore spot he looked around stupidly, and saw Matt leering over him, holding a tuft of dark brown hair up to Curt's face. It was a moment before Curt realized what he was seeing, and when he did he felt a surge of white-hot anger course through him.

Matt's face combined with a small shoulder shrug asked him, 'What are you going to do about it?'

Curt averted his eyes and buried his anger deep within him since there was no use trying to fight the bigger kid. This seemed to disappoint Matt who waited for a reaction he wasn't going to get.

After a few moments he sullenly motioned, 'Miss Feanor wants you to go take a shower.'

Curt nodded and was just getting up when Matt shoved the smaller boy backwards off the bed with sudden viciousness. Though his mind might have been flirting with a fear and stress induced madness, Curt's body was still agile and lithe. Falling backwards, he twisted, cat-like so that he landed on his hands and then pushing off the bed with a delicate kick from his trailing leg, he guided his body around in an ungainly, but quiet cartwheel.

Matt seemed cheated by the way Curt had landed so noiselessly and in a flash of insight he saw that Matt was somehow jealous of his quietness.

Though he didn't doubt the truth of this, it still seemed preposterous to Curt because the older boy did everything in virtual silence. His clothes never rustled when he walked, his spoon never scraped against the side of his bowl, and the pages of his book never made even the slightest crinkle sound as he turned them. If Curt were to close his eyes, Matt would disappear from the universe as if he never were.

That is, if it wasn't for his cruelty. His cruelty disturbed the air around him and it was only during those times when he was acting on that base emotion that he could ever be heard at all.

The insight went through Curt in a flash as the two boys froze in position staring at each other. At first he thought the older boy would come around the bed for him, but Matt stood just as he had when he had pushed Curt; bent over at the waist with his arms extended.

He locked his brown eyes onto Curt's blue ones and glared into them ferociously. It seemed as if they had entered into an odd contest of wills. Not much earlier, Curt's mental state had the structural fortitude of a snowflake, and if Matt had woke him with that same glare, Curt might have broke down crying right then. But the stinging pain in his neck and the hard shove that followed had him reacting physically, not mentally and he had ended his vulgar cartwheel in a low crouch.

[101]

A comfortable crouch, one that he could dart in any direction from, and one that he could maintain for a long time if need be. In contrast, Matt looked uncomfortable and when ten seconds had elapsed, Curt knew the boy would have to straighten soon and when he did, Curt stood as well, in one graceful move. Matt's eyes narrowed further at this and Curt saw another reason for the jealousy. The little thief made it look too easy. Curt was such a natural, and he adapted so well to extreme circumstances that even though he had only been in the house barely four days, he could already move nearly as quietly as Paul, who had been there well past three years.

But there was more to Matt's anger than merely being quiet, however what it was, Curt didn't know just yet and he wasn't going to get a chance to find out right then. After holding his glare a moment longer, Matt left in a huff as quietly as he had come.

Curt drooped in fatigue and sat back on his bed, feeling exhausted and it was a few minutes before he could force himself to go into the bathroom for his shower.

4

Curt still didn't read the note left by Paul. Just after stripping down and turning on the shower, he actually decided that he would, but as he walked past the mirror he caught sight of his bruised body. It stopped him in his tracks and he stared hard.

The colors of his skin were turning a nasty green-yellow and it gave him a queasy sensation to look at his own body, but he also became morbidly curious as to the bite marks. With the help of the mirror, he counted fifty-three of them and as he counted, his skin broke out in large goose bumps.

Dazed by what he'd seen, he forgot the note.

As one would expect, showering in Miss Feanor's house was a noiseless endeavor. The water came from the showerhead in something slightly heavier than a fine spray and instead of the usual gurgling, it slid down the drain as if disappearing down a black hole. Even the curtain sighed back on cloth sleeves, still noise could be made if care wasn't taken. Therefore, Curt moved through his toileting routine with deliberate slowness, yet still he made tiny noises and each caused his anxiety to flare. However, this was nothing compared to the anxiousness he felt after he had dried himself and slid with increasing skillful silence to his room.

There he found another purposeful chaotic mess.

His few belonging were strewn widely about and his sheetless bed lay overturned. In the doorway he stood for a long time staring in disbelief and ever so gradually, the suppressed scream that had been with him earlier came back, thickening and squirming in his chest like a live snake. It wanted out. It demanded out.

This time it would come bursting from him and there was nothing he could do to stop it. He felt the urgency of it as if he were about to vomit and he staggered into his room, shutting the door behind him. Knowing that he only had seconds, he grabbed up his pillow and then taking his blanket he used it to wrap the pillow to his face and only then did he scream.

"Mmmmmhhhrr!"

Chapter 7

Déjà Vu

1

Curt had no way of knowing how loud the scream had been, since it had been muffled even in his own ears. He could do nothing but wait for his punishment. It was not long in coming.

Perhaps no more than a minute went by before his door opened with dreadful slowness, but it was only Paul who stood there. He surveyed the scene of the trashed out room and with a look of reproach he came in uninvited and began to clean. Oddly, this grated on Curt, who after days of insanity felt nothing but a crushing despair. He didn't want to be rescued, he wanted to give up, and though he didn't really know what giving up entailed in such a perverse house, he knew that cleaning wasn't a part of it.

Taking the older boy gently but firmly, Curt guided him out of the room and then went and sat down on his bed to await his doom. The house was all a stir over his scream apparently, because Amber came up stairs next and peeked dully past his door. Curt had been crying silent tears, and when he saw the blonde girl he attempted to wipe them away, however his face was so wet that it was a useless gesture. For some unknown reason she looked even more dejected than Curt, and he felt a stirring of sympathetic emotion for her. He tried to ask her what was wrong but in her state Amber missed his hand gestures and just as suddenly as she appeared, she left again.

Despite his own issues, a spasm of worry for her went through him. She wasn't moving as silently as she should have and he heard her walking away instead of gliding. He got up to look down the hall after her, but nearly ran into the silent menacing form of Matt, who had come back just then.

Surprise at seeing him there sent a shockwave through Curt, he backed into his room, and it wasn't playacting that made his face morph into a mask of dread. However, he needn't have feared. Matt seemed only to want to make sure that Curt was suffering, and he merely glanced into the room, happily seeing that the mess he'd made was still there.

The house was usually so subdued that Curt's brain was whirling with all the activity of the last few minutes, but as he sat there on his bed, letting the despair take a good grip of him, the mouse made her appearance. He heard someone coming. Unlike the others, she generally crept about instead of sliding, and though she was nearly as quiet as Paul, she still made very soft sounds. The mouse gave him the willies, and he slipped off his bed, darting to the other side of it, hoping that she was only heading for the stairs. He wasn't that lucky. She came into his room and he saw that she had added a new dimension to the outward aspect of her insanity. In addition to her horrible rolling eyes, her lips formed long strings of words that kept the thin pink lines of her mouth moving ceaselessly.

With her hands out, the brown haired girl came around the bed toward him and it looked as though she wanted to tell him a secret, or perhaps hand something to him. However to Curt, all that she looked capable of giving him was a disease and he put his hand out, telling her to stop, this she ignored it and kept coming. Fear of her insanity blossomed within him. He knew little about mental illness, save only that the insane were horrible and disgusting and stank of urine or regurgitated beer. Though the mouse looked clean enough, he guessed that if she were ever to escape, it wouldn't be long before she resembled the rest of the bums sleeping in the alleys.

But this wasn't the streets, where if he had met her, he could elude her with ease; instead it was a rather small bedroom. Therefore, he let her come nearer and as she approached, he noticed the words that formed on her lips were all in her head and no noise escaped her. When she was close enough, he calmly dodged to the side and vaulted neatly over his bed before scurrying to the bathroom, locking the door behind him.

The lock was a cheap one and Curt, with the help of his Swiss Army knife that as of four days ago he carried about with him, could have popped it easily, but he figured it would hold against the mouse. Just in case he took a firm grip of it, hoping that a shut bathroom door was enough of a discouragement and that she would go away and perhaps bother Matt. But clearly she wanted something from Curt and it was with a sickening feeling in the pit of his stomach that he felt the doorknob twitch beneath his fingers. She wanted in bad enough to make noise and the knob rattled back and forth as she jerked at it from the other side of the door. Fear of the insane girl had Curt's hands damp with sweat and now he worried that if the lock failed he wouldn't be able to hold her back.

Without any forewarning the movement against the knob vanished and there was absolute silence from the other side of the door. Curt immediately dropped down to the floor, pressing his face against it, hoping to see the mouse's feet through the crack. However, the angle wasn't a good one and he couldn't see even a shadow. He had no way of knowing if she were skulking about on the other side of the door—he was trapped in the bathroom.

After a few minutes of boredom he went for the note.

Hi Curt,
i know how you are feeling. i have been there. You want to screem and yell at the top of your lungs, but don't. It won't do you any good. You will be punished and an hour later you will want to screem some more. My first time, i talked myself into thinking that the punishment wouldn't be so bad, it was a hunderd times worse. Stay cool it will pass.

When Curt finished, he wished he hadn't read the note. The activity of the last few minutes had caused the need to scream to recede, but now with the notes reminder it was there in the forefront of his mind. He had to do something to take his mind off his need, so he wrote Paul back.

Hi Paul,
i didn't make the mess in my room, Mat did. He hates me for some reson. i didn't do anything to him. i think i have to scream. It feels like my throat and lungs are atached to my brain and it is telling me to scream. Does Miss Feenor ever leave? Can we scream then, or will Mat rat us out? What's wrong with Beth? She came after me just now in weird way. Will she try to hurt me? i think the windows will break if we hit them with something hard enouf. Sorry about my hand righting but i haven't been going to school much.

He reread both notes before putting his in the secret hiding spot and flushing Paul's. In order to kill time and take his mind off the need to scream, he went through the closet and the cabinet beneath the sink again. These held nothing but cleaning supplies and he wished he knew something about chemistry, thinking that if he did, he could make a bomb out of what he had found there. From long ago he remembered a vague warning from one of his foster parents not to mix bleach with something. But he couldn't remember whether it was ammonia or comet. At the time in that far away home he hadn't planned on touching any of the chemicals, since he hadn't planned on doing any cleaning.

There wasn't any bleach in the bathroom either way, but still he read the warnings on the back of the various bottles until he became bored silly. At that point he got up and paced back and forth, his anxiety building in him along with the scream. Finally, he couldn't stand the little white room any longer and went to the door and opened it in a silent rush.

The mouse wasn't in sight. Nobody was. Curt looked into his room and saw that it had been cleaned up and everything sat perfectly placed just as it had been on his first day.

He wished it wasn't.

He liked the mess. The lack of structure. Part of him, the part that naturally rebelled and could stand up to the scream and maybe even stand up to Matt, wanted to go in and destroy the room again. But the weak part of him, the part that felt fear and needed friends, thought it would be disrespectful and so instead he went and sat on his bed.

2

He wanted a note from Paul, and he wanted to scream. His leg bounced up and down in a frenzy of jiggling as he waited to see which would come first. Thankfully, Paul came out of his room, just as the silence of the house began to overwhelm Curt. He smiled at the older boy, but Paul didn't return the smile, in fact, he gave Curt an exaggerated purposeful frown.

Curt got the hint and cast his features back into dour somber look. Smiling in Miss Feanor's house was clearly a suspicious activity. Paul went to the bathroom and a few minutes later came out, moving with very deliberate slowness.

'Don't go running for the bathroom.' Paul's body language told him. So Curt forced himself to again count to a thousand, or rather that was his aim, but he gave up around five hundred and scooted into the tiled room.

Hi Curt,
You can never screem, or make any noise. EVER! You can't escape throogh the windows and doors, don't even try. Mat hates everyone. He has to be Mr. Perfect and thinks that the only way to be perfect is if everyone isn't. You know what i mean? But there is another reason that he is after you. He wants you to crack. He wants you to get punished and soon, so be on the lookout for him. When i first got here he said that he held the record for going the longest without being punished- three and half days. Beth won't hurt you, but she will get you both punished.

Three and a half days without being punished? That didn't seem right to Curt, who hadn't seen or heard anyone being punished yet.

Paul,

i've been here four days and haven't seen anyone get punished yet. How much noise does it take to get punished? i screamed into my pillow earlier, but nothing happened. Will i be punished tonite? Beth came after me with her hands out, i think she was going to try to tell me something or grab me. When is lunch?

After Curt planted his note, Paul studiously avoided the bathroom for what must've been an hour. This drove the younger boy up the wall and he took to pacing in his room and counting for as long as he could. He had hoped that waiting for the notes would help to stem the need for him to scream, and it did, but only for those brief moments when he was reading or writing them. The rest of the time, the scream was right there with him, hiding just below the surface of his throat, biding its time. Threatening to explode.

Finally, the blonde boy went to the bathroom.

Curt felt as if he were dancing on fire to get the note he was certain that Paul would leave him. It seemed that his precarious sanity rode on getting that little piece of toilet paper and it was all that he could do, not to go rushing into the bathroom after Paul had left. He forced himself to wait, but he waited too long and Amber, looking very mopey slid in before him.

He nearly cursed aloud, but held it in by the barest margins and was obliged to pace his room a hundred times after Amber had left.

Hi Curt,
i'm sorry, but we don't get lunch. Diner and brekfast are
always the same, except at odd times like once we had two
feet of snow and we ate some of the other food. Beth will try
to grab you sometimes, just push her away. i don't know if
you will be punished tonite. If you screemed, i didn't hear it,
maybe they didn't either. The record is for who lasts the
longest when they first get here. As far as i know, everyone
gets punished there first nite, so that doesn't count. This is
your fourth day, so if you make it through to tommoro you
will have the record.

Why Curt wanted these notes so badly, he didn't know.
As usual, the note hurt more than it helped. This was due
mainly to the idea of not having lunch and his stomach
growled insistently from then on at the notion of eating. Not
that he expected any food prepared in the house to be any
good, but it would at least break up his day, which since
there was nothing to do, seemed so dreadfully long.

For the first time in his life, he wished mightily for a
watch. Before he had been a prisoner of Miss Feanor's, in his
previous existence as a hustling thief, he had always hated
watches. To him, they were a symbol of laws and rules, and
he scoffed at people who lived their lives as if the little piece
of metal and glass on their wrists should dictate where they
went and whom they saw.

Now time seemed twisted out of shape by the evil house,
so that hours turned into days and days into weeks. In his
mind he felt that a clock of some sort would bend it back.

Paul,

What do i get if i break the record? A cookie? Ha-ha How long did you last? Do you know anything about sun dials? I want to make one. i'm wishing i stayed in school longer. Did i ask about a telephone already? What about the mailman, have you tried to signal him in any way? i don't think i can last here, i'm going crazy trying not to talk.

He planted the note and waited, and waited, trying his best to ignore his all-consuming need to talk. This was how it went for the rest of the afternoon, planting notes and then pacing his room endlessly with his fingers shoved into his mouth to keep from speaking. During that long afternoon, he would have frequent visitors from the other children, all of whom would stop by to eye him closely and other than Paul, they all looked as if they expected, as well as hoped that he would crack at any moment.

When Curt would go to the bathroom and see the strange red-eyed boy with the wild tangled hair looking back at him from the mirror above the sink, he'd think he was on the verge of cracking up as well. For the time being, the notes kept him going.

Hi Curt,
Braking the record means putting off punishment, which is worth a millyon cookies! It will get better in a day or two, just try to hold on. We never get mail here, so there isn't a mailman. i've never heard a telephone ring, but once i heard Miss F talking quietly in the down stares bed room once, so there mite be one, but i never go in that room. i don't know anything about sundials, but i've seen them. i was in the 5th grade when they put me here, so i'm not so smart either.

Paul,

Your a brain compared to me, i only got threw the second grade before i quit going to class, it was to boring. But i have lived in a couple of schools and i read a lot, including text books which is kinda funny when you think about it. You said it will get better in a day or two, what happens then? Hold on to what? Theres nothing here but crazy people and silence(no ofence) i think i'm going crazy too. i can't think straight half the time and i feel like i'm about to explode. You never told me how long you lasted when you first got here.

This was the last note that he wrote before Matt, with a hard look on his face, came up to tell him that it was time for dinner.

3

Dinner was not as expected.

Curtis sat down knowing full well he would see the same plate of food that he had already seen twice before and would again many times well into the future. Yet that foreknowledge didn't matter much since really, there was no preparing a person for a break with reality.

It all happened so fast. Sitting down, he saw the white plate with its unkempt piles of carrots and rice, and its formed slabs of spam and suddenly the table fell away from him. Reality spun into the unknown, leaving behind only that plate with its rambling mounds of eternal bland sameness. Déjà vu became layered upon déjà vu and seeing his plate as it always was and always would be sent a picture-echo rampaging through his mind, upsetting the carefully arrange teacups of his sanity.

His plate seemed stacked upon another that looked just like it, and that was stacked upon another still.

And then suddenly, his entire world turned into layers of spam and rice.

It was impossible to blink away the image, and there was no seeing past the plate and now it was as if he was looking upon it for the hundredth time and then the two-hundredth. His eyes bugged out and his jaw worked in silent protest at what he was seeing. Thousands of plates stretched down before him, stilted and stacked, making stairs that twirled and twisted.

He began to lose the feeling of the chair beneath him, and dimly he was aware of his chest expanding, filling with the air of a scream that was all but unstoppable. But he didn't care about a scream, not in the slightest, not then. That plate was the only thing in his universe.

Thankfully, Matt, unable to wait for Curt to implode on his own, rescued him once again. From nowhere, according to Curt's warped senses, a small round carrot slapped him coldly, dead center in the middle of the forehead. It bounced off him and rolled away, like a little orange wagon wheel, and as it did so, Curt's eyes followed it hungrily.

It seemed improbable, that someone would throw a carrot at his head, yet to his fragile mind this was far more real than seeing hundreds of plates of spam and rice, accordioning up and down in front of him. Therefore, he turned to the carrot, which acted in the most normal fashion—rolling from the table, it bounced a few times before coming to rest a few feet away.

When he looked up, still attempting to right his mind, he saw the other children staring at him as they shoveled food into their mouths as fast as they could. Miss Feanor bent and picked up the carrot and looked at it strangely for a moment before she calmly put it on his plate. He almost protested this and would have, save for the fact that his mind still seemed only distantly connected to his body.

Instead of protesting, he reached down without looking at his plate and picking up a carrot, stuck it in his mouth and chewed. He finished his meal this way; bare handed, afraid to look down at what he was eating, afraid that his mind would fly away again. Slowly his mind came back to him as he ate, and with it came the sane fear of insanity.

If one didn't counted his first day, which he slept through most of, he had been there only three days and already he was having mental issues. It was like his brain was a living mass of grey worms, each struggling against the next so that all his thoughts were starting to jumble and work at cross-purposes.

What he did after dinner helped a lot; he cleaned.

Even though he was just cleaning things that were still clean from the day before, he was at least doing something physical and it helped, not only to pass the time, but to focus him as well. His hands touched and knew each of the figurines on the hall runners; he traced the lines of theirs features, convincing himself of their reality. Soon he no longer doubted his eyes and rapidly, his mind was once again closer to what it had been and he thought with greater clarity during those two hours of useless cleaning than he had all day and as he worked himself into a sweat, he realized that Matt was not done with him yet.

Because of that stupid record, Matt would want to break him as soon as possible, which meant either a physical attack or another round of destroying his room. Curt guessed the latter as the most obvious point of attack, and hurried through his chores hoping to have time to set his room straight. With maybe ten minutes to go, he finished and zipped quietly down the hallway and up the stairs. At the top, a cold look from Paul greeted him and he knew without looking that his room was trashed and so without pausing, he skated past the blonde boy but not toward his own room.

Strangely, he felt good. His issue with Matt was a dilemma, a puzzle to be solved, a battle to be won. His keen mind and agile body reacted well to this sort of pressure and moving quickly with the barest whisper of his feet on the gleaming wood he went straight for Matt's room and barged in.

Thankfully, the older boy wasn't there. Curt opened the top dresser drawer, scooped out the clothes, turned for the hallway, and heaved them down the backstairs. The contents of the next drawer were thrown around the room, while the third drawer he took with him and zipped back to his room.

There he went about setting his room to rights and with Paul's help, they were done just as Matt came in seething with silent rage. Curt dive rolled over his newly made bed and grabbed up the stolen drawer that sat just on the other side of it and threatened to unload the contents of it onto his floor.

Matt stopped in his tracks.

Curt was not very good at pantomiming yet, still he managed to get his point across.

'I...look...downstairs table...clean...you get drawer...messy?...I dump drawer.' His room wasn't his only vulnerable spot.

Matt glared fiercely, but sourly as well and he hurried off down the stairs. Curt followed slowly after with the drawer lifted ready to be dumped and watched as Matt arranged the nick-nacks properly on the running tables in the hall. Curt then pointed to the powder room.

'I didn't touch that room,' the older boy said with a quick headshake. Curt believed him and in an effort to make peace between them, he handed the drawer to Matt, though he could have let it fly. And what's more, he followed after and picked up the clothes he had dumped down the stairs. Matt's face was unreadable at this.

There was no time to read into it further, Paul stood glaring at him from down the hall and Curt suddenly remembered that the blonde boy had to finish as well. On winged feet, he noiselessly made it to the bathroom and brushed his teeth while watching Amber's bottom shimmy toward him.

Feeling good, even triumphant at his small victory, he let himself become distracted by the sight of her delicate curves. A moment later, Paul punched him the arm.

'Move it,' the blow told Curt. Sheepishly he did so and was in bed minutes later with his lights out. One by one, he saw the other lights in the house wink out and then suddenly, one flicked back on for a moment and then it too went out for good. It had been Paul's and he worried for the boy.

And then he worried for himself.

Chapter 8

The Record

1

Curt had much to worry about as he laid in the dark with the covers up over his head.

There was still a chance that Matt had been lying about messing up the powder room, as well the older boy could've cleaned his own room up quickly and went back down stairs for more mischief. Also he probably knew Miss Feanor's schedule so well that he could be, even then, slipping up silently to Curt's door and that any second he could expect an attack from the older boy.

In alarm, Curt jerked the covers back and looked about. His now darkened room was empty, but just then a shadow loomed outside his doorway and he had to make a snap decision. Was it better to be hit by Matt or caught with his covers down by Miss Feanor?

He slipped beneath his blanket.

Hot sweaty minutes passed and when no sound came from the other side of his covers, Curt allowed himself to move but only enough to build his little breathing tunnel.

Now he could worry in earnest.

Lying there, he wondered if his scream from earlier had been too loud or if all of his little noises had added up enough to mark him as the child in need of punishment. Only time would tell and it took a very long time indeed. It felt like hours before Curt heard the first tell tale noise.

Crreik.

This was his fourth night and he knew now the number of the stairs. There were twelve and each heralded a coming doom with a slightly different call. Some were louder, others higher pitched and the fifth, held on to its sinister Crrrreik much longer than the rest. Together the twelve sly sounds were enough to push a boy over the brink of insanity if he were near enough to the edge.

And Curt had his feet dangling out over that terrible abyss.

Earlier, as he had cleaned, he had marveled at how quickly he was succumbing to the insanity of the house. Foolishly, he had just assumed that he would possess a mental toughness that was superior to the other children, and this was mainly due to the fact that he hadn't started out as a well-adjusted All-American boy from a normal family. He thought that his life on the street would've hardened him in some way and he supposed that since he was nearing some sort of stupid record, it had.

All the same, there he was huddled in a ball beneath his covers and at that first sound his thumb had come unbidden to his mouth and he began to suck. In no way was he embarrassed by this, in fact he didn't even realize he was doing it. His whole mind was taken up with the coming teeth and the huge possibility that tonight he would be punished. The dread noise from the stairs was a countdown to this and his terror mounted as the sound came closer and closer. Crreik, crreik, crreik.

Wwhhhhhh. His door opened in that near soundless way and somehow he forced his trembling body to go absolutely still.

Again, the sly footsteps walked around his bed and then back, and for a moment Curt thought that she had passed on him once again, but then there was a new sound in his room. A soft little sigh; the breath of air that the plastic runners of his dresser drawers made as they were being pulled back.

New fear flared within him as he worried about how well he and Paul had put his drawers back in order, but they must have done a good enough job because soon the drawers were pushed back into place and Miss Feanor left.

Tonight she visited every room in turn staying a long time in each, and Curt refused to stir a muscle until well after she had moved on toward Matt and Beth's rooms. Even then, he did little but shift his position and wipe away the tears. He always cried.

Thinking that the danger of the night had passed, Curt slept.

2

The next morning, Miss Feanor woke him again and just as she had the previous day, she pulled up his shirt and looked at his chest. She gave a small unreadable shrug at what she saw there and motioned that breakfast was ready. Curt nodded and tried to prepare himself for what was coming. Not the lukewarm oatmeal, that he could take, but it was the certain feeling of déjà vu that would accompany it.

Heading into the nook, he decided that last night's policy of just not looking at the food was his best option. It wasn't easy keeping his head high while he ate, yet it worked. Unfortunately, since he wasn't looking at his food, he was forced to look at his fellow inmates and that turned out to be nearly as upsetting. There was something decidedly wrong with all of them. Each of their personal eccentricities were more pronounced. Matt, who once wore a look of sour peevishness, now looked straight up angry, and not just at Curt, but at everyone.

The mouse, he could barely stand to even look upon. Her lips moved ceaselessly, even as she ate, and small bits of oatmeal flew out toward whomever she was currently rolling her eyes at. She was simply disgusting and the sight of her turned his stomach.

It bothered him to look at Paul as well.

The twitching of his right eye had started to now affect his left and Curt wondered how the boy would be able to see if this kept up. Curt looked away from him as well and his eyes sought out the girl whom he fancied. Amber appeared ill. Her pale features were practically paper white, and the lethargy that she had displayed at times was now more pronounced, so that she ate her breakfast almost as a sleepwalker would. Slow and deliberate, but without noticing at all what it was she put into her mouth.

Seeing them this way made him wonder what he looked like and after breakfast, he hurried upstairs to get to the shower first. He didn't like what he saw in the mirror. Curt would be thirteen years old in a few weeks; however he had the dark circles and bags beneath his eyes of a forty-year old career alcoholic. At first, he rubbed at them and splashed water on his face, but soon he had to give up, and he turned away from the mirror, hoping to forget what he saw. It nagged at him though and he felt a weight growing in him.

With the depression of seeing his own haggard face in the mirror, Curt didn't much feel like reading the note that Paul had left for him. However, he read it on the off chance that it could hold something that would cheer him up.

Hi Curt,

i only lasted part of the first day. i didn't mention it cause i was embearassed. Miss F told me about the punishment and a hour later i went crazy and tried to escape, first by trying to run out the front door and then by trying to bash in the family room window. To get throogh this, you have to find something to hold on to or things won't go well.

Curt shook his head tiredly at the note. It had only made him more depressed. Things didn't seem to be going well for any of them. Before he got into the shower, he wrote a quick response.

Paul,
Everyone seems more depresed then normal today. Is there something going on?

A large part of him didn't want to know.

He stayed in the shower for a very long time. The water wasn't exactly soothing, but it was warm and there was the slightest fuzzy sound that accompanied it. That small noise caressed his ears gently and after a while, he thought he could hear odd sounds in it. Rhythms or mechanical echoes and sometimes he fancied he could hear tiny voices as well. He strained to catch these, but they were the auditory equivalent of a willow-o-wisp and were always just out of his reach.

3

Matt met him at the door when he finished with the bathroom. And after he finished getting dressed, Matt met him outside his bedroom. And when Curt went downstairs to be around the others, Matt followed him there as well.

He seemed determined to hound Curt into breaking and with his unrelenting stare, he gave off waves of negative energy that nearly made it happen. Everywhere Curt went that morning he was shadowed by the angry boy and he couldn't seem to sit still for very long, because of it. Hiding in his bedroom was his only point of refuge, but soon it felt more like a jail cell. Just as the day before, he found himself pacing while sucking on his fingers, however now there was no waiting on a note, rather he waited on a boy who had learned patience through years of being a prisoner in that wicked house. Matt sat outside his door, waiting. Waiting. Waiting.

Curt felt the edges of his world begin to slip. It was a long morning that turned into an eternal day. The silence slowly became too much for him to handle. After hours trapped in his room, he took another turn about the house and as before, Matt was there but now he began to push Curt or jostled him. The little thief fled back to his room.

There he heard the silence. It radiated in his head until finally, he gave in to the pressure building inside him, and just like the day before, he pulled his blanket and pillow from his bed, and headed for his closet.

The closet held a small but very clear path.

The path would start as a trifling thing; however it would ultimately become a wide boulevard that led, if one kept to it, eventually and invariably to insanity. He knew this and feared it as well; still his need to speak and be heard, if only by himself alone was too great. Therefore he headed for his closet so he could hear the sound of his own voice and he knew logically it wouldn't stop with a simple humming or a few whispered words. He had seen too many whacked out bums not to know that they carried on long dialogues with themselves and he guessed that they too began in some simple way such as this.

But just as he went to close his closet door for the first of what he guessed would be thousands of conversations with himself, a flash of light lit up his room, and it froze him in place. His breath caught in his throat at this, and when the great bang of thunder followed it, his body jerked in fear. The vibrations of the sound ran through the panel of the closet door and he marveled at it. A second flash of light that was even brighter than the first came moments later and this time he felt mild alarm. The thunder arrived instantaneously with the light and the house seemed to shake around him.

Could the house have been hit by lightning? Forgetting about Matt momentarily, he went to his door and looked out—the house appeared unharmed. As he stood there, Matt glared at him as he had all day, but when a new sound came, the glare slipped and became instead disappointment.

The new sound was a very heavy rain. It drummed with a wonderful intensity upon the roof of the house and Curt felt sudden giddiness at it. He even went to smile at Matt, who seemed oddly unnerved by the sound and within moments of the beginning of the deluge, the older boy wandered away, heading for his room.

Just then, Paul and Amber came out of their bedrooms and both wore a mixed look of relief and awe. Upon seeing Curt, Paul began heading his way, but Amber came rushing up with a determined look on her face and grabbed Curt's hand.

"Get away, he's mine," she said out loud. Curt's heart leapt into his throat at the sound of the words and he stepped back from her in complete shock.

4

Even for a girl, her voice was surprisingly high, but her commanding manner and the possessive way she spoke about Curt were more surprising still. There was a dangerous look on her face and Paul backed away, leaving the two of them alone in the hall. She wasted little time and yanked him into his room. Shutting the door behind her, she crossed to his window, dragging him along.

"It's best right here," she said in a high breathy whisper and pulled him down to a sitting position on the floor, the dangerous look now completely gone from her face. Curt's mind was a jumbled confusion of questions, starting with: *what's best right here*, but these would have to wait as she went on speaking, quickly.

"I'm Amber Vandermark, I'm fourteen...I think. Do you know what day it is? I'm pretty sure that I'm fourteen, it's so hard to tell, but my birthday is February tenth and I think there have been like, three Christmases that I spent here. Oh, but don't get your hopes up, you could barely tell that it was Christmas, though we do get a bit of chocolate, which was nice. You didn't happen to like, go to Greenfield elementary did you?"

Now she paused, waiting for an answer but the moment was a little too much for Curt and he must have looked as stunned as he felt.

"It's ok," she assured him, nodding her head vigorously. "You can talk low...or quietly I mean, when it rains, it's allowed cuz nobody can hear it."

Still he hesitated.

The mindset needed to keep from speaking under these dangerous conditions wasn't something that he could turn off and on so simply. Little things had slipped from his lips under great pressure or when he wasn't thinking about it, or when he felt his mind was coming unglued, yet now it seemed he could speak as a normal person would, if only he could overcome the inertia of the last four days. It was difficult to find his tongue with so much mental friction.

"It's uh..." Curt counted days quickly in his head. "It's February 28...1997." He added this last part just in case she was confused as to the year as well. "And I have..."

She interrupted, "The twenty-eighth of February? Is that all? That's weird. Don't you think that's weird? Shouldn't it be like, almost July fourth? You know you can so totally hear the fire works on the fourth of July. But I don't like the fourth or New Years. Those days suck, but it is good to know what day it is, you know?"

Curt actually loved Independence Day. As a thief, the distraction of the pretty lights, the beer drinking, and the press of bodies made for easy pick pocketing. Last year he had come away from the night with well over three hundred dollars.

He smiled at the memory, "Actually I..."

"Time is so like weird here, you know?" She looked dreamy for a moment, "I'm supposed to be a freshman at Carrick high. I was so looking forward to high school. My mom, before you know, told me I would make the cheerleading sqawk...sq...I mean *team* easily, but I never really believed her. Now, I don't know if I want to be a cheerleader, I think I do, but I'm not sure, you know?"

Even though there was a temporary halt to her speaking, Curt only nodded vaguely, knowing already that she wasn't actually asking him a question and sure enough she began talking again after barely a second.

"You never told me if you went to Greenfield or not. I did. I miss that school. It was so much fun. Did you know I was Glenda in the Wizard of Oz? I was. My mom died then and my dad, like disappeared. I kept my magic wand from the play. I used to think it was like a real wand and I kept it until I came here. Were you ever in a play? You could of been like...the scarecrow. I was going to say Toto the dog, but I bet you would've thought that would be...uh angry? Or rude, I think I mean. But it really wouldn't have been rude of me, since we had a boy play that part too."

Curt blinked wondering if he was supposed to answer this time and as she didn't start talking again, he said, "I didn't go to Greenfield, but I visited there a few times. Did your mom...die during your play?"

"No, she died at work. Bam, just like that. It was a...uh brain asperinism or aspearnism or something like that. I forget the word. It's weird, I forget lots of words lately, you know when you're talking to your sel..." Suddenly she stopped speaking and snapped her mouth up closed with a little clicking sound. Her eyes went wide and there was embarrassment in them.

He guessed that she secretly talked to herself, just as he had planned to do, only minutes before. So not wanting to humiliate her, he started speaking as if he didn't notice her sudden silence.

"I know what you mean, it happens all the time to me. But speaking of the Wizard of Oz...*are you a good witch or a bad witch?*" he asked her with a smile.

For a moment, she looked blankly at him before light came back into her eyes and remembering the lines answered, "Who, me? Why, I'm not a witch at all. I'm Dorothy Gale from Kansas." She giggled then and grabbed his arm. "So you were in the story...uh, I mean the play? What part were you?"

There was a warm needy grip to her hands and he didn't mind it at all, in fact, he rather liked it and he liked as well the smile that she had for him. It made his heart begin to race.

"I wasn't in any play, but I saw The Wizard of Oz a lot. It's one of my favorites." This was true on both accounts. Going to see plays and stealing from the people attending them was one of his favorite past times. Frequently there was free food, or rather, food that was free for him and everyone seemed to be in such a good mood. The kids ran around with abandon and the parents took picture after picture of their little darlings.

People always enjoyed the illusion of warmth and security that being in an elementary school gave them. However, in Curt's opinion, that was when a person was in the most danger—when they thought they were safe.

While at these plays, he'd linger in the back of the auditorium, finding his marks, waiting for the lights to go low, or for the moment when the Wicked Witch of the West would be doused with water.

'I'm melting! I'm melting,' little Suzie would say to great applause and then Curt would casually fish through a purse, or rifle through the coat that invariably hung from the back of a chair, easily finding the wallet where it always lay, in the inside left pocket. He'd then slip away, perhaps hiding the now empty wallet in someone else's coat or just tossing it, depending on his mood and then he would enjoy the rest of the play, or if the week had been a spare one, he'd go for seconds on another mark.

His least favorite plays were the ones celebrating diversity, or the environment or worst of all, celebrating the greatness of the state of Pennsylvania. The kids and parents never seemed to enjoy these as much and it was harder to steal from someone who wasn't relaxed and watching the show with their full attention. There was one time however, when a kid dressed as the Liberty Bell fell off the stage and in all the ruckus, Curt cleared two hundred dollars.

Amber broke in on his thinking, "Can you guess what my favorite line in the play was?" She only paused long enough for him to open his mouth. "I'll give you hint, the chair, I mean the care...the person I played, Glenda said it."

"Would you be mad if I told you that the good witch's name was actually 'Glinda'?" He asked, noticing that she did indeed have trouble with words, especially the larger ones.

"It was?" Her pale face screwed up prettily and he saw that she could very well be a cheerleader, if only she could ever be allowed to see the sun again. "You're probably right, but you didn't guess!"

"Uh...how bout when Glinda tells Dorothy all she has to do is tap her feet and say, *There's no place like home*?"

"Nope. It's like just after Dorothy gets to Oz, when the other witch shows up, and Glen...Glinda says to her, 'Oh, rubbish! You have no power here. Be gone, before somebody drops a house on you, too.' I just love it how powerful she is; like she was just waving away a fly. I wish I could drop a house on somebody." She seemed to cloud up for a moment and turned her head at an angle to see through the shutters into the gloomy afternoon sky.

His spirits had been rising with the conversation and the warm touch of her hand on his arm, which had never left. But now Curt felt a trace of gloominess settle back on him and it reminded him of where he was.

"Tell me, do you know why this is all happening? Why Miss Feanor keeps us locked away? Do you..." he stopped in mid-sentence; she had turned from the window and looked back to him with a hard cast to her very white face. He leaned away from her at this, thinking she was seconds from exploding in wrath, but instead she slumped.

"I've always loved the sound of the rain. Even before...this. I liked to fall asleep to it," she said in her high voice. It was like a little girls voice, not a teenager's. "When it rained like this, I would go cuddle with my mom. She liked it as well. Until she died that is. Now she probably hates it. Her hole probably fills up with muddy water and I'm sure the worms just have a field day. You know what I used to like a lot? Gummy worms..."

She chattered on like this for quite a while. No aspect of her former life went unspoken about, right down to the number of shoes she owned on her last day before foster-care. Curt marveled at her and not only that, he reveled in her. His overwhelming need to speak, which mere minutes before had been all-consuming, now disappeared completely. He spoke only a little but it was enough and he realized that what he needed more than speaking was simple contact with another human.

The notes from Paul had been barely keeping him from drowning, but this long talk and the innocent touch on his arm that came with it, buoyed him, lifting his spirits and he sat back smiling and nodding as Amber spoke. Every once in a while he would comment or make a joke and only a single time did he again bring up their present circumstances.

In a lull, he asked a question that had been with him since they first started talking. He didn't have a burning need to ask it, since he didn't expect much from her answer, but he had to at least try.

"Have you ever tried to escape?"

He hadn't read her well at all, because her reaction was a complete surprise. Her perky demeanor dried up in a heartbeat, replaced by coldness that seemed very adult.

"You want to know about escape? Why don't you go to the front door and give it just a touch, just a little wiggle and see what happens. They will know. Even with the rain, they will know. Go on, I'll wait right here. Go get it over with. You know you can't last forever." Her eyes were pale blue circles of deadly ice and looking into them, he saw that she truly did want him to go and just as Matt did, she wanted him punished.

His mind swam in circles over this and he tried to pull his arm back from her grip, but she held tighter, her fingernails digging into his skin, even through the long sleeves of his shirt. Thankfully, the change that came over her lasted for but a moment and she smiled suddenly.

"I like, so didn't mean that," she lied to him through her smile. "Really. Why don't you tell me something about you?"

He began to talk about himself in only the most general way and the odd moment passed as Amber quickly took over the conversation, steering it toward boy-bands that she once had crushes on. Curt let himself relax and once again, he enjoyed her very closeness and the sound of her high little girl's voice and the way she used the word 'like' every fourth or fifth word.

Amber had a slim and very pink tongue that came out and showed itself to him when she said the word. He couldn't stop staring at it, and it so captivated him that he barely heard the slight change in the tone of her voice a few minutes later. She had been talking about some movie star when she mentioned Curt's eyes.

"Your eyes are a nice blue just like his," she said and now her voice wasn't nearly as high as it had been. "Don't you like so totally think so?"

Curt loved going to the movies, but whom she was talking about, he hadn't a clue. "You're right. I never noticed before," he replied. Having your eyes compared to a movie star's, no matter who's was very nice and he felt a little warm glow at this.

"You have better lips than he does," she continued and now her eyes were full on Curt's lips and the warm feeling that had been filling him evaporated. "Your lips are like so much bigger...or fuller I think I mean."

She licked her lips then, and he knew they were about to kiss.

5

His chest seized up at the thought. He had never kissed a girl before, not even his mother as far as he could remember. Amber bent slowly toward him and he licked his own dry lips with a tongue that was drier still and tried not to think about the strange excitement which had laid a hold of him, it felt distinctly like a form of panic.

They kissed and he was certain that he'd been terrible. It was a long, very wet, open mouth kissed and when he pulled away with a desperate need for oxygen, she wiped her mouth with the back of her hand as if a Great Dane had slobbered all over her. But despite this, she smiled at him.

He smiled back as if it had been the most remarkable thing, though in truth he didn't know what to think of his first kiss.

His body had failed him in such a way that it almost seemed like it wasn't his at all. For one he hadn't been able to breathe, and then there were his hands, which had suddenly felt oversized and ungainly; he hadn't known what to do with them. His heart had pounded and he had been hyper-aware of it and was certain that Amber could feel it beating through his chest, yet at the same time, he had gone numb from the waist down.

Still he was eager for more.

Their second kiss felt in no way different from the first and Curt knew instinctively he was doing something wrong. It was like there was too much work involved and what's more, there didn't seem to be any *passion* to his kiss. He wasn't certain he knew what passion was, but he did know that he wasn't feeling it.

When it came to kissing, his only frame of reference came from what he saw at the movies and so he tried to emulate the actions he'd seen there—to disastrous effect. Many times the actors appeared to be so passionate about their kissing that it looked as if they were practically chewing the face off their partner.

"Oh! Ow! Hey that hurt a little," Amber pulled back holding her mouth. Their teeth had clashed together with painful force. Curt grabbed his mouth as well, it was more to hide his tremendous embarrassment from the older girl.

"That didn't go..." Curt started to say, but as frequently was the case, was interrupted.

"I'm so sorry," Amber cut in, blushing. "I've like, never kissed anyone before."

Curt wanted to say something to reassure Amber, however the blush in her cheeks had done wonders for her and she suddenly became beautiful. She looked alive and healthy and normal. Her blue eyes were deeper in color than he had at first thought and they reminded him of a picture he had seen of a beautiful white beach running along the bluest water imaginable. Her eyes were just like that, the blue sitting in the porcelain white china of her skin. It made him want to kiss her again and so he did, but this time he just wanted to feel the red of her lips with his.

So he planted a small gentle kiss on her lips and this time he understood what all the fuss over kissing was about. There was an instant connection between them, one that was awash in feeling and nearly endless possibilities. They kissed for some time like this and as they did, Curt relaxed becoming less aware of the ungainliness of his body. But as that left him, he began to feel the first stirring of his sexuality. Strangely, the heart stopping fever of his lust that he figured he was supposed to be feeling was nowhere within him, instead all he felt was a growing concern that Amber would notice his...thing.

It would be difficult for her not to, they were sitting very close together, and *it* was pointing up, right at her through his jeans.

He shifted his position, laying his arm across his lap and broke away from the kiss hoping to take his mind off of *it*. "Wow, for someone who hasn't kissed anyone before, you're a really good kisser," he said. He had no idea if this was actually true, but he did enjoy the kiss. She wiped her mouth again with the back of her hand and smiled her thanks at him.

"Really? I thought I was so terrible and..." She stopped talking abruptly. She had grabbed his hand from his lap to hold it and not only did her hand actually touch *it*, worse, she then looked down in confusion at *it*. Her eyes went wide and her mouth came open in surprise.

But Curt's eyes positively bugged and he felt his cheeks go instantly red, while his ears burned with the embarrassed heat of a blast furnace. In a flash he half-turned away crossing his legs, "I...I...it...I, uh." This was all he could splutter as he watched her face go from surprise to confusion. He was completely mortified about what he assumed was the improper way his body had reacted.

Having not been raised with parents, or an older brother, or even with actual friends, his understanding of sex was contorted to say the least. In his mind, people didn't have sex with their clothes on. Sure they could 'make-out', while dressed, but then they'd have to go to a bedroom to do that thing that so confused him.

Everything about sex was a puzzle to Curt, even the mechanics of it left him feeling stupid. He knew that his thing would go into the girl, but his went straight out, at least most of the time, while a girl's thing was more upward and he pictured their bodies forming an odd T. This was in direct contradiction to a bit of a dirty movie he'd seen and he felt certain his thing was broken. As evidence of this, his thing would frequently grow for absolutely no reason, sometimes painfully so and it would remain that way for a long time.

Not only that, his thing was weird looking, at least to him it was.

6

All this went through his mind in a wink and Curt felt a strong desire to apologize, but also an even stronger desire to hide. However, he was perfectly petrified in his shame and could only sit in his awkward position and seconds ticked by uncomfortably.

At first, Amber stared at the floor, then an uneasy look came over her and she darted her eyes up to his face a couple of times.

Standing up abruptly, she said, "Come on, I...uh want to show you something."

"No, that's ok, I'm good right here," Curt replied, still covering up. His petrifaction wasn't entirely metaphorical and there was no way he was going to stand up anytime soon. But Amber had other ideas.

Turning around she said very quietly, "I won't look, I promise."

"Maybe you can show me later."

"Uh-uh, it'll be too late, now come on," she insisted. Curt scrambled up and self-consciously pulled his shirt out to cover his erection. Amber turned around and immediately broke her promise by glancing down with nervous eyes at his crotch. She then peeked back to his face with a guilty look.

'Come on,' she motioned and then taking one more quick look toward his thing, she slid silently out of his room. Curt looked down as well and shook his head at the lump pushing out.

"Jeez," he whispered in frustration and then slid after her. She waited in the hallway, just outside the bathroom door.

'Be very quiet,' she motioned with her large eyes while her index finger went to her lips. Then taking more care than was usual for her, she slid to Paul's door, nine feet away and with a delicate slow twist of the knob, she cracked it open an inch.

Now Curt was very confused. He stood there waiting for further instruction from Amber, but she had her eye to the crack. When she turned back, it was with an almost sick look on her face.

'Come here and see,' she pointed.

What he saw through the door was unnerving and though he had spied on hundreds of people, perhaps even thousands, he felt a guilty shame at this particular view. Stretched out onto each other and totally naked were Paul and the mouse. They were making love in the most graceless and inelegant fashion. Not that Curt was in any way an expert, but what they were doing seemed altogether uncompelling. They ground their sad and dreadfully skinny bodies together, their faces contorting in what looked like pain. Similar to Curt, they seemed unable to overcome the inertia of the strictly enforced silence of the house and they moved against each other without noise, but also without any passion or even enjoyment as far as he could tell.

He stared for all of two seconds, before Amber pulled him away, taking him by the hand, and drawing him back to his room. She looked at him still with that slight sick look on her face, but now he re-interpreted it as nervousness bordering on fear.

"Do you want to do that?" she asked in a low whisper.

Her question sent a tremor of anxiety so deep into him that he felt it in his bones and now it was his turn to look sick. The idea of being naked in front of Amber, especially now that he was covered in nasty green and yellow fading bruises was almost enough to make him wish for an end to the rain.

"I don't know, do you want to?" He figured that she did, otherwise why else would she have shown him Paul and the mouse. His question was a delaying tactic only and he struggled hard to find a cool sounding reason not to.

His desire for sex was as immature as he was. He had only just begun to look at girls in that way and to progress from his first kiss to making love in the course of an afternoon was too much for him and there was now a trickle of nervous sweat running down his back.

"I don't know...maybe. I thought you did, cause of your...thing," she retorted with another glance at his crotch.

His thing, in the space of the last minute had shrunk smaller than its usual size and was currently in hiding. He didn't know what to say to her. There was no way he was going to explain the defective nature of his penis to her, but it turned out he wouldn't have to, because almost immediately she started talking again.

"We don't have too if you don't want to...I don't know if I want to. I like kinda do, but...I'm a little scared. You know what I mean?"

"I..." was all he could get out before she began to speak again.

"Matt and Paul both want to do *it* with me, but I can't. Matt is like way too much of a jerk and Paul...he's like a brother to me. He helped me out so much at first, you know."

"I..."

"But I don't want you going to Beth." She took a deep breath, "So...if you want to, we can do it."

She paused longer than usual, but it was only from nervousness, not from a lack of something to say.

"I..." he said again.

"Have you done *it* before? You're awfully cute and you're such a good kisser..." She left off and Curt waited for the pause to draw out a long time before he even considered answering her.

Awfully cute? He had never been called that by a girl before and it did wonders for his confidence, which had faded to nothing over the last few minutes.

"I've never done it before...I'm only thirteen you see," he lied casually, since he was only a few weeks away. "I don't think I want to do *it* just yet...I mean, I've only just kissed you after all, but I promise not to go to Beth."

"You won't? Good, good. Thanks a lot," she was practically in tears with relief, which had him wondering, what all this meant. "You don't know what this means to me," she added as if she were a mind reader.

"I guess, I really don't," he said truthfully. She gave him a sharp worried look at this, as if she suspected him of attempting something underhanded.

"What do you mean? Everyone needs someone...I need someone," she began to sound desperate to the point of being in pain. "Beth already has Matt and Paul, and I know she has her eye on you. I can do the...uh, that...uh, the same things she does, ok? We can do it right now..."

She began to paw at him and he was forced to hold her hands, "Amber, please. It's ok. We don't have to do anything just now. I'm just trying to understand. Are you trying to say you want to be my girlfriend?"

Her eyes were wet with tears. "Yes...please, I need someone. She's trying to get me all...uh, all...what's the word? When there is nobody, uh, like near you?"

"Alone?"

"Yes, she wants me to be alone, all by myself."

"Why would she want that? Maybe she's just lonely too," Curt said reasonably.

Amber looked around the room, or so Curt thought at first, but then he realized that she was listening. It was with a much softer voice that she continued.

"She wants me crazier than her. She wants me to be punished, all the time."

Curt was finally getting some real information from her. "Why? Did you do something to her?"

At first Amber seemed insulted by this question and before answering she looked at him as if he were being terribly rude. "No of course not. How could you ask that?"

"Then why..."

"Why is she trying to get me punished?" she asked, shocked that he wouldn't know. "You may be cute but you aren't too...brittle? Or uh, smart I mean. She wants me punished so she won't be." His look must have shown his confusion, because she only paused a second before going on, "Somebody has to be punished, right?"

"No, I don't think so."

To this she gave him a queer look. "I guess you're still...frag...is it fragile? When you're new to a place? Darn it! I mean new, that's the word I wanted. You're still new here." She shook her head with angry frustration over forgetting her words. "The others all use the word punishment, but it's not really punishment. You can be like perfect in every way but the teeth will still come, they are...I don't know the right word to describe this, but I think that hungry is close. They *have* to come, like it's a need. That's why the first day after someone gets punished, it's usually more relaxing around here. The need is gone."

"They have to come? That doesn't make any sense!" he exclaimed and she only shrugged. Curt wanted to get mad at what appeared to be an uncaring reaction, but then he realized he was getting actual information so he continued, "Paul said that I should hold on to something to get through this. What do you hold on to?"

She started to answer, "I always try..." Suddenly her eyes narrowed at him and little lines creased her forehead, but then she turned unnaturally cheery. "Just stuff really, nothing much. You should ask Paul about this anyways, I'm sure he'll tell you."

She was easily the worst liar he had ever encountered. Quite possibly from lack of practice, yet either way he didn't want to upset his new friendship and said, "I will, thanks."

"Does Paul write you notes and leave them in a book?" Her manner was far too casual.

"He did at first, but..." he trailed off purposely, hoping to draw information from her instead of giving any away. Her eyes narrowed at first and then she nodded as if understanding.

"He's fine right now, but if he ever stops writing notes that means he'll want you punished pretty soon...but please don't hold it against him," she said in honesty. "He's normandy...norm...uh, usually such a good guy, but there's a lot of pressure you know and he gets kinda," she waggled her hand a little suggesting Paul would go slightly crazy.

Curt believed her. In fact, he was sure they all were a little crazy. "Should I hold it against Matt?" he asked, knowing that he would, regardless of her answer.

"Yeah...you should, he's so nasty about everything." Her delicate pale face darkened at this, but then she grew sad, "I don't want to talk about him or the house. The rain sounds like it getting...lesser? Is that the word? Lighter? Either way it could end soon and I don't want to waste my time... how bout you tell me more about you. You don't do much talking do you?"

7

For a little while he spoke about inconsequential aspects of his life, however as he expected, she again took over the conversation and he happily listened to her chatter on sweetly. He would have rather went back to kissing, but it seemed the mood had left her, though she still held his hand with a warm needy grip and it was enough.

Unfortunately, the feeling of being on vacation ended soon after. The heavy rain gave way slowly to a much quieter snow shower and this drifted into a fall of fine white powder. As it did, Amber's voice sank lower with each passing minute, until finally she stopped talking altogether and only sat in the growing dark, staring at the floor. Eventually, Curt got up and switched on the overhead light and saw that at some point in the last few minutes she had transformed.

Sitting so still as to appear lifeless and with her perfectly white skin, Amber now resembled a manikin in a store window. She barely even blinked. It was unnerving having her sit like that on his bed, and Curt was a little afraid to touch her or in fact to move at all. With the passing of the rain, the house had once again gloved itself in its constricting silence, but along with it came a dreadful feeling of anticipation. It felt as though the house was waiting for something to happen and the feeling sent an army of goose bumps marching across his flesh. He decided to wait out this odd feeling in absolute silence but that was not to be.

Matt showed up then. As usual, he was absolutely soundless as he approached and only the small feeling of moving air announced his sneering presence. The relaxing rain had done nothing to calm Matt's hate for Curt, but he was surprised at how fiercely angry the boy became once he saw Amber sitting upon the bed.

He lost all control.

His face turned instantly red and there was a murderous jealousy in his eyes. He advanced on Curt, his face contorting and his throat working up and down, when he did, the smaller boy set his feet against the frame of his bed, and just as Matt reached out for him, Curt eluded his grasp with a beautiful backwards somersault. Regaining his feet with only a small thud on the floor, he sized up the situation, it didn't look good. He was trapped in his own bedroom, but just then the unspeakable happened.

Matt spoke.

In frustration and rage, he said, "Hugn!"

It wasn't much of a word, yet it was loud and had a tremendous effect on the moment. Almost immediately, Matt lost the ability to organize the muscles of his face and they took his features through every range of human emotion in a matter of seconds. Finally, they settled on something that looked like a constipation attack and he turned from the room and fled the sound of his own voice.

[142]

Curt stared in amazement, and then slipped around his bed with a wide toothy; it was then he saw Amber hadn't stirred in the least and still sat staring at the floor. In a heartbeat, Curt's elation turned upside down and he became alarmed for her. It was one thing to zone out, but this was scary.

No longer did she look like a manikin; her muscles had become slack, and now she seemed rather a corpse. Forgetting all about Matt and indeed about where he was, he spoke.

"Amb..." Though he caught himself in mid-word, still he sucked in a sharp breath as a stab of fear sunk into his chest. Twisting around to look at the door, he froze in place for many seconds, waiting for the dread sounds of approaching doom, but when nothing happened, he turned back to the blonde girl. Her eyes were as wide and empty as a Montana sky and just as blue. With a growing fear for her, he waved his hands in front of them; nothing happened.

However, when he gave her a little shake, she came instantly awake.

"With the yarn. Did you see..."

The volume of the words unexpectedly spilling out of her mouth froze him in place and it took over a second for him to lunge forward and clamp a hand over her mouth.

Those six words were the loudest thing he had heard in the house since Miss Gladys left five days before and the air in the room came straight away alive with fear. Moreover, that horrid feeling of malignant anticipation grew about them.

Amber was all too aware of what she had done and her pale blue eyes grew huge as she stared over Curt's shoulder at the doorway leading to the darkening hallway. Curt desperately wanted to turn back and look as well, but there was a voice within him telling him to remain completely still and quiet. He could only kneel, looking into her eyes, hoping he would see what was coming from her expression.

Amber seemed like a rabbit in her fright and he could feel her heart thudding crazily beneath his right arm. He knew for certain that if he moved, even the slightest, she would bolt out of the room and so he held to his position long after he had lost feeling in both legs.

Finally, the air around them seemed to relax and as it did, he let his shoulders droop, letting go a huge pent up breath. It felt to him as though they had dodged a bullet and he tried to give her a smile of reassurance, but Amber shook it off, leaving the room in a hurry, her face still marred by fright.

As frequently happened, when others grew more afraid, Curt had a tendency to become less so and despite the fact that he was still damp with the sweat of his recent fear, Curt wondered whether they were all being ridiculous about this whole thing.

Together the four teenagers could overpower Miss Feanor with relative ease. In fact he could kill her himself, under the right circumstances. He had never killed anyone before and had never thought of himself as that sort of criminal, but he was sure that any jury would see it as a clear case of self-defense.

He decided to write to Paul on the subject, but minutes later as he read the older boy's note that had been left earlier that day, he had second thoughts about whether he could trust the blonde boy so wholeheartedly with such a delicate subject.

Chapter 9

Set Up

1

Hi Curt,
Everyone is on the edge cause it's been 4 days since the
last punishment and everyone gets to feeling presure. Since i
got here, the longest we have gone between punishments is 8
days and normally its around 5-6 days. You don't look good
and if you feel the need to crack and just scream, no one will
think badly of you. Actually they may like you better cause
you will have gotten it out of your system. if you do, try to do
it in your room. its a little bit better.

It almost seemed to him that Paul was hinting for him to
crack; like it would be good thing. Was this wishful thinking
on Paul's part? Or perhaps a very subtle attack—a way of
undermining his resolve? With the note wilting in his sweaty
palm, Curt feared to bring up the idea of murder. He could
imagine the note being 'accidently' left where Miss Feanor
could find it, maybe slipped under her door, or left casually
next to the coffee maker. That was a queasy thought.

Curt decided to adopt a wait and see attitude where
murder involved. Instead he asked about Matt. There was too
much animosity between the two older boys to worry about a
lack of trust on that subject.

Paul,

i dont think i will crack just yet. The rain really saved me and i feel much better. Hopefully, i will last a little while longer. How do we deal with Matt? if the presure is on, he will only get meener. What do you do? Do you know anything about moris code? i'm trying to come up with a plan for dealing with matt. Whats SOS? Amber says, you two used to rite notes, do you still?

Curt didn't like the note.

Writing was a poor medium for lying, especially on single ply toilet paper. He had no plan concerning Matt and Morse code but he realized that certain dangerous truths should be guarded, just in case. He actually wanted the information in order to signal the outside world using his ceiling light. The idea had come to him the night before when Paul's light had flicked on briefly. He had wondered if he were being signaled in that way and he recalled the use of Morse code he had read about in one of his many stolen textbooks. However, other than the fact that dots and dashes had been used to signify letters, and that ships had sent out SOS calls when they were sinking, he knew next to nothing.

After writing the note, Curt wanted to go to the family room to see if there were any books there that might mention Morse code, instead he ran into Amber, who unfortunately told him it was time for dinner. Curt wasn't hungry. He should've been starving, but the idea of spam and carrots killed the hunger pains neatly. Setting aside his mission to the family room, he slid on reluctant feet down to the kitchen.

As he had at breakfast, Curt kept his eyes off his dinner plate and for the most part only looked at Amber. To look at the others was far too upsetting. Paul's twitch had progressed, Matt was still Matt, and the mouse kept shooting bits of rice and carrot out through her constantly moving lips. To Curt's surprise, whispers came out as well. They were barely over the sound of her breathing, but they were still in the low range of audible. He tried to catch what it was that she was saying, however the whisper seemed mostly composed of the letter "S" or the "Sh" sound.

She sat right next to Miss Feanor, but the mad woman appeared not even to notice the tiny noise. Her muddy brown eyes were far away in another world.

So Curt ignored the others and did his best to make eye contact with the blonde he now thought of as his girl friend, but she ate robotic like and her eyes never came around in his direction. In fact, her eyes never focused on anything and he noticed that she missed her mouth with her fork frequently, it was disturbing.

There was a lot that was disturbing about the dinner. Chiefly, it was how the others were clearly feeling the pressure of the upcoming punishment. The rain and his ability to talk and be close to Amber had helped Curt's state of mind tremendously, but seeing the other children's anxiety only increased his own. He decided to wolf down the hated meal as quickly as he could and get to his chores before he began to feel that sense of *losing it* as he had before the rain came.

2

The chores that night were difficult for him. He was supposed to be hurrying, but his mind wandered ceaselessly, hopping from memory to make-believe and then to his grim reality in a painful loop. Eventually he fell into a nice fantasy about escaping the house with Amber.

In his imagination, he had just been showing off his legendary lock-picking skills to the helpless blonde girl, when he heard a whisper behind him. He was in the downstairs hall wiping off the microscopic particles that he couldn't see, but assumed had gathered on the knick-knacks during the last day, when he heard the noise. It wasn't the sound of sock covered feet swishing towards him, but that of a breathy whisper.

Startled out of his daydream, he turned and saw the crazy-eyed mouse heading toward him. She moved slowly, yet not very quietly and was easy to duck around, which he did, twisting away from her. Paul had suggested pushing her away, however the idea of touching her disgusted him, however in the end he was forced to. She kept coming at him over and over, no matter how much he dodged. Finally, he gave her a hard shove and it was like turning a wind-up car, she walked off in the direction in which she had been pushed and knocked face first into a wall. Thankfully, she bounced off it and then kept going down the hall.

It was a horrible sight and the spam in his gut shifted, threatening to come back up.

Returning to his dreary repetitive work, he forced himself not to daydream and to be more on guard, which proved useful in two ways. First, he finished his chores quickly and second, he caught sight of Matt on two separate occasions and neither time did the older boy look as if he were just out for a stroll. Curt felt like a sparrow stalked by a mountain lion and it set him on edge.

For as long as he could remember he had been a thief, and he had fancied himself the quietest, the slickest, and the coolest under pressure. But Matt, and his constant nasty presence had Curt second-guessing himself. With his chores finished early, Curt decided to turn the tables on Matt.

He found the older boy in the dining room dusting like crazy and at first he didn't see Curt in the doorway. When he finally did, Curt fought hard to suppress a huge smile at the older boy's look of shock. Matt glared at him for a moment, looked slightly confused for another, glared again, and then went back to work.

Curt decided to test the older boy. Leaving the room, he stopped just outside of it, stripped off his long sleeve turtleneck, waited a moment, and tossed it down the hallway. It made only a very small sound. Within seconds, Matt had crept to the doorway and peeked around the corner, but jumped again startled at the sight of Curt standing there half-naked.

Curt snorted quietly and retreated as Matt turned toward him. There was an urge within him to turn and slide off down the hall, however five days with the older boy had taught Curt never to turn his back on him, since that was when Matt was most dangerous. So he stood his ground, and sure enough after another bout of glaring, Matt eventually went back into the dining room.

Curt allowed himself a moment of elation at this and then took off in a quiet fast slide up the stairs to his room grabbing his shirt on the way. He would change and get ready for his ridiculously early bedtime and then zip back down to keep an eye on Matt. Oddly, there was a bag sitting on his bed and when he looked into it, he saw that all of his borrowed clothes were neatly folded up in it.

Could he be moving out? His heart jumped happily at the thought and he pictured himself smiling and waving goodbye to Paul and Amber as he stepped out the front door. However, he then saw a little note on top of the clothes.

Put your dirty clothes in the bag and set it outside in the hall. Put these where they belong.

Curt deflated at this. Feeling stupid for even thinking he'd ever be allowed to leave, he went through the motions of putting the clothes away. He almost forgot how he was going to keep watch over Matt and when he remembered, he went down the stairs in a gloom. He could tell his emotions were getting away from him again, because inadvertently he startled the older boy for a third time, yet despite the panicky twitchy jump Matt performed at being startled again, Curt could only look at him dully.

This was probably a good thing, since Curt wasn't trying to irritate the older boy; he just wanted to keep an eye on him. But he didn't have long to do that either, Matt finished cleaning the living room a few minutes later and scurried upstairs in a huff. Curt trailed after him, making sure to leave plenty of space between them, but the older boy simply went into his room, shutting the door behind him.

Curt then went to use the bathroom that he shared with Paul and Amber, pausing only to watch the shimmying bottom of the blonde girl. He wished that she'd turn around and acknowledge him, but she went on cleaning and he knew that if she had turned, he would have only seen the dead eyes of her listless self. When he was in the bathroom, he found Paul's note and the paranoid kid within Curt saw it as a reaffirmation that Paul wanted him punished.

Hi Curt,

I read a book and they used Morse code, I think SOS is three long, three short, three long, but those were sounds not lights. What are you thinking about doing? Matt is hard to take, I guess you just have to get used to him. Amber and I used to write notes back and forth, but she got caught and got punished and now she won't do it any more. I'm happy that the rain made you feel better, but sometimes after it makes it worse, because you remember the sound and it starts to become a fuzzing noise in your head. Fuzzz! It can drive you nuts.

Just as soon as he finished reading the note the first time, Curt could suddenly hear the fuzz sound that Paul referred to. The house was so dead silent that the fuzz, which reminded him of static from an improperly tuned radio, grew louder filling the void where normal sound should have been.

It seemed to grow very loud, very quick, forcing Curt to cover his ears, but this did no good. The sound now seemed to fill the inside of his skull and it shifted, suddenly forming a long, apparently endless tone, much like a dial tone. It raged hugely in his mind. He knew the noise wasn't real, but that didn't stop the need within him to scream it away and he was very close to crying out.

He pulled at his hair. He paced back and forth in the small white tiled room and he even began slapping his head, but nothing stopped the eternal tone from ringing. At length, he turned on the water in the sink to splash his face, but he paused as his ears finally found something real they could hold onto.

The tiny sound of the water trickling out of the faucet. Amazingly, it had the strength to push back against the ringing in his head and for a long time he stood, bent over with his head in the sink.

Paul had done this to him on purpose.

Curt knew it as a fact, not as part of his paranoia. He'd even been warned by Amber that Paul might try something. And he remembered how she had pleaded with him not to hold it against Paul. It was absurd to think Curt wouldn't, in fact, just then he hated Paul more than he hated Matt. The eldest boy at least hadn't pretended to befriend him.

He seethed in a silent rage at the betrayal, and began plotting all sorts of improbable revenge scenarios, but a minute later, he heard a voice in his own mind speak a single word.

'*Hypocrite.*'

3

It's not the same, he thought to himself. But it was the same, essentially.

There had been many times over the past six years that Curt had falsely befriended all sorts of people, and in the last four months, this number had been growing. He had discovered an interesting tactic to breaking and entering—he called it befriending and entering. It had become nothing for him to search out lonely marks at the different schools that he made rounds at. Curt would get chummy with them, hinting at how long it had been since he was invited to a sleep over. The power of suggestion was a strong force and usually within a day, he would have his invite. The parents of these unfortunate loners would always be gung-ho for junior's new best friend or in many cases, first best friend to come for a sleep over, not realizing they were opening the chicken coop to the fox. It may seem counter-intuitive, but Curt made it a point never to steal during these all night bore-a-thons, instead he used the time to eat and make discreet inquiries.

"Do both your parents work?"

"Do you have any older brothers and sisters?"

"What are you doing for summer vacation...winter break...spring break?"

Later, just before sunrise, he'd 'lift' a set of the keys, normally the mother's, and make sure that he was out of the house with a proper 'thank you' just after breakfast. A week or two later, he'd then burgle the home, usually in the middle of the day, making sure to gouge at the lock with a screwdriver, disguising the fact that a key had been used to gain entrance. No one ever suspected a twelve-year-old boy was behind these break-ins.

This sort of B&E was quite profitable as well as easy.

Now trapped in Miss Feanor's house, he cursed the ease of it all. It had made him lazy and he'd done little to learn how to pick a lock. He knew only the very basics; pins, tumblers and such, but he had never tried more than to pick the simplest locks.

He could always ask his new 'best friend' Paul, if he knew anything about picking locks.

The sarcastic thought made him shake his head in frustration and he wondered if the older boy knew anything about Morse code at all, as he had mentioned in his note. Perhaps three long, three short, three long meant something else entirely...something bad.

Now suddenly everything Paul had ever said or done became suspect in Curt's eyes, and he began to see conspiracy and duplicity in the boy's every action. Then he remembered the fight Paul had with Matt. The two boys had fought simply because Paul was helping Curt out and he would've cracked for certain that night without intervention. Where was the scheme behind that?

He breathed out tiredly, not knowing the truth behind anything and left the bathroom without a glance at Paul, who stood patiently outside it. Going to his room, he was pleasantly surprised to see it still in one piece. But he no longer trusted anyone or anything and went through it inch by inch, making certain that it was indeed perfect. He then slunk about the house re-checking his areas and only just climbed into bed when the hall light shut off behind him.

4

The night should have been his most worry free since he arrived. He had after all, been quieter than on any previous day, yet he worried regardless, and not just for himself, for Amber too.

She'd been so loud when she came out of her little trance that Miss Feanor must have heard it, even from downstairs. Still, the mouse had been noisy as well, with her constant whispering and Curt shamefully found himself hoping that she would be punished that night.

He had a long time to hope.

Just as the previous night, it took hours before the first of the twelve steps began to crreik and in that time, he decided that the next day he would confront Paul about setting him up with that fuzz business.

"Don't think about a pink elephant." Some kid had said that to him once and sure enough, all he could think about was a pink elephant. What Paul did was virtually the same concept, he had implanted the idea of a noise within Curt and with the dead silence of the house, that noise had grown in his mind and nearly caused him to break. To Curt, who now barely felt the effects of the punishment he'd suffered through while asleep, five nights previous, this was inexcusable. But he was willing to give Paul a second chance simply for Amber's sake. That and the fact that he had a sinking feeling that he didn't know the full ramifications of the punishment.

Having seen the horrible teeth marks on his own body and the awful bruising, he knew that the bites would hurt terribly, but he was missing something from the equation. There were four teenagers against one lady, why didn't they ever try to overpower her? Even if she carried a weapon during the punishments, she certainly didn't carry one about the house with her during the day. Something wasn't right about all of this, and he decided that figuring it out was almost as important as escaping. Tomorrow he would find out the truth.

First he had to get through the night. When the stairs started their ominous crreiking, Curt froze in fear beneath the blanket. Later, he would wonder about that as well. After five days, he should have been used to the feel of Miss Feanor creeping around his room, opening his drawers and circling his bed. However, it was with the same exact dread that he felt his first night, that he cowered there in the dark. It was inexplicable.

She moved on, after what seemed like an endless time going through his meager belongings and when she did, he breathed a near silent sigh of relief. Miss Feanor then repeated this same routine in each room. There were no punishments that night, but Curt would not have long to wait for the next one.

Chapter 10

On The Sixth Day When All Else Was Complete, God Created Death

1

Day 6 was a nightmare and Curt spent the hours of the morning praying for a return of the rain. Clouds came in and tortured him with their teasing presence, but not a drop fell from the sky. That didn't stop him from taking the trip up to his room every half hour or so, where the view between the shutters afforded him a glimpse of the low grey ceiling on the world.

They seemed too light in color for rain.

He sat up there brooding, gazing at the sky until the silence became too loud, and then he would go back down to be with the others. Curt found he needed to be around them, even around Paul, whom he still felt animosity towards.

Straight away after breakfast, he had written a note to Paul, but the blonde boy had yet to touch it, which seemed for now to be a good idea. His twitch had become so great, that reading or writing wouldn't be easy for him. Paul wasn't the only one feeling the pressure to be perfect. The mouse was easily the worst, her eyes zigzagged an unending "S" pattern, up and down, up and down, all the while her whispering had picked up so that if you bent near enough to her, you could barely hear the words:

"You'll be next."

When Curt had come down from writing his note, she had come through the family room door just behind him and grabbed him around the waist.

"You'll be next," she whispered, he nearly screamed right then but held it back by the barest margins. Her hands went exploring toward the front of his pants and in revulsion, he forced her away from him. It was then he saw her eyes.

He wished desperately that she would blink. She looked possessed and so frightful that he backed away from her, falling over Amber, who sat on the floor. He thudded loudly onto the carpet and scrambled to right himself just as the mouse came toward him again.

"You'll be next," she whispered a second time. He hopped up and shoved her very hard toward the hallway and she walked off in that inhuman way of hers.

Curt went to signal an apology to Amber, but it was as if she hadn't noticed any of what just happened. She lay sprawled from when he had tripped over her and had yet to move. Curt knew better than to touch her, since the last time she had erupted loudly, and so he only sat staring at her in growing envy. If this was how she dealt with pressure, she was certain never to be punished—or so he thought at first. Within three minutes of his arrival, she started as if being jerked out of a dream and spoke out loud.

"Miss Snitters caught the balloon! Look Ma..."

She blurted the words out happily as if she were at a picnic instead of trapped in that infernal house, but the next second she looked like she were about to vomit. Understanding of where she was and what she had just done struck her and sudden fear warped her face, turning it into something that more resembled a cartoon mask. Everyone waited on pins and needles to see if this was the final straw for Miss Feanor, but when nothing happened, Matt showed how the pressure was eating at him as well.

He jumped up angrily and smacked the fist of his right hand into the palm of his left. It made a high slapping sound that was louder by far than Amber's words, but he didn't seem to care, he gesticulated rapidly.

'She should be punished for that.' Matt wanted her in pain; it was sick. He looked on the verge of exploding further, and a glaring challenge formed on his face. No one wanted that sort of trouble and they all froze in place, keeping their eyes to the floor, until he sat back down, his torso ramrod straight.

The air in the room had become charged with tension during this and it was sometime before it calmed enough for them to move about. When it did Matt was the first to get up, and with a knowing look at Curt, he went to the bookshelves and began to thumb through each book, one after the other. Curt assumed he was looking for hidden notes.

Amber returned to work on her etch-o-sketch and Paul attempted to read his book with only one eye. It was very sad to see him like this and Curt felt his anger toward the boy drop a few degrees. Curt tried to read Oliver Twist. Only he found he couldn't concentrate enough and so he then went to the bookshelves and trailed after Matt, looking for anything that might have Morse code in it. But after unexpectedly being punched by the older boy for not re-aligning the books *exactly*, he left again to check on the weather.

Still no rain.

This was how his morning went, until sometime after noon things got worse.

They were all sitting in the family room again, where the sameness was overpowering and the silence was dreadful, when the mouse for just a few moments, became Beth. It was the sudden lack of movement coming from her direction that caused Curt to look up from the book he wasn't really reading and he saw her as she could have been without her ever-present insanity.

Beth had her chin canted upwards and cocked slightly to the side, while her brown eyes, for once, were still and held to the wall, the one that adjoined Miss Feanor's room.

She acted as though she had heard something, and at first Curt felt certain that this affectation on her part was another sign of her ongoing craziness. Then he heard it as well.

There was a very low, fuzzy murmur coming through the wall. In a flash, Curt hopped up and pressed his ear against it, and the sound became more distinct, yet still was indecipherable. The others, apart from Amber, who had spoken twice since her first outburst concerning Miss Snitters and was currently staring trance like again, saw his movement and stared at him as if expecting a report on what he had heard.

He could only shrug, which earned him a hard shove from Matt, who took his place at the wall and listened. The brown haired boy stood there with his eyes partially closed for a few seconds, but then turned suddenly and sat back down on the floor. There, he picked up Curt's book and pretended to read it.

By this, Curt knew Miss Feanor was coming and he too snatched up the first book at hand and read it...the cover upside down.

2

She walked through the doorway a moment later, her face aged and pinched with nervous strain.

'Look at me,' she indicated, waving her arms and pointing at herself. To Curt she gestured, 'You, wake up Amber, quietly.'

He made a great show of putting the book back perfectly, but this only seemed to anger her and she signaled for him to go faster. Feeling a mounting fear, he slipped behind the near comatose girl and with a sudden movement put his hand gently around her mouth, while giving her a little shake.

"Mmmhh," she said through his fingers. She struggled briefly, yet without any true strength and stopped altogether at the sight of Miss Feanor; going rigid beneath Curt's small hands.

Once she had their complete attention, the lady then began to communicate through gestures but Curt was still very new at this sort of thing and only understood a small part of it.

'Ok. ...visitor...Amber...we...ok.'

This was all he was clear on and in bewilderment he glanced at the other children; everyone else appeared to understand what was being suggested, and their emotions ran an amazing gambit. Amber seemed to melt out of his hands and laid down upon the floor in the greatest misery. Tears seeped from her eyes and ran a silent course down her face as she stared up at the ceiling, gently shaking her head back and forth in disbelief.

Paul, whose nasty tic disappeared in the space of those seconds, at first seemed relieved and then came shame at his relief and then oddly, sadness. Just as that first morning Curt had seen him, he was not sad for himself, only for Amber.

Matt looked positively happy, he even gave Curt a perky smile, complete with a little eyebrow raise, but what this was supposed to signify, he didn't know. The mouse on the other hand, seemed to be without emotion and still looked like Beth, the girl she once was. Her lips had become quiet and at rest, while her eyes still moved about, but slowly as if she were curious about the world, rather than insane. She looked exactly as she had when Curt first laid eyes on her in the living room six days previous.

Seeing them all this way, so suddenly, made his head spin and he turned to Miss Feanor shrugging his shoulders.

'Matt talk to Curt,' Miss Feanor indicated.

Matt's happy look faltered, but nonetheless, he obeyed her. Only he did it in the strangest manner. Grabbing Curt by the sleeve of his shirt, the older boy dragged him back upstairs to his own room and shut the door behind them.

Curt couldn't help but be afraid at being trapped there with the bigger boy, however Matt didn't hurt him, he only took Curt by the shoulders and leaned in close with his mouth coming open slightly. Curt had a wild thought that Matt was going to kiss him, but instead he whispered in his ear.

"Amber's social worker is coming here for a visit," he said very slowly and quietly, feeling the words out as if they were a foreign language to him. "Do not talk to her unless she speaks directly at you. Do not try to signal her in any form. If you do, you will be punished. If she looks at you, smile. If she talks to you, say that you enjoy it here. Follow Miss Feanor's directions."

Matt leaned back and looked him hard in the eyes, checking to see that Curt understood.

Curt was still very confused and he moved in close, "Why is Amber so upset?"

Matt didn't answer except to snort at the foolish question. Curt realized then that Amber was going to be punished, just as he had that first day. This was monstrously unfair and he became instantly angry over the stupidity of the house. Matt saw the look, but didn't care a whit and only pushed the little thief from his room. Curt wandered down the backstairs and incredibly found himself alone in the kitchen. This had never happened before and despite the thousand thoughts he had over the coming social worker, he jumped at the opportunity.

Since he arrived, he had felt naked without a weapon and he figured a knife would do nicely. With a quick glance down the hall, he went to the first drawer by the refrigerator, which was where most people kept their utensils—but that one wouldn't budge, it seemed glued shut. Working his way down the line, he found that they all were. He gave the last drawer as mighty a tug as he could, but it felt welded in place.

Next, he tried the cabinets and they were all equally impossible to open, all except the ones in the far bottom, where he found some cleaning supplies, and a small store of the same food that he had been eating for the last six days. Exasperated and afraid that he had spent too much time in the kitchen than was wise, he went looking for Paul.

Curt found him exiting the bathroom. Paul's drooping face and down cast eyes told him that he had read the note that Curt had left earlier. The older boy didn't stop to make eye contact with Curt, but only slunk to his bedroom and shut the door.

This is what he had written Paul earlier.

Paul,
You tried to set me up with that 'Fuzz' bisness. Trying to get someone punished is nearly unforgivabal. You are a backstabbing snake!!! Tell me why i should forgive you and then beg me for forgiveness or we will be enemies from here on.

Just at the moment, with the coming of the social worker, Curt wished he hadn't written the note at all. Despite Matt's warnings, he saw this as his best chance to get out of the house, however he didn't think that he could do it alone and he hoped to enlist Paul's help.

Plans were shooting through his mind at an amazing rate, but each was discarded just as quickly.

The problem stemmed from how the other children had acted on his first day. They had stood far back away from Miss Gladys, as if afraid to get too near her and none of them seemed to look in her direction much at all. Amber had stared at the floor listlessly, the mouse had done her usual, looking everywhere, seeing nothing, while Matt and Paul, only looked at him. Curt had barely noticed it then; when around adults, teenagers were like that after all. But he saw now that they had been coached to behave that way and he was sure they would do so again.

This was his dilemma.

He didn't think he could get close enough to the social worker to pass her a note, so Curt needed to find some way to signal her. However, *he* couldn't do the signaling since it would be not only obvious, but expected by Miss Feanor. Therefore, the best option was for him to draw Miss Feanor's attention, and Matt's as well for that matter, and have Paul do the signaling. He'd have chosen Amber, but with the stress, she was a very fragile thing and couldn't be trusted.

It would have to be Paul.

Having no clue when the lady would arrive, Curt went straight into the bathroom. He nearly ignored Paul's response to his earlier accusation, he didn't think he had time for flimsy excuses, pathetic denials, or bogus apologies, but despite that, he read it.

Curt,

You were rite, i did set you up. A boy named Trey did the same thing to me when i was new and i went crazy with the noise in my head and i was punished. i wanted you punished as well. i AM sorry that i did this. When the presure starts to grow, this little voice in my head starts telling me all sorts of ways to sabatage everyone around me. i warned you to trust no one. And that goes for me as well. i fight the voice as much as i can, but sometimes i cant tell if it is me thinking or it. i want you as my friend and in my next note i will tell you all the ways that i have hurt people so you can be on guard against me. About the social worker...DO NOT try to talk to her or signal her or pass her a note. She will DIE if you do.

Flabbergasted, Curt stared at the note. He was so keyed up about his plan that he ignored the threat to the social worker, thinking it highly unlikely and instead focused on what Paul had said about himself. Curt certainly hadn't been expecting Paul to admit to insanity. For a moment, he wondered whether he could trust Paul enough to pull off what he had planned, but he felt he had little choice in the matter and sat down on the toilet and quickly wrote out two notes.

The first was for Paul, the other for the social worker. Curt wasn't going to leave them in the bathroom; that would take too long, he was going to hand them to the blonde boy directly. The note addressed to Paul outlined his simple idea.

When the social worker arrived, he wanted Paul to take up a position next to the far side of the couch. When he judged the moment right, Curt planned on taking a few steps in the direction of the lady. Not enough to get her attention, but enough to focus Matt's and Miss Feanor's eyes on him. At that point, Paul was to give a little wave to the social worker and make a show of putting a note behind the couch pillow, which always sat on that end of the couch. Then he was to signal her that this was their little secret, by putting his finger to his lips.

Curt was a fine judge of human reactions and he felt that this was a good plan for getting her a note. He was sure that she would be very curious by Paul's actions and what's more, social workers had a tendency to view foster parents almost in an adversarial manner. He hoped this would be enough to draw her into their little conspiracy.

The second note he'd give Paul—the one that he was supposed to slip behind the pillow—read:

Lady, we are being held in this house against our will. Miss Feenor is sick in the head and violent. Beneath the shirt i wear, i am cover in bruises and bite marks. She threatens us daily with terribul punishments. Do not try to confront her yourself, but bring the police, she carries wepons.

With the notes done, he went to Paul's room where Curt found him sitting on his bed. Curt thought it a good sign that both of his eyes were twitch free and he brazenly held out the two notes for the older boy to take. Paul did so without looking up into Curt's face and after reading the first, he shocked Curt by tearing both of them up. Curt became livid and his blue eyes shone out harshly from his reddening face.

'Why?' he mouthed the word angrily at Paul.

Paul came close. "Listen to me," he said. The sound of the words was shockingly clear, as if Paul had given up fighting the silence. "You will kill her if you try this. You might even kill yourself and believe me, dying here is the worst thing that can happen to you."

Not only was it the volume of his voice, it was the tone of the words and the look in Paul's eyes that made Curt realize that he wasn't lying about this. But what he said next killed his plan completely.

"Two years ago, I tried to pass a note to my case worker and was forced to watch helplessly as...as...she died in front of me screaming endlessly and then it was my turn...I dream about it often."

Paul's twitch began again, and in moments took over his face, so that he looked like he was being ravaged by a seizure. Puzzled and horror stricken, Curt left him alone a minute later, still twitching. Did Miss Feanor really do that? Kill someone in her own living room? Or was this Paul's voice feeding him lies? There was no way to know and so in despair, the little thief went back to his room.

Chapter 11

Darla

1

It seemed like ages before he heard the knock vibrate, not only through the air, along the walls as well. Curt felt it run across the frame of his bed and he marveled at it. Then he was up, hurrying down the stairs, stopping just at the last step as Miss Feanor came down the hall wearing a look of icy warning.

A moment later, Matt appeared from the family room and wore the same look. With deliberate intent, he stepped between Curt and the door, causing the smaller boy's heart to sink. His mind might have understood that escape this way wasn't possible, but his heart was another matter altogether and it ached in its desire to be free as Miss Feanor crossed to the front door.

When it opened, Curt tried to stop himself from staring out with a look of longing, only that proved impossible. He gazed past a little frumpy looking lady, with his face hanging slack and his mouth open as if hungry. The world beyond her called to him demandingly and it took everything not to run or make a mad dash in that direction, to escape before the door could shut in his face. If he were any closer, maybe only a step or two, he probably would've tried it, as it was, he felt himself leaning forward.

The day outside was grey and dull, overcast and chilly. It was the kind of a day where children sat huddled around the TV, and moms brewed an extra cup of coffee; Curt longed for it and wished he could breathe in the cool air of the fading winter. But it was not to be, and the caseworker stepped into the house. She was nothing special.

He had hoped for a twin to Miss Gladys. *She* wouldn't have put up with any of Miss Feanor's funny business if she had known about it. Instead, this social worker looked a little like a young schoolteacher, enthusiastic and stupid.

"Hi Miss Feanor? I'm Darla Heines. I'm Amber's new caseworker. Hello Amber," she spoke loud and cheerfully, looking past Miss Feanor at the blonde girl, who came down the stairs, slowly dreading each step. Darla had short brown hair and thin close-set features which made her head look smaller than a normal head. Curt couldn't stop gawking at it.

In his periphery, he saw Amber come to stand next to him, a full ten feet from Darla. When he pulled his eyes off the small head of the caseworker and glanced at her, he saw the girl had attempted a smile, but it sat mangled on her delicate features and was nearly all grimace.

"I told you on the phone that she wasn't feeling well," Miss Feanor said reproachfully to the social worker. Darla gave her a shrug and a, *what can you do,* smile.

"I know," Darla commiserated. "I'm so sorry, but it's been over six months since anyone has been out to see Amber..."

"That's not true," Miss Feanor cut across her. Curt noted how dry and quiet her voice was. She stood very close to the caseworker. "I sent you a copy of the last report and it was dated only three months ago."

Darla smiled, "But I don't have the original and the state won't accept a copy. Either way, Amber has been on my case load for three weeks and I couldn't put off seeing her any longer."

"I suppose," Miss Feanor said with condescension. "Why don't we sit in the living room?"

Darla went to the couch, while Amber and Miss Feanor came and sat close, one on either side of her. They started a small talk that normally would've had Curt bored silly in seconds had it been in any other setting, but in that house, where words were almost priceless, he listened intently. The boys hadn't been invited to sit, so he stood next to Matt, by one of the two tall chairs that flanked the love seat opposite the couch. Matt seemed to act as his personal guard and kept an eye on him at all times, but he did so unobtrusively, keeping his body canted toward him.

The logical part of Curt didn't know exactly what he was doing there. If there was to be a punishment, he didn't want to be anywhere near it when it happened, but he supposed it was the irrational that had a hold of him. That part of him was very interested in Ms Darla Heines and everything she had to say.

From her small head to a little white scar on the back of her wrist, he took in everything about her. Her appearance at first seemed drab and frumpy, but the more he looked at her, the more he saw a horde of interesting details. But in truth, all he really saw was someone different. Someone new. Though he had been in the house less than a week, he was already tired of looking at the same people and so this woman, a person that he would have barely noticed at any other time, captivated him.

A sigh escaped his lips and with it came the realization of just how much he missed hearing the English language spoken so freely without the slightest touch of fear. And Darla used it with abandon, keeping up a steady stream of chirping sounding words. He loved it and her voice made him a little giggly. It went up and down like a musical yo-yo and when she pronounced the word 'water', he had to smile. *What-er* is how it came out, and he mouthed it after she said it.

She didn't notice it, but Matt did. He must have thought that Curt was trying to signal Darla and gave him a sharp poke in the ribs.

The movement caught her eye and she directed her attention at the two boys. "Hi, what's your name?" She asked this rather generically and neither boy knew to whom the question was put. They turned to each other, hoping the other would speak first.

"This is Matt and Curt," Miss Feanor spoke for them, much to their relief.

"Oh, the famous Curtis Regis," Darla said with a knowing look at him. "I applaud you, Miss Feanor for keeping him here for practically an entire week. There's a pool going on for how long he'll stay put this time. Do you like it here?" she asked him.

He paused only long enough to see if Miss Feanor would answer this for him as well, and in that second and a half, the tension in the room mounted hugely. All eyes were upon him and if ever there was a chance to say something damning, this was it. But Amber's look of total horror stayed his tongue.

"I like it a lot," he answered in a very quiet voice and he forced a smile onto his face.

Miss Feanor and Amber let out matching sighs of relief, Darla didn't seem to notice.

"I'm so happy for you," she said cheerily, but loudly in her exuberance.

Curt tried to hold onto his smile a little bit longer, but it became increasingly difficult as the air in the room suddenly felt charged, just as it had on his first day. Now Curt realized the charge was like electric fear, clearly Miss Feanor felt it as well.

"Do you mind if we cut this short?" she asked Darla. "Amber's not feeling well and I'm starting to get a migraine..." She trailed off hoping the caseworker would act as Miss Gladys had.

"Sure, how about I just take her out for a little bit and get to know her. I have always thought that ice cream cures everything." Darla was young and still optimistic about her job. At the suggestion of leaving, Amber's skin went as pale and dry as a dying birch.

"I'm really not feeling well," she begged off and just then she looked truly sick in her fear.

"Ok sure...I'm sorry. Maybe next time," Darla said and for a moment, this seemed to be the end of the conversation, but suddenly she turned to Curt. "What about you? Would you like some ice cream? I heard a rumor about how you stole ten gallons of chocolate..."

Crazed wild hope surged through him at the thought, but Miss Feanor interrupted Darla's invitation, "He's sick as well."

At this, the caseworker's brows came down on her small head. "Is there something wrong here?" There was more than a touch of suspicion coloring her voice.

Quite suddenly, Curt felt queer, like there was something wrong, and he was amazed that Darla didn't feel it. The air had become heavy, thick, worse than it had been on his first day. He looked back toward the doorway of the living room and felt a touch of panic when he saw it blocked by Paul and the mouse. It wasn't as if they were guarding it, still he had a sense of being trapped nonetheless. He was beginning to feel an overwhelming need to move in that direction, to get out of the room, but all of his senses told him not to move a muscle.

Miss Feanor appeared sick with worry and her eyes shot about. "No, there's nothing wrong, just a bug going around the house is all."

Darla's face took on a sour, odd appearance, as if she didn't fully believe Miss Feanor's statement. "I think I want to speak with Amber alone. It'll be only for a minute or two."

"I'm really not feeling..." Amber started to say, and indeed her face was greening as if she were about to vomit.

Darla stood up. "I'm going to speak to you either way," she announced with authority. "Let's go outside where we can be alone."

Amber climbed to her feet, her hands shaking noticeably as she did. "In my room...please." There was a scared whiny sound when she said please, like she was begging. It caused Darla to look closely at her for a second and then the caseworker grabbed the girl's pale shaking hand and headed for the front door.

"No, outside I want to speak to you in private."

Miss Feanor hopped up, her face full of panic. "I'm sure that isn't needed, the girl said she wasn't feeling well, why don't you go up stairs. Please," she implored hurrying after the caseworker. Matt and Curt came along in their wake.

Curt felt the charge of the house as a physical thing every time he breathed in. It made his heart thump hugely and his lungs constrict, as if his chest was shrinking, or being compressed from the outside.

Dragging Amber along, Darla made it to the front door and tried the knob. It wouldn't budge under her hand and she shook it fiercely.

"What's going on? Unlock this door!" she demanded angrily yanking on the door. Besides the anger, there was also a touch of fear in her voice and in her eye.

There was more than just a touch in Curt, he was suddenly more afraid than he could ever remember being and looking around, he knew that it wasn't only him. Paul and the mouse stood frozen in place, halfway to the stairs, their eyes huge as saucers; Amber had her fingers stuffed in her mouth and tears rained down from her chin. But what scared Curt the most was the fact that not only Matt looked frightened, Miss Feanor did as well. She had her head craned around as if listening for something from the other side of the house and abject terror stretched across her face.

Feeling suddenly dizzy, Curt put his hand out to the frame of the living room doorway. It pulsed beneath his skin.

He snatched his hand away, clutching it to his chest and felt a flash of adrenaline shoot through his entire body, as if his soul had exploded. The frame had moved beneath his fingers, like a heartbeat or a breath of an enormous creature. It felt as though the house were alive, or possessed by something monstrously wicked.

At that moment, Darla cried out and pulled her own hand back from the doorknob. "It just moved! Did you see that? It moved! What the hell is..."

Thum...thum...thum!

2

Despite all that had happened in the last minute or so, the house was still an amazingly quiet place and so the sound coming from the basement was frightfully loud. It was the sound of someone...a very large someone with heavy footsteps charging up the stairs. Curt's mind tilted over in confusion and he was unable to grasp clearly how it was possible that someone had got into the house, while he'd been so desperate to get out.

"Run!"

Miss Feanor screamed the word in a shrill panic. Pandemonium broke out. Paul and the mouse took off running for the stairs, Amber went wild in Darla's grip, straining and jumping in the air like a bass on the line, and even Miss Feanor began to run.

Thum...thum...thum!

Curt made to follow, but his head had swiveled in the direction of the mudroom door, visible down the long hallway, through the kitchen and he didn't see Matt. The older boy hadn't run at that single screamed word and instead took that fraction of a second to shove Curt hard over. The smaller boy went sprawling onto the gleaming hardwood floors. Bewildered, he looked back at the cause of his fall.

Thum...thum...thum!

He saw Matt streaking for the stairs, Paul and the mouse already halfway up, and now Miss Feanor turned on the first stair and she wore a surprising look over her fear. Her face showed concern.

It was a motherly concern and it was for Curt.

"Curt run!" she screamed at him as Matt shot past her. She then turned and pulled hard on Amber's outstretched pleading hand and the blonde girl became extended between the two older ladies.

Curt heard and felt the last thum...thum...thum! And these were louder than the rest. Curt scrambled to his feet but instead of running, he froze in place and his skin shot through with gigantic goose bumps. He was about to see it. The thing from the basement. He knew he was supposed to run, yet he couldn't. He saw the handle of the mudroom door turning as if in slow motion, but just then he felt a hand grab him.

It pulled him away from the hypnotic sight and yanked him with considerable force toward the stairs. It was Miss Feanor. Looking past Curt, her face was riveted in horror at what she saw down the hall. She went whiter than ever and took off in a blind panic, no longer with any concern for him or for anything, but escape.

Amber was running too. She had broken away from Darla and raced up the stairs, her light feet churning wildly. Frantic not to be left behind, Curt blazed past the stunned caseworker and dashed up the stairs. He had no clue as to who it was coming from the basement, but the fear of everyone in the household had become his in an instant.

He was halfway up when the first scream split the air.

Turning as he ran, he saw Darla staring in disbelief down the hall, her face unrecognizable in her terror. She screamed again and just as he got to the top of the stairs, something rushed full upon her.

It wasn't a man as he had expected it to be, but it was shaped as one. It was grey and translucent, at least parts of it were, other parts seemed to form from within it and looked far more solid. And nothing seemed more solid than its teeth. These shown large and white through the grey of its ghostly skull and they opened wildly as they came at Darla, the caseworker.

Chapter 12

The Disposable Body

1

Blessedly, Curt was yanked around then and the sight of those awful teeth digging into the soft flesh of Darla's face was lost to him. Her screams on the other hand were not, they were clear and exact, loud with the agony of slow death.

They pierced his mind and he had trouble thinking past them. He blinked stupidly at the person in front of him. Miss Feanor had left him and it was Paul, who had turned him around; his face was a warzone. A battlefield where rational fear and insane panic fought for control of his features, Curt caught only a flash of this before Paul shoved him into his room and threw him bodily onto his now familiar bed.

Curt struggled up thinking what a tremendously stupid thing to be doing just then. He should be running for his life, but Paul pushed him back down again and covered him over with his blanket.

"No matter what, don't come out."

The words were hissed in his ear through his covers and the desperation in Paul's voice made him stop struggling at least physically. Mentally he felt besieged. The endless screams echoing in the otherwise silent hallways, the vision of the larger than life teeth and the near certainty that the house was alive, washed relentlessly over his mind, making him feel as though his brain was being squeezed into nothingness.

He could sense his ability to think clearly, diminishing. All that came to him were a series of questions but hardly any answers.

Was he really going to hide from that creature, that thing, beneath his blankets as his five-year-old self would have? Where were the others? Were they hiding like a bunch of moronic children as well? Shouldn't they all be hightailing it out of there while the thing ate Darla? Was that thing an actual ghost or perhaps something worse?

His own failing logic could only answer one of those questions and that was the first one. Yes, he would lie under his blankets and keep absolutely still. He realized he had been doing this, hiding from this creature, every night since he arrived... every night but the first that is. All along, he had thought it had been Miss Feanor, who came at night, but in reality it was this thing and she was afraid of it as much as he was.

How hiding under a blanket kept the creature at bay, he didn't know, or how sound played any part in this, he didn't know that either. Nor the fastidious cleaning. Nothing made sense.

And nothing would as long as Darla's shrieks continued.

At first, her misery struck him so keenly that he cried beneath his covers, sobbing in empathetic fear for her. But her screams went on for so long that ultimately, his tears dried up and he could only clamp his hands over his ears and hope that they would end before he went mad.

They did end eventually and then his fear was no longer empathetic, but personal, selfish and he became afraid only for himself.

Crreik.

He should've expected this. The creature crept up the stairs and as it did, Curt began to shake beneath his covers. By the long fifth step, he was nearly in a panic, because his muscles wouldn't stop shimmying about. In desperation, he curled into a ball and grabbed his knees with all of his remaining strength. This helped, but oddly seemed to forced the shaking into his chest, where it felt as though his heart were about to explode.

About his bed the creature moved, slowly as always. Curt lay there on the verge of screaming in madness. His world became the creature. He could see it. Somehow enough light came through his window that the thing was able to cast a feeble shadow through the blankets. It turned him cold knowing it was only inches from him.

But then it moved away.

Like a bizarre and demented postman, the thing went about the house on its usual rounds, and as it did, Curt lay there sweating freely, petrified by fear, and he stayed this way long after the last sly sound of the thing had disappeared. Eventually, his brain became disconnected and he didn't think, or question or remember, but instead slipped into a waking trance.

And judging by how dry the pool of blood would later feel, he laid there for hours.

2

What brought him around was a sharp jab of fingers through the blanket, directly into his cheek. His mind switched back on and his brain started thinking exactly where he had left off and he sucked his breath in sharply with fright. A second later, the fingers jabbed him again, harder. He waited hoping to be left alone, but then suddenly his covers were ripped off of him and he saw Matt standing there. The boy wore unreadable expression. It was certainly not a happy one, nor was it the usual sneering superiority.

With a snapping hand gesture, he motioned for Curt to follow him. They went down stairs and immediately visible was the body of Darla. It lay contorted and crushed looking, sprawled in a hellishly unnatural position by the front door, surrounded by an undisturbed pool of dried blood.

Before he saw the body, Curt had wished in his heart that Darla would be alive and hoped that she would only have the terrible bruises and sharp pains as he did on his first morning, but she was very much dead. Very, very dead. He had seen dead bodies before, four of them; none could compare to this.

The creature's large teeth had shredded her clothing and had bitten through her skin in hundreds of places and even where the skin hadn't been ripped open, he could see that the bones beneath had been broken. In many spots, splinters of bone erupted up out of her flesh and these appeared sharp and jagged. It looked as though she had fallen into a trash compactor on the back of a garbage truck or into some piece of heavy machinery. He grew light headed and felt sick at the sight.

He wasn't the only one. Miss Feanor had a green complexion under an expression of worry and Matt, who had followed him down, couldn't stop staring at the body and swallowed repeatedly as he did. Only Paul, the only other person there, didn't seem like he was going to vomit. He had other problems. His twitch had returned with a vengeance and no part of his face wasn't affected. He was as difficult to look upon as the body. But they weren't there to look.

Miss Feanor laid out a heavy blanket and directed Curt and Matt to put the body of Darla Heines onto it. Curt was terribly afraid to touch it, but Paul, who was practically blind from his twitch was clearly useless and so the youngest boy went to the women's feet. Along with Matt, he made to pick her up, but her legs bent inward, that is to say the wrong way and feeling the strength in his arms disappear at the sight, he dropped her.

"Oh God," he mumbled and knew there was no stopping the vomit shooting up his throat.

Turning toward the staircase, he heaved and retched loudly, but since breakfast had been hours before, only a nasty watery spew came up. The others waited for him in the dead silence, looking greener if that were possible. Finally, shaking and sweating as if he were in a fever, Curt bent to his horrid task and with a face twisted and ugly, he helped Matt move the body onto the blanket. They moved her to the garage then, and that was much easier since they could hold the blanket instead of her.

Darla was small, like a child herself and lighter than he expected. Her body went into the trunk of Miss Feanor's car, which was very tiny, but since she was so horribly bendable, she fit with ease.

Matt shut the trunk with a dull thump and just then, Curt's knees gave out and he fell heavily to the cement floor of the garage. He couldn't get up. There was no strength left in his mind or body and his head swam making the room spin and his stomach wavered. Matt didn't help him, yet he didn't hurt him either, he simply turned his face, dead white and shining with sweat, to the door and left.

With a slack jaw, Curt watched him walk through the mudroom and then the older boy was gone and he was all alone. The horror of the day had left him dazed and apathetic. He gazed around and saw the garage just as it looked the other time he'd been there. Save for a car, it sat empty. No tools, no bikes, no boxes, no nothing. Nothing but the cold. The cement beneath him was like ice, yet his body was numb and had been since he had watched Darla's knees bend backwards, and therefore he only felt the cold cement vaguely.

Now he turned his lifeless gaze back to the door and looked into the mudroom and only then did he see what sat catty-corner to the garage door. It was the door that lead into the black pit of the basement, that lead to the creature, the thing. He felt the cold then. It raced up through the hard floor shooting up the sweat of his back.

He was trapped.

If the creature came then he would have nowhere to go, nowhere to hide. In the space of time it took for his heart to boom once mightily in his chest, he was up off the floor and flying out of the garage and he didn't check his speed until he was all the way down the long hall, standing with the others breathing noisily and staring back at the mudroom door.

The creature didn't come up from where it lurked in the basement.

A few minutes later, Miss Feanor left, presumably to dispose of the body of Darla the Caseworker; however, before she did, she ordered them to clean up the blood and of course his vomit.

Compared to handling the mangled body this was simple; nothing in his life would be difficult after that. They were done quickly, Matt going on his hands and knees to inspect. When they were finished, and despite not having had dinner, Matt ordered all of them, the girls included to start on their chores. This was fine with Curt because he needed something to do, something physical, something to keep him occupied so he wouldn't think about how easily they had rolled Darla's broken body up to get her into the trunk, and besides, he didn't imagine he would be able to eat anytime soon.

It seemed very strange and highly inappropriate to Curt, but as the other four children went about their chores, they all acted in the most relieved and relaxed fashion. They cleaned and polished and dusted with smiles on their faces and in the case of Amber, occasionally hummed. On the other hand, Curt felt mired in a stagnant pool of depression.

He saw himself at least partially to blame for the death of Darla. It had been her interest in him, which seemed to have been the final straw. If he hadn't hung around, she might still be alive. Not only that, he now found himself living in a house that had some terrible ghoulish fiend in its basement. The others might have been living like this for years, but he was too new to the situation for him to think past it and the vision of the thing haunted him as he worked.

At one point, while Curt was cleaning the main hallway, Amber skipped quietly by expecting to see a smile on his face, but when all she got was a frown, she stopped.

'What's wrong?' she gestured. Curt couldn't believe how insensitive she was being.

'Bite, bite. Death. Monster.' This was all he could communicate to her with his hands, but it seemed to be enough.

Looking close into his eyes, she gave him a little sad shrug barely a lifting if her shoulders that told him, 'This is the way it is.' She then pointed at him with one hand and shook her head, while pantomiming biting with her other hand, 'At least it wasn't you that was killed.'

Bitterly, he wanted to ask her if she would act this way after his next punishment, but the concept was far too complex for his ability to communicate with his hands and all he could do was sigh tiredly. Hearing it, she reached out and formed his face into a smile, matching it with one of her own.

When she let go, his face drooped, and she repeated the process, being so cute about it, he had to smile for real. The blonde then kissed him sweetly on the lips and left.

With her departure, he immediately became depressed again, yet it was less than it had been and it allowed him to think a little clearer. Unfortunately his very first thought was, 'I wonder where Miss Feanor is dumping the body?' He groaned aloud at his own morbid thinking and sagged against the wall.

Looking up he noticed that he was just outside Miss Feanor's bedroom and the door stood partially open.

What was in that room? What secrets?

3

Answers could be in there...something that would help him understand what was going on—perhaps even the key to their salvation was in that room.

After a very quick glance in both directions, he crossed to the door, measured the opening at four fingers of his right hand, and slipped in. He closed the door nearly completely behind him.

Curt had peeked into every one of the bedrooms on the upstairs floor, but had never done more than glance at Miss Feanor's room. Like the rest of the house, it was decorated in a girlish manner, or so he thought at first. After a closer look, he reconsidered and a vague notion of 'Grand Ma' came into his mind.

Though he had never known a single relative other than his mother, he'd been in enough homes to associate the decorations in the room as those belonging to an elderly woman. Far more elderly than Miss Feanor. Even the pictures appeared decades old and though he looked, he did not see a young Miss Feanor in any of them.

There was another thing about the room that seemed out of place and that was the smell. The room gleamed as if it were regularly cleaned like the rest of the house, but it smelled musty and unused. Rifling through the dresser drawers, something that was quite literally beyond his ability to control, Curt discovered the source of the smell.

All the clothes were clean, but clearly hadn't been worn or washed in years. Moreover, none of the outfits looked like anything Miss Feanor had yet worn or would ever wear for that matter. On a hunch, he went to the bed and discovered this too had an unused smell. His gut told him that this wasn't her room at all, as he had assumed.

Curt, even though he was just shy of thirteen years of age, was an efficient thief and had zipped through the drawers and looked about very thoroughly in only a matter of minutes. He then went for what he had truly come into the room for, the telephone.

Ever since he'd heard the muted mumblings of Miss Feanor's conversation through the wall of the family room, the phone had been in the back of his mind, and ghost or no ghost he was going to use it. Yet he hesitated. The reason being was how the doorframe pulsed just before Darla had been attacked. The house had felt alive, and not as a plant or a turtle were alive, but as something intelligent and aware and very evil.

In the hour or so, since he had moved the dead body, Curt had frequently put out his hand and had gingerly felt the walls. Now that he knew what he was feeling for, the aliveness of the house was readily apparent, though it was far more subdued than it had been...it seemed sleepy.

But just then, in that room it was as if the house had cracked an eye at him. His nerves had jangled with alarm as he had gone through the dresser and the bed, however it seemed as if the house, was satiated and again Curt's intuition told him to proceed. Still he knew the phone would be a different story all together. It was a link to the outside world and he felt it in his bones that using it wouldn't be permitted.

Yet, like all thieves, Curt was a gambler. His chosen profession was all about taking risks and he weighed the pros and cons and decided if ever there would be a time to attempt the phone, it would be at that moment. Miss Feanor was out, the ghost had just killed, and the house drowsed around him.

Now was the time. Still he didn't rush.

Putting out his hand, he laid it on the phone and simply rested it there for a moment, feeling it as if taking the pulse of the house. There seemed to be only the slightest uptick of awareness, but not enough to turn back. With a deep breath, he pulled the phone up and heard the soft reassuring hum of the dial tone. So far so good.

The phone was an older rotary style and he drew the 'nine' all the way around and watched in agony as it slowly rattled back to its starting point. Then he pulled the much closer 'one' around in a short arc, and repeated it a second time. Anxiety filled moments went by as the phone clicked and ticked in his ear, but finally it rang. The phone rang once and then went dead in his hand.

The house suddenly seemed very much aware of him and he realized at that point, that he had gambled and lost.

4

In complete dread Curt put the phone back in its cradle, and slipped out of the room as his heart began to beat gigantically in his thin chest. With all the quiet he could muster, he slid down the hall toward the stairs and although he didn't want to look back toward the mudroom, he couldn't help it. There the light glinted as the knob began a slow motion turn just as it had earlier that afternoon and as it did his world went grey and static filled his ears.

Vaguely, he thought about running, but it seemed so useless, his knees were shaking and his muscles trembled, all he could do was stand there and wait for his punishment. But unbelievably it wasn't the creature. Like a miracle, Miss Feanor walked into the kitchen just then from the mudroom and in her hands, she carried white bags and he could see the McDonalds logo imprinted on them even from that distance.

Curt blinked and shook his head, not believing his eyes and he honestly thought that for just a moment, he was dreaming. Nervously he touched the wall next to him and discerned that the house's awareness was diminishing and for the second time that day, his legs gave out from beneath him and he plunked heavily onto the second step of the main stairs.

In his relief, it seemed that there was nothing to him, like he was only a ghost himself, and he simply sat there staring at the floor that earlier had been filled with blood. His mind tried, but failed at forming thoughts and sometime later, minutes probably, Paul appeared and touched his shoulder. Curt didn't jump, he only looked up, his mind empty.

Paul, giving him a huge grin, pulled him to a standing position, and the two of them slid down the hall and as they went, Curt's became aware of the wonderful smell of McDonald's French fries.

This simple thing had him suddenly ravenous and his hunger was a reminder that he was still alive and still had a chance at life. His spirit became re-animated and he hurried forward.

The atmosphere in the kitchen bordered on Christmas morning, something Amber had told him not to expect much from. There was tons of food, too much food in fact and Curt ate his fill for the first time in a week and as he did, the cheery mood of the others further awakened him. Everyone but Miss Feanor seemed in the gayest of moods. She looked horrible and appeared to have aged another ten years, but no one seemed to pay her any mind. Eventually, she waved for them to finish and moments later they moved as silent ghosts to their bedrooms.

Full, but not sleepy, Curt contemplated his predicament. There was a chance he would be punished that very night for the crime of touching the phone, still he also knew that he wouldn't die as Darla had, and it was a nasty shock that he realized that this wasn't a good thing. The house wanted the children alive so that they could be punished over and over again—the conception of endless punishments, endless torture, seemed far worse than one death, no matter how horrible it might be.

The creature came that night moving with the indolent slothful ease of a person fresh from a tremendous feast. It went about the house making far more noise than usual, but it did not tarry in any of the rooms and was back in the basement quicker than it ever had. For the other children, this was probably considered a good night. For Curt who now knew what it was lurking in the house at night, it wasn't, his bladder had let go at the first *crreik* and his tears flowed greater than his urine. Still, he wasn't punished.

Chapter 13

The New Pauls

1

Now the creature was in Curt.

From the moment he'd seen it rushing at Darla it was in him. Beneath his breast, it sat as a cold hard lump of fear and in his every thought and action, it was there making its presence felt. That feeling caused each moment to drag by in protracted agony and the seconds of his life elongated, stretching out and out. His days became slow motion monotonous hell.

Besides the notes that he and Paul would write back and forth to each other, the next four days were so dreadfully repetitive that Curt had trouble remembering which day was which. As they progressed, the increasing pressure to be perfectly quiet and to have their areas of responsibility exactly as the photos indicated, marked the only real difference between them.

That and the level of insanity in the house.

As in the prior week, as the days advanced each child continued to exhibit a growing madness that had Curt wondering what his would look like. Logically it had to happen and everyday he'd stare at his reflection in the mirror checking for tell tale signs.

For now the mirror only showed him an increasingly haggard looking boy. His eyes became more and more red, the circles beneath them growing darker with each passing day, but still no insanity. He had begun figuring out little tricks to stave off the inevitable lunacy. When the silence in his head began to take on that great empty ringing tone, he would run water, or slide his hands gently over his blanket listening to the tiny sound it would make. When he felt the overwhelming urge to talk or to scream, or to shout, he'd seek out one of the other children and force them to converse in their made up sign language. Even the mouse he'd corner in order to break up the monotony, ignoring the vacancy behind her spinning eyes.

When the pressure to be perfect in his duties became unbearable, and he found himself checking and rechecking and re-rechecking the exact position of the porcelain cats, or the angle of the satin pillows, he'd purposely leave some items improperly placed. Obviously so. For instance, once he left one of the cats with its paws hanging egregiously over the edge of a runner. All day it sat like that, secretly amusing him and he'd walk by and have to suppress a giggle at his own audacity.

The toughest thing to remain sane over, other than the thought of the creature and its horrible tortures, turned out to be the food. Curt couldn't imagine his way into liking spam or carrots, while the rice was so dull it was déjà vu in every bite! He tried mixing up his eating patterns, one day eating his carrots first and then the rice and then the spam. The next he would reverse the order and the next he'd alternate bites of each, but by the fifth day, he dreaded the sight of his dinner plate, scared to death that he would snap and fly into a screaming fit if he saw one more pale slab of pink spam.

He saved himself, by eating that meal completely blind. Closing his eyes tightly before walking into the kitchen, he kept them closed until not a single grain of rice was left on his plate. Feeling quite foolishly proud of his minor accomplishment, he opened his eyes and was surprised to find the table completely empty, save for a blank staring Miss Feanor.

2

Despite the fact that the blonde boy had set him up and had tried to get him to break, Curt had a tremendous need to know what was going on in the house and it wasn't a matter of curiosity, but of survival.

His first note, of the week he wrote on the morning after their McDonalds feast.

Paul,
Please tell me everything you know about that creeture that attacked the case worker. Why didn't you tell me what it was before? Was this one of the things the voice in your head told you not to tell me about?

Hi Curt,
you wouldn't have believed me. You would've thought i was crazy. Yes, i know i'm crazy sometimes, but in this i'm completely sane. i don't know much about the creeture, besides that it bites and bites and chews on you hungrily in the worst way. It hides in the basement, so never go down there. its not a ghost, or i think its not a ghost...it feels worse than a ghost. Never touch the doors leading outside. ive told you before, but hopefully you will take it to hart now.

Paul,

How is the creeture connected to the house? is it part of the house? Does it feed on us or the house? Do you think if we burned down the house, it would kill the creeture?

Hi Curt,
I'm surprised you know about the house being alive. It took me months to figure it out, of course I was in shock for most of those months. My first few months, I was punished a lot and I was so thankful when Amber finally showed up and she started to get punished. I know that is a mean thing to say, but I'm just trying to be honest. I'm sure she is thinking the same about you.

Curt read this on the morning of the second day after Darla had been killed and his eyes had narrowed at it. Paul had totally blown off answering his questions.

Paul,
i don't mean to be rude, but you answered none of my questions. i repeet, how is the creeture connected to the house? Is it part of the house? Does it feed on us or the house? Do you think if we burned down the house, it would kill the creeture?

Paul's note took a long time in coming and Curt checked the hiding spot four times before finding a message there just before dinner.

Curt,
Perhaps you don't mean to be rude, but you are anyways. You assume that I have to tell you these things but I don't. Maybe if you were nicer to me, we would be more inclined to answer directly.

This note sent a shiver down Curt's spine. It was as if someone other than Paul had written it—not even the handwriting was the same. For a moment, Curt looked around the bathroom as if expecting the house itself to suddenly confess to leaving the note. But he knew logically it had to be Paul and he wondered about the extent of this 'voice' the older boy had mentioned. Perhaps it wasn't a voice at all. Perhaps he had a split personality problem as he had silently accused Miss Feanor of having. In this house, it was a painfully real possibility; he would have to tread carefully.

Hi Paul,

Your right. i have been demanding alot from you and i'm sorry. i think the house is getting to me and making me cranky. You have been an excelent friend and i never thanked you properly the other day for saving me from the creeture. i would have been punished for sure, or worse.

Your friend,

Curt.

He wanted to write sincerely at the end, but the spelling of the word was beyond him and he didn't want to come across as stupid.

The dinner that night, the second one since Darla's death, was a most difficult affair. Because of what he suspected about Paul's mental state, Curt was afraid to look too closely at him, yet time and again his eyes were drawn to the boy's face. What he saw there only confirmed his suspicion of the idea of Paul's schizophrenia. Part of the time he looked fearful or sad and at other times he'd glower angrily at his food and his lips would start to move as if he were talking to his plate.

Curt began to be afraid of Paul and after the way the notes had progressed, he sadly had to begin considering the possibility that the blonde boy was now as much an enemy as Matt. The thought sent his soul sinking low. Two older boys—bigger boys, both working to see that he was punished rather than they; it was hard to take. His mind went into overdrive attempting to discover some way to deal with both of them at once and that night was the first that he began practicing his purposeful deception.

With no one looking, he took the contents of his own dresser drawer and threw it around the room.

After which, he snuck down the back stairs and went about his chores, making sure to leave enough time to clean up his own mess. He found it hard to keep a straight face when Matt came by and gave him a quick look, the older boy's lips were barely holding back a smirk, and his eyes held a malevolent glee. It was clear that he had seen the mess and was himself trying to keep a straight face. After Curt finished his chores he nonchalantly went upstairs preparing himself to make a great silent fuss, but what he saw in his room killed that idea.

Paul knelt busily folding the clothes and when he saw Curt, a look of intense guilt swept across the aspects of his face. The blonde boy clearly didn't know if he had made the mess or not and as he folded, his eye began to twitch badly.

In a sense, this was part of Curt's plan. He could deal with messes when he knew where they were, these weren't a problem. It was the secret attacks that he feared. The boys could come at him from any angle, while his back was turned and he would never know for certain who was after him and what exactly they were doing. So by purposely sabotaging his own areas of responsibility he hoped each of the older boys would think that the other was setting him up, with the idea that both would then sit back and let the other destroy the new kid. When all the while neither was.

Seeing Paul's sad face sent a little pang of guilt through him, but Curt stuffed that away; he'd rather see that sad look than the creature's teeth any day. In keeping with his plan, he left to blame Matt and gesticulated in front of him in fake indignation. The older boy only professed silent smug innocence.

On the third day, Paul started with an apology.

Hi Curt,
i think i might have given into the voice in my head and messed up your room last nite. i told you about how I sometimes do bad things to get people punished and this is one of them. i will do things and blame others, usually Matt. i'm sorry that i did this. i don't know much about the creeture. It is connected to the house, but i don't know how. i don't think you could burn down the house even if you had matches, which we don't and even then, i don't know if it would kill the thing. i don't think it is alive.

Not alive?

In his heart, Curt had known this to be truth, but his mind nearly went into open rebellion at the very notion; he stared at the small white tiles of the bathroom floor for a long time trying to get it to sink in. At length, he decided that although the creature may not be alive like a person was, he was certain that it could at least be destroyed. Everything could be destroyed.

The house certainly could be, it was made of wood after all. For a while Curtis pondered how it could be done. Fire seemed the best option, but realistically he didn't see it happening. There were no matches or lighters about the place and since the house was somehow alive, then in all likelihood it could control the electricity just as it did the phone, so the idea of an electrical fire went out the window. There was the possibly as well that the house might be able to flood itself, making it a moot point either way.

A bomb could do the trick, Curt reasoned, and not only that, it would be much more fun to watch. This brought a smile to his weary face and he spent a good hour, sitting in the bathroom, imagining how he could make a bomb out of normal household goods. It was fun to make believe but eventually he had to turn to more immediate matters.

Hi Paul,

Thank you for your note. im sorry to hear about your 'voice' i hope we can all get out of here soon and im sure that we can get it fixed. i only have a few more questions, if you don't mind. How is Miss Feenor connected to all this? She was very afraid of the creeture, why doesn't she run away while she is out? Does she sleep down stairs?

Your friend

Curt.

Paul again took a long time in answering and in the slow hours of that third day, his twitch worsened noticeably.

Hello Curt,

I honestly don't know how she is connected. From the information I have gleaned, she has been here fourteen years and has been doing foster care the entire time. She sleeps upstairs in the attic, but that really shouldn't be your concern. I understand the desire to escape, but you should really concentrate on surviving. Last night I heard voices coming from your room, I think you were talking in your sleep.

3

The little piece of toilet paper fluttered to the cold tile of the floor. Talking in his sleep? He was going to die. He couldn't control what happened in his sleep. Nobody could. He was going to die. He would be punished night after night and he knew that if that ever happened, he would never survive.

"Oh my God!" Curt whispered. He was going to die.

Getting up suddenly, he began pacing the room in weird jerking motions, sucking on his fingers once again...unable to stop himself. Unaware. He pictured how it would be, laying in bed, fighting to stay awake, his eyes getting heavier with each passing second, going crazy.

An idea struck him, maybe if he slept in the day and had Amber or Paul wake him if he began to talk. They could all look out for each...sudden realization stopped him in his tracks. Paul had set him up, again! He wasn't talking in his sleep, the boy only wanted him to think so.

This new aspect of Paul was just so diabolical that Curt wondered why he hadn't shown himself before. It hadn't been in evidence at all in the last week. Perhaps it came and went with the amount of stress he was feeling. Or maybe the death of Darla triggered it. Or maybe it was there all along and the nice Paul was the fake one.

Curt hated this. There was no way of knowing what was true and what wasn't, and because of that he had to lie as well.

Hi Paul,
Thanks for the heads up. Now im really afraid to go to sleep. Do you have any advice? How do you stop somthing like this. im so scared.
Thanks
Curt.

[196]

He left the note and wasn't eager to get one in return and didn't bother to check for it until the next morning.

That evening, he pulled his same trick, throwing his own clothes about, but he was very wary of Paul. When he came up the stairs again, just as the night before, there was the blonde boy folding his clothes. In a huff, Curt again went to Matt, who was getting nastier as the pressure again began to mount and so he didn't push his luck and only glared, acting his part.

That night, as the lights were being turned out all over the house, Curt did a recheck of his drawers and saw numerous glaring errors; obvious, purposeful mistakes just underneath the facade of the top layers. The sight made him cold. In a rush, he fixed it as best as he could.

A little while later, Crreik...

Every night the creature came, and every night Curt hid beneath his covers, picturing it looming over him and he would shiver in fright and sweat with anxiety.

But that night was exceptionally hard on him.

There were just too many ways for him to get in trouble and having both Matt and Paul working against him left him feeling small and helpless. In truth, Matt seemed not to be doing much to hurt Curt at all. It was as if he knew what was going on with Paul and was content to sit by and let him destroy Curt.

Crreik, crreik...

That night the creature stayed long in Curt's room, but eventually moved on and no one was punished for the third day in a row.

4

Day four since the death of Darla, showed pressure building in everyone. This was exactly how Curt thought of the days since he already had trouble remembering how long he'd been in the house.

He knew this would get worse as weeks turned into months, and that eventually he'd be like Amber and walk about wondering why it was snowing in August. But that didn't bother him too much since he rather enjoyed being surprised by the weather. Being caught in a rainstorm was a delight to him.

Once, a deluge had sprung up out of nowhere and he had been obliged to take shelter in a small cafe with dozens of other people. As if he were working a jackhammer, Curt had forced his body to shiver and thus within minutes, using only the power of sympathy and without a nickel to his name, he was sitting drinking hot cocoa and eating a large sandwich and doing what he liked best, people watching.

They fascinated him.

The people in that cafe, for the most part, were peppy, even buoyant. The rain had forced them out of the dull routine of their lives and they were happy about it. This made Curt wonder why they didn't break with their routines more often.

Curt had no routine.

Other than waking up, usually while it was still technically morning and begging on Wednesdays, when the need arose, everyday was nearly completely different from the last. His life was one small adventure after another. He gloried in it.

Not everyone in that cafe was feeling so elated at the change in their lives. There were some with pinched expressions who sat near the door and allowed their anxiety to express itself in a jangling knee or constantly drumming fingers. These people would eventually duck into the sheets of the cold grey rain, desperate to get back to dull sameness that marked their every moment. These people he pitied, they were ants to him, unable to deviate from their pathetic ruts even when Mother Nature forced the gift of change down their throats.

Curt missed the rain. Just then, lying in his bed with the covers over his head as the sun came up on that fourth day of the week, he missed the rain. Of course, he missed everything about his old life, but now he missed the rain most of all since it seemed to have magical properties over the house.

His mind ranged over this. What part did the rain play in calming the creature? Or was it only about the house's ability to sense, to hear? With that thought in his mind, he leaned over and felt the wall. He could feel the aliveness of the house, it seemed...normal. At least normal for it, content, but unhappily so. And its awareness seemed no greater than on the evening after Darla had been killed.

This was strange as well. The pressure to be "good" was fueled by a building hunger, and really the word hunger only barely covered the perversity and unwholesome desire and need of the house. That nasty feeling grew in the air all around him, but not in the walls.

Strange.

A minute later Curt got up and went about his now hated morning routine, and as he did he considered the possibility that whatever spirit or ghost haunted the place might very well have a split personality too.

Hi Curt,
i dont remember what i wrote in my last note. isn't that strange? i need to know something that may sound stranger. it's very importent. Did you hear something from my room last nite? A voice, or someone talking? i woke up with words in my head just as if they were spoken to me. it was a boy's voice and at first i thought it was yours, but it wasn't. im freaking out. Please help.

If ever there was a time to get revenge and have Paul punished it was then. A simple: *Yes, I heard you talking about your mom, you were crying for her to come back,* would very likely send him completely off the deep end. However, the note was written in the handwriting of the old Paul, the one that had fought for him, the one that he still couldn't help but like and pity.

Hi Paul,
i didn't hear anything and i think i would have cause this house is so dang quite. Maybe it was that voice in your head only. Try not to worry about it. Worrying will only make things worse. When you read this come see me and we will thum restle. That's always quite and fun too!
Curt.

Paul never showed up to thumb wrestle.

That was a worry. Curt spent that fourth morning sitting next to Amber, despite how much it angered Matt. Starting the day before, she had again begun slipping into her trances and now they were progressing for longer and longer periods and as before she always came out of them in the middle of conversations.

The first one had sent everyone in the family room jumping back, startled. After that, Curt sat near to her, ready to clamp a hand over her mouth at the first sound. Matt was furious about this, wanting Amber to be punished, but Curt paid him no mind except to keep watch more closely for the sneak attacks that were soon in coming. It seemed as long as he kept the older boy in front of him, Curt was relatively safe. Matt was taller by six inches and heavier by forty pounds, but was basically a coward.

On Amber's third outburst, "Why don't...mmmnh..." Matt showed that he would've made a good thief if it weren't for that yellow streak running down his back. Curt clamped his hand over Amber's mouth just as before, and at that precise moment, Matt punched him in the face.

Matt, like a good thief, saw the opportunity coming a mile away and knew that Curt, with his hands occupied, would be defenseless. The older boy was quick and accurate as well and if it weren't for the stinging pain that erupted across the bridge of his nose, Curt would have admired the blow.

As it was he stumbled away, his eyes watering in pain. Curt was still at that age when he'd sometimes cry when hurt and he didn't want anyone one to know. Embarrassed and angry, he went upstairs to the bathroom and sobbed as quietly as he could. When his eyes had dried somewhat he checked for a note. Paul's second note was strange; it was as if he didn't realize he'd already sent one that morning.

Curt,

Thanks for your kind note. I believe my issue with that voice is a thing of the past. I haven't heard it for awhile. About you talking in your sleep, Just try to sleep as light as possible. I heard you last night. It wasn't bad, but it will get worse. Did you try the SOS thing yet? I know that you weren't trying to signal me concerning Matt. You want to contact the outside world. That's very smart. No one has tried that yet, to my knowledge. My window faces nothing or I would try it. Give it a shot tonight.

A sigh escaped the young thief and his hands ran their way through the mass of brown curls atop his head. Obviously, the wrong Paul had written this note. There was no way he was going to try the SOS, now that he knew the house was aware and not after the near disaster with the phone.

The little letter, with its evil intent depressed him worse that he had been, and for a long time he sat there feeling empty of all thoughts and emotions—his state similar to what he went through on the day Darla died. He felt neither alive nor dead during this time. It was as if he was trapped between heartbeats and he wanted to stay trapped. Though he knew that time ticked away around him, this feeling of being nothing and knowing nothing had a soothing quality and he hoped it would last forever.

Sometime later Amber snapped him out of his state, though she did not mean to.

From the family room: "Where's the yarn, mom? I can't see it..." her voice carried clear as a bell and sweet as cream all the way to Curt, who sat in his trance on the tiled floor of the bathroom.

It was as if a little girl Amber were calling up the stairs to him. Her voice had that adorable innocent tone that all mother's loved, and wished would last forever. It startled Curt back into his body, only his mind had trouble focusing. The words had been so alive, and without even the smallest trace of fear that for a few seconds he wondered if someone had called from outside the house.

Then it clicked into place as to who had spoken and why, he froze waiting and worrying, fearing that he would hear those dreadful footsteps charging up from the basement. The air stirred with hungry anticipation and on a hunch, Curt reached out and felt the tiled wall next to him.

The house seemed to be coming awake, and if he were to describe what he felt, he would've said it was a growing anger and below that an unmistakable evil. He wanted to go to Amber just then to comfort her, but knew that any movement or noise would only make everything worse. Therefore he sat, feeling the tile and slowly, eventually, the house drowsed again. Before going to check on Amber He wrote a hurried return note to Paul.

He didn't really want to, but he'd read a saying once before, "Keep your friends close, but your enemies closer." At the time, he had thought this to be a stupid thing to do, now it seemed a necessity.

Just like trailing closely around after Matt to keep him supervised, Curt had to keep Paul as a "friend" and allow the boy to try to undermine him in that sly way of his. If he didn't, Paul would surely become more overt in his attempts to have Curt punished and there was no way he could keep an eye on both the older boys at once.

So for now, he'd have to act worried that he was cracking up around Paul, it wasn't much of an act.

Hi Paul,

You heard me last nite? i thought for sure that it was only a dream. i was thinking about trying to signal with my light, but now I'm too afraid too. i will try to sleep lighter tonite, but i already sleep so little that i don't know what to do. thanks for your help. Can i ask another question? Som of the kids seem much weirder this week than last. like the pressure is worse on them or somthing.

Curt.

With this done, he rushed down stairs to be with Amber.

Her pale blue eyes were large and fearful and she cried silent tears in relief at the sight of him, but otherwise didn't move a muscle. She was too afraid to budge an inch and he had to pull her from the room. He took her to his.

There they sat together—in silence—and in order to pass the time while they waited for the next punishment or for dinner, they played little games. However, the stress was still too great for her and during their second thumb-war, she escaped into one of her trances.

That's how it went for the remainder of the afternoon of the fourth day of the week. She would startle awake with some word or another on her lips and he'd clamp his hand down over her mouth again fast. Each time she wore a look of increasing fear, as well as gratitude, while he hid a worried one of his own.

She'd been very loud that one time she called out to her dead mom concerning the yarn, and the other words that she had spoken, though brief seemed to be adding up. Curt fretted that even though it was only the fourth day she was just on verge of being punished. Yet dinner came and went and then chores; somehow she was able to hold it together.

That night the creature barely looked into his room, but it stayed so long in hers that Curt felt convinced it would attack at any moment. Eventually it moved on and the punishment was staved off for one more day.

Chapter 14

The Punishment

1

The fifth day after Darla died, the house seemed to be a home for lunatics.

This included Curt.

He decided to try a new tactic to keep the older boys from ganging up on him and went to breakfast that morning wearing his pajamas under his clothes and he made sure they stuck out oddly here and there. As well, he spiked his hair purposely and arranged his face to suggest he hadn't slept a wink. The stress on him was massive, but his facade was all a fake so Paul would think that his mind games were working.

The other children weren't faking and as usual, the mouse looked the craziest and in truth, it wasn't just a look. It was a fact, a very sad fact. Next on the list was Amber, she went in and out of trances, becoming a living manikin in a second, even while she was eating and sometimes when walking. Paul appeared as if he was having an endless seizure and Matt had become a mute, raging drill sergeant.

Every infraction or even supposed infraction was enough to set the boy off and he would frequently make more noise being silently furious than the person who had broken his rule. By the time normal people were sitting down for lunch, Curt thought Matt was for certain going to be punished that night.

The older boy must have felt it too and went to his room to hide.

Curt could only wish the mouse would do the same thing. This time it wasn't her crazy eyes that were bothering him, it was her overt sexual nature.

"You'll be next," took on a new meaning when she grabbed his crotch and rubbed her bone-skinny body against his while she whispered it in her dead voice. He pushed her away in complete disgust, wondering how she could possibly be thinking about sex. Or if she were thinking at all.

This was something that he had wondered a great deal about.

Did the mouse have any of her mind left? Other than showing her empty plate to Miss Feanor, she never tried to converse with anyone. And besides being crazy, all that Curt had ever seen her do was the same cat puzzle. She worked on it day after day. She never finished it either, but would only get so far depending on how crazy she currently was and then she'd start all over the next day.

On this fifth day, with the pressure running so high, she had done little more than pull the box down and open it up. There it sat looking lonely and ignored as the mouse seemed quite fixated on Curt. Time after time, he would have to push her away, only to see her bounce off the walls and come zombie-walking back at him.

Finally, he took Amber by the hand to his room.

At this point, mentally, the blonde girl was only so much better than the mouse. Her trances were coming on very fast, but unfortunately they wouldn't last long, sometimes only a minute or two and then she would be talking to the air, in a loud conversational manner. Curt was hard pressed to keep her quiet and he was only partially successful. Because of this, an hour or two before dinner, his betting odds on who would be punished next became almost even between Matt, Amber, and the mouse.

His own chance at cracking that day was virtually nil. He had invested so much of himself into protecting Amber that the little things that had been haunting him were overshadowed by this and he barely noticed the oppressive silence, the terrible food, or the hungry desire for pain in the air that sat unmoving in the house.

Paul wasn't in the running either and this was mostly due to the fact that he kept to himself most of the time, sitting in his room with his door shut. Curt assumed that the blonde boy would make it another day, but he hadn't taken into consideration the deterioration of Paul's mental state

Just before dinner, the boy had walked boldly into Curt's room. "You think you're so great, don't you?" Paul asked in accusatory tone and Curt scarcely had time to grab Amber's mouth.

"Mknnha," she mumbled as she popped out of her trance at the sound of the boy's voice. She looked about and when she saw Paul, her eyes went wide in alarm. Curt must have worn the same surprised expression.

With both hands, Paul had a hold of the skin around his eyes and was pulling back on it; stretching the skin to the rear of his face. He was trying to control his twitch this way; it looked freakish and made Curt's skin crawl.

"Do you?" Paul asked. "Is that why you think you can tell everyone, who can and can't be punished. We heard you talking to the house. We know what you said about me."

Curt could say nothing to this. Not only because the atmosphere in the room had charged instantly, but also because he hadn't spoken to the house, and denying it to an insane person would've been useless and perhaps dangerous. Paul looked as if violence lay just beneath his skin.

Meekly Curt shrugged his shoulders.

"Fine, be that way," Paul growled, but thankfully he said it quietly in a vindictive way. "You know what you are? You're a fucker. That's what you are." He turned and went back to his own room.

2

The first real punishment since the one that Curt had slept in a drug-induced coma through occurred that night.

Dinner in the house was normally a somber affair, but that evening it seemed deader than usual. Other than the mouse, everyone ate with a minimum of movement and barely made eye contact with each other. Curt saw that each of the children thought they were going to be punished that night.

Again, except the mouse. She didn't seem capable of thinking to such an extent.

There was only one upside to this. Matt and Paul blazed through their chores and then each went to hide in their rooms, hoping to draw as little attention to themselves as possible. The downside was the two girls.

During his chores, the mouse kept appearing out of nowhere, whispering that he would be next, and attempting to grab him, while Amber seized up with such frequency that by the time Curt finished brushing his teeth, she had yet to start cleaning the hallway.

A minute later, he found himself sweating through his pajamas, working in a near panic to get her chores done. At one point, he even dragged her stiff and useless body to the end of the hall just to get her out of the way. And he still wasn't done, when Miss Feanor began turning off the downstairs lights.

He had to fight a great temptation to leave her there and run to his room.

Instead, he tried to work faster, but seconds later he saw Miss Feanor glaring at him as she walked slowly up the stairs. He bent to the chore harder but sloppier. Surprisingly, the lady began helping, going on her hands and knees to get the work finished. Before this, he never noticed before how much tougher Amber's chores were compared to his, and hers were nothing compared to Matt's, who had a million little trinkets to dust, twenty pictures to clean, and many yards of floor to sweep, wax, and buff.

At some point, Amber was back next to him crying and scrubbing at the same time. But a minute later, she had frozen up again, a single tear hanging from her pert little nose.

'Go put her in bed,' Miss Feanor motioned with uncharacteristic charity. 'I will finish up here.'

Curt had a small lithe, sleekly muscled body and like most active twelve-year-olds didn't carry an ounce of fat on him. Yet compared to Amber, he was a hippopotamus. She felt like little more than bundled twigs in his arms and when her head lolled backward, he could see the cartilage of her larynx and the rings of her trachea clearly beneath the skin of her neck.

How long could a person survive off a diet of oatmeal, spam, carrots, and rice and expect to live? The very sad answer came to him quickly, a ten year old like Amber had been when she had first arrived, could probably make it to her eighteenth birthday and no more. All that was needed. He sighed as a heavy depression weighed him down more than the mass of the girl.

Placing her in bed, she came back to her terrible reality with a start.

"I, mnhh," she said beneath his quick hand, she struggled for half a second before going limp. He then kissed her goodnight, rather as a father should have and after turning off the lights, he asked her a question with his hands.

'Is this good? Or more?' He wanted to know at what width the door should be shut.

'A little more,' she informed him, her fingers an inch apart. He did as she directed and then she smiled and buried herself, burrowing beneath her covers more like an animal than a person.

3

Miss Feanor stood across the hall at the door that led to the attic. Her room and all her belongings lay beyond that door and up some stairs. The thought of them and all their possibilities caused him to pause a moment, but she pointed to his room and then to her wrist.

'Go get in bed and hurry,' the moves indicated.

He did as he was told, still that didn't stop his great curiosity about what lay beyond that door. Very likely it held the answers to why they were in the house and more importantly how to get out.

He sensed her watching him and he kept his head carefully neutral and forward. Even when he entered his room, he didn't look back, but when he got into bed, he made sure to be in a position to look through the crack of his door.

Unfortunately, all he saw was the door to the attic slowly coming to a silent close.

Crreik.

The sound of the thing moving up the stairs had occurred within seconds of Miss Feanor having shut her door and Curt still had his covers down under his arms. In a flash, he had them over his head. Because of the very evil nature of the creature, Curt was afraid, but logically he didn't see himself as a likely candidate for punishment. For that reason, his body didn't vibrate in fear as it normally did as he hunkered down.

[210]

The creature barely looked into his room. It paused outside of it, as if this was day one instead of day five, and then it moved on to Amber's. There, not only did it go into her room, it moved about loudly, knocking into things, shutting her drawers with heavy thumps. Curt hadn't been afraid minutes before, however now he felt a pain in his chest—if Amber was to come out from one of her trances just then, she'd be attacked for certain.

Eventually it moved on, going to each of the other rooms and lingering as it had with Ambers. Amazingly, after four or five minutes, the time it took to go through the other rooms, there were no screams as Curt had expected. This made him feel weird all of a sudden. He actually had anticipated the coming punishment, not as a pleasurable thing, only as something he could count on.

All the children, except him, had made a great deal of noise and there was no way a punishment should've been avoided. He was beginning to think he had been working far too hard at being quiet; he had practically driven himself crazy trying to keep...

Suddenly, there came a small creeping noise in the hallway, and this focused his razor sharp mind. The sly sound was no child moving about, nor was it Miss Feanor...

A scream rent the air.

"Noooooooooo!" The word was so unreal in its terror that Curt didn't recognize who it was tearing out their own throat in order to make it.

"Stop! Please, nooooo!"

He rolled over, orienting on the sound and guessed it was Paul screaming. His screams went straight to Curt's gut and he felt he was about to hurl up his hated dinner. He clutched himself; first his stomach and then his ears. Paul's screams rang out with amazing clarity in the otherwise silent house and no matter how hard Curt thrust his hands to his ears, the noise snuck through. They went on and on, and after a minute, he found himself sobbing and he suddenly realized that he'd actually been saying something.

In horror, he now abandoned his ears and struck his hands over his mouth. He had been mimicking the sounds as they came to him, Paul's no's were his no's, Paul's pleading whiny voice had been his whiny voice.

Curt wanted the torture to end as much as Paul did and he began to picture the creature with its huge teeth, and the urge to vomit came again, stronger. He also felt that he couldn't breathe and with fear in his heart, he pulled his covers back and gasped for breath.

Now that he was out of the covers, the screams were more vivid and carried a weight to them. They struck his exposed skin and seemed to leave a residue on him. In anguish, Curt moaned miserably and rubbed at himself for just a second or two, before ducking back under the covers.

He realized he'd rather suffocate than be outside his blanket.

The air beneath quickly became hot and stale—it made him listless and he felt himself slipping into his fugue state where time would blessedly pass him by. But the thief in him had felt something out of place and pulled himself back from that blissful nothingness.

Thinking past the hateful sounds, he became conscious of the fact that when he had been out of the covers, he had not felt the atmosphere of the room as he thought he would. His curiosity, as it sometimes did, overcame his prudence and while the screams of Paul raged on, Curt forced himself, with a mental toughness well beyond his years, to reach his arm out of the covers and feel the wall next to his bed.

His breath came in sharply. He barely felt the evil hating force that made the house seem so alive. It was there, but distant. Was it so caught up in the punishment that it might not notice a small boy such as himself heading down the stairs? With that thought came a weak urge to make a break for the front door, but the ongoing screams and his own common sense quelled it easily. Now was not the time. He knew too little of the truth of his situation and the creature scared him too much to take that sort of risk on a wild fancy.

He was a gambler, just not a reckless one.

4

Soon after this the screams ended, and then came a long, miserable soulless blubbering, punctuated by periodic shrieks. He could picture the creature still in the room hovering over Paul, nibbling on him as if full, but unable to resist the treat.

Eventually this ended as well and Curt heard the soft sounds of the creature moving away down the stairs. After it did, there came a lingering shameful weeping from Paul's room that had Curt embarrassed for his friend. He didn't know what to do. Was he supposed to go to him? Should he stay in bed? As far as he knew, no one got up to check on Paul and Curt understood so little about first aide that he would've been the last person Paul would want near him. This last was just a flimsy excuse he used to cover his fear and in the end Curt did nothing.

The next morning Curt laid in bed awake well before the sun's light snuck past the slats of his shutters. He stared at the ceiling, watching as it slowly transformed from a dull grey to a bright white, remembering each of Paul's screams. They replayed themselves in his mind, one by one.

He wanted to cry them away, yet all he could do was swallow them and push them down into his soul, where he knew they would rot and fester. Eventually he knew those fermenting screams would poison him, killing him from the inside out, but first they would change him into someone new. Someone unrecognizable, someone insane. There was no getting around it. Curt saw it happening to the people of the house and it would happen to him as well.

He got up for breakfast...oatmeal again. And again, and again. Always oatmeal. They had to wait on Paul who took forever coming down to eat. Matt rolled his eyes as the blonde boy came limping in and Curt felt his hatred for Matt double.

Paul looked awful. The poor boy seemed like the walking dead. His face was stark white and he moved about unsteadily. Fresh bruises and bite marks could be seen just at the edges of his long sleeve shirt and Curt knew that beneath the shirt, there'd be a laundry list of more. The boy's skin would be like wallpaper depicting his torture. Curt swallowed the image along with his hated oatmeal and both went to join the screams that were churning in his stomach.

Worse than the bruising were the boy's eyes. They were haunted like Curt had never seen. Not in any of the street crazies he had known or the strung out prostitutes pushing their scuzzy wares. No, nothing compared. They had seen something unspeakable and it showed in the way he looked at the world around him as if it were part of a dream; that after last night, nothing could be real. Every object that he came in contact with, he touched consciously; his bowl, his plastic spoon, even the table he'd grip, or run his hands over, and his head would give a little nod as if he had just convinced himself that these were real.

At one point in the tasteless meal, Paul looked up at him and Curt had to look away in embarrassment. He felt tremendous overwhelming guilt, which he knew was stupid. None of what happened to Paul had been his fault, but still the feeling was there.

Part of it was his memory of Paul calling him a 'Fucker'.

It was such a childlike and childish thing to say. Only grade schoolers, just learning about cussing would ever say something like that. This made him realize that Paul had been ten years old when he came into the home and in some ways, the boy was still ten. The crying for instance. It had been that of a small child, not a teenager and as it had gone on, Curt had pictured a much younger Paul lying in bed.

But he knew there was another, greater reason for his guilt—Paul had been his friend. In his life, Curt had few friends, still he knew how to treat them, and he felt that he had somehow profoundly let the boy down.

After the meal and before anyone got up to leave, Miss Feanor gave them each a red pill.

'Vit-a-min,' she mouthed the word at his questioning look.

'Ok,' his return smile said, however it was anything but ok. Taking pills from her scared him and the red pill went into his cheek and eventually it sank beneath the waters of the toilet. The others took theirs easily enough and Paul received two more large white ones, which he eagerly swallowed.

As usual, after breakfast the long dull day was theirs. Curt moved listlessly through his monotonous morning routine and then wandered into the family room and noticed the familiar first day gaiety was back. He sensed the relief at being passed over for punishment as much as any of them, but the way they acted seemed so tactless. Just as quickly as he had entered, he left again hating how everyone pretended to ignore the fact that Paul had just gone through a terrible experience.

Amber skipped quietly after him, but he ignored her, however she proved difficult to ignore.

'What's wrong?' her shrug and questioning look asked.

'Everything,' his hands waved about, indicating the house and all that it contained.

The girl commiserated and motioned with her patented shrug, 'This is the way it is.' She seemed to be right, but he still didn't like it. Thinking he wanted to be left alone he gave her a little smile and gently pushed her away, pointing at himself and then at his room; she understood and he went to his bedroom. For a while, he pondered on the house and the creature and about Miss Feanor, and the puzzle she represented. And he thought about the screams.

Paul's screams and Darla's.

With those beginning to replay themselves, he decided he didn't want to be alone after all. Amber was there outside his door waiting for him as if she knew he wouldn't be long. She smiled at him as sweet as a child. When he didn't return her smile, she forced him to.

Pushing her very pale face into his, she poked her nose at his lips, until they pulled back and his white teeth shown from behind them. She then yanked him around, directing him to the family room where he could enjoy the company of the other children, while they were still halfway enjoyable. Even on their best behavior, Matt and the mouse were hard to take. Paul came in a little later and Curt had trouble looking him in the eye, but the older boy was persistent.

'There is a message upstairs for you,' he communicated this to Curt with a very small movement of his eyes upwards, towards the bathroom. Curt didn't want a note just then. He felt sure that it would be heavy on blame, but it wasn't.

Hi Curt,
im so sorry for the way i acted. You have every rite to hate me and i desserved completely what happened to me last night. The last couple of days, it was like i was posessed. It has never been this bad and it scared me. i see that you and Amber are an item, be careful about this. She will become more and more needy and will want to spend too much time in her weird trances knowing you will bale her out. I don't remeber any questions you mite have asked, so please ask again.

After Curt read the note, he couldn't remember what questions he had asked either. He did have a thousand questions concerning the creature and what happened last night, however these were questions he'd never ask. If Paul was to volunteer information, well that would be ok, but otherwise it seemed too personal and too painful a subject to bring up.

Curt pondered the question of questions for a while. So many of his questions had been answered by Paul with, *I don't know,* that he was little hesitant about bothering with any more. He had already asked about the attic, Miss Feanor, the house, and the creature; all that seemed to be left was asking about the basement. Even considering asking about that gave Curt a lasting case of the goose bumps.

He pushed past the goose bumps.

Hi Paul,
The house can make us be a little crazy and you are forgiven. i just wish i had been able to help you better. Maybe if it starts happening again, you can give me a more direct signal. Maybe tap the top of your head. What's in the basement, did Beth ever tell you? Is there a door to the outside down there? Are there windows? Miss Feenor can run away but doesn't. She helps the creeture, but helps us to. Why? Have you been in the atic? Does she ever leave her keys around? Why was everyone weirder this last week than the week before?
Your friend,
Curt.

Fighting what felt like an eternal depression, he sighed heavily when he left the note, wondering how long he'd consider Paul his friend, or Amber his girlfriend for that matter. People changed under average circumstances, Matt had, in all probability, just been a normal kid when he first came to the house and now he was a psychotic monster. The mouse as well had started off as a girl named Beth.

How long before Paul's voice became a permanent part of him, or how long before Amber slipped into a trance and stayed there for good? Curt went to his room, considering what would happen if these two things came to pass, and it was then that his day became more interesting.

The police knocked on their front door.

Chapter 15

Love Letters

1

Curt had just entered his room, when the hall light behind him flashed on and off twice. In a house where uniformity and consistency ruled, this little thing was equivalent to an earthquake. It caused as much fear as one as well. Poking his head out of his bedroom door, Curt was just in time to see Miss Feanor streak down the main floor hallway, gliding effortlessly and as silently as an ice-skater. She peered through the little peephole for a fraction of a second and when she pulled her eye away, her face had gone grey.

'Get down here, now!' she motioned to Curt. The others hadn't needed prompting and were gathered around her before he'd got halfway down, even Paul, who could only limp along slowly, beat him there. As he came up to them, the lights blinked again.

"It's the police," she said in her dry quiet voice. "They've already called about Ms Heines once. I told them she never showed for our meeting. If..."

Donk, donk, donk...

The police were knocking on the front door. Curt should've been feeling elated, but instead a sick dread had crawled into his belly.

"...If they ask any of you, she never showed up. You've never seen her. Matt..." Miss Feanor looked at Curt oddly with her tongue out and then jerked her head upwards.

Curt's face showed confusion at this, but before he could say or do anything, Matt spun him around and began pulling him up the stairs, which crreiked alarmingly. The other children scattered like roaches. Matt had him by the collar of his long sleeve shirt, and in seconds brought him into his room.

"You're sick, vomiting, have a sore throat," Matt whispered into his ear. "You've never seen the caseworker, if they ask. Got it?"

Curt nodded. The air in the house had already begun to feel angry, but he couldn't stop a sliver of hope from coming out. "Maybe the police might..."

Matt shut him up with a terrific glare. "Don't be stupid. Bullets won't affect the monster," Matt hissed with rising anger and fear in his voice. He then bodily pushed Curt into bed. The younger boy ducked down and started to cover his head, but Matt yanked the covers down and tucked them beneath his chin. It felt strange, even foreign to lie like that, like a normal person.

When Matt left, Curt began imagining all sorts of scenarios playing out, and found he couldn't just lay in the bed waiting. Cautious as always, Curt extended his hand to feel the wall. The house was definitely aware and awake, but as expected it wasn't focused on him. Warily, he pulled himself up and around and put down one of his white socked feet. Just at that moment there came a change in the air in the house and Curt recognized the feel: the front door had opened. Now the house seemed really to come alive and with his heart in his throat, Curt ducked back down like a frightened squirrel, this time burying himself beneath the covers.

Seconds passed.

He heard murmuring, which he strained at and soon his curiosity had his head out from under his blanket and in moments, when he still couldn't catch the words, he stood just behind his door craning his neck to see through the crack. The police and Miss Feanor were nowhere in sight.

The air around him had relaxed which was puzzling. He reached his hand out to his doorframe and took the pulse of the house; it had calmed a little, and this was odd as well. He had expected the house to be riled and getting more so.

The murmuring came again, it sounded muffled to his ear, and so he slipped out of his room and squatted down on the top step so he could see the front door properly.

It stood open by a few inches.

The sight sent blood rushing to his ears and he could feel his own heart beat there. It was loud and fast. Those few inches represented an amazing opportunity, not only was this a chance at escape, but protection as well. Bullets might not stop the monster, but they would certainly aggravate it and with the monster focused on the cop, Curt could run and if he did, he wouldn't look back.

So it was that on feet that were feather light, he went down the stairs, moving in complete silence. His hand trailing on the wall felt the angry awareness in it grow with each of his careful steps. He had the impression that eyes were in the walls watching him, but what he didn't feel was the growing sense of perverse hunger, which more than anything else about the place scared him.

It was there, yet distant and uncaring, still replete from the night before. Later he would remark upon this as another sign of the dual nature of the house, but just then the lack of feeling added impetus to his anxious feet. It allowed him to move forward despite the watchfulness coming to center on him.

At the bottom step, he took a quick glance into the family room and saw the other children had set up the monopoly board. They sat about it nervously, no one moving any of the pieces or rolling dice. It was only a prop and like actors, they were waiting on their cue: the entrance of the police, to begin their scene.

His sudden appearance caught their attention, they all turned and looked at him in shock. Yet in a flash their expressions collapsed into dread, every one of them, the mouse included and this made him pause, his fear doubling within him. However, unlike them, he wasn't faking a game, he was gambling for high stakes. Putting steel in his spine, he stepped boldly toward the door.

"No," Amber said. It was only a tiny squeak of a word, but it stopped Curt three feet from his objective. Behind him, he heard a rustle of cloth and a dull smacking sound. He shot a look back and saw the girl holding her arm and fighting against tears. Matt had hit her for trying to stop Curt. Fury coursed through Curt in an instant, sweeping aside his fear, yet not his common sense. He glared hard at the boy and vowed his revenge silently, but knew it would have to wait.

Freedom was too near at hand to waste this chance. The door was so close that he could hear Miss Feanor plainly.

"I don't know, Officer. We only spoke twice and she seemed fine. Not at all anxious or suicidal, but you can never really tell." By her tone, Curt could tell the conversation was going the way she wanted and that she wasn't a suspect in the disappearance of Darla Heines.

She soon would be, Curt thought and his feeling of revenge grew within him.

As a good gambler, he knew the risks involved with trying to make an attempt at the door, but like so many bad gamblers he was letting his emotions overrule his thinking. Revenge, anger, and hate clouded his judgment; yet even greater than those was a simple desire for freedom.

It burned, overpowering everything, including his jangling nerves, which were trying desperately to warn him about the house. The house was very aware and angry that the boy wasn't in its proper place. And now the hunger for pain began to awaken within it. Curt sensed all this, however he didn't care, and at that moment, he put his life, as well as the police officer's on a lucky roll of the dice.

But just like in Vegas, the house always wins in the end.

2

He stretched out his hand to grab the knob, thinking that nothing could stop him from simply yanking the door open.

"Miss Feanor, I'm going to Jonny's now. Oh, and thanks for setting up this play date. I'll be back by dinner."

This is what Curt planned on saying to Miss Feanor when he stepped out onto the small cover porch. He also planned to move quickly, skipping elusively by her as if they were playing a game. He was certain that she would try to grab at him.

But none of this happened.

The house was more alive than Curt had counted on. As he stretched out his hand, the door retreated before him. It was as if the door and his hand had the wrong end of magnets within them and the closer he got, the further the door closed. It hadn't been open much to begin with, but with a sinking heart, Curt's advancing hand chased the door closed.

It shut with an empty silence. Now the whole house seemed focused on the little space left between his hand and the knob. There was an energy in that small gap, very much like electricity. Curt hesitated at grabbing it, wondering if that force would actually stop his hand from touching it. He moved his hand a hair closer, without feeling any resistance and he knew he could grab the knob if he wanted. Would he be allowed to open the door? Probably not, yet that great longing for freedom filled him, demanding that he throw caution to the wind and take the chance, anyway.

The thief in him suddenly spoke out against this, quiet and authoritative: *Don't. It's a sucker's bet.*

That voice inside his mind seemed older and far wiser and was certainly right. Curt curled his fingers in toward himself, making a fist. He realized, he couldn't win this way, cop, or no cop and now he pulled his hand back. And as if by magic, the house seemed to turn its focus away from him, it again centered on what was occurring on the porch.

The thief began to shake, feeling as though he had narrowly averted a certain disaster, and it was with a crazed, giddy sensation running through him that he turned from the door. He saw that the other children had frozen in place staring at him. Amber smiled, happy that he made the right decision, while the mouse roved her eyes over his body and if she had a thought, he couldn't tell what it was. Matt, meanwhile looked only curious, which gave Curt a nervous thrill in his stomach.

The last person he turned his attention to was Paul, who slumped his shoulders in sweating relief. He smiled at Curt, and Curt smiled back, feeling wired as the tension dissolved out of him. Thinking it would be wise to be in bed when Miss Feanor came back in, he gave the children a small wave and then headed upstairs, missing an opportunity that he'd regret later. Just then, he had no way of knowing that he would see this sweet version of Paul only a few more times before the blonde boy died. If he had known, he would've stayed longer and played fake monopoly with him.

The police officer was gone a few minutes later, but Curt was oblivious to it. The very long, sad night listening to Paul being punished, coupled with his own near catastrophe, had left him exhausted and he slept half the day away.

When he woke, he read the note Paul had left for him earlier.

Hi Curt,

You have to stop thinking you are going to escape. The house can feel! It's alive! Miss Feenor is the only one who can leeve and that's if the house lets her. i don't know why this is so but it is and you are right, the house and her do seem to work together. i already told you, i don't know whats in the atic and Beth has always refused to talk about what happened to her in the basement. i dont think she can anymore. About the difference between your first week here. im sorry but we all thought you'd be punished and it took the pressure off us a little. im glad you weren't.

Curt wasn't going to stop thinking of escape; he was only going to stop asking Paul about it. Every lock has a key, he thought to himself, but with a queer turn to his stomach, he worried that his key might be found in the basement. With that unsettling notion, he left to see the others.

He spent the remainder of the afternoon sitting with Amber, reading, sniffing her hair when the desire came upon him and she would stroke his arm softly when the desire came on her. Paul kept to himself during this time, locked away in his room and Curt at first thought that it was an after effect of the punishment. However, minutes before dinner, he heard a noise from Paul's room. He had just come from the bathroom when the sound of murmuring came to him, he crept closer.

"I don't think that's a good idea." It was Paul speaking to himself barely above a whisper. "Quiet down or they'll hear us."

Embarrassed for his friend, Curt wanted to slip away, but since Paul's 'voice' was easily as malignant as Matt, he felt it best to stay and eavesdrop. In order to listen better he pressed his ear to the boy's door.

"Please don't...or...how bout you do it to Matt," Paul continued. "You hate Matt."

There came a long pause. "He's one of us already...Will you at least tell me what you're planning? I won't tell, I..." another long silence and then Paul's voice rose slightly higher and more desperate, "No please I want to stay. I told you I wouldn't..."

Now a long pause was accompanied by a light step from within the room and this had Curt hurrying down the hall toward the backstairs. Not wanting it known that he'd been listening, he ducked into the first room that he came to; it belonged to the mouse. Thankfully, she wasn't in and he dodged behind her door. Paul slipped by seconds later, oblivious to the boy standing in the shadows of the room.

Curt breathed a gentle sigh of relief, but his relief didn't last long as he bent his mind to the partial conversation he had heard. Paul had a plan working, very likely to have Curt punished. Had it been Matt, Curt would've very much considered going on the offensive, doing damage of his own, but he couldn't with Paul. The blonde boy had just been punished the night before and Curt felt sorry for him.

He was almost about to step out of the room, when he realized he'd never properly inspected the mouse's bedroom. This was an innate part of Curt's nature. He snooped. No matter where he was or with whom. Inside him was a constant need to study humanity and there was no better way of doing this than to look where they least wanted you to. Find what a person had hidden away and you find their true selves.

The mouse had secrets.

She'd been in the basement at least once, and she might know if there was a way out in that direction. However, with her insanity, those secrets could be locked away, beyond the ability of any thief, but there could be clues, pictures, drawings, perhaps even a diary.

Her room was as austere and bare as everyone else's, which made his quick search easier. The mattress and box spring were first to undergo his close scrutiny, and then the bed frame and finally the little dresser, none of these revealed a thing...at first.

On his second go round, he became far more methodical and eventually discovered a veritable treasure, pinned under the bottom of the dresser. Not knowing how much time there was until dinner, he moved with haste, tilting the dresser back he saw a slim stack of wrinkled notebook paper. The one on top was visible to him and had writing all over it. His heart leaped with excitement, not just at the paper, but more at what held the paper in place. Four bent paper clips had been pushed into the soft wood of the dressers frame.

Every lock has a key! he thought happily to himself and lowered the dresser without touching anything.

There was no sense grabbing the papers just then and risk being caught when he would have no time to read any of it with dinner so close. The papers weren't going anywhere; he'd get the papers the next morning. It would only be day two since Paul's punishment and the pressure would have barely begun. This meant that the mouse would be hard at work on her stupid cat puzzle for at least two hours. That would be the right time.

He stepped unseen from her room and almost chortled going down to dinner. It was the thought of those paper clips. Before that moment, if any locks had stood in his way to escape he would've been helpless against them. Now he would have at least a chance and happily he pictured the door to the attic, but his happy thought died at the sight of Paul.

3

The boy's twitch had already begun, but what was worse was the ill-concealed hatred in his eyes. It was there for only a second before he replaced it with an oily smile. Curt smiled back, pretending he hadn't noticed the look, all the while feeling ill at the thought of it.

What did it portend? All through dinner he tried to predict exactly what Paul would do and more importantly when. Normally Curt wouldn't have expected a day one attack, since it didn't make any sense. Nobody was on the verge of cracking so soon after a punishment and the creature hadn't yet built up its demented lusts, however Paul's look had not been entirely sane. And that evening after he had completed his chores, Curt found subtle evidence of someone tampering with his possessions.

It wasn't much, just enough to have him second-guessing everything else and he sped about checking, and re-checking all his areas, which was likely Paul's intention. He wanted Curt on edge, unable to relax.

Another aspect of the boy's psychological warfare came in a very subtle but unnerving manner.

Out of habit, Curt checked to see if there was a note in the toilet paper dispenser, only to find the pen missing altogether. He remembered then how Amber had been punished when a pen had been found in her belongings and with doubt gnawing at his insides, Curt checked his things again, but didn't find the pen.

Of course that didn't mean it couldn't be planted at any time.

There was no sleep in him that night and when the stairs began to crreik, crreik, crreik, his hands and arms commenced to shiver, and he had to force himself to remain completely still, hugging them about his body.

No punishment occurred that night.

The second day following Paul's punishment he felt the pressure far greater than he should have and he worried endlessly over what Paul was up to.

But his day was not all bad, the high point came late in the afternoon when he stole the paper clips from the mouse's room. He took also the papers and read each but they held little of interest. In fact, they were sad and painful. They were love letters from Matt to Beth—the girl who would eventually become the mouse. After reading them, he couldn't help but feel sorry for Matt. He seemed to have really loved her, but in the end she'd asked too much of him. Even though Curt could only read one side of their correspondence, it was plain that eventually Beth had pleaded with Matt to be punished for her.

It hadn't even been for something specific, it seemed that she was just feeling the overwhelming pressure and had worried that she was about the break. It was an utterly impossible thing to ask, and Matt had declined and tried to explain to the girl, Beth that if he did it that one time, it would become a never-ending thing. She would expect it of him always. Curt had to agree. If Amber ever asked him to be punished for her...he dreaded the very idea.

Thinking that the mouse's idea of where to store the papers was a good one, he put them under his dresser and when they were safely hid, he went to join the others. Dinner followed soon and the low point of his day came during the meal, as Paul's twitchy eyes never left his face. It was so disturbing that Curt decided he couldn't sit back any longer and scarfing down his hated meal he raced up stairs to the bathroom.

Back Off!

Using soap, he wrote this on the bathroom mirror and fully expected Paul to see it first, but Amber came upstairs after dinner and went straight away into the bathroom. She left the room minutes later with big eyes.

'You wrote that?' she pantomimed. He could only shrug and look sheepish. At this she hurried off, not wanting to get in the middle of an escalating war. Knowing he couldn't protect two places at once, Curt sped through his chores downstairs and came puffing back up in record time. He then commenced to follow Paul about just as he had Matt the week before. Poor Paul slipped back and forth between personalities and couldn't decide which way he was going, but longer and longer he spent time seething in the hate personality.

Curt managed to avoid punished that night, however the next night would find him downstairs well after the lights had been turned down, racing in horrible darkness toward the very creature itself.

4

The third day after Paul's punishment started off with a great deal of promise, the trapped children woke to a steady drizzle of rain. Curt ate breakfast wearing a broad grin, but the promise was a false one and when it turned to snow an hour later everyone felt the pressure of the house and its near insatiable hunger intensify.

No one felt it more than Curt, though from an outward appearance, one would've thought Paul and his terrible twitch might have. But if one could look past the spazzing muscles of his face, they'd see an awful insanity in his eyes. He seemed hell bent on making Curt break.

The only solace Curt could find was that Matt had become aware of the sudden enmity between the one-time allies and had stepped back from any mischief, the eldest child in the house appeared not just content, but happy to see the two younger boys destroy themselves. Disappointingly, Amber wasn't exactly broken up by the situation. He understood it from her point of view, Paul was like a brother to her, and he was her boyfriend. It would be nearly impossible for her to choose sides and what's more, she would escape punishment yet again. Still it stung that she refused to even help with little things like keeping a watch over Paul.

Nevertheless, above all things, Curt was a survivor and he changed his routine that day just to befuddle Paul's attempts. Before dinner, he went up to the bathroom, but left as soon as he arrived and ducked down the stairs leading to the kitchen. In secret, he then began to work on his downstairs chores and completed everything except the backstairs.

After dinner, he kept his eye on Paul, following him around for so long that the boy almost screamed at him to go away. Eventually he had to; streaking down stairs, he tore through his one remaining chore as fast as possible. But he wasn't fast enough, yet in truth, there was no way he could've been. It took less than a minute for Paul to dump the contents of his drawers around his room. Curt wasn't fazed by this at all, in fact, he had expected this very thing, and with a minute to spare, he had his room ship shape.

For some reason, now Paul seemed more relaxed.

This sudden change worried Curt and he began to second-guess what the downstairs looked like. Was his area of responsibility ransacked? Was Matt involved? Anxiously, he raced to the first floor and scanned over everything—nothing appeared amiss.

Minutes later, he was lying in bed thinking he had made it through another day without being punished. Lights were being turned off downstairs, and he laid back, pulling his covers over his head.

"Aren't you forgetting something?" Paul asked.

Curt yanked them back down in an instant.

Paul stood there and in his hand was a porcelain figurine of a kitten. The boy tossed it in the air in a relaxed fashion as if it were of no more value than a stone. To Curt it was worth a small fortune. He knew that figurine very well and it certainly didn't belong in Paul's hands. He knew exactly where it belonged and he knew as well, the precise angle at which its ears aligned with those of its fellow frolicking kittens and he knew also just how close to the edge of the wall its tail should lay.

It belonged on a shelf above the sink in the powder room on the first floor. Curt's heart went into his throat.

"Paul may have never told you this, but you don't want to be out of bed when the lights are off," the boy he knew as 'Paul' said this quietly, just above a whisper. "The house knows and sends out its creature and then...it's play time." Another light, somewhere downstairs went out behind him. "I think we should start the games now, here catch." He casually tossed the figurine well over Curt's head toward the far wall.

Trapped mostly under his blankets, there was no way Curt could catch it, and in his mind he saw it hit the hardwood floor and explode into a thousand pieces. But his body reacted faster than his imagination and with his face turning, following the flight of the kitten, which arced high enough to nearly hit the ceiling, his hand grabbed the end of his pillow.

In a flash, his sharp blue eyes judged the trajectory of the figurine and with a dexterity few could match he tossed the pillow and to his delight the kitten landed square upon it, but to his horror, it bounced off. *Snink* was the sound it made when it hit the floor. Curt couldn't tell if it had been damaged. He turned back to Paul and saw the blonde boy shaking his head in disbelief.

"That's not right," Paul said mostly to himself and just then the final light went off behind him. Now he slunk away, knowing that Miss Feanor would be heading up the stairs any second. As he did Curt was out of bed in a blink and scrambled to find the cat in the dark. In horror he found two pieces; a small one and a larger one. The kitten had lost an ear and to Curt it was as if his own child had been injured. Grabbing his pillow he was back in bed in an instant.

Under his covers in the pitch black, he strove to figure out if the ear would sit back on the kitten's head without falling off. It wasn't easy. Breathing heavily in his fright and the suffocating heat beneath the covers, he found that it would stay if it were angled right. Now all he had to do was go all the way down to the powder room and set it back up on the shelf.

But there were both Miss Feanor and the creature to worry about. The lady would be relatively simple to elude. Though she moved very quietly, she still made noise if you knew what to listen for and Curt had memorized her routine days ago, it was eerily similar to that of the creature. But would it matter? If Paul was being in the least bit truthful, Curt could expect the creature to come up out of the basement the second he got out of bed.

What choice did he have?

Miss Feanor came up a moment later and Curt began counting as he had almost every night. In his mind, habits were made to be exploited and he knew that when she turned toward Matt and the mouse's rooms, he'd have a window of between twelve to sixteen seconds, to get down stairs. After that, she would turn back around and come along the hall, heading for the door to the attic.

After peeking into his room, she went next to Amber's and as she did, he slipped out of bed. Now all he waited on was for her to turn away from Paul's room and when she did, he ghosted out past his door and down the stairs. He made little more noise than his barely visible shadow, but he had to sacrifice speed in order to move that quietly. Therefore, he was just getting to the bottom of the stairs when she began heading for the attic and he paused—sweat running down his cheeks—as she passed by only a few feet above his head.

The downstairs was nearly perfectly the color of pitch and Curt had to reach out for the end of the banister to know where he was. In shock, he snatched his hand back, holding it to his chest. The house was awake, and worse, aware. It knew that he was out of bed.

It had a sharp tang of anger to it, outraged that one of the vermin could think of strolling around her house anytime it wished. The entity within the house was feminine, but bitterly so, with a hateful streak when it came to children. All of this, Curt could feel and understand with that single touch of his on the banister, yet there was one more thing that overrode all of that. The house was demanding a punishment.

It was eager for it.

So horrible was that feeling that Curt almost turned and ran to his room, but the kitten still sat in his hand and the empty spot on the shelf where it belonged would stand out, glaringly. Just then Curt felt something through the white socks of his feet: a vibration in the wood of the dark gleaming floor. On impulse, he reached down.

It was as if he could hear with his hand and what he heard scared him down to the pit of his stomach. It was the sound of heavy footsteps coming up the basement stairs. They weren't charging up them like they had when Darla the very dead caseworker had touched the door; no these were slow, measured and seemed to gain weight with every step.

Curt's heart thundered huge in his chest, coinciding with each of the villain's steps, and he could feel the surge of blood rushing along his arteries in a wave that went all the way to his fingertips. He felt three of these giant beats and then without thinking or considering any consequence, Curt took off sliding into the inky blackness of the main floor hallway, into the very heart of the house. He raced in complete silence on numb feet heading straight for where the creature would emerge from the basement a few seconds from that very moment.

If he had any chance whatsoever of avoiding the punishment, he'd have to place that kitten onto its shelf and then get back in bed, faster than the creature could climb those stairs. Despite flying down that hallway in a silent blaze he would never make it and he knew this to be fact. And he was right.

The steps of the creature grew louder in the stillness of the house as they advance upwards and Curt was still in the bathroom trying to put the kitten's ear back on it, when he felt the creature near the top of the basement stairs.

The damned ear kept sliding off of the kitten and Curt was close to crying in his frustration, finally inspiration struck and he ran the porcelain ear over his very dry tongue and stuck it where it belonged. Now it stayed in place.

In dread and knowing he was out of time, Curt then slid out of the powder room, taking a single glance through the kitchen. What small amount of light there was, seemed to gather on the shining metal of the doorknob to the mudroom and it glinted as the door swung slowly outward. Even at a dead sprint Curt would never make it halfway down the hall without being seen and so, desperate to put off his punishment for a few more seconds, he slid into the dining room and stood against the wall.

5

His body's reaction to his circumstance amazed Curt. He no longer felt his heart pound or his pulse race, nor was his breath coming out in great gasps of fear. Rather the air seemed to drift in and out of him on its own accord. He didn't sweat, or even shake or shiver. Instead, he became intensely focused on the creature.

It moved with deliberate slowness through the kitchen toward the main hall and now Curt heard it pause only feet from him at the junction where the three doors met. The gambler in him weighed the odds and they weren't good. If the creature took a left, into the dining room, Curt was done for, there was simply nowhere to hide. If the creature moved straight down the hall, Curt would have to race in complete silence into the kitchen, up the backstairs, and then along the upstairs hall, before the creature reached the main stairs twenty feet away.

That was impossible.

Thankfully the creature chose to go to its right, into the powder room. Hearing its sly footsteps, Curt peeked around the corner and saw it as a shadow moving in the blackness. He couldn't tell which direction it faced, but he had no time to worry...it would either see him or it wouldn't. With all his considerable stealth he crept from the dining room and slid down the hall, and as he did he began to feel again the heart pounding fear that had left him momentarily. The terrible thing was behind him and could, at any moment, turn and spot him outlined in the hall. The very notion made his testicles pull up practically into his body.

But the creature didn't turn in those few seconds, and Curt made it to the stairs. He was so close to making it back to his bed, where he hoped that he'd be safe, that he hurried up the stairs...too quickly.

Crreik!

A single misstep and the sound carried clearly in the still, black air of the house.

Once again Curt's body overrode the spastic fear-ridden thinking of his mind. He raced up the remaining steps, and even in the dark the memory stored in his muscles of where to place each foot was true, and he made it to the top in complete silence. The same could not be said of the creature.

At the sound of the crreik, it charged down the hallway with thundering feet and turned up the stairs; it barely slowed until it reached the halfway point. There it inexplicably stopped, perhaps confused to find the upper hallway deserted.

Curt of course hadn't stopped at the top of the stairs, but had zipped into his room, slowing just enough to close his door the proper distance. When he did, he saw the ghost white face of Paul staring out at him from the crack of his own door. In the dim light the boy's expression was of vindictive hate. Curt didn't have time to care.

Crreik

The creature's pause had been short and it began to move in its sneaky manner again. It came up the remaining stairs slowly and, as every night, it paused in front of Curt's door. As always he was under his covers, but now he steeled himself for what was coming. He would run if he could and fight if he couldn't. When Paul had been attacked, it sounded as if had just laid there doing nothing as the creature bit into him. That wouldn't be Curt.

Though the creature's pause in front of his door was probably no longer than on any other night, it felt to take an eternity to the frightened thief and it seemed as if the creature enjoyed this moment and dragged it out purposely. Perhaps it was hoping Curt wouldn't be able to take the pressure, knowing that he was only moments away from pain like he had never experienced before.

But Curt was made of tougher stuff than even he understood and he didn't break, but he did shake and he did cry, but in silence. The creature then came into his room and slowly drifted around his bed and Curt kept his body tense, ready to spring up at the slightest touch. With every second the thing was in his room his fear grew and he began to sweat freely beneath his blankets. The creature was different that night. Perhaps it was all the excitement of running around, but it seemed especially hungry and a great anticipation hung in the air about it. Curt could feel it even beneath his covers. He was sure that it would attack at any second, yet after a few moments the thing left.

Curt didn't relax even then. It had done something similar to Paul three nights before, teasing him, drawing out the expectation of misery. It seemed to love the fear as much as the pain that it caused and Curt knew that after it made a cursory inspection of the other bedrooms, the thing would be back. His stomach went suddenly very queasy.

'Run, while there is still time!' Curt's fear stricken mind screamed at him. He didn't run, inside him was still the childish hope that the creature would just go away like it had on so many other nights.

The creature went next to Amber's room, entered, stayed for a very short time, and then moved on to Paul's. When it opened Paul's door, the boy unexpectedly shrieked in excitement.

"I saw him, it was Curt! He was out of bed! Get him."

The sound of Paul's voice, shrill and loud, paralyzed Curt. There seemed to be cement flooding through his body and even his lungs ceased to expand and contract. He was so sure the creature had turned on the spot and was even then heading right for his door that it came as a huge surprise that Paul screamed again.

"No! No! It wasn't me, it was Curt...get Curt, not me. Nooooooo!"

If Paul had just remained quiet, it would've been Curt that was punished. Instead, it was the older boy's cries that went on and on, and it was far worse than the other night, at least to Curt it was. Paul wouldn't stop blaming him, nor would he stop begging that Curt be punished next. It made it that much harder to endure.

After what felt like an hour, when the creature finally finished with its torture of Paul, Curt had a long moment of painful nervousness as the thing left the older boy's room. There was a pause in the sly sound of its footsteps outside his door, but it only went back to its hideout in the basement.

Chapter 16

The Thief as Savior

1

Perhaps the saddest thing of all for Paul was that the rains came the next day.

Breakfast was a somber affair, more so than Curt had expected. Normally first days were peppy and what with the rain, he expected the others to be practically throwing a party, though he was certainly in no mood for such things.

The way Paul had gone on begging for Curt to be punished had made it into his dreams. All the rest of that night he had dream after dream of hiding from the creature, only to have Paul show up and point him out to the thing. By daybreak he was exhausted, but was surely better off than Paul, who didn't come down for breakfast at all.

They were forced to divvy up his oatmeal between them and this soured Curt's mood even more. Only the mouse appeared truly content. Matt, who was normally at his finest on first days, disliked the rain and seemed as angry as usual, while Amber ate her oatmeal as if in a race with someone Curt couldn't see, and when he chewed the dull paste slowly, she crinkled her forehead at him and gestured upwards with her eyes. She wanted to talk and this was fine with Curt, since he missed the sound of her voice.

"What happened last night?" she asked, sitting on his bed. He made to speak, but she didn't give him a chance to answer. "Were you, like out of bed, or was it Paul? Someone was up. I heard them on the stairs."

"We both were," he said tiredly and told her what had happened.

"Are you crazy, or what? You could've been..." she stopped talking abruptly and wet her pink lips. "Kiss me, ok?" Curt happily obliged, however, there was an odd desperation to Amber's kiss that made the moment feel strained.

Breaking away, he eyed her closely and she smiled but it tilted unhappily. "Amber, what's wrong?" His question alarmed her.

"I'm sorry...I'll do it better." She bent in to kiss him again and he held her back.

"Really, what's wrong?" he asked her gently. "You don't seem your normal self." This question caused tears to instantly well in her eyes and she gripped his arms fiercely.

"Please..."

This was all she had time to say, before Paul came into his room uninvited. He was the saddest thing Curt had ever seen. As always, he wore his blue jeans and his grey turtleneck, but now bruises and bite marks could be seen all along the edges of his shirt and one stood out along his jaw line as well. The teeth marks looked impossibly big. Darker stains of what had to be blood, soaked his shirt along his arms and even at his neck, near his right collarbone.

"Pleeeese...pleeese," Paul begged coming down on his hands and knees in front of Curt. He was crying through very red eyes, both of which were still twitching, despite the rain and the first day. The tears tracked a well-laid course; he had been crying for a while, perhaps all night.

"Please, Curt...it's your turn. You have to break," Paul said in a frantic blubbering rush.

Alarmed, Curt tried to back away, but Paul grabbed his legs, hugging them to his chest. "I'm sorry, I didn't mean it ok? The cat and...and the shirt, those were accidents."

Curt wiggled out of the scarecrow-sized arms of Paul. "Those weren't accidents. You did them on purpose."

"I know I did...uh, what?" Paul paused for a second, tears dripping from his chin. "No, I already said that. I did. I just did. Fine. Please Curt, it's your turn, ok? Will that be all right?"

"Are you asking me to volunteer myself for punishment? The answer's no." Curt wore a hard look, but his insides were harder still. Pity was one thing, self-mutilation at the hands of the fiend was another altogether.

Still crying and wearing his fear-twitching mask, Paul paused, clearly listening to a voice within him for the answer he was supposed to give. To Curt he seemed like a major league pitcher shaking off the signs from his catcher.

"No. No...uh-uh...ok," Paul said to himself. "We...I mean, I'm only asking that you give it a try...it's not that bad really and then you can become one of us."

Curt shook his head, firm but with real sadness. "Paul, I can't. But if you can just stop listening to that voice, we can be friends again..."

"I don't want to be your God damned friend, you fucker!" Paul screamed, his twitching face a vision of insanity.

Even with the rain, which was a steady drumming on the roof of the house, that scream had been tremendous. Paul knew it and in instant, turned and ran from the room, leaving the air charged with that familiar anger. It was hard to even breathe it in.

Curt and Amber sat perfectly still for a time, letting the house drowse once again. When he felt the time was ripe, Curt asked her. "Has he always heard that voice, or is this something new?"

Amber pulled him back down on the bed and she laid her head in the pocket where his chest and shoulder came together. "*Voices*, really. I think there might be like three or four in there. They come and go and I can never keep track of them. They are always what gets him in trouble, but he's generally quite harmed...uh harmless and he sometimes, like sticks up for me."

Sniffing her hair had a relaxing quality and he breathed her in deeply, feeling the stress of his little encounter with Paul slip out of him. He enjoyed this closeness, it was warm and comforting.

"He stuck up for me also, at first. But now he's so weird."

"I think it's because Paul expected something different from you," Amber said, tilting her head to look up at him. He smiled in confusion.

"Different than what? How would he know what I was going to be like?" She took a long time to answer this and her body stiffened as if anticipating that Curt would become angry

"I think he expected for you to be normal that's all," she had her shoulders hunched a little at this, but her nervousness only made him smile at her.

"I am normal. What do you mean?"

"Don't be mad, it's a good thing. But...you're not normal. You don't break. You don't even look close to breaking. I can see it in your eyes. But...but how? How can you be this way?" she pleaded suddenly, grabbing his shirt in both hands. He became a trifle nervous at this. However she didn't seem to notice and only went on talking quickly with a growing desperation. "How do you do it? You have a secret, I know it...please, you have to tell me what it is. I told you I'd do anything. I will, I'll do anything."

At this, her hands went right to his crotch.

Under any other circumstances, it would have tickled and he might have laughed. However, he had become frightened at her manic behavior and unnerved at how suddenly she reminded him of his mom. It had been seven years, but he could still remember how needy and whiny she would get if she had to wait too long for whatever drug she was taking at the time. Her eyes would go wild and Curt knew she'd be capable of the most vile acts with the dealers that hung around her.

He grabbed her hands. "I don't really have any secrets..."

"Don't lie to me!" she practically yelled, but then her eyes went wide at the sound of her own voice. The two of them paused, feeling the air with the sensitive skin of their necks and trying to hear beneath the rain. "I mean, I won't tell anyone, I promise. It'll just be our secret."

Curt didn't know what to say. His little tricks for dealing with the pressure, he hadn't considered to be actual secrets, but that was all he had.

He gave her a shrug and spoke in a hushed tone, "When the sound of the silence gets, you know, really big, I'll go to the bathroom and run some water, or I drag my hand along the wall and listen to the sound..."

Her eyes had narrowed at this and she interrupted, "No...everyone does these things. I'm talking about how you ignore the pressure, dealing with the knowledge that...that the thing could burst in any time...and the teeth..." Her face went as white as it could go and she broke off staring at the floor.

"I don't have any secrets, I'm just new here is all," Curt insisted.

"No. You're a liar," a boy's voice spoke, it was quiet but full of emotion. Matt stood in the doorway. He seemed very big. "You got some secret and you *have* to tell the rest of us. It's only fair."

A flight of butterflies took off and swirled about his insides at the sight of Matt. "I don't have any secrets...I swear," Curt asserted. "When I feel the need to talk, I go and be around you guys and when it's too quiet, I make little noises. I read or daydream the rest of the time, that's all I do, I swear. I don't have any se..."

"Don't give me that. Like Amber said, we all do these things, but the difference is, we break and you don't." Matt walked into the room and shut the door behind him. At this Curt rolled off his bed, and stood up, preparing himself.

"Look, I'm just new here and I..."

"Cut the crap. I was new too. And Amber and Paul and Beth...we were all new and the kids before us were new. We all broke and after that we broke some more. Amber, how many times did you break in your first week?"

She pursed her lips at this, refusing to speak, so Matt spoke for her, "Three times she broke. It was awful for her. The rest of us broke twice in the first week, but you...like she said, you aren't even close. You look like you're on vacation, strutting around here, cuddling with your new little bitch."

Amber hopped up into his face quick. "Just because you'e jealous..." He shoved her hard onto the bed.

Anger warped Curt's handsome features and he took a step forward, coming between the two. "Matt, get the hell out of here."

"Sticking up for your girlfriend? How manly. What happens if I don't want to leave?" Curt wasn't exactly nervous about the situation, Matt had proved himself a chicken on too many occasions. He thought that as long as he kept Matt in front of him there wouldn't be a problem. He was quite wrong.

Stepping up to Matt, Curt was about to tell the bigger boy to leave again, when Matt attempted a sucker punch. Lightning fast, Curt dodged it easily and assumed a fighting stance, anticipating this to be the end of their confrontation, but Matt attacked in a head-on charge that Curt wasn't expecting in the least.

Later he realized that he should've known better. The rain and the fact that it was the first day gave Matt a courage he wouldn't normally have had. The older boy threw himself into Curt and they fell to the bed in a swirling melee of arms and legs. Unfortunately, Curt's couldn't benefit from his natural advantage in quickness and was soon pinned by the much bigger boy. Matt then began to pummel Curt mercilessly in the face and rapidly the younger boy's world started to grey.

In great pain, and bleeding profusely, he did the only thing he could think of. He lashed out and kicked the wall as hard as he could. Thump!

The vibration could be felt throughout the entire house, including the basement.

2

Matt let up his attack immediately and froze in position, listening with all his being for the dread sound of footsteps on the stairs.

"Get off or I do it again," Curt threatened.

"You don't have the guts to," Matt whispered, but when the younger boy drew back his foot, Matt rolled off him in a hurry. "You're an idiot! Protecting this girl, calling the monster. I should..." He let off in midsentence and Curt, whose vision was a bleary red from the blood that poured into his eyes, missed the look of sudden excitement on Matt's face.

By the time Curt had blinked away the blood, he was surprised to see Matt had left the room. At first he thought that Amber had as well, but turning, he saw that she had backed herself into a corner and stared at him in fear.

"Are you and the monster...uh, al...uh, together, like on the same team? Is that it?"

The pounding in his head, made comprehending her question difficult. "You mean are we allies?" he asked, moving to sit on his bed. Dizziness had him swaying slightly and he feared he would fall over.

"Yeah, allies."

"Uhhh," he groaned as he lay back. Feeling his face gingerly, he discovered a cut above his right eyebrow and another across his nose. "Of course not, that's stupid," he answered uncharitably, his pain making him irritable.

She kept to the corner. "It's not stupid. First, you're out of bed at night and you don't get punished? That has never happened, and then you try to bring the monster here... were you going to have it attack Matt? And...and also you never break, and... and you aren't afraid of it."

"Uhhh," he groaned a second time, not wanting to deal with this at the moment. Yet seeing no choice, he said, "I am afraid of it, very, very afraid of it. And I would've been punished last night, I know it, but Paul yelled out with the thing right there. And about this breaking business. Why is everyone so hung up on me breaking? It doesn't make any sense."

"Yes it does," she said, casting her face to the floor. "If you don't break, that means there's a higher per...percenter?"

"Percentage," he suggested.

"Yeah, a higher percentage that I'll be punished, ya know what I mean?" she asked.

"I guess I do. But what do you want me to do? Get punished on purpose?" Her eyes changed levels at the notion and Curt shook his head tiredly. "Would you do that for me? Would you get punished for me?" At this, her eyes went down to the floor.

"No," she whispered clasping her hands to her chest. She looked small and vulnerable. It made Curt's heart break a little.

"I wish I were strong enough to be able to do that for you," he said blinking largely. When he blinked there was a pain in the bone of his right cheek. He worried that it was broken and he began testing it, wriggling his face.

"I think that you're strong," she murmured from the corner. "You're stronger than anyone here."

"Did you have your eyes closed when Matt beat me up just now?" He meant it as a joke, but he didn't know if it came across that way. Thankfully, she smiled.

"Not that kind of strength." She finally moved from the corner to sit beside him on the bed. "I meant like spear...uh in your soul, spirit. That part of you. That's the part that counts in this house. You have a good soul."

"A good..." His mind jiggled while it boggled and he laid there snorting back blood for a time before he decided to tell Amber just how wrong she was. "I'm not good at all. I didn't tell you this before, but I lie...a lot and I'm a thief."

"We've all done little things like that..." she started to say.

"No you don't understand. I'm really a thief. I don't live in foster homes like you guys. I live where I want to and get money by, you know stealing...breaking into people's houses, pick-pocketing, that kind of thing."

"You don't need to eg...eg...exaggerate," she said with a cloudy look of disbelief about her. "No kid lives like that."

"No kid lives like this either, but here we are," he replied with his arms out indicating the whole house. She still looked skeptical and so he added, "Do you remember what Darla...your caseworker said to me? She called me the 'Famous Curtis Regis' and it's because they know I'm a thief."

"That's right she did," Amber eyed him dubiously. "You're really a thief? Can you pick a lock and uh, hot...hot," she looked up at the ceiling, trying to remember a word. "Uh, hot-wire! Can you hot-wire a car?"

"I can only a pick a few kinds of locks, simple ones, and I haven't stolen a car yet...well actually I did, but I stole the keys first, so I don't think that counts."

Her eyes popped at this. "Wow, you stole a car. Can you drive? Is it hard to do? From what I remember it looks very hard." She took on a dreamy look as if recalling something long forgotten. Curt enjoyed the look. Her worries and her very real fears dropped away, revealing a much prettier girl beneath. She was the kind of girl that outside this house would've looked down her nose at a boy such as Curt.

"It was hard at first," he said and smiled at his own memory. "I kept running into the curbs, back and forth like pinball! And I couldn't figure out how to turn the lights on or how to work the seat controls or nothing. Part of the problem was that it was this huge long Cadillac and I couldn't even see the front of it. But the next car that I stole was this 'rice-burner.' That's what all the guys call these little Hondas. Anyways I could see better in that and I crashed it a lot less."

"Whoa, how many cars have you stolen?" she no longer seemed impressed and her brows knit together looking suddenly a trifle disgusted with him. He remembered now why he rarely told anyone of his career choice.

"Just the two...I was trying to teach myself how to drive," he added defensively.

"That doesn't make it right. You can take driver's-ed, you know." Because of her tone, which he thought of as 'snotty', and the way she looked upon him then, with superiority, he only nodded knowing she would never understand him. She would never understand his life or where he came from, or how his mind worked, or the fact that he wasn't the same as everyone else.

"I gotta clean this up," he pointed at himself. Getting up, he went to the bathroom and once the layers of dried blood had been washed away, he was surprised to see that his face wasn't nearly as awful looking as it felt. The cuts were small and the bruises were in the early stages of blooming, but they would heal just fine.

This wasn't his first time on the wrong end of a fist. Life on the streets wasn't always fun and games. Curt had been cut before, pegged with rocks, kicked in the face, and very nearly stabbed as well. He peered closely and could see the tiny white scars that marked many of these moments of his tumultuous childhood. The mirror captivated him and for some time as he looked at the boy framed within it.

He wasn't like everyone else and that was just fine with him.

Upon leaving the bathroom, he nearly collided with Amber, who was standing close to the door. Curt had expected her there, after all where else would she have gone? He just hadn't thought she'd be that close.

"Look, I didn't mean to be all like high and mighty, ok? I'm really sorry," her voice a notch above a whisper. He had expected this as well, she could count on no one, not even herself when things got rough. The only thing he hadn't counted on was her hushed tone and he cocked an ear at the ceiling of the hallway.

The rain had begun to slacken already.

He sighed, feeling the first weight of depression. Amber seemed to think it was about her and moved in very close, her new state of neediness, unmistakable.

"I'm sorry...I looked down on you. I know kids get into all sorts of trouble. Will you forgive me?" Her whispering was very warm against his neck and her body leaned in, touching his. She began kissing him and he kissed back, feeling the warmth where their bodies touched become heat.

During the long kiss, he started to understand that indefinable word passion and soon his *thing* had pushed itself out. He didn't care then if she knew, he was too caught up in the kiss. However, he was so caught up that he didn't see Miss Feanor coming up the stairs until she was practically on top of them. Her face was a steady neutral at the sight of the two kissing, but when she glanced down and saw the obvious bulge in his pants, her eyes narrowed. Feeling his ears go hot, he stepped a little to his right and hid himself behind Amber.

Amber hadn't noticed his thing yet and the light pink color that slipped into her cheeks, had only to do with the fact that they had been caught kissing. The older lady ignored her and only pursed her lips irritably at Curt, and was just about to head toward the attic door, when she noticed Curt's battered face.

With a touch of concern, she moved in close to inspect the small wounds.

Curt was absolutely mortified. His thing refused to go back down and it stood just an inch or two from Miss Feanor's belly. He couldn't look her in the face and so he turned toward Amber, but she had finally noticed *it* as well.

It was hard not to miss.

And *it* seemed hard not to look at as well, at least for Amber who stared at it with her mouth gaping as if her jaw had become unhinged. Her cheeks were the color of ripe apples and her eyes were huge with embarrassment.

"Humph," Miss Feanor said, turning his face this way and that so the light could catch the lacerations there. She seemed content with what she saw, and with one more look down at *him*, she turned away.

The moment Miss Feanor took a single step, Amber, giggling like the child she was, pulled him to his bedroom where he immediately went to his bed and sat a pillow on his lap. Amber snorted with suppressed laughter.

Soon she was rolling about on the floor, tears streaming from her very red, red face. Her entire body couldn't seem to stop quivering and she gasped for air in between holding down her laughter. Curt began laughing as well and finally this caused his *thing* to go back down. The heavy laughter inside them eventually diminished, but they still chuckled weakly for many minutes after this.

"Is it safe to join you?" Amber asked from the floor, giving his crotch a quick look.

"Yes!"

They cuddled again and every once in a while, they would giggle for a moment, but for the most part, they just sat back and stared at the ceiling.

"You never answered my question from earlier, what's going on with you. You seemed different," he asked her.

Air blew hard through her nostrils. "Beth was in your room yesterday before dinner...don't deny it. I saw her coming out with my own two eyes."

"Mmmm," Curt mused, wondering if the mouse had been searching his things, looking for her papers. They had been so dusty, that he had assumed that she had forgotten them in her insanity.

"Well?" Amber's voice had risen.

"Hmm? What? Oh, the mouse...I was doing my chores early yesterday, so I would have time to deal with Paul after dinner. I don't know if she came in here or not."

"Oh," she didn't look exactly like she believed him.

"Why would I want the mouse when I have someone as beautiful and as *sane* as you," he said and kissed her on the nose.

"Then what was she doing in here?" Amber asked, propping herself up on one elbow. "And don't call her mouse. Her name is Beth. She's a person."

"I don't know why she was in here." Curt smiled falsely at her.

Amber settled down again and relaxed in his arms and the more she relaxed, the more she talked. This was fine with Curt; he loved her voice regardless if he actually listened to the words she was saying.

He wasn't.

Instead, he pondered upon the girl he still thought of as the mouse, wondering if she had more going on upstairs than he knew. He wondered and she talked for a long time, but eventually the heavens gave all that it could and the rains petered out. Amber's voice gradually sunk as low as it could go and with a final kiss, she left as quietly as the rains had.

Curt immediately hopped up and fished under his dresser. The papers and the all-important paperclips were gone.

Figuring that the mouse had taken them back to her room, he forced himself to be calm—a very difficult thing—and went about the rest of the late afternoon and evening as he normally would, knowing that he'd get them back eventually. The next day was a different story altogether and a light panic fluttered about inside him, making him feel queasy. He had searched the girl's room top to bottom, the papers were nowhere to be found.

Chapter 17

Obsession

1

That fourth week in the home, Curt dwelled obsessively on two overriding matters.

Now, he had not actually been there for four weeks, but with the dreary consistencies of the days, each as dull and repetitious as the last, he had already lost track of them. He could only keep the punishments clear in his mind. His had been the first, and a few days followed that and then Darla had been killed. The beginning of the third week had commenced with Paul's first punishment and now with Paul's second, they were on to their fourth week according to his distorted reckoning.

The first obsession that he had to confront was an amazing hunger that nagged at him endlessly during that long week. It caused him to think about food constantly and he especially craved anything salty. His mind strayed to his past life where he would eat potato chips by the bag-full, sitting behind the Seven-Eleven. He dreamed of the huge pretzels at the ballpark, watching the Pirates play. Or popcorn with extra butter at the movies.

He found himself daydreaming of everything he would eat, once he got out of Miss Feanor's home; the list was very long. Curt had been hungry on many occasions, he was a boy after all, but since leaving his mother it had become a rarity.

Save for a few ancient cans of soup and some inedible dust-bunnies, his mother's cupboards were always barren. In her miserable world, food wasn't a priority; her only concern had been when and where she would get her next fix, and it was out of hunger, that tiny four-year old Curt had begun his life as a thief.

On the streets, food was far more plentiful than the average person realized; one just had to know where to look for it. Not that Curt would ever dig through the trash for food, not anymore at least. The last time he'd done that, he had still been living with his mother and hadn't yet fully grasped certain concepts. The chief of these was that if opportunity didn't present itself, one would have to create the circumstances to allow it to.

But even with his growing skills as a thief, sometimes things got tight and there had been a few times when he had gone a couple of days without eating. Thankfully, the super market seemed always to carry plenty of food.

His favorite trick was to grab a cart and follow around after a lady pushing a full one, he would make sure to engage her in conversation, asking in the most polite manner about different products. To all appearances, they were mother and son. He would add things to his cart, generally large household items, paper towels and the like, but also snacks. These he'd munch away at, as if he had a perfect right to and no one ever said a thing concerning it, believing that "mom" would be paying for the items at the counter.

If that didn't work, he'd just shoplift. With his keen eyes and quick hands, he was exceptional at shoplifting and had never been caught, yet it rankled him having to do it. There was nothing to it, no artistry was needed and very little skill. He felt himself above it.

However, during that fourth week he would've done it in a heartbeat.

Walking about the beautiful home of Miss Feanor's, his stomach growled almost non-stop and for the first time since arriving, he ate the monotonous food with gusto. He couldn't seem to get enough, but since the lady never offered a second helping, by the third day of the week, he felt shaky and frail. Having to fight the pain in his stomach in some fashion Curt began eating, of all things, toilet paper.

Always he kept a handful of it in his pocket and nibbled at it, rat-like, constantly. Creating little spit balls, he rolled them around his tongue until they had practically faded away before he swallowed the remainder. Whether it helped in any way, he couldn't tell, but once he had started the gross habit, he couldn't stop. His hunger also made him jittery and anxious, neither of which helped his other fascination that week, the missing paperclips. The love letters were of absolutely no interest to him, but those paperclips occupied his mind and he searched relentlessly for them.

In a way, he began to think of them as his salvation.

On the second day of the week, he explored all the bedrooms, including Amber's room—obviously without her knowledge—and came away empty-handed. Slinking out of Amber's room he spied the door to the attic just across the hall and on impulse went to it, in the hope that it would be unlocked.

It wasn't.

The knob was different than every other doorknob in the house; he had of course noted this long before, the others were all original, large and ornate, but without proper modern locks. The one to the attic however had a lock dead center in it, and it looked relatively new. With the paperclips and enough time he could pick it, he was sure of this.

Beyond that door lay wondrous possibilities that ensnared his imagination. He was certain almost with the zeal of religion that he'd find the key to defeating the creature there. The boy in him hoped that he would find a weapon, a great shining sword perhaps, while a slightly more logical side of him considered the possibility that he could find a charm or potion to ward it away.

After all, Miss Feanor, though afraid of the creature had never been attacked at least as far as Curt knew. There had to be some reason behind this and his active imagination conjured up a vision of a laboratory, filled with bubbling beakers and tubes that squirreled their way about.

But what he hoped to find most of all was simply a window. When he had arrived with Miss Gladys, he hadn't given the house more than a cursory glance and hadn't bothered to count exactly how many stories it consisted of. There could be a chance that the attic would hold a window, a normal glass one. One that hadn't been nailed shut, one that he could slip out of, sliding down knotted sheets to the soft green grass of the yard below.

That was his wish.

And there was a definite possibility that it might come true. It was unlikely that Miss Feanor would've ever suspected that a child could not only pick a lock, but would have the guts to attempt to escape out a window that high up. That was why he spent almost every waking moment of that very long week, casually and not so casually looking for the spot in which Matt had hid the clips.

It had to have been Matt. Curtis fully believed the mouse incapable of hiding them in any but the simplest of places, while Matt walked around the house day after day with a smarmy grin on his face. The older boy acted as though he had some great secret knowledge and since the paperclips were paramount in Curt's mind, he automatically presumed to believe that Matt's secret concerned these.

It did not.

2

That week lasted a total of five days.

The rains came on the first day and the rest of the week was marked only by Curt's growing hunger and obsession, but the nights were claimed by doubt.

There was something important going on that he was missing. The first two nights he felt it, though it was only a nagging unnamed feeling. By the third however, he began to realize the problem. The pressure had begun to build as always, but it was how everyone in the house was reacting to it that was different, and by the fourth night, Curt was downright scared by the change.

Matt and his nasty grin seemed as relaxed at the end of the fourth day as Curt had ever seen him, and whatever secret he carried around, he had obviously shared with Paul. After that second punishment in a row, the blonde boy had taken to keeping a hand stuffed in his mouth to keep himself from talking. It was only at meal times that he'd remove it. He was a wreck and looked as if he hadn't slept since his punishment.

But sometime during the afternoon of the fourth day, Paul perked up and stopped his unsettling habit and started a new one, which in Curt's mind was far worse. He began to look upon Curt with wide expectant eyes and he watched the younger boy eagerly. There was a savageness to him. Clearly, Paul looked forward to something unpleasant occurring to his one time friend.

Amber changed as well.

She fully believed that Curt had it in him to protect her from the punishments. Her trances were shorter, quieter, and less frequent and this should've been for the better, and it was for her, but not for Curt. By the evening of the fourth day, the stress of protecting them both, while guarding over his areas of responsibility, as well as finding the paperclips began to overwhelm him. He felt as though he had to be in too many places at once, and he zipped about dodging the new frightening look of Paul's, as well as the wild eyes and strange whisperings of the mouse.

The mouse was a sad thing and a part of him wished he'd left the love letters and paperclips where he had found them. She was just as crazy as always, however in that fourth week, life seemed to drain from her. Not that she had much of a life to begin with, but now she moped about, unable to concentrate even on her ridiculous cat puzzle. Every day she took it down from the shelf yet left it unopened and only knelt in front of the box, while her eyes whipped across its fading cover.

He couldn't feel too much sadness for her.

"The teeth are coming."

These were the whispered words that the mouse greeted Curt with on the morning of the fourth day. Hearing that, along with everything else going on, made that day the longest since he had arrived. She wouldn't stop. All day long she repeated the sentence, and he began to fear that she was having a premonition, yet no one was punished that night.

"The teeth are coming, tonight," the mouse said an hour after breakfast on the morning of the fifth day.

Curt pushed her away with more gentleness than he usually did, but still she knocked into a wall. After bouncing off it, she then forgot about him completely and went to her cat puzzle. There she whispered to the box with sad monotony.

"The teeth are coming, tonight. The teeth are coming, tonight..."

The words should've been upsetting, or even frightening, but now they only angered Curt.

Right after breakfast that morning, he had ducked covertly into the living room, once again in search of his own personal holy grail: the paperclips. He had only just started running his fingers lightly along the underside of the couch when a shadow in the hallway alerted him of someone moving in his direction. He ducked behind the large piece of furniture and watched as Matt pulled the mouse into the room.

The eldest child whispered into her ear, but his voice was so low that Curt couldn't make out the words. The whispering took a number of minutes and as it progressed, he saw that soon the movement of Matt's lips was being matched by the mouse's. Before this, Curt had thought the mouse was just being crazy as always, but now he understood that Matt had been using the poor girl to get at him.

He cursed under his breath, hating Matt, but fearing him as well; it seemed that he'd stoop to nothing.

Perhaps the older boy would use Amber as well. If Matt did, Curt worried that he wouldn't be able to put off his first real punishment much longer.

With that in mind, he kept the blonde close to him all through that fifth day. To keep his hunger at bay, as well as to keep his mind off the deep thrumming anxiety within him, Curt spent the dull hours between breakfast and dinner cleaning. The perfection demanded of him, whether it was by Miss Feanor, the creature or the house itself, meant that he frequently had to dust drapes, polish brass, wax floors, and clean baseboards among other things.

Normally this was all done in those couple of hours during the evening, but he feared that there wouldn't be time that night. He worried he'd have his hands full just staving off the combine efforts of the other children to have him punished. Therefore he worked diligently on both his areas as well as Amber's. She was very sweet to be with, but wasn't much of a help as she went in and out of her trances.

With all the work, the day went by surprisingly quickly and now Curt steeled himself for what he figured would be an evening of harassment.

The previous four evenings had come and gone without any mischief—he felt as though he were being lulled purposefully into letting down his guard. Yet his guard was as high as ever.

In order to spoil whatever monkey business Matt was planning, right after dinner he set Amber to guard over their areas up stairs while he watched over the lower floor. Nothing at first seemed amiss, however after a few minutes he realized the house was too quiet.

This might seem like an impossibility to the average person who would think the house, at its loudest, no more noisy than a tomb, but Curt knew otherwise. He had become attuned to it and knew that after dinner the air should've been stirring slightly with the movement of the young bodies passing through it. He should have heard the soft swish of a broom, the whisper of cloth on metal and the occasional tiny tap, tap, tap sound of water colliding with tile after a brief plunge from the end of a rag. Only ears, hypersensitive and starved for the slightest sound, could have heard these noises and when Curt didn't, his anxiety doubled.

Reaching out and touching the wall of the main floor hall, he went perfectly still. With his eyes closed, he concentrated with all his mind to feel even the slightest vibration, but there was nothing in the wall, and he felt only his heart, which began to pick up the tempo.

After first peeking into the dining room and finding it empty, he moved down the hall with more than his usual silence, stopping to glance into the living room. It was empty as well, as was the family room.

Was the creature coming and he missed the signs?

That thought caused sweat to breakout down his back and just then his anxiety no longer made any pretence and showed itself for what it truly was, fear. Curt crouched quickly, putting his hand to the cool polished wood. His body was a coiled spring, ready to fly at the first indication that the creature was heading up the stairs.

But again, nothing.

Confused, he stood back up and glanced down the hall toward the mudroom door. It sat unmoving, as was Miss Feanor. He could see her still in her customary chair, still staring at her customary coffee mug.

"Hmm," he murmured.

Whatever was occurring, if anything really was, didn't have to do with the creature or the house. Perhaps this had to do with Amber, perhaps the other children were trying to get her to conspire against him. The thought sent a coal of hot anger burning at his insides and he went creeping up the stairs.

The second floor he found as lifeless as the first. None of the other kids were there as they should've been, moving about in that noiseless but efficient way of theirs. Now Curt was sure he'd find them holed up in one of the rooms, plotting his downfall.

He went first to Paul's room; they weren't there, but something was so out of place that he had to look back in a second time. The boy's blankets weren't flat, neatly tucked in, as they should have been, instead the huddled form of a body lay beneath them. Curt's mind was a confusion of thoughts at the scene. Had the creature come and gone in the fifteen minutes since dinner? Had there been a false alarm? Had someone come that close to breaking, and he and Miss Feanor had been the only ones not aware? Had Paul finished his chores early and had gone to bed?

The last question was easiest to answer and he stepped back a few feet and peeked into the bathroom. The first thing he noticed was that the towels sat uneven on the bar. He didn't bother to look further. Paul hadn't gone to bed early, he was afraid that the creature would be coming soon.

This sent Curt crouching a second time, his palm to the floor and his head cocked, still there was nothing to suggest the creature was on the move. However, the house seemed distinctly more aware than it had on the first floor. That awareness sent a stab of fear so strongly into his slim chest that it felt like pain.

It wasn't a fear for himself that he held within his breast, but rather for Amber and he hurried to her room, his fingers trailing the wall as he went. The feeling that the house was aware grew beneath them as he closed on her doorway, and his hands went numb at what he saw there.

On the floor near the closet, Matt knelt on one knee, half-straddling Amber's chest. His left hand, he had entwined in the silk of her platinum blonde hair, while in his right, he held a large shard of wood. It was maybe a foot long and looked as if had once belonged on the underside of a bed. Its edges were jagged and nasty and it tapered to a sharp point, which hovered only inches from the blue of Amber's right eye.

Chapter 18

The Thief's Punishment

1

"Come in, asshole," Matt whispered.

Curt stood in the doorway, as if he had grown roots. "What's going..."

Matt interrupted, "I said get in here...go stand in that corner." He nodded towards the corner furthest from the door and when Curt hesitated the older boy growled low like a dangerous animal, "I said go, or she loses an eye."

The large sliver of wood, a veritable stake, sat poised just above Amber's face and the poor girl fixated upon it as if nothing else in the room mattered. At the words, *or she loses an eye*, she whimpered pathetically. Curt had noticed that his hands had gone numb just as he had entered, but he didn't realize that the rest of him had as well until he started walking in a queer jerking motion toward the corner. The floor could have been strewn with glass and he wouldn't have known.

"Matt, what are you doing?" Curt asked in a little kids quavering voice. Like Amber, he couldn't take his eyes off the tip of the stake.

"You're going to call the monster," the older boy replied, still speaking barely above a whisper. Despite this, the energy of the room began to intensify. "You're going to call it or she loses an eye."

"No...please no," Amber moaned the words. Her blue eyes were practically crossed staring at the tip of the stake. Matt's grip in her hair tightened and he gave her shake, bringing the shard dangerously close to her eye, so that now she finally shut them, grimacing.

"Shut up!" Matt snarled savagely into her ear. He said it loud and this made him pause for a second, realizing that he could inadvertently bring the creature down on himself. After a few moments his head came back up at Curt and he wore a black look. "Call it now or else."

Curt, who had unknowingly turned thirteen the day before, had always thought of himself as smart, mentally agile, and quick on his feet, but at that moment he was none of these things.

"Matt...I...I...Matt," he stammered. The enormity of what was being asked of him, coupled with a chest tightening fear that there was no way out of this, froze the gears of his mind.

"That's not what I want to hear," Matt said, smiling incongruously, as if hearing Curt spluttering was exactly what he wanted to hear. "Now call it in three seconds or else." Amber's face, looking like it had been glazed in tears by a potter, turned toward him and she pleaded with fearful eyes.

"I..." This was all Curt could force out of his mouth. He wanted desperately to help her, but the dying screams of Darla the caseworker and the tortured ones of Paul filled his mind and cowardice held his throat closed. Three seconds came and went quickly.

"Fine," Matt muttered.

Screwing up his features into a grimace, he stabbed Amber in the face.

Curt's vision spun for a heartbeat at this and he fell to his knees, unable to breathe. He hadn't truly expected Matt to carry through with his threat—the two of them had practically lived as brother and sister for over three years. But despite that fact, Matt had, with terrific malice, aimed the stake directly for Amber's right eye.

At the last second she squirmed and the stake drove a gaping red furrow in the side of her head.

"Aaiighhh..." Her scream of pain had started loudly, but somehow she had been able to bite it back. Now she cried in near silent misery as Matt looked with fury on the smaller boy.

"Coward. That is your fault. Call it or I'll take her eye, I swear!" He gave her head another violent little shake.

"Mmmhh," Amber managed to hold back a second cry and now the room was on the verge of bursting with what felt like a furious electrical charge. The house was very aware of what was happening and it wasn't pleased that its perfection was being marred by tears and blood and screams not of its own making.

'Call it,' Matt mouthed the words and slowly raised the stake for a second time.

There was no choice. Curt's heart had felt the pain of the gash in Amber's head and her tears were his tears. He hadn't known it before this last minute, but now he knew: he was in love.

"Aaaaahhh," his yell warbled up and down a little bit, as if he were unsure exactly how he was supposed to call the creature.

Still it was enough. The air in the room felt black with anger and beneath his knees, the floor came alive, seeming to twitch and heat up oddly. A second later, a familiar vibration came up through the wood. The creature was on its way.

A span of unnumbered heartbeats went by as Curt and Matt stared at each other, both aghast at what they had unleashed and then Matt jumped up running for the door. Foolishly, Curt held out his hand to the older boy in supplication, hoping Matt would wait for him. But Matt wasn't looking and was gone even before Curt had gotten to his feet.

Through his white socks, Curt could feel the thrumming heavy tread of the creature making its way from the basement. It wasn't running as it had been with Darla, but it was moving quickly with determination. There were other vibrations in the floor as well, frantic ones and he could envision Miss Feanor running like mad up the stairs.

Terror drove a bolt right through him and without thinking, he charged to the door, desperate to make it back to his bed, hoping there was yet a chance that he'd get lucky and the creature would bypass him once again. Turning into the hall, he paused, looking back for fraction of a second and saw Amber motionless on the ground where Matt had left her.

The horror of the situation had thrown her into one of her trances and she lay upon the living wood of the floor, staring out at him with beautiful, china-blue eyes. But her eyes were vacant and unseeing and would remain that way until the creature was at her with its teeth and its horrendous desire.

Curt was in ghastly luck. He saw that he could make it back to his bed if he hurried and knowing the creature as he did, there was good chance that if he remained perfectly still under his covers it would go on to the other rooms before coming back to his. And it would certainly attack Amber if it found her lying on the floor. Sudden hope, like a lighting strike went through him and he took off for his bed, but he stopped after only two steps.

"Jeeeez," he whined low and more tears sprang up in his eyes.

He couldn't leave her like that

Turning back, he ran to her limp form and attempted to wrestle her back into the bed. He had picked her up with ease once before when she had been like this, but now with absolutely not a second to spare, she was like a plate of noodles. Twice she slipped out of his grasp. Finally he grabbed her by the pockets of her jeans and threw her onto his shoulder. Heaving her onto the bed, unmindful of any injury he might have caused, he yanked the blanket over her and dashed out of the room.

Again, he stopped after only two steps.

Crreik...crreik...crreik...

The creature was already practically to the top of the stairs and now Curt was trapped.

2

The white walls with its fancy crown molding, the gleaming hardwood floors, and the polished railing with its hand carved leaf pattern all disappeared as Curt's world tunneled in on the creature.

Seeing it so clearly for the first time, he couldn't call it a monster, since obviously it wasn't alive, it was more what he would consider a ghost. It had all the hallmarks of one. It was translucent and Curt could almost see the stairs through its grey form. Its body seemed amorphous and appeared ragged, with the edges of it shifting constantly as if it was being subjugated by an unfelt wind.

But the greatest reason that he saw it as a ghost was the terror it induced in his young mind. His fear became all-encompassing, superimposing itself over every aspect of his personality until there was nothing left to him, but his fear. And except for the shaking of his limbs, he stood unmoving as the ghost drifted up the stairs.

Though there seemed nothing physical to the thing, it made sounds on the stairs as if it were a live being, and interacted with the house as a person would. If it had a back, it was to Curt and didn't seem to notice him standing frozen in place, caught far from the ridiculous safety of his bed. Curt's bedroom door hung partially open and instead of floating through the gap, it reached out an appendage, what looked like an arm, and pushed the door back. It then moved in, 'stepping' quietly.

Once the thing was out of sight, Curt's mind threw off a good deal of the fear that had practically paralyzed him and he dashed across the hall to the attic door. It was locked. He turned and was just about to race down the hall, hoping to get to the back stairs, but saw the grey shadow loom in his doorway.

In a flash, he zipped back into Amber's room. There he had three choices: hide under the bed, in the bed, or in the closet. Despite his entire being desperate to get in the bed with Amber, he chose the closet. If he went to the bed, they might both be punished.

The closet door had barely shut when Curt heard the soft sly sounds of the ghost walking into Amber's room. There was little preamble to what occurred next, the ghost was there to inflict punishment and it was Curt's turn; he could sense the thing just on the other side of the door and the thing sensed him as well.

The door of the closet flew open and the creature floated there seeming huge, filling the doorway with its ragged body. Curt tried to dive past it, but it shot out one of its long arms and pinned him face first to the floor. The hand at the end of the arm felt terribly real and he cried out in pain as fingernails dug into his flesh. The arm was strong as well and flipped him over as if he were more of a child than he was. Now Curt could look upon the full horror of the ghost and the madness of the thing staggered his mind and froze his joints.

It half-floated, half-swarmed over his numb body and as it did something happened to the misty nature of the ghost's form. Parts of it started to solidify.

To his horror, he saw a face forming on the grey and within the face there were teeth, which began to look more and more substantial. Now the mouth opened and stretched toward him and as it did, the mouth took on color and texture in horrifying reality. The lips were blackened and rotting, but protruding from them and sticking out further than possible, were the great, yellowed teeth, and as the mouth opened, a stench blasted out of it. It smelled like the rotting filth from a sewer.

The half-formed face and its fully formed mouth hovered over him for only a second and then it struck, biting down onto the flesh of Curt's stomach. The pain was intense and he screamed. It was the highest scream that his throat could endure and in an instant, his vocal cords seemed to tear and then no sound came out but a high keen rush of air.

In a frenzy, Curt tried to fight back, swinging his small fists with all his might at the slowly materializing head of the ghost. The half-formed flesh and thin limp hair of the thing's head hung off of it in long strips and as Curt swung at it with desperate strength, great wet clumps of it fell upon him.

Due to his panic and terror, Curt only barely saw this and kept swinging, fighting with instinctual savagery, covering himself in grey half-rotted flesh.

Finally, the ghost, which had begun to take on the condition of a living corpse, released its jaws. But this wasn't due to the blows that struck it so feebly, it wanted to taste new flesh and pain, it bit down again. And now the huge teeth dug into him, penetrating his skin and Curt could feel the teeth grate horribly against the hardness of one of his ribs. Unexpectedly, he found his voice again and he cried out loud with tremendous anguish. The pain was excruciating and he didn't care what the thing was or how disgusting it smelled or felt, all he cared about was getting it off of him and Curt dug his fingers into the putrefied flesh of the creatures jaw and frantically began to work the teeth loose from its rotting gums.

In a moment, he felt the jaws come open slightly and he pulled his body back. The ghost thing reared up again and Curt knew it he was about to be bitten, but some part of his mind was still operating at a basic level and had already noted this pattern of the creature. It would rear up, animal like, before it bit down.

When it did, Curt's body came alive and without needing any real commands from his mind, it acted instinctually. Bringing his legs up, he kicked out at the solidifying mass of the thing's face, not in any hope of hurting something so clearly and horribly dead, but rather to push himself back away from it. His hard strike and its momentum allowed him to turn a small back summersault and then he was up and running with absolutely no idea where he was going.

But it hardly mattered.

Behind him, the creature thundered after and Curt only had time to let out a long terrified scream as he ran, before it was on him once more. He went down in a jumbled heap of rotting arms and grey mist. Squirming mightily, he kicked and punched as the ghost re-formed parts of itself and for a second, he pulled himself clear again but could only backup to the nearest wall. There he was cornered.

A scabbed-over blackened hand came out of the grey mist of the ghost. It had yellowed claws where its fingernails should have been and it smelled of long fermenting death. The rancid odor was enough to tip him over the edge of madness he'd been flirting with and now Curt could no longer fight back even at an instinctual level.

He could only scream.

His screams echoed, reverberating throughout the entire house, bouncing off the walls, unanswered and unattended. But they weren't entirely useless. There is a purpose to screams in these sorts of situations. They occupy the mind, filling it with sound, focusing it away, if only partially from the pain and horror.

But the creature ended Curt's screams very quickly.

The blackened hand pinned him to the wall by his throat and squeezed, sending its talons deep into Curt's flesh. Now there was no screaming, or breathing for that matter. His lungs were shut off from air and his face went red in a second, yet he barely even noticed this or the pain for that matter, for now the face of the ghost began to form again.

The blackened burnt looking lips and the large yellowed teeth grew out of it. But worse, behind the teeth, a tongue black and cracked slithered out and when the thing bit Curt on the shoulder there was the unmistakable sound of sucking and slurping.

However, in all this, there was a single mercy. The creature had held onto Curt's throat too long and his pain and horror became muted and distant, until finally he slumped over and knew no more.

Chapter 19

Pain

1

Within the boundaries of the house, time had no meaning.

How long he lay there before he came awake, Curt had no idea. And he didn't come awake all at once in a start, but rather slowly, one sluggish blink at a time.

For a while, he couldn't feel his body, and the only one of his five senses that seemed in order was his eyesight and that was blurry at best. He could see the lines that made up the individual boards of the polished hardwood floors and were amazed at how they had been placed so neatly, so seamlessly together. They started off straight and true, and then they trailed off into a distant hazy brown horizon.

It seemed far away and that struck his dull witted mind as not right, he attempted to sit up to see how far the boards really went. That was when the pain began. It flared first in his neck, then his shoulder, then his right arm and so on, until he felt it all over his body. The pain brought with it the horrific memory of what had caused it and Curt cried.

Because of his pain, he cried weakly but the tears came without much effort and he saw them splash heavily onto the wood. They began to form a tiny puddle beneath his face and Curt tried to concentrate on that instead of the horrible memories. This worked, for a time, but then he saw that within the puddle there was a tinge of pink.

It was the smallest amount of blood.

There should have been more. Curt wagged his head this way and that, looking for the spattering of blood that logically he knew should have been there. Before he had passed out, he had felt it draining down his neck where the creature had laid a hold of him with its foul talons and he had felt it coming from the wound in his shoulder where he had been bitten.

He touched these spots and the pain burned at him, but strangely the wounds, instead of being wet or tacky with blood, were crusted over with fresh scabs. There should've been blood. There should have been quite a bit of blood in fact and he puzzled over this briefly, but a rational part of him, one that seemed very adult spoke into his mind, 'The creature drank your blood, lapping it up with its huge black tongue.'

It was a horrendous thought, yet likely a correct one and he envisioned the tongue and the mouth—it gave him the shivers. Then he remembered the smell of the creature and foolishly, he sniffed at his torn shirt. The smell was there. The rot. The horrible stench of a decomposing body.

Curt knew he was about to be sick, yet he lacked the strength to make it past a kneeling position and he vomited up a great gout of spam and rice. The pain and effort to vomit left him even weaker than before, but he couldn't stand the smell of the creature for another second and crawled toward the bathroom.

Blessedly it was only a few feet away.

The bathroom still hadn't been cleaned. It made him wonder, in a groggy sort of way, what time it was and how long he had lain upon the floor. For a second he worried that he should be in bed, lest the creature come again. This thought made him want to puke a second time, but he fought the urge and felt the floor instead. The house only had a vague awareness of him and if it was angry or annoyed, it was focused on something else. What was more, the creature drowsed, its lust satiated, at least for the time being.

Curt realized just then that there were two separate distinct beings haunting the house. If indeed haunting was the correct term. While they both felt dreadfully evil and unnatural, he could discern that one was male and the other female.

Or at least had once been so.

The essence of the female resided in the very structure of the house. She existed in the floors, the ceilings, the walls, and he wondered if he ever took an axe to the house, would it bleed? That she would feel it, he had no doubt. She could sense almost everything within her, even the doors and their knobs and hinges. But not the windows. The sills and frames, yes, however he had never felt her presence in the heavy plexiglass. Nor was she at all obvious in the furniture, except as an extension of the floor and Curt now equated the furnishings of the home with her hair or fingernails.

The creature, on the other hand had been a man at one time. A foul evil man. A perverse one as well. The creature had bitten him with such a nasty pleasure that it couldn't have been anything but sexual. The term perverse, he'd read and heard on a number of occasions and had only a vague notion of its meaning. Now however, he may have understood it on a fundamental level better than most adults.

Curt stripped down, groaning in pain as he did. Just thinking of the ghost like creature made him want to shower badly and he wished there was some way to turn up the shower so that water would rinse away the stench of the thing quicker.

He cried again in the shower.

Either that or he had never stopped crying.

2

After his shower, Curt forced himself not to look in the mirror above the sink. The glass would surely show a wreck of boy staring back at him. His face had swollen next to his right eye and he felt a curving row of scabs under his questing fingers. He feared that the swelling would appear grotesque, and that the bite marks would perhaps leave him with great ugly scars and in his delicate state of mind, he was too afraid to look at himself.

As an old man would, he hobbled into his room, slowly, feeling pain with every step. Exhaustion laid a hold of him and he crawled gingerly into his bed, moaning with the effort. He was asleep in minutes, unmindful of the house or its occupants and uncaring whether it was seven in the evening or ten in the morning.

It was in fact only a few minutes past six. He'd been attacked at about five and had lain on the floor unconscious for only a half hour, before he had headed to the shower.

The night for Curt was a long misery.

Frequently over the next twelve hours, he would come awake with half-suppressed groans as sharp pains lanced through his body. But what had him jumping up in a cold sweat, despite the pain were the endless dreams of the creature. It was all he dreamed about. In each, he would hide and always the thing found him.

The next morning when Miss Feanor tapped his blankets to wake him, he dried his eyes before poking his face from beneath the covers. He had been awake for some time, crying quietly in self-pity. Though it was well-deserved self-pity, he was still embarrassed. When his covers had been pulled back, Miss Feanor's eyes went wide in astonishment and then her features took on a frown of concentration as she turned his cheek one way and then the other, after which she peered closely at the wounds. She then shrugged dismissively as if his injuries were of no concern of hers.

Through a series of hand motions as well as mouthing of words, she said, 'Next time make sure you get punished in your bed. It won't be as bad. Now get up it's time to eat.'

Angry tears filled his eyes at her uncaring attitude and he pulled himself up, keeping his head down hiding his fury. But his anger doubled when he turned back toward her.

Her face was suddenly heavy with concern, not for him, but for his pillowcase and his pajamas. Sometime during the night, his scabs had weeped a pinkish fluid or had bled outright and left stains. She glared at the stains in anger and then at Curt as if any of this had been his fault.

With a sour look, she left. He sat back down feeling lightheaded, not at all sure he could stomach looking at either his oatmeal or Miss Feanor just then. Paul hadn't gone to breakfast after his last punishment, why should he? Groaning in his pain, he laid down beneath his covers but it seemed he had slept only moments before Amber came and pulled them back.

Her blue eyes were rimmed red and bloodshot all the way through, it was clear that at least she was concerned for him. At the sight of his face, she started crying and at the sight of her tears, he did as well. They hugged each other gently for a moment and then she kissed him delicately.

"Thank you," her words came so softly that they tickled his ear and though it hurt to, he smiled at her. 'You need to eat,' she gestured to him and tried to gently pull him up.

'No,' he shook his head. 'Sleep.' His ability to converse in their improvised sign language hadn't progressed much.

'No, you need to eat,' she signed. 'You will get better, faster.'

Curt didn't care much about getting better just at the moment. His body ached from head to toe and the trip down to the kitchen nook seemed too far to even try. And then there was the fact that he would have to face Matt.

The very thought of the boy turned his mind black as night and he swore silently to himself that he'd kill the older boy somehow. At that moment, it wasn't an idle threat, it was survival. Curt knew there was little he could do to stop Matt from having him punished whenever the older boy felt like it, and if he were to suffer a few more nights like the last one, Curt would be ready for the loony bin just as the mouse was.

Miss Feanor was another reason he wished to stay in bed, he despised her nearly as much as he did Matt. And then there was Paul. Curt was sure to see a look of gloating triumph on Paul's face.

The only person he actually wanted to see, besides Amber, was the mouse. With a punishment out of the way and the pressure diminished, he hoped that she would be less likely to obsess over her lost love letters. Still the mouse wasn't enough for him to go down stairs and he refused to move under the straining arms of Amber.

Curt thought he would stay right where he was, but Amber was more resourceful than he realized.

First, she tried pouting. Then she tried an assortment of cute looks. Neither budged him. Next, she went with a move that surprised him. Stepping to his doorway, she slowly lifted up her shirt.

His eyes, swollen and puffy bugged at this and she had his full attention. She stopped just shy of exposing herself and then gestured, 'Come on if you want to see more.'

She backed into the hall and like an automaton, he followed, dragging himself along. Only from the perspective of a thirteen-year-old boy could Amber's malnourished body be considered sexy. She was flat as a board, with hips that were slimmer than Curt's but the promise of a peek was enough to get him moving.

She wasn't a liar or a tease and when she saw that he was actually going to follow him down the stairs, she turned and flashed him.

3

It was worth it, Curt decided.

But that was before he started down the stairs. Each stair was a reminder of his torture and he grimaced and groaned with every step. At length, he made it to the kitchen nook, where upon he kept his face down for the most part, embarrassed by the swelling that he had yet to see.

Sitting down, his stomach rolled over at the sight of the sticky grey paste in the bowl in front of him. It looked thicker than usual, but he knew he would have to get at least some of it down if he were going to take the two large white pain pills and the smaller red vitamin that sat just above his bowl on the table. Grabbing his spoon, he glanced up only long enough to see that his hatred for Matt was well justified, the smug look the boy wore burned at Curt's heart.

He turned his battered face toward Paul and if he gloated, Curt couldn't tell as the blonde boy kept his eyes averted staring down into his oatmeal. Thankfully, the mouse looked more relaxed. It assuaged his guilt somewhat, but unfortunately, she wouldn't stop wandering her eyes over his misshapen face and it started to bother him a great deal.

However, what bothered him most of all was Miss Feanor.

As they came into the kitchen she only sat staring at her coffee mug as always, yet eventually she looked up and saw the red, scabbed over gouge on the side of Amber's face. She flew into a silent rage over this and astonished Curt by slapping Matt across the face, but his astonishment went even further when she turned and slapped him as well.

The pain made his eyes water and before he knew it, Curt was weeping again. The tears were impossible to control, as was his breath which came out hitching as he sobbed. All of his frustration and anger and hate and fear came out right there at the breakfast table. He was terribly embarrassed, and it was long minutes before he could control himself. Miss Feanor waited patiently in an angry stew until he did.

'No more of this!' Her gestures were hard and swift. 'Anymore and I put the Teeth on you both.' They all nodded solemnly and then Matt made sure to catch Curt's eye making it clear their little feud wasn't over.

Everyone except Curt went back to eating their breakfast. At first, he could only stare at his oatmeal in disbelief at how unfair Miss Feanor was being. All of his being wanted to say something to her. To protest her ill treatment of him, but then he caught Matt's look. He wanted Curt to say something as well.

Curt wouldn't give him the satisfaction and went back to his breakfast, but Matt wasn't done trying to hurt the youngest child just yet. He ate quickly and a second before he showed his empty bowl to Miss Feanor, he showed Curt something as well. In a quick, unobtrusive way, Matt opened his right hand and there in his palm sat two large white pills and a smaller red one. Before Curt's eyes could finish widening in surprise, Matt had popped the pills into his mouth in a single fluid motion.

"Hey..." Curt started to protest the theft of his pain pills, but stopped himself and bit back the useless accusation that had formed on his lips. It wouldn't have done any good to tattle on Matt; at best they would both be punished, but more likely, it would just be Curt. Matt got up a second later and in defeat, Curt kept his face down like an abused dog, not wanting to see whatever look the older boy had for him. Deep depression began to settle over the mind of the young man.

Matt was just too good. There had only been a couple of instances when he could have taken the pills and each would have taken both daring and skill. Curt was no longer impressed with Matt's abilities as a thief, rather he was now deeply afraid of them.

He started to eat again, but ate so slowly that everyone finished ahead of him and left the room, all save Miss Feanor, who except for a couple of trips to the attic, would sit in the kitchen for the remainder of the day. During his long meal, he turned over in his mind every possible way that he could deal with Matt, but Curt saw that he'd always be on the defensive with him and sooner rather than later, the older boy would get him punished again.

The thought gave him such a nasty turn, that once again he began toying with the idea of killing Matt. But it was little more than wishful thinking. The bigger boy had already proved that he was more than a match for Curt physically, while mentally Matt was cunning and devious.

He sighed loudly, causing Miss Feanor to glance up from her mug with a glare. The look turned his hatred from Matt to her and in a stew he left the room a moment later, slowly, painfully making his way to the family room to find Amber.

She was there, but so was Matt, who was practically sitting on her lap. He smiled at Curt as if they were good friends and toyed idly with the girl's blonde hair—the same girl he had stabbed in the face only the evening before.

Curt lowered his head in defeat. He was helpless to stop Matt in anyway, especially in the shape he was in. Matt knew this as well and pressed his advantage, running his hands up Amber's leg. She squirmed away from him but he followed, backing her up against one of the ornate couches. This was too much for the thief. Before coming to the home, Curt had never before been a hero in any way and after the previous night, he didn't ever want to be one again. Nevertheless, he found himself stepping into the room towards Matt. The older boy sprang up eagerly.

Their fight was short, over within seconds, but it had long-term fatal ramifications, all stemming from the fact that when he was lying upon the floor, bleeding into the lines of the wood, Curt found the lost paperclips.

Chapter 20

The Treasure

1

In truth, Curt couldn't remember much of the fight.

He remembered Amber dashing out of the room the moment Matt stood up and he remembered how it hurt even to raise his arms in his normal fighting stance and finally he remembered how hard it was to see out of his right eye due to all the swelling there. He even recalled a distant hope that a punch wouldn't come from that direction, because he would never see it coming.

That was about it.

And now he was trying to figure out why they were fighting in the first place and where he was exactly. His mind felt as coherent as a scramble of leaves in an October wind, but slowly two things came to him: he was in the family room and he was bleeding. Looking down, he saw his blood drain from him, trickling in a steady stream from a cut somewhere on his face. It formed a swiftly growing puddle on the pretty hardwood floors.

The puddle began to spin rapidly and Curt who was on his hands and knees collapsed into it, smearing the side of his head with his own fluids. He laid like that for a while, trying to think with any semblance of clarity and eventually he felt a tiny bit stronger and rolled over.

"Uhhh," he groaned as he went to his back. He did this without any of his usual grace and his right hand swung out and smacked the floor with a wet sound. His hands were slick with his own blood. Just then, he noticed that the mouse was in the room and his brain told him that she'd been there the whole time. She shied away from his reddened hand, and eyed him in her crazy way. Thankfully, it wasn't fifth day crazy, only first day crazy so it was at least bearable. Not that Curt could do much about it either way, he didn't think that he had the strength to even stand.

His head lolled back and forth for a moment and he saw that that he and the mouse were alone. She knelt in her usual spot, leaning over the box that held her cat puzzle. Since this was the first of the week, he found it strange that she hadn't taken it out and begun work on it yet. Though she could still be broken up over the loss of her letters, her demeanor that morning didn't really suggest that. He felt as though he was missing something and he wished his head would stop pounding so that he could think clearly.

Out of the fog of his mind, an idea came to him to get her back into her usual routine. Perhaps if he could help the mouse start the puzzle, she could take it from there and who knows, maybe he could help her actually finish the thing for once. Not that morning certainly, but possibly the next if she were still having problems and if he felt any better. It seemed like a good plan and his guilt over what he had done to her dropped a degree.

At least something felt right.

Absently, he put out his hand to touch the box, which was only a couple feet away, but the mouse snatched it up protectively, her eyes weaving up and down him were cloudy with emotion. She then took the puzzle box and put it back on the shelf, burying it among the other games and puzzles that sat there. It seemed so childish of her to hide the box in plain sight with him just there. The scene was so naive in its innocence that he found it endearing really and for a moment, he liked her.

He would've like her even more if she would get some paper towels and help him clean up the mess of his blood, but she was crazy and he'd have to do it himself.

Too bad Amber wasn't here to help... He suddenly remembered what he had fought Matt over and a brief surge of fear-laden energy infused his muscles.

"Uhh." More groans escaped him as he pushed himself up to a sitting position. His head swam, but he struggled to his feet. He trembled as he walked, yet made it to the doorway, leaving great bloody smears as he gripped the frame. Resting there for a moment, he glanced back and a wave of shock came over him. The pool of blood he had created was much bigger than he had realized and he put his hand to his face. The older cuts on his face had reopened, and he had a new one on the bridge of his nose. It bled freely.

He didn't care.

He was too afraid for Amber to care. Stepping into the hall, he looked up the stairs and saw that his immediate fears could now become secondary. Matt leaned against the bathroom door and Curt knew that Amber had made it safely inside. Good.

Unfortunately, Matt had all the patience of a cat waiting outside a mouse-hole and could be there for a few hours without a problem. With his head spinning, Curt decided he would have to worry about that later and not knowing what else to do, he went back inside the family room, deciding to keep his mess to a single location rather than bleed all over the house.

2

The mouse stood with her back to the games.

But just then Curt didn't care about her. At the moment, he cared about his huge headache and the blood that still ran down his face. Dragging his feet, he stood next to the puddle, which was already becoming tacky at the edges. It looked very dark. A deep maroon, while the fresh blood on his shirt seemed a cheery bright red. His shirt was ruined. He pulled it off and held it to his face, staunching the flow of blood, it hurt, but there was nothing he could do about that. His head felt heavy and despite all the blood pattering to the floor, it seemed sodden and he wobbled in place, tilting back and forth, before he found the sense to sit down. For a long time he sat there and his only companion was the mouse standing as if she were guarding her stupid puzzle box.

Again, her actions struck him as strange even for her, with sudden interest, he peered closer at her, and the weirdest thing happened...their eyes met for a moment.

He looked into hers, while she looked into his. A normal event if they had been two normal people, but the mouse wasn't anything close to normal. And what he saw in her eyes was a bit of a shock as well. She clearly didn't like him, or trust him for that matter, the knowledge made him blink away first from their locked gaze. At that moment he realized she was indeed guarding over her puzzle box. On a certain level, she knew that he'd been the one who had taken her love letters and now she was afraid he would take the puzzle as well, or...

Or the love letters were in that box.

He was suddenly sure of it. And he was sure as well, the paperclips would be right there with them. As far as he knew, she hadn't opened that box since the day he had discovered the letters were missing from his possession. She had only sat over it like a mother hen.

For the first time since he had lost the paperclips, excitement flooded his body and he began to think hard about what he had to do. Step one was to clean up his mess, and stifling a groan, he got up heading for the kitchen, giving a timid look up the stairs as he passed. In truth he felt far from timid, therefore he masked his true feelings and gave Matt the expression he had expected to see.

Once in the kitchen, he ignored Miss Feanor, who ignored him right back, despite his being covered in blood, and he went to the cabinet low down on the right where extra cleaning supplies were kept. Reaching over about a dozen containers of comet, he grabbed a roll of paper towels and then a bucket, which he filled with hot water. In a minute, he was back in the family room, noting the mouse hadn't budged. He began cleaning and became so absorbed in it that it was a few seconds before he noticed movement to his right.

Paul stood in the doorway, cleaning the smear of blood that Curt's hand had left. Seeing this stunned Curt and he only sat watching his one time friend clean, soon the blonde boy with the dull grey eyes finished and came over to Curt.

Kneeling down, he began to clean the drying blood there as well. "I'm sorry," the boy said softly under his breath. "I can't seem to help it...the voices, sometimes just take over." The last word came out in a strangled choking manner and Curt saw Paul's tears intermingling with the blood on the floor. Paul cried and cleaned, while Curt only sat near to him feeling sorrow for the boy. Greater sorrow than he had felt over anything and when Curt finally bent back over to clean again, his own tears dripped down as well.

From then on, they worked in silence and when the mess had been cleaned, the two boys looked at each other. Curt smiled a swollen lopsided smile at Paul, hoping to convey the fact that even after all that had happened, Curt still liked the boy...at least when he was like this...like Paul. The blonde gave him a half-smile in return while his right eye went through a series of twitches, a reminder to Curt that though he sometimes liked Paul, he could never trust him again.

Curt left a few seconds later, and saw that since Matt still lingered outside the bathroom upstairs, he would have to use the forbidden powder room to finish cleaning up. The forbidden rooms weren't precisely forbidden. Curt could go into them and stay for a while, just as long as kept all motion or noise to a minimum. If he didn't, he would the feel the annoyed hanger-over like anger of the house build quickly. It did that morning as he cleaned himself up, and he did his best to hurry, however this proved difficult, there was a lot of blood, caked and dried all over him. Underneath it, Curt found a boy he barely recognized.

His face felt shaped like a potato. The right side was indeed swollen, large. His eyelid stuck out about half an inch and was the color of a grape. His nose, which at one time was small and slim was now puffed up and looked too big for his face, a little like an old man's nose. The scabbed over teeth marks were the worst.

They made him shiver as he gawked at the size of them and for a second, the scared child in him wanted him to forget the paperclips and the insane risks that came with them. He buried the frightened voice in his mind, deep within him and when he finished cleaning off the blood, he looked past his injuries and into his own blue eyes. They were not the eyes of a thirteen-year-old. They were hard, surprisingly so, and filled with hate and anger, emotions that he rarely felt.

But the look in his eyes couldn't match the feeling of the house, the anger of which was stirring the air about him. He'd made too much of a commotion and had overstayed whatever small amount of welcome he might've had in the powder room and left as soon as he could.

Now he would be tested in one of the few areas in which he didn't excel. Patience.

With no more noise than a sighing baby, Curt slipped into the living room and ducked behind one of the couches. Positioning himself so that he could see into the hallway, he got comfortable, thinking he might have a long wait on his hands.

He was waiting on the mouse, knowing that she would have to leave the family room at some point. For what, he didn't know, perhaps to get a drink, use the bathroom, or even just take a stroll. In truth, because he had labeled her as crazy, he hadn't ever given her much thought. The other children's patterns and routines, he knew fairly well, but other than her fixation with the cat puzzle, he really didn't know her or what she did with her day.

It turned out to be a long wait. It seemed being crazy was a time consuming endeavor. At first, Curt spent the time planning on how he was going to get into the attic, but his plan was so simple that he got bored mulling over the same thoughts repeatedly. Then Curt spent quite a bit of time worrying. What if he got caught? What if Miss Feanor sicced the creature on him? What if he got up to the attic and found there weren't any windows or glowing swords or frothing potions? What if all that was up there, was a bed and some cobwebs? What if Amber was in trouble right at that moment, being raped by Matt?

He sighed and blew the tiniest particle of dust across the floor, where it scampered out of reach, deep under the couch. Amber was going to have to take care of herself, at least for the time being. It hurt for him to even think this way, but it would be pointless for Curt to get beat around again for nothing. Besides, he was pretty sure that she hadn't moved from the bathroom, and by staying there, she was providing an excellent distraction for Matt, keeping him out of Curt's hair.

These were not his only worries, which were almost beyond count, but it was what he dwelt upon for the most part, before he entered the third phase of his long wait. The napping phase.

Judging by the size of the drool puddle in which he woke, Curt guessed he had been asleep for at least an hour. But despite that, he came awake in an instant, his eyes flying open in alarm. The floor under his face had vibrated as if someone was moving in a stealthy manner along it.

3

His first instinct was to run to his bed, and his nimble young body tensed, preparing to spring up, however just then he saw the mouse go by. The sight stopped his muscles from contracting and he laid there, motionless, listening as she went up the stairs.

Though he felt a terrific desire to dash to the family room, he forced himself to count slowly to ten and then did so again, before he pushed himself up. With only a slight wobble as he stood, Curt listened for a second and then moved in his graceful way, with far more silence than the mouse had, sliding to the unoccupied family room. There he wasted no time and was at the puzzle box in a matter of seconds.

The love letters lay atop the jumbled pieces, and beneath them, mixed with the jig-sawed picture of a happy frolicking cat were four paper clips. The sight of them caused him to breathe in sharply with excitement and in a near reverential manner, he pulled them one by one from the box.

Seconds later the box was back exactly where he had found it and he was slipping noiselessly up the stairs...or almost so. Crrrreik!

When he had left the family room, he saw the bathroom door sat ajar and neither Amber nor Matt was in sight. His heart knew a touch of panic and worry for his girlfriend, and this had caused him to hurry up the stairs faster than he wanted to and he misjudged the step. Goose bumps flared across his skin at the noise but he threw aside any fear he had for the creature and slid as fast as he could to Amber's room. The door stood closed and it caused Curt's heart to thump all the harder in fear as he pictured the horrible things that Matt was doing to Amber. Without thinking of the consequences, he burst into the room, ready to fight Matt again if need be, yet the scene which greeted him drained all feeling from his body and all the blood from his head so that he staggered and held to the door for support.

Amber and Matt were locked in a deep kiss, which they ended with a jerk the second he charged in.

'Get out and shut the door,' Matt gestured casually, not at all angry for the interruption. His arrogant look had Curt coming back around and he began to see red. In a jealous rage, he stepped into the room but Amber hopped up quick and put herself between them; her face was crimson, but also blotchy with her guilt.

'No,' her hand was out to stop him and she pleaded to him with silent tear-filled eyes. He stopped as she wished and could only shake his head in misery and confusion, as he felt great shards of his heart break off and fall into the pit of his stomach.

Amber turned and motioned something to Matt, who only gave a small thin lipped smile. He wagged his fingers at her in dismissal and then pointed at his wrist and then to the bed, 'Go, but be back quick.'

She dragged Curt bodily from the room and once the door was closed behind her, she pressed herself close to him, "I'm doing this for you...he promised not to hurt you anymore if I do it." He could feel her tears wet his cheek as she whispered the dreadful words.

"No, I don't care. You can't let him..."

She interrupted, "You saved me last night, now I'm going to save you." He started to protest, but she pressed her lips to his to shut him up. They kissed for only a second and when they separated, she said, "I think I love you, Curt."

Stunned by the words, he was easily pushed back and with a last look, she went into her room where his hated rival eagerly awaited her.

Chapter 21

The Thief's Punishment-2

1

In a daze, he stood there unable to make sense of his emotions, his thoughts, or even his life. He was aware of dreadful pain, and his body ached and so too did his soul. His heart had been beating at a thunderous pace, but as he stood there outside the closed door, it became slower and slower; so slow that he felt each individual beat hammer cruelly within him. He began to hate that thumping organ and he wished it would stop all together.

Curt sank to his knees, with such an empty feeling that it was as though he were deflating and soon even kneeling felt like too much effort and he laid down upon the cool floor. There was nothing more than he wished but to close his eyes and follow a dream into another world, however the house was aware of him. Their quiet voices had beckoned its petulant scrutiny. It was so hateful that Curt found he couldn't lay his head down for very long and soon he sat up with the question of killing Matt on his mind. There was no choice in the matter for him and the sooner he did it the better.

It wouldn't be easy. There were no weapons in the house, not even knives and without something, Curt knew it would only mean another beating for him...or worse, he thought of the terrifying creature and what had happened the night before.

The stake!

Excitement stirred within Curt as he suddenly remembered the shard of wood, He got up and began sliding down the hall, but the more he visualized the thing, the slower he went. It was a pathetic weapon, especially against a bigger opponent like Matt. He could count on only a single strike with it and if it wasn't a fatal one, there was a good chance the older boy would simply take it from him and then Curt would be on the receiving end of it. This thought stopped him completely and his disappointment drifted into depression.

Then he remembered the paperclips.

Seeing the empty bathroom had sent them straight out of his mind, now he dug in his pocket and yanked them out. They were a dull grey and the slim twisted metal barely gleamed, yet to Curt they were wonderful and he balled his fist around them as he slid back down the hall. The attic door stood directly across the hall from Amber's room and Curt cast a long look in that direction before dropping to his knees and peering at the lock within the door's knob. This was where his hope laid waiting for him, this was where he could find something to defeat the monster and escape with Amber.

He forced the painful thoughts of what was happening just a few feet behind him out of his head and concentrated on picking the lock. Unfortunately, he knew only a little about the process.

Within a lock such as this one, were pins, which sat on tiny springs. In order to pick the lock, he'd have to push each of the pins down and then twist the clips as he would a key. Curt had seen it done once before, or rather, he had seen the back of a boy's hands as it was done but all the same, it had seemed an easy thing to accomplish.

Taking a deep breath to steady his nerves, he took each of the paper clips and bent them at the tip into the shape of an 'L' and then he went to work digging away at the lock.

It wasn't easy at all.

Again and again, he reached in with the tiny tools, feeling things move within the lock, but never did it turn. After a few minutes, sweat began to trickle from the wild tangle of his thick hair and he had to pause frequently to wipe it from his face. After ten minutes, he was no closer to opening the door than he had been when he first started and he paused to collect his thoughts. He worried that each pin could only be depressed to a certain depth and that if he pressed down too far, or didn't press down far enough, it would keep the lock from turning.

Just then, a soft cry of pain came from Amber's room.

Curt grimaced and groaned in misery as tears sprang to his eyes, he felt her pain, it was a keen knife in his chest, and it overrode the dull ache of his many injuries. It brought with it a sense of hopeless defeat and he sagged in front of the defiant lock, crying. It was minutes before he mastered his emotions enough to make another try at the lock.

This time, he took a different approach. Part of his problem lay in the fact that he had no clue to the number of pins that were in that particular lock and so he took only a single clip and placed it into the keyhole.

Closing his eyes and breathing lightly, he gently went back and forth, pressing at the pins, feeling them move up and down. In this way, he mapped out the interior of the lock and decided that there were five pins within it. For a second he sat wondering where he could get a fifth paper clip, but then he saw the answer was right in his hands. There was enough of the twisted metal for ten picks! Swearing at his own stupidity, he took one of the paper clips, straightened it out fully, and went to work bending it back and forth until the metal weakened enough to break. He then formed it as the others were and stuck them all into the lock.

Another ten minutes passed and the door remained locked.

Curt wanted to scream out his frustration. Nothing was working. If he had the pins depressed to the correct depth, he had no way of knowing, and he discovered a new problem, every time he attempted to turn the 'key', all of the paperclips would shift out of place. He lost count how many times he had tried and each attempt ended in failure and each failure weighed him down.

Again, for the fiftieth time, he leaned back and blew out a heavy blast of air. His fingers hurt and he had to pee. He needed a break.

Going to the bathroom, he mulled over what he would need to turn the lock. Simple, a slim piece of metal. Of course, if he had one, he wouldn't have needed the paperclips in the first place. His mind went over every aspect of the house wondering what he could use, but nothing came to him. After he urinated, he looked under the sink, and saw nothing useful, then he went to the cabinet where the cleaning supplies were kept. The answer was right in front of him.

"Oh my God," he whispered.

The lid to the comet cleaner was made of metal. Simultaneously, he wanted to jump for joy as well as kick himself for being so stupid. The means to form a crude set of lock picking tools and been hiding in plain sight since he had arrived. Snatching up the container he studied it for a moment, the metal was perfect, even better than the paperclips, since it was a slightly heavier weight and wouldn't bend so easily. But for now, he wasn't going to attempt to fashion anything more than a shim, which would act as the barrel of the key and allow him to turn the lock easier.

Fiercely, he strained at the lid until he tore it off, he then went to work bending the lid this way and that until he broke off a small piece. Unfortunately, the bending left a curved lip to it, which would keep it from fitting into the lock. This proved difficult to bend back flat, and after tearing his fingers to ribbons, he was forced to use his teeth. The vague taste of comet and the feel of the metal on his teeth made for a most unpleasant time.

When he was done, Curt zipped back to the attic door, and he was so focused on what he was doing that he didn't even look around for any of the other children or Miss Feanor. It was a terrible breach of operational security, something that he prided himself on, but he got lucky and no one was about.

The piece of metal from the container went in first, he kept it high in the lock and applying a light amount of pressure, in a clockwise direction, he then inserted the paperclips, and he had barely begun fiddling with them, when to his astonishment the lock turned slightly to the right. Lightly, he jiggled at the clips attempting to get the pins depressed correctly and the lock turned all the way.

2

Curt sat back staring at it with his mouth hung open.

He had done it, but instead of elation, he felt a cold dread and now that the possibility of escape was just barely in his grasp, he scarcely had the temerity to seize it. This was one of those moments in life when decisions could have fatal consequences and Curt fully understood this. Going through that door could very well mean his death, still the lure of escape was stronger than his fear.

With a light breath in, he opened the door slightly and peeked through the gap. There wasn't much to see, only a set of stairs leading up and a dim light coming from somewhere in the attic. In his mind, he pictured the window that he had been hoping for and his heart began to thump heavily inside him.

Shutting the door only partially, he pocketed the homemade keys and zipped to the bathroom. Now his senses were on full alert, his ears straining to catch even the smallest noise, the soles of his feet sensitive to the least vibration. Furtively, he checked in every direction before he grabbed a large stack of sheets and slunk with more than his usual caution to the attic door. There he stepped in and watched as the door swung gently and silently shut behind him. It locked by itself. This gave Curt a heavy feeling in his stomach and he reached out and tried the door. It opened beneath his hand and he let out a sigh of relief.

Turning back to the stairs, he paused to let his eyes adjust to the dim light, and for his heart to cease its tremendous pounding. Curt had broken into and explored many places in his short life, but had never felt so strangely out of place than he did at that moment.

The dust, the cobwebs, the little bits of trash strewn about the steps, and the musty smell, all made him feel like he had just stepped into a stairwell leading to an attic. It was of course exactly what he had done, but after so many days spent in the perfectly ordered and near sterile cleanliness of the rest of the house, it felt out of place; wrong even.

He was tempted to open the attic door behind him just to see if it would somehow magically lead to another home. Logic stayed his hand, he knew he hadn't left the house, he could still feel its angry presence in the air. It was less, however. Almost he could describe the feeling as faint and taking up his habit once again, he reached out a hand to the wall.

The house's attention was focused elsewhere, if it was indeed focused at all and beneath the dim and distant vitriol of it, Curt sensed the creature deep in the basement. It seemed to slumber as an old man would after a feast. The fact steadied Curt and he began moving up the grimy steps quickly, feeling a mounting desperation to be finally rid of the place.

Gaining the top stair, he saw that the attic was a large one, with a diagonally sloping unfinished ceiling. The rafters were exposed, criss-crossing the area high above his head and forming an 'A' with the sides of the roof. Whether the walls were also unfinished, he couldn't tell since the dark attic was filled with the belongings of a person who had clearly lived through the great depression.

There were heaps of magazines from a remote time, decaying and broken furniture, bookshelves lined with books whose pages were yellow with age, and perhaps a hundred fading and dusty boxes heaped in great piles stacked higher than his head. There was more, a lot more, and Curt's head swiveled round and round at it all. Normally this was the kind place that he would have loved to hunker down and explore at his leisure, but his sense of urgency kept him from tarrying. However, he did pause at a great jumbled mound of children's toys, nothing seemed more out of place, and there was something about them that made his stomach knot up.

Gladly, he turned away from the pile and made his way through the maze of junk, moving toward the light. As he walked, his eyes darted about the mountains and stacks of unkempt items, but his mind was on escape. The first thing he would do is call the police. And then an ambulance and then the fire department, he'd even call Miss Gladys.

A smile lit his face at that, picturing the great brown form of Miss Gladys in a towering rage, storming up to the house and hammering on the door with her large man-sized hands. He would pay good money to see that.

3

His smile faltered though, when he found the source of the light.

It wasn't coming in from a window. In fact, there were no windows in the attic at all. The illumination came from a hanging bulb suspended over a pair of simple steel framed beds. Two people, a young man of maybe twenty, and a girl of perhaps sixteen lay in the beds. At the sight of them, he stepped back in shock, prepared to run, but he hesitated, unsure whether they were dead or simply asleep. For all the world they looked like corpses to him.

They were dead pale, white to the point of translucency and thin blue veins could be seen making a map at their temples. Though their skin seemed young, unblemished by the slightest wrinkle or crease, their hair, which was a light sandy brown was exceedingly thin. So thin that Curt could see their scalps clearly through it.

If they breathed at all, he couldn't tell, despite his watching for any movement of their thin chests. Cautiously, he took a few careful steps closer, and still couldn't decide if they breathed or even lived. Knowing that the dead soon began to stink, he gave them a tentative sniff, but the musty air of the attic only held the penned up aroma of an antiquated house.

The smell was wonderful. He breathed in deeper. Filling his lungs with the stale air and enjoying it. It was an odd moment, he had been so keyed up with getting into the attic and finding a way to escape that he hadn't taken the time to truly notice the fragrance. At any other time, the attic would have smelled as just that, but deprivation had turned it into a circus of smells, bubbling with scraps of memories.

Curt took the time to breathe in deeply once more, closing his eyes as he did, relishing the air as if he were at a feast instead of in a musty attic standing over two bodies. But the moment passed as his sense of urgency forced him to the task at hand and he walked around the two beds. Even up close, he couldn't tell if they alive or dead and in truth his curiosity over them waned with each passing second. His need to escape eclipsed his inquisitiveness and soon he left them and went about exploring the rest of the attic.

Unfortunately, there wasn't much else to it.

Just beyond the bodies, in a dark corner, he found where Miss Feanor slept. Here, there was another simple bed, a chest of drawers, a filing cabinet and a computer. But no windows.

Feeling a touch of desperation, Curt began peeking behind the towering stacks of junk. Going from wall to wall, he moved with more haste than silence and within minutes had attracted unwanted attention. Not from the house, but from Miss Feanor. Curt finished checking the last of the walls and decided to see if Miss Feanor had a weapon stashed in her belongings. There were no thoughts of swords left in him, he was all logic now and hoped to find a gun. But as he went, he paused to stare again at the two people.

They appeared harmless. However nothing about the place was, as it seemed and Curt started to wonder what part they played in the weird nature of the house.

"Get away from them!" A voice hissed out of the darkness just behind him. With a little cry, Curt dropped the sheets he'd been carrying about and spun to face the angry sound. At first, all he saw was a looming shadow and involuntarily he stepped back.

"I said, get away." It was Miss Feanor. She moved forward into the light of the single bulb and in her hands she brandished a baseball bat.

The bat had been sitting in with the pile of children's toys; he remembered the handle sticking out, and now he wished he'd had the foresight to have grabbed it. Miss Feanor waved it over her head threateningly and he stepped away from the bodies, never taking his eyes from the bat.

It was old. It was chipped and nicked, and in places gouged where some boy from long ago had used it to hit rocks instead of baseballs. The Louisville Slugger logo that had been branded onto it was faded practically to nothing. The knob at the end was notched, and despite all of this, Miss Feanor could cave in his head with a single swing. It occupied most of Curt's mind, but there was still a part of him that could think past the fear of that skull-crushing bat.

"Who are these people?" he asked her with eyes as big as saucers.

"None of your damn business." Her voice stayed low and menacing. "Now, give me the key and get the hell out of here. If I ever catch you up here again..." Her eyes, black and malignant finished her sentence for her.

"I...I...I don't have a key...I picked the lock with this." He pulled from his pocket a single paperclip.

Her hateful eyes focused on the tiny piece of metal. "You picked...? You can't do that. Where did you get that?"

"Matt gave it to me," he lied smoothly, the words tumbling out of his mouth, naturally like a leaf in blowing wind. The lie strangely enough calmed his nerves somewhat and he was able to continue, "He beat me up when I told him I wouldn't do it. See look." He showed her his battered face.

Confusion entered her mind; Curt could see it cooling the anger in her eyes. "You're lying, the monster did that to you, and... and Matt wouldn't..." She stopped, knowing in truth it was something Matt might do. "Empty your pockets," she ordered suddenly.

His lie was going to become quickly obvious.

Worry over what would happen next, made his breath hitch and his heartbeat hugely, booming in his slim chest, while his stomach formed itself into knots. All that was on the inside, on the outside, he demonstrated the very interpretation of serenity.

"Matt gave me these ones too," he said, handing over the remaining paper clips, as if he were eager to get rid of them.

He wasn't of course, but the piece of bent metal from the lid to the comet container was far more important. This he palmed as he handed over the paperclips. It was another slick move; showing her, what she expected to see all the while hiding the truth. The paperclips had been good for the small pins in the lock of the attic door, but now that he had found the attic devoid of windows, he'd have to summon the courage to tackle one of the doors leading to the outside. With the large pins and tumblers in the workings of the antique locks, those would take something more substantial.

As well, there was the fact that if she found out where the little piece of metal had come from, his newly discovered source of picks would surely disappear. He'd be trapped, completely without hope.

Miss Feanor took the small pieces of metal and her fury mounted. "Where did...?" She stopped and stared at the bent clips. "Matt didn't give these to you...you're a thief. That big social worker told me all about what you are. What you are capable of. Now, I said turn out your pockets."

Curt did so, but he had to do it slowly lest he make it obvious that he held a slim piece of metal in the palm of his right hand. To distract her, he asked a few questions, though he wasn't expecting any real answer.

"Who are these two people?" he tried for the second time as he pulled out his pockets.

"Nobody," she retorted in flat anger.

"Are they kids like me...are they foster kids that got too old? Is this what happens to us?" Curt hadn't thought about this until the words had actually darted from between his lips. The idea was terrifying.

"I told you they're nobody." Even though she was clearly in a great fury, she kept her voice amazingly controlled and quiet. "You forget about them, damn it. Now turn around, let me see those back pockets."

Putting his back to her was the last thing he wanted to do—the very idea sent a cold shiver down his spine. Turning slowly, he faced the two people in the beds; he thought they were definitely foster kids who had turned eighteen. Instead of being released, where they would surely tell somebody, they had been stuck up here.

For what purpose?

Miss Feanor dug roughly at his back pockets for a few moments, pushing him closer to the bed occupied by the older male. Curt looked at him, wondering if this was the boy who he'd replaced and if this would be his fate as well. But it struck him suddenly that this couldn't have been the boy. Amber had described him as blonde, also the person in the bed was too old, he was obviously older than eighteen.

"Who is this?" he asked aloud, but more to himself than to Miss Feanor.

She yanked him about, and held the bat to his face. "You leave them alone and stay out of here, or I'll have you punished for a week straight! Do you hear me?"

Without waiting for a reply, she started pushing him roughly to the stairs and as he got to the bottom, his jumbled thoughts came together and he turned back to her. She stood two steps up and from there she looked huge. Curt was frightened of her and of the punishments she had threatened, but his need to know why he was there at all overrode his fear and he asked a last question.

"Are those two the reason we're trapped here?"

Her eyes told him that they were. She tried to hide it, but he read it clearly before she could cast her face into hard-set marble.

"You won't leave it alone, will you?" Her countenance grew splotchy and red. "You need a punishment, not to mention a fucking spanking!"

He had gone too far and fear blasted through him. "I'm sorry, Miss Feanor. I'm just trying to understand." His pleading tone was wasted on her and she only eyed him with a look that Curt had trouble reading. She jerked her head toward the door leading to the second floor hallway, the one that he had picked triumphantly not even ten minutes earlier. Now he'd go through it with a punishment looming over his head and perhaps worse, Miss Feanor as his enemy. She would be impossible to stop.

As he opened the door, he turned back to give her one last apology and caught just the blur of motion as the bat came slicing through the air at his head.

Chapter 22

Legacy of the Bat

1

At first he was kicked, though not cruelly so, it was more of a quick nudge.

Then he was shaken, but it was for seconds only. It brought him around...barely. His first vision, when his eyes cracked briefly was a blurry view of the hardwood floors. For some reason he lay upon them, yet Curt lacked any sort of curiosity as to why. He closed his eyes for a span of time that couldn't be accounted, at least not by him. When he opened them, he saw again the floors just as before and felt vibrations running through the wood. A part of him thought that he should care about these vibrations...he used to care; he understood that much, but just then the vibrations were without context or meaning and he only closed his eyes once more.

Amber shook him awake some time later. Maybe it was a second later, or two or perhaps an hour, he couldn't tell, however he did notice that she'd changed into her pajamas.

"Curt, get up! You have to get up...Curt, please," she whispered to him, shaking his shoulders. His eyes had a great deal of trouble focusing and the shaking only made the world around him spin.

"Huh?" he half groaned the word.

"Curt, look at me. You have to get in bed it's..." She stopped all of a sudden and turned her head, listening. The bat had rattled him so much that though he heard her words, he couldn't understand their meaning, still the hysteria in her voice helped to concentrate his mind.

"It's almost time! Get up, please," she pleaded.

And then she was gone. One second her teary-eyed face was above him, the next all he saw was a pink blur, fading into a great distance. He blinked his eyes, trying to focus them, but everything more than a few feet away came to him as only vague colors.

There seemed to be a remote voice within him telling him to get up and so he rolled to his side and saw again the hardwood floors, they were close to his face and now he understood that he was laying full upon them. Still, he didn't care. His mind had not progressed to that point yet, it was only now processing the simplest facts.

However, when the lights went out and he sensed new vibrations running along the floor and up into his cheek, he started to care. The voice within him became more urgent, but the loss of the light effectively blinded him and he only felt about on the floor as if looking for something.

"Good luck tonight with the monster."

Miss Feanor's dry quiet voice came out of the dark and he rolled back over with a low groan. She leered above him. With his vision impaired, she appeared nothing but a head floating in the darkness.

"Perhaps now you'll learn your place here and obey the rules," she whispered and then, just like with Amber she seemed to disappear. Through the floor he heard her moving and then came the tiny sound of the attic door closing.

With that soft noise, the voice within him began an urgent cry, 'Get up!'

Curt pushed himself over, and slowly, very slowly got to his hands and knees, but he couldn't find it within him to go any further. Even when he felt the first vibrations of something moving deep in the house, he couldn't push himself up. Instead, he swayed as if in a heavy wind, back and forth on all fours.

"Come on," a voice whispered in the dark.

Someone appeared next to him, and now hands roughly yanked him to his feet. Unable to hold himself up, Curt pitched forward onto the person and didn't recognize that it was Paul. In the older boy's anxiety and fear, his twitch had distorted his face into a horrifying mask, and Curt shrank back away from it in dismay.

"Come on!" a second time Paul implored with terrific urgency and now Curt understood who it was that was helping him and as he did, he became conscious of a tremendous fear running throughout the house. There was a real terror rippling through the air. Curt had felt this once before, when he had been out of bed after dark, it meant the creature was coming and with it came a ball of ice in his stomach.

They could feel it moving purposely through the main floor and now Paul began pushing him along the hallway in a silent rush. Curt felt like the Scarecrow from the Wizard of Oz and wobbled about, scarcely in control of his limbs and as a result, they fell into the walls heavily time and again. Each time Paul would haul him back up and propel them forward once more. His bravery was fantastic, but not infinite.

When at last Curt stumbled against the bathroom door and slid down to the floor, there was a moment's hesitation on Paul's part. The creature, just below them would turn up the stairs at any second and catch them out of bed. And then it would be a tossup, which of the two would be punished and who would be allowed to slink off and hide in their bed.

Paul took a single glance down the steps and fled without another look back.

Curt didn't blame him. When he peered down, he caught a swirl of movement among the shadows, the sight of which sent him into a spasm of panic. Lacking the strength to stand, he crawled like a drunken sailor after a runaway bottle. Because of his concussion, the floor seemed to heave up and down as he went but his dread had him hurrying despite that. At that moment with his back to the stairs, what he most feared was the sound of the creature charging up them.

However, he didn't hear that sound, but only the long slow *Crreik* of the creature coming up, in its usual sly fashion and this he heard precisely a bare second after he had his door closed to the proper width.

Crreik...Crreik...Crreik, Crrrreik, Crreik.

To his addled mind, the creature seemed to moving faster than normal. Curt struggled madly to climb the short distance into his bed, but the tilting room and the spinning walls made it a mountain and a trial that he only barely surmounted.

Wwhhhhhh.

His door opened just as he pulled himself under the covers and the creature came into his room, slowly, menacingly. It seemed to enjoy the terror it caused and Curt, who was properly terrorized, began to shake and quiver uncontrollably. Perhaps it was for that reason the creature hovered over him for so long. It hadn't left as it should have; he could hear it moving furtively about his bed, as if waiting for something.

For the creature to linger there, wasn't ordinary for a first day. Normally, it just had a quick look around before moving on to the next room yet for some reason now it wouldn't leave. The building panic in Curt was becoming too much and it made him want to scream, but then he remembered what happened to Paul and he wondered if this was what the creature was waiting for.

It wanted Curt to scream. He was suddenly quite sure of this. In fact so confident was he that this was all it needed to trigger an attack, Curt bit down on the inside of his cheeks and held on. Slowly his body ceased its shivering and began to relax and before a half a minute had passed, the creature moved away from his bed and left his room. When it did, an unconquerable exhaustion swept over Curt and he only had time enough to remember that people who had suffered a concussion weren't supposed to be allowed to sleep, before he fell deeply asleep.

2

Curt had a wonderful sleep. It was deep and refreshingly free of pain, fear, or anxiety.

Upon waking, he felt all of these in abundance.

Miss Feanor yanked back his covers, startling him out of sleep. She stared hard at him, while he could only blink stupidly, trying to focus his eyes well enough to see her. In a second, she pulled up his shirt, taking in his dark blue bruises from his punishment two days before. She was disappointed there weren't fresher ones.

The lady leaned in very close. "Don't bother cleaning this evening. It won't make any difference. You're going to get the punishment you deserve." With a final glare, she slid out of the room.

Depression struck him like a kick to the stomach. It laid him flat on his back and he lacked the will to move. Though in truth, even without the depression he wouldn't have wanted to budge. He hurt up and down his body and was hard put to find an area that was free from pain.

Gently he touched the foul swollen teeth marks left by his last punishment. They were everywhere upon him and they still stung, he then felt his face, and had the impression that he had been hit by Matt, more than he realized. All about his jaw, and the bones in his cheeks ached, but this was nothing compared to pain in the back of his head.

There was a lump half the size of his fist back there and he could scarcely touch it without crying out. He almost did. His depression made it so that he didn't care when his punishment came. In fact, he wanted it sooner rather than later. Since it was currently raining, he decided to get the punishment out of the way so that he could at least relax the rest of the day instead of worrying over the coming night.

"What a waste of a good rainy day," he mumbled to himself, before attempting to get up. Despite what everyone had said, he couldn't see himself just laying there waiting to be attacked, he would fight back, even if the odds were against him.

"Holy crap," he moaned through gritted teeth. The pain throughout his body was exquisite and it took a great deal of will power just to sit up. He tried to concentrate on the rain, thinking how he would lie there the rest of the day, simply listening to the soothing sound.

Swinging his legs around, he grunted loudly—he didn't care since he was just about to get louder still. Amber cared and she came rushing in. The look in her eyes told him all he needed to know about what he must have looked like. She stared and stared, her eyes dancing over his many bruises and cuts while her face betrayed her misery.

He became embarrassed at her scrutiny. "Why don't you go get in bed. I..."

"Shush!" she hissed at him, covering his mouth at the same time. He pulled back from her touch and almost fell over in the process.

"It's ok," he murmured, quietly this time just to mollify her. "First, it's raining and second...I have to be punished."

She looked confused and cocked an ear. After a moment she mouthed, 'It's not raining.'

"Sure it is..." He paused listening. Just then, he noticed that the rain sounded fuzzy, more like a poorly tuned radio. Curt looked toward the window and light streamed in through the slits of the shutters, confusing him.

Working his jaw around, he said, "Weird."

However, the words came out in a much quieter voice. It wasn't raining, instead there was something wrong with his hearing. This sudden realization gave him a scare and he started to have second thoughts about being punished just then.

"You don't have to be punished...this is my fault," she whispered in a voice only slightly louder than her normal exhaling. "I'm sorry for last night, for everything." Her hair fell in front of her face and she didn't try to move it, but hid herself behind the blonde curtain. She started to cry and he held her, not having a clue as to what she was talking about, then he suddenly remembered Matt and he stiffened against her. She had nothing to apologize for.

"You were just being brave...for me. You don't need to apologize for that," he whispered in reply. "But when I have my revenge on Matt...don't try to interfere." His battered face was hard and menacing as he said the last.

She stepped back from him and he was glad to see the slight apprehension in her eyes, but he was gladder still that she didn't try to argue with him about it. After a moment, she told him what it was that she was sorry for.

"I'm not sorry for that...I'm sorry because..." She paused looking around, blinking back more tears. "I'm sorry that I didn't get out of bed to help you. I couldn't...I tried, but I just couldn't. Once the lights went down..."

This time she paused in alarm. The room had become charged with that nasty awareness as the house focused on their whispered discussion. Curt shushed her lips by putting his swollen ones to hers and they kissed with gentleness until the feeling died away.

'Come eat,' she motioned. 'You have to keep your strength up.'

She helped him along the hall to the backstairs and the more they moved the better his legs felt beneath him. Conversely however, the more they moved, the more his head pounded. Curt had never had such a throbbing headache in his life and he was suddenly thankful for the quiet of the house.

There was no way he'd be able to eat breakfast that morning. The very thought curdled his stomach and he worried that this would be another strike against him with Miss Feanor. But he needn't have worried. When the two finally got to the nook, he saw that his bowl was empty and not because someone else had eaten his food. Miss Feanor had left it purposely so and she wore a nasty look that had a touch of maternal vindictiveness that he associated with the feeling of the house.

Despite the fact that she'd inadvertently done him a favor by not making him eat, she was being over the top cruel in her desire to punish him. As if being hit over the head with a bat wasn't enough, she was going to sic the creature on him, and as a final straw she wasn't going to feed him.

He turned from the table quickly, not wanting his emotions to betray him. Feeling overwhelmed, he put a hand to his eyes as if to wipe away a tear and tottered slowly out of the room. He wasn't at all sad.

He was angry.

More angry than he'd ever been. Angry enough to kill.

Chapter 23

A Night Out

1

Curt, by nature was not a killer.

By nature, he was thief. Not only was he genetically gifted with all the physical abilities of one, he was gifted mentally as well. His mind was as nimble as his fingers and his wit quicker than his feet. However, no thief becomes one through genetics but rather through happenstance.

Had Curt's first foster-care placement been to one of the many, many loving homes in the system, he would most assuredly look like the very picture of a normal happy kid. Unfortunately, his first placement was in a foster-farm.

A foster-farm is one where the children are treated as little more than human livestock. They aren't there to be raised in a normal family environment while they await adoption or re-unification with their own families, as the system intends. Rather, the children are simply a way for the 'foster-parents' to get easy money with little or no effort.

Six-year-old Curt found himself as one of seven children, living in squalor that was only a small step up from what his drug-addicted prostitute of a mom had provided. He was inadequately fed, clothed, bathed, and most importantly supervised. Little Curt was the youngest of the children and as such his belongings, meager as they were, became the property of others. That included his food. Once again, he turned to petty crime and begging to survive.

Just then, sitting on his bed gently massaging the pain in his face, he missed that house. He even missed the 'foster-mom', Mrs. Frailey. She did nothing all day, but smoke, eat, and watch soap operas. She was horribly repulsive, with greasy unwashed hair and a black moustache and Curt would've kissed her face if she would just walk in the front door and take him out of there.

Curt didn't want to be a killer.

In fact, he was a little afraid to even start down that path. Up to the moment when he walked out of the kitchen everything in his life had reinforced and supported his future as a thief. It was as if the universe wanted it that way and had structured events and circumstances to nurture the rogue within him. He saw it as destiny. But he knew his destiny could change in the blink of an eye. His mother was a fine example. One moment on the fast track of life, the next a waste of space, using up oxygen.

Killing could be like that. He saw it as walking through a grated subway entrance. It was one way only. Go through those doors and you were a killer for life, and a part of him knew that if he were to kill just once, the next murder would be easier and the one after that easier still. There was a resistance to killing within each person, ingrained not only morally, but also on a level far deeper than that. Deeper even than genetically and he suspected there was a spiritual aspect that kept man from killing his fellows with ease.

It was for this reason that Curt went to his room and despite his thumping head, worked through every possible method he could think of to escape. It was a futile exercise, one that he'd gone over a thousand times prior to that morning. Giving up, he laid himself down and was soon fast asleep.

Sometime later, he woke feeling much better. His arms were numb from lying on them and the drool puddle on his pillow was very large so that he suspected he had slept a few hours at least. He found Amber guarding over the outside of his bedroom and he actually teared up at the sight of her there. No one had ever cared for him that much before.

They kissed gently for a few moments when he finally came out and then she pushed him back into his room. She was desperate to know what had happened to him. With painful slowness he whispered the story into her ear so as not to awaken the house's anger. When he was done, she looked very sad for him.

"She-must-have-figured-out-where-you-got-the-piece-of-metal-from. She-has- taken-all-the-lids-from-the-comet-containers." Amber whispered these two short sentences over a period of a minute, one word at a time. The news sank his spirits even though he had suspected that his secret hadn't remained one for long. The tiny piece of metal hadn't been lying near the attic door, he had checked.

"I was afraid of that," he said slow and soft. "Who do you think those two people are up there?" he asked pointing to the ceiling.

She shrugged.

"What should we do?" he asked.

He already knew what they should do, he had known it from the second he saw that baseball bat coming at his head. The two people in the attic had to die. Oh, so badly he wanted revenge on both Miss Feanor and Matt, but even more he longed for freedom and he figured that the two people were connected to the house in some way, and he felt confident they had something to do with the horrid feminine and masculine spirits haunting the place. His gut told him they were likely the physical bodies of the two, and simply put, that meant they'd have to die. From his point of view, it was a choice between his slow horrible death and their quick ones.

But he didn't really want to come out and say it. He wanted Amber to tell him to kill the two; he thought it would make him feel less...guilty. However, she only shrugged again.

An exasperated sigh escaped him. Slightly angry with her he whispered, "I think we should kill them."

That she didn't ask why, told him she agreed with his assessment of who they were. She looked down for a time, "I d-d-don't think I c-c-can."

He glared hard at her and she began to cry, ashamed of her cowardice. This wasn't her fault, he reminded himself; she'd been trapped here from the age of ten, in many ways she was more of a child than he was.

"Do you at least think it's a good idea?" he asked gently, hoping for a little support. She nodded timidly. It was better than nothing.

2

Now that he decided he would kill the two, he set his considerable intellect against the various barriers in his way. First he'd need a weapon and second, a way to get past the attic door.

The weapon was the easiest to get.

His initial thought was to use the same stake which had been used to scar up the face of his girlfriend and setting Amber to keep watch, he ducked into Matt's room. The stake had looked exactly like a part of the underside of the box spring in a bed frame. Even as he searched Matt's bed, his intuition told him he was searching in the wrong place. Matt was too devious to be so obvious.

He was correct. The underside of Matt's bed was unblemished. With a snort, he went back to his own room and checking his bed, saw the stake. It was aligned nicely but the cracks along its edges were obvious when looked for and in a second, he had yanked it out. With Ambers dried blood running along one edge, it was nasty looking.

The sight of the brown discoloration turned his stomach and he wondered if he'd be able to stab it into a live person. There was little choice in the matter and he decided he would just have to find a way.

Next, he bent his mind on a way to get into the attic. Taking up a position in Amber's room with a view of the attic door, he studied it and his options. After an hour, he had discovered what he already knew; it was a plain white door with a lock that he had no way to pick. Curt was out of options, save for knocking on the door and asking to be let in.

Another hour of sitting and staring came and went without him being any closer to a solution and anxiety over his coming punishment added to a depression which threatened to sink him. For the first part of his vigil, Amber lay on the bed looking pensive, her face even more anxious than his, but then she fell asleep. Just like that, her worries were gone and without them, she was more beautiful than ever. Curt reclaimed his optimism in the way her hair shimmered and looked so soft, and in the way her angular face would make a model jealous, and perhaps more importantly in the fact that she was his.

He was lucky and he'd find a way in.

Minutes later, he found the means to access the attic. As Miss Feanor made the second of her two daily visits to check on the people up there, he saw the smallest opportunity. It was a horribly dangerous way and it possibly meant more bloodshed, but there was no other choice. Waking Amber, he told her what he considered doing and she sat back saying little, only thinking about the ramifications of his failure.

After a few minutes, she gave him a piercing look. "Can-you-really-do-it?" she asked in their slow way. He nodded and she nodded in return, which was her way of agreeing with his plan. It surprised him a little, he had assumed that she would attempt to talk him out of going through with it and was very glad that she hadn't.

Now came perhaps the worst part of his plan: the wait. Things wouldn't be in position until the lights had been turned down right before bed and that was still a few hours away. Even in the best of circumstances, he wasn't good at waiting. But in a house where there was absolutely nothing to do, it was the purest tedium. He paced, until his head hurt. He listened to Amber talk, one slow word at a time, until his head hurt. He even showered until he ran out of hot water, and then his head hurt.

The one productive thing that he wanted to accomplish backfired and yes, it made his head hurt. Curt went to find Paul, and Amber, who seemed afraid to be left alone, went with him. They found a boy who looked like Paul sitting on his bed.

"What do you want, ugly? George ain't here," the boy with dirty blonde hair and dull grey eyes spoke loudly in an offensive manner.

The volume of his voice stopped Curt for a second and then he responded as if he were in church, "I wanted to thank you for last night."

"Are you saying I'm gay?" the boy asked, again with anger in his whisper.

Confused Curt could only shake his head at first, "No...I meant thank you for saving my life."

"No, I won't fucker," the blonde boy suddenly hissed at his dresser. "I won't, George, and you can't make me." The air in the room was fast becoming thick and Curt's head began to pound with Paul's craziness. He started to leave, but Amber strode up close to Paul and knelt in front of him.

"What did George say?" she spoke so low that Curt had trouble hearing her.

"None of your..." he began to say to her, but paused for a second looking back to the dresser, "I'm handling this, so shut up George, you fucker. I won't say it...I won't...your welcome? No, that's the last thing..."

With the air becoming charged as if it hummed with a swarm of invisible bees, Curt grabbed Amber by the arm and pulled her out of the room, leaving Paul to argue with himself. At least on some level Paul had heard his thanks, but he worried that the boy was seconds away from paying a heavy price for hearing it. They hurried back to Curt's room and knelt there, sweating in fear, feeling the floor, trying to figure out if the creature was coming. It wasn't. Paul must've felt the air as well and once more dead silence reigned throughout the house.

Curt went back to pacing, glum at the near disaster he had almost caused.

3

Two very long hours later, dinner was served.

It was served to everyone but Curt. By this point, he'd gone nearly two days without eating and his body was starting to get the shakes. He sat down at the table hoping Amber would have the guts to give him a bite or two. She earned a series of unpleasant glares from Miss Feanor and Matt when she gave up most of her spam and carrots to Curt.

Despite the monotonous blandness of the food, he ate ravenously and the dirty looks only made the food go down easier. After dinner, he took Miss Feanor's advice and ignored his cleaning. Instead, he warmed up and then began stretching. This was a habit he'd begun a year before, just prior to a break-in of a second floor window—one that had practically demanded a contortionist to enter.

Since then he'd increased his stretching routine and now there were very few people outside a gymnastic school who were more limber than the little thief.

That night waiting for his slim opportunity, he took his time, allowing his mind to focus on the many small things he'd have to make sure would go right for the night to end well. He was risking much. More than he'd ever risked before. It was not just a punishment that was on the line, there was a chance that if things went terribly wrong, his life would be taken from him one bite at a time.

Finally, when he'd stretched all he could, he took the stake and put it in his bed. Turning off his light, he climbed in as well. As a *just-in-case* he wore three shirts and below that he left his jeans on—protection against biting.

In order to calm his nerves, he began breathing in slow and deep, waiting for the arrival of Miss Feanor, which would mark the opening move in his gambit for freedom. She would say something, probably a nasty something and just then that would be preferable to something nice. If she were to suddenly apologize, he didn't know what he would do.

Another light went down and Curt took a big breath and slipped beneath his covers, giving himself an extra big tunnel to breathe through. The layers of pajama shirts were making him sweat already and he didn't want to overheat. He squirmed suddenly. The layers of shirts had ridden down his back and were choking him, forcing him to pull down hard at his collar.

Just then he heard his door open, it was too early for Miss Feanor by at least fifteen seconds, so he popped his head out. The very white face of Amber seemed to shine in the growing darkness. She stood in his doorway for just a moment until another light, a closer light went out behind her. Upon her face, she wore a tight worried smile and her eyes were filled with fear for him—her lips held something else and she leaned in to kiss him.

"Good luck," she whispered and then she was gone. The feel of her warm lips stayed on his—they had been so soft, and they had spoken to him soundlessly as they kissed. They told him of the love she held within her. The feeling made him slightly giddy and he was slow to duck beneath his covers when the final light went down. It didn't matter though. Miss Feanor was going to have him punished, a torture that would slowly drive him insane over time. What more could she do?

His mind started to go down all the nasty things she could do, but luckily, she interrupted his dour thinking.

"You won't be getting out of your punishment tonight. I've made sure of this and for your own sake, don't get out of bed. Take the punishment right here," she advised in a rather loud voice as if she weren't particularly worried about the creature coming for her. "And do me a favor; try not to scream to much. I'm a little tired and need my rest. Sweet dreams." The last words she added with fake syrupy insincerity.

Curt just nodded under the covers, feeling the welcome burn of his anger. Good, he thought to himself. It would make everything that much easier to do with his hatred for her running so high.

Now he pulled back the covers and listened intently as the lady of the house went from room to room. When she made it to Paul's he slipped from his bed and when she left the blonde boy's room three seconds later, Curt stepped out into the darkened hallway.

Chapter 24

The Thief of Life

1

Being out of bed after the lights were down was a perverse thrill. Curt felt it and fed off it, knowing few kids his age in all the world would have the guts to attempt his audacious plan.

A second after Miss Feanor left Paul's room, Curt was ghosting down the hallway towards Amber's door. He moved fluidly, silently, the stake clutched in his left hand, his mind a whirl of *What ifs*. What if she were to turn around just then and see him plain as day out of bed? What if he were to trip or simply knock the wall with the stake and make some noise? What if instead of going straight away to the attic as he counted on, she went to his room for a last snide remark and saw him out of bed.

What if...

What if...

Curt ignored these nagging questions and concentrated on what was. Miss Feanor, who lived her life with more routine than a ticking watch was moving right on schedule. Good. The house seemed aware of him being out of bed, he could feel it in the air and in the floorboards through his white socks. Not good, but expected. This was only the second day of the fifth week, as Curt reckoned the days, and the creature wasn't even moving yet. Better than average.

All in all, he felt good as he made it to Amber's room without alerting Miss Feanor. Of course, this was the very simplest part of his plan and if he'd been caught just then, he would've added a great deal of shame to the pain of his punishment. But he had learned to make his plans in stages and enjoyed the small feeling of triumph that accomplishing each afforded him.

Now he'd wait eight seconds.

That was how long it would take Miss Feanor to get to the attic door. In the interim, he glanced back at Amber. She looked tiny under her covers. It was a shock to see her so small and vulnerable. And like a child afraid of the dark, she quivered and shook in silence. Oddly, considering what he was about to do, he felt sorry for her, empathizing with her fear. He wanted to go to her and tell her that everything would work out and that she wouldn't have to be afraid any longer. But he couldn't spare the seconds nor could he risk the possibility of noise.

Feeling hard hearted, he turned away and peeked from her slightly opened door. Miss Feanor came into view just then and he cast aside all thoughts of Amber and waited in a light bath of perspiration, ready to dart forward. The attic door came open with the tiniest sound of metal, something Curt hadn't expected. She had a key. This he hadn't realized before. He had assumed that like the rest of the doors in the place, the house had just let her in and out of the attic as it pleased.

It was interesting, yet not worth dwelling over, especially not just then. Curt had literally one second to get from Amber's room to the attic door before it closed. As soon as Miss Feanor stepped through the doorway and disappeared up the stairs, Curt darted out. Moving as quickly and silently as he could, he pushed off hard with his left leg, gliding forward across the hall, his right arm held outstretched.

With the knob a bare inch from the frame, he caught it and stopped the door from closing all the way. It was a simple easy move of about eight feet, all the same his breath gusted in and out as if he had run a mile and his perspiration had become a glaze of fear-induced sweat that had his face glistening. With the sleeve of his left hand, Curt swiped at his eyes and counted silently to ten.

In a perfect world he would've waited longer, letting Miss Feanor get comfortable but the creature would be up and about soon and he figured he'd have a minute at the most to accomplish his grizzly tasks. When the thief got to ten, he pulled back on the knob and looked up into the attic. Compared to the shadow struck hall it seemed bright up there, almost cheery and stepping in, he let the door close behind him. Now he shouldn't have let anything delay him, but a sight just to his right made him pause.

The baseball bat that Miss Feanor had used against him sat leaning against the wall. Laying the stake aside, he took up the bat, liking the feel of it, the heft. He felt a heavy sense of revenge go through him as he held it and made no effort to quell the cruel feeling.

There was a sound from above him, somewhere in the attic. It was a voice that at first he didn't recognize. It got him moving up the stairs, like a cat, attuned to everything about him, ready to run or pounce without the slightest hesitation. Curt, in his ultimate thief mode slunk around the stacks of ancient rubbish, moving stealthily, until he hid just feet from the circle of light.

From there he could see Miss Feanor moving about the two people lying in their beds. She spoke softly to them, practically crooning to them in a motherly way, but they remained as he had seen them before, unmoving and maybe not truly alive. It sickened Curt to see her acting this way toward the pair, while she had been perfectly content to starve him and have him tortured.

It burned him up inside. And the feeling made it easier for him to do what he came for. When next she turned away from him, he gauged it was time to pounce and he stepped boldly forward. Bringing the bat back, he let it fly in a snapping arc aimed at the back of her head.

2

Even in his extreme anger, Curt hadn't been able to commit murder. At the last moment, he pulled his swing so that he only sent Miss Feanor sprawling to the floor, dazed.

One of her eyes came open, blinked and then rolled about unfocused before it closed again. Curt was reassured by this; still when he knelt to feel the floor, he did so purposely out of reach of the woman. The house was aware and focused on the attic, but wasn't greatly angered yet. It seemed stuck midway between confused and curious. The creature he could barely feel at all, it seemed still to drowse far away.

He took this as a good sign and straitening up he moved around Miss Feanor—in a wide arc heading for the nearest bed, the one that held the young man. This unknown person would have to die first.

The man with the thin brown hair looked at peace lying there. Curt brought the bat up and grimaced as if he were the one in pain. The bat went further back. Further. A pause. Further back.

And Curt slumped his shoulders.

He kept picturing the man's head exploding under the impact of the bat. It left him weak and gagging, forcing him to pull down once again on his pajama top. It kept sliding back up for some reason, choking him. A noise behind him caused him to jump around quickly. It was Miss Feanor groaning slightly. He would have to kill the man quickly, either that or brain Miss Feanor again. That thought had him pulling on his collar once more, sickened that he was being forced to do any of this.

But it also gave him an idea.

In a second, he pulled off the first of his three pajama tops, spun it quickly as if he was in a locker room and planned to snap somebody's bottom with it, and turned back to the man. This would be far less messy.

"I'm sorry," Curt whispered and then leaning over the sleeping figure, he wrapped the spun top around the man's neck and after another moment's hesitation, he yanked it down tight.

The man's very white face went from pink to red in seconds. After half a minute it was a deep magenta and Curt began to wonder how long he would have to keep it up. He didn't think he could for very much longer, both for physical and mental reasons. His straining arms were already getting tired and his soul ached with what he was doing. But still he held on.

"Uhhn." Another soft groan from Miss Feanor. She now had both eyes open. However, they were unfocused and her face was slack without understanding of where she was. There was still time for murder.

Turning back to the man, Curt honestly couldn't tell if he was alive or dead. For a few more seconds he strained with all his might and then he bent his head and listened at the man's chest. There was nothing, no sounds at all. With a distressingly empty feeling inside, Curt released the grip on the shirt and watched as the man's head went limp over. With only a single look back at Miss Feanor, he then dashed to the girl.

With his arms already tired he worried that he wouldn't be able to hold and pull the ends of the shirt for long enough to kill her; he was right. Curt barely had the make shift noose on her for thirty seconds before he had to stop, feeling weak and feeble.

"Wha...?" Miss Feanor mumbled.

Curt went back to the noose. Wrapping it around the girl once again, he pulled, but saw that if he were to twist it, the noose would stay very tight against the girl's throat. When he did this, it was with sadness—he could now kill her one handed.

Already he was a more efficient killer.

The thought bothered him greatly, making it so he could barely look at the girl as he killed her.

"Huh?" Miss Feanor slowly crawled up the side of the man's bed, using it to support her weight. She looked very confused and at first didn't see Curt and didn't seem to notice anything unusual. Finally, her eyes drifted over towards him and went wide in shock.

Curt had frozen in place, still holding the strangling noose, and now he reached over with his free hand and plucked up the bat. Miss Feanor looked at it, perplexed, but for only a moment and then she ran to the girl.

"My baby!"

Her what? Curt's mind screamed the question and it echoed throughout his empty core, the place where his soul had once resided. His soul felt to have shriveled to nothing in the last few minutes. Curt backed away from the dead girl, brandishing the bat. Miss Feanor ignored both the bat and him, having only eyes for the girl, her daughter. She yanked away the pajama top and looked into the girl's empty eyes; immediately the older lady began crying.

"Why? Why? Why would you do this?" Miss Feanor wailed at him. Her grief was heavy and loud—out of habit, Curt knelt and touched the floor. The house was definitely more aware than it had been and beginning to become angry too.

"That can't be right," he muttered to himself. There should have been no feeling left in the house whatsoever. An unexpected pain erupted in his stomach and then he felt his throat tighten up so that he couldn't swallow. It dawned on him that he might've killed two innocent people.

"Doesn't she control the house?" he asked Miss Feanor, who sat rocking back and forth crooning to the girl, dripping tears upon her face.

"No! No, Susan is too sweet...she's so sweet, she's so, so sweet."

"And what about him? Does he have anything to do with the monster?" Curt pointed to the man, instinctively already knowing the answers. Miss Feanor looked over, horrified at seeing the odd unnatural tilt to the man's neck.

"Oh...uhh-uh." She made sounds of deepest grief and moaned in anguish, tears falling in an amazing torrent from her chin.

Now it felt to Curt that all of his tendons abruptly let go of his bones and he collapsed onto the floor. His guilt became over powering and he began to cry along with Miss Feanor. He wasn't just a killer now, he was a murderer of innocents, and it was a few minutes before he was able to hitch out an apology to the mother of the people he had murdered.

"I'm sorry...I really am. I didn't know. I thought that they were controlling the house." The sound of his voice appeared to bring her around to their surroundings: the dreadful house.

She wiped away tears and it seemed as well that she wiped away the will to live. She looked blank and dead herself. "No...it's not them."

"Then who is it...or what is it?"

"Something terrible. Something that has held my babies prisoner for so long, for so many years, but I guess I don't have to worry about them now." She gave him a haunted smile that set him on edge. It held a look that suggested she had nothing left to live for and nothing left to fear. "Come on."

Kissing her children once on their pale cheeks, she left them, going to the very back of the attic where she kept her meager belongings. Curt followed after and he did so warily, despite the feeling in his heart that told him she was no longer a threat to him.

Going to the filing cabinet, she rummaged around in it for a moment and then pulled from one of the neat little files a newspaper clipping. Beside the headline, was a picture of a large man and other than having shadowed dark eyes, he seemed completely normal. Curt looked at the picture for a while before turning to the article.

Havacheck's Death Ruled Homicide

Allegheny County authorities have reversed their original ruling in the poisoning death of Darren Havacheck. It had been thought to be a classic murder-suicide, but new evidence points rather to murder-murder.

After brutally killing his wife, Sonja Havacheck, sixty-eight, by biting her to death, Havacheck succumbed to the poison Tetra-phenol-HC, a highly toxic compound with uses only in petroleum distillation. The poison was originally found on his hands and this led to the first report of suicide. Later, however the coroner is reported to have found the poison "smeared" on the neck and arms of Mrs. Havacheck. It appears that she knew she was going to be bitten the night of her murder and due to faded bruising on her body, it has been suspected that she had been bitten on numerous occasions prior to this. It is unclear whether these bruises were indicative of abuse since unnamed authorities have speculated that the bites might have been sexual in nature.

Mr. Havacheck who had been under an investigation for the disappearance of a seven year old in his care...

Before he had a chance to finish, he was a slow reader after all, Miss Feanor snatched away the clipping and handed him another.

'Cemetery' Found in Havacheck Basement

Police authorities, early Tuesday morning, announced that the bodies of eight children, ranging from six to seventeen, have been unearthed in a hidden crawl space beneath the home of Darren Havacheck. Alerted to the presence of the bodies by what one officer, who asked to remain anonymous, called, 'The atrocious odor of decomposition.' Detectives have been working around the clock to discover who exactly the children were.

The wet soil found beneath the home has made identification difficult and authorities have been using dental impressions in their attempt. A spokesman is asking that anyone with knowledge of...

Again, without warning, Miss Feanor took the clipping from him. She stared at it for a moment and then crumpled it up, dropping it to the floor.

"You wanted to know," she said listlessly, her eyes staring down at the paper.

Curt felt adrift in confusion. "The man was a killer? How did he come to haunt this place?"

She shrugged.

"What about the lady...Mrs. Havacheck. Why is she here? She didn't do anything wrong, except for maybe kill that guy."

This question finally burned through her apathy and Miss Feanor stared at him as if he were the stupidest thing. "Nothing wrong? She was worse than that sick pervert. All she cared about was this house and living in style. He was rich and kept her in this fine home and gave her everything she wanted. And when she found out what he was up to...did she go to the police? Noooo! She would've lost her pretty home and all her fancy crap and more importantly, her status."

Curt began to get frightfully worried, he'd been out of bed far longer than he had thought he would be and Miss Feanor was becoming very loud. And now, he felt the air building slowly up around them and he made to shush the lady, but she was compelled to rant and wouldn't quiet down.

"No, Mrs. Havacheck was way worse. She was the one who would go and find the children. She just seemed to have a knack at luring them in; despite the fact that she hated them...you can feel it right?" Curt was about to answer, but it was a rhetorical question and Miss Feanor went right on talking. "She hated everything about children. The way they made messes, and broke things. And how much noise they made and how much they ate and how they smelled. The only thing she liked about them was their screams. Can you believe that?"

Curt nodded and stepped back a little. The air was becoming brittle with the energy in it. Miss Feanor seemed to notice as well.

"I guess you won't have to worry about punishments tonight, Curt," she said this with a sad smile. "Tomorrow yes, but not tonight." She walked behind her desk as she spoke and began to yank on something.

"Why not? Didn't you do something to my area of responsibility?"

"I did, but that bastard Havacheck will be coming for me soon...the house will make sure of it," she sighed when she said this and looked deathly tired. It was an odd feeling that came over him then. He felt sad for her. The woman who had imprisoned him and who had sought to have him tortured. It was strange, yet Curt's soul rebelled at having caused her so much pain.

"I thought he only attacked children," Curt said to her.

"No...it only gets off on attacking children, but that doesn't mean it won't attack someone else. Remember that stupid caseworker? You know how many times I tried to put her off, to keep her from coming over. The new ones are the worst. They think..." she paused as she pulled an extension cord free of its socket.

"They think they can change the world, but give them six months and they'll find any excuse not to leave their tiny little offices. You know that the average social worker barely last three years doing what they do? The burnout rate is ridiculous." She sighed again and looked up at one of the rafters, she then went to the desk and gave it a shove.

The noise was very loud and alarmed by it, Curt hurried to the other side of the desk to help move it. She smiled and said, "Thanks. When Havacheck comes, you'll want to be somewhere else."

Curt wanted to be somewhere else even then, but he had more questions. "What is Havacheck? Is he a ghost?"

"I don't know. I don't know what either of them are really. I was twenty-six when I bought this house. I thought I was getting the best deal of my life and suddenly, I was trapped..." All emotion appeared to drain from her face. "My husband had left me with two kids and no job. I started doing foster-care, but then there was a fire and I had nothing. I needed a furnished house and this place came on the market. No one would take it, because of what had happened here, but I was desperate. I didn't even need to put any money down; all I had to do was take over making payments. What a deal I was getting. What a fucking deal! That first night the monster came. It was just me and four kids. I heard him sneaking around and I went to call the police, but the line went dead. Just like that." She snapped her fingers and perhaps out of habit, they barely made a sound.

"I tried to get out, only I couldn't, you know?" At this, she looked for Curt to agree and he nodded his head, knowing exactly what she meant. "I tried and tried, but everything was locked and the windows wouldn't budge. I took the children and hid up here. The next morning we snuck downstairs and the house had been cleaned. All the little messes were picked up and everything looked just like it had when we moved in. It was so bizarre. We tried to get out again, but the house seemed to wake up and...you know how it is. You can feel it in the air, in the wood. I didn't know what to do so we went and hid again in the attic.

"That night the monster came again, but this time it came all the way up here. And so we hid in the junk, but one of the foster kids began to cry and the monster was on her just like that. I was so afraid. I didn't do anything. I just sat behind that desk and held my two babies. It was horrible. The little girl had been chewed on..."

Hearing the tale made his skin crawl and his injuries sting just a little more.

Miss Feanor went on, "The same thing happened the next night to the same little girl. By this time, I was crazy with fear. We had barely had anything to drink and no food what's so ever and I thought we would all starve and I was so afraid for my children. They were so good throughout the ordeal, but not the other two. The other two whined and cried all the time and I knew this was only making the house angrier. I told them to stay quiet but they wouldn't. At the time I thought it was all their fault and I became really angry that my babies were in such trouble because of them, so...so I went downstairs and..." She paused and swallowed hard. Her words had been growing louder as her story progressed, but the last sentence was a whisper as if she really didn't want Curt to hear what she had done.

"...And I went to the basement where I knew they were hiding, down in those wet pits. I begged them. I begged the Havachecks to spare my babies. I said they could have the other two, if only they would spare my babies. But it wasn't enough. They wanted more. And Curt, you have to believe me I was so desperate, I was so afraid and...and I told them I could get them more."

"You mean more children?" His mind felt as if had become unglued.

She nodded without looking him in the eyes. "What was I supposed to do? The Havachecks wouldn't just take the lives of my children. They would take their souls as well. You know this. Deep down, you know this and I knew it too. So I told them I would get more children. And I did. Mrs. Havacheck...or her ghost I guess laid down the rules, how everything had to be exactly perfect. How the children had to be quiet at all times...you know the rest."

Curt did. "But why were your children like this? Why did they just sleep up here all the time?" he asked.

"Because I tried to run away with them once. It was about a year after we moved in and I was going crazy. Really, really crazy. If you think it was easy for me to have done what I've done, then you're wrong. I couldn't stand what I had become, so I tried to run. They stopped me and Havacheck would've killed us all but I begged them again and so Mrs. Havacheck took their souls as hostage and somehow they were kept alive, but like this. And their souls...oh, now their souls are hers forever! My poor babies. And all this was for nothing...I wish..." She looked down and tears came again from her eyes. "I wish you had been my first foster child, Curt. I wish I hadn't wasted fourteen years watching my children wither away. I wish I hadn't become just as evil as those two bastards. I'm sorry about that...I really am. Do you believe me?"

He did, and he felt bad for her too, but he couldn't exactly forgive her. She'd been a large part of so much hurt and misery. "I believe you."

"I am sorry. Tell the others, ok? Tell them I'm sorry." He nodded again, and Miss Feanor, with a little grunt, climbed onto the desk and threw the cord over one of the rafters. "It's time you went back to your room; I can feel the monster moving about."

"You're going to kill yourself?" he asked incredulously. "Why don't we make a run for it? You have no reason to stay anymore."

Miss Feanor started to tie knots in the extension cord and soon had fashioned a noose. "The house knows what's happened...it won't let me leave now and I don't want to stay here causing more misery than I already have." She then began stacking books on the desk and when they were a foot high she stepped up on them, placing the cord about her neck.

"Please, wait! You have to tell me how to get out." Now Curt could feel the monster coming. It was charging up the stairs in a fury even as it had when it had attacked Darla the caseworker.

"There is no way out," she said simply and kicked away the books.

Chapter 25

The Punished Alone

1

Despite the heavy tread of the creature rushing in a savage anger toward the attic, Curt stood mesmerized by the spectacle of Miss Feanor hanging from the extension cord. He had never seen such a horrible sight in his life. She twitched and kicked in the most gruesome manner.

Finally, he heard the thunderous feet of the creature coming up the stairs of the attic. This got him moving. But he was essentially trapped. His one choice was to hide, however his delay had left him no time between thought and action. With his natural speed propelled by an unnatural fear, he took two quick strides and slid beneath a roll top desk a few feet away.

Now his greatest worry was that Miss Feanor would die too quickly, leaving him to face the creature and its inhuman desires alone in the attic. The thought made every pore on his body open up and sweat ran down him in sheets. Craning his neck, he saw the unfortunate Miss Feanor a second before the creature came rushing full upon her with its teeth already fully formed in its ghost like mouth.

Sadly, she lived longer than she had planned. The extension cord stretched beneath her weight and her toes were touched the top of the desk. It was a hideous sight when the creature came upon her and began to bite without mercy. She was still very much alive, fully aware of the shocking pain inflicted by the great teeth and she jerked about making a nasty gurgling sound deep in her throat. Hanging by the neck as she was, the sight of her flopping in spasms, reminded Curt of fish at the end of a line.

Stricken in horror, he sat huddled beneath the desk, captivated by the sadistic cruelty in front of him until he felt his dinner rising up in his throat. It broke the spell and he crawled away, without looking back. As he moved on hands and knees, he could feel the terrible evil glee of the house emanating through the rough floorboards. He flew along faster.

Miss Feanor had been right. The woman, Mrs. Havacheck was worse. The spirit of the man, the creature, Mr. Havacheck was practically an animal in its lusts, he gloated on a horrifying perversion and got off on pain and fear, but not necessarily death. And what's more it would become satiated, where as the woman was never satisfied. She was evil. Hating and angry and bitter. In addition, it was clearly the dominating force in the house and it seemed to dictate or control the creature at least to some extent.

This all went through his mind as he crawled away, but he didn't crawl for long, the moment he felt he could, he got up and ran as if his life depended on it. His greatest fear was that the house would hold the attic door closed against him, but when he came sailing down the stairs, the knob turned easily.

Curt's relief was short lived, however. Above him, a great crash shook the bones of the house and a second later Miss Feanor's gurgle became a soul-searing scream. Feeling her pain running through him, he slid to his room and crawled beneath his covers, crying.

2

She wasn't just being killed, she was being punished, and the screams lasted a very long time.

Each sent a dagger of guilt lancing his heart and through it all, he wept like the child he was. For the other children, it was likely a mercy when it finally ended, but for Curt, the guilt had just begun. Alone in his bed he laid for hours replaying everything that led him up those stairs, seeing vividly with the benefit of hindsight how he had stupidly jumped to wrongful conclusions.

His cowardice was on full display as well. Curt had known all along that the evil things haunting the place resided in the basement, not the attic. Yet he had killed innocent people based on little more than wishful thinking; he had wanted it to be as simple as killing two invalids in their sleep. Pathetically, he'd fancied himself this great thief, but now he knew he was nothing more than a killer.

Eventually he dozed, but awoke frequently with Miss Feanor's screams echoing in his head. They were so sharp and real that he'd start up gasping, yet always the house was silent. With the coming of the morning, his guilt only increased. Now, he'd have to tell the others exactly what had happened and he dreaded the looks he'd get from them and the accusations they'd hurl his way.

He began with Amber.

When he judged the sun high enough, he slipped out of bed and found the house amazingly still. Out of habit he went to one knee, feeling the spirits residing in the very molecules of the wood. The creature was well satisfied with the misery it had caused, and it seemed to slumber. The house, that mockery of a feminine spirit was alert, but waiting as if unsure how things would proceed.

Curt wished he knew as well.

His steps were light and agile, so smooth that he slipped into Amber's room barely disturbing the air around him. As all the children in the house were, she was an extremely light sleeper and his very presence woke her. Beneath the blanket, he saw her stiffen and he gave her a little shake. She came out from under the covers very slowly, afraid, 'What happened?' she mouthed the words.

"I-made-a-mistake," he told her the story, whispering or mouthing it one word at a time, sniffing back tears as he did. By the end, she cried as well, but her tears were those of a frightened little girl.

'What are we going to do?' she gestured the question; remarkably the movements were able to convey her great fear. Curt could only shrug, unwilling to come out and state the reality of their situation; the day before, their future looked bleak, filled with impending punishments and horrible stress, but now their future was downright terrifying.

Miss Feanor's last words had been correct. The house was sentient and had an intellect that was smart enough to know it couldn't let any of them leave. Curt could envision them slowly starving to death while punishments came with greater and greater frequency. The biting would go from leaving bruises to leaving jagged wounds and then to death.

With these thoughts weighing him down, he went to Paul's room and tapped at his blanket under which he hid, until the boy's twitching paranoid face emerged. There was a caution to him that told Curt that Paul knew something very wrong had occurred last night.

'Come with me. I talk to everyone.' Curt's gestures were still pathetic, like those of a three year old. In truth he didn't care, they weren't likely to get much better in the time he had left in the house. Paul glanced sharply to the side and then shook his head 'no', he then shook it even harder. He was having an unheard conversation with an unseen person. Curt waited. Finally, Paul nodded and Curt pointed him toward Amber's room where the blonde girl waited.

Giving in to the coward within him, he put off going to Matt's room and instead went to the mouse's. Due to her advanced state of mental illness, he felt that it was a waste of time including her in his confession, but he didn't know how the others would feel about her not being there.

The old sense of guilt at the pain he'd caused the mouse came back to him when he stepped into her room. It layered thickly on the fresh guilt in his soul and for a moment he wanted to give up and go hide in his bed, letting the others figure out what happened as best as they could. But he mastered that childish feeling, perhaps because of the visual in his mind of hiding in his bed. He'd done that too much already.

If the mouse were already awake, it wasn't obvious since she could be very still at times.

"Ahem," he cleared his throat softly, he didn't want to touch her. Her insanity repulsed him. When she didn't budge a muscle, Curt gave her a squeamish little poke, however the girl only laid there. After a few seconds, he pulled down her covers. He wished he hadn't. She was awake and her eyes spun in lunacy as if it was a fifth or sixth day rather than a first.

"Why? Why? Why would you do this?" The mouse whispered the words, barely breathing them out. Again, a normal fifth day sign. She'd heard the commotion and the screams clearly, but what wasn't clear was why she would assume it was Curt that had done anything wrong. Could she sense his guilt?

He felt himself freaking out, and he had to get out of the room. The mouse however was surprisingly fast and hopped up quick, grabbing him by one of his pajama tops. She pulled him in close.

"No! No, Susan is too sweet...she's so sweet," the mouse whispered to him. Curt remembered the words that Miss Feanor had used. They pained him greatly to hear them again and in his anguish, he shoved the mouse roughly away. She fell back on her bed, her eyes turning circles and her lips moving non-stop.

He fled from the room.

Instead of going to Matt's, he ran to the bathroom and tried to hold back the tears that were on the verge of over-powering him. Looking into the mirror helped, he hated the boy he saw there. That boy was a killer. He was ugly and looked beaten. The scabs on his face were nasty and raw, and the rainbow of bruises made him a little queasy but he felt that he deserved each one.

Eventually, his tears dried up and when at last he had control of himself, he went to Matt's room and found the boy, whom he hated even more than himself, was already awake and out of his bed. He gave Curt a piercing look, not an angry one as expected. His eyes were cold, calculating and Curt's insides squirmed beneath them. Not knowing what to say and not wanting to argue or fight, Curt simply jerked his head back down the hall and then left. Matt would come.

3

"I say we tie him up and throw him into the basement," Paul said with deadly intensity, twenty minutes later. Curt had slowly, using whispers and pantomime, explained what had happened the previous night.

It wasn't quite the reaction Curt was hoping for. Especially from Paul. Except it wasn't really Paul, the boy who had twice saved him. It was one of his personalities, every one of which was more awful than the last.

An uncomfortable silence settled on the five of them until the mouse broke it. "Why? Why? Why would you do this?" she intoned. Her reminders of Miss Feanor's words weren't exactly helping Curt's explanation of what had happened, they seemed designed to heap upon his soul more guilt. The eyes of the children surrounding him glittered with increased anger every time she whispered.

"That's enough, Beth," Matt said in a kind voice. It sounded weird coming from him, but it shut the mouse up quick. She had been driving Curt so crazy with her whisperings that he actually wanted to thank the older boy just then.

"But what are going to do?" Amber said leaning in close. It was the only thing that she had added to the near silent conversation, and she had added it three times already. Each time everyone had simply looked at one another cluelessly.

This time though, Matt had an answer. "We don't *do* anything. We carry on just like we always have. The house expects us to clean and behave just like before and that's what we're going to do."

Curt wanted to protest this bit of lunacy, only he was afraid of the older boy and instead glanced around to see who else would challenge the boy's nonsense answer. No one said a word. He hadn't expected anything from the mouse, but Amber only looked at her hands and Paul was staring into the closet.

"No...that won't work," Curt murmured, summoning a scrap of courage.

'Oh really? Then what's your great plan?' Matt glared across Amber's bed at him.

'We go escape. Right now...' Curt's sign language was cut off by Matt.

"Are you insane? That's how you got us into this mess in the first..." he paused looking around. They could all feel it in the air and they each sat back and waited and waited and waited. The house took a long time to calm and Curt began to wonder if it had heard and understood the word escape.

When it felt safe to communicate, Matt leaned in to the little group and gestured, 'No escape, that's final.'

'You aren't in charge,' Amber motioned to Matt. 'I want to know his plan.'

Curt was thankful for her confidence in him, but he had decided already that it was best for him to keep mum about his intentions. For one, the plan he'd been considering would never work without everyone's complete participation, and that included Matt. Without him, it would be a waste of time and certainly would only end in horrible punishments, if not death. It had to be all of them going in full force or nothing.

The second reason he wished to remain silent was that the plan was immoral, full of black sin. It crossed the line well into evil and after the previous night's wickedness, Curt was ashamed that it came to him at all and that he actually entertained the idea. Paul hadn't been the first to envision tying someone up and throwing them into the basement. For Curt's plan to work, that horrible deed would have to be done and he had chosen the poor mouse as his offering to the creature. She was just plain useless and the others would be needed.

He hated himself just for thinking it.

Curt's unspoken plan centered on using the ornate love seat from the living room as a ram. It was heavy and would take the three boys and maybe Amber to lift it and slam it repeatedly against one of the plexiglass windows. He figured it would take at most three minutes to break down the window, but without something occupying the creature, they'd be lucky to have thirty seconds. That was where the mouse came in. She'd have to go into the basement to buy the time needed.

It was a sound plan—a loathsome criminal plan, for sure, but one that he felt in the end would result in less pain, and death for everyone, the mouse included. There was no denying that like everyone else she would be dead soon, regardless if they carried through with his plan or not.

A few days before, in his search for the missing paperclips, Curt had seen the kitchen cabinet where the food was kept. There had been lots of rice, but only maybe seven or eight tins of spam and an even smaller stack of carrots. Even if they made that last, they were looking at three weeks before their bodies would start to disintegrate from lack of protein.

And this didn't take into account their body's need for nourishment after one of the terrible punishments. Curt suspected that without Miss Feanor there, the punishments would begin to increase in frequency and if that happened, then that three weeks would likely drop to two.

All of this was logical and should've been within the limits of the discussion, however, Curt's shrewd reasoning told him to stay silent. Fear held sway over common sense in that room and he could tell Matt was going to use that fear to sink any plan that wasn't his own. Unfortunately, he didn't have one.

Curt sat unspeaking for a time, pondering their situation and considering ways to get his plan into action. Matt took his hesitation as a sign that Curt didn't have a plan at all. The older boy sighed.

'Well?' The mouthed word was drawn out, annoyingly and Matt's question came with a self-satisfied look. Curt shrugged and looked glum, not at all faking the emotion. With that, Matt declared in a whisper, "Escape is out of the question, and anyways I think we'll be rescued soon."

Curt's mind boggled at the very unlikely concept of rescue and he was sure his face must have registered just that. If it did, Matt didn't seem to notice and went on whispering, "Until then, we go about our day like nothing happened. Except for you Curt. From now on, you'll do my chores *and* yours, and..."

Amber interrupted gesturing, 'That's not fair.'

"I'm in charge and I'll tell you what's fair and what's not." Matt stood up, his face becoming dark, he looked very tall, and Amber shrunk back, wilting before him. "I'll do Miss Feanor's chores...he'll do mine. And another thing. I'm getting tired of you sticking up for your *old* boyfriend and if I get any more back talk from you, Amber, I'm going to break your legs." The calm way he said it made them all realize that he was deadly serious.

Chapter 26

The Thief Alone

1

Breakfast that morning, the first day of "week" six, was as always oatmeal. However, it was ineptly prepared by Matt, being so thick that actual chewing was required before any attempt at swallowing could be made. At one point early on, Amber spent nearly thirty seconds choking on a large glump of it, turning a frightful shade of red before she finally managed to swallow it. In addition to the thickness of the oatmeal, it set a record in blandness and Curt, who would've rather been chewing on toilet paper again, thought it likely that Matt had forgot to add the salt.

Curt wasn't about to mention this. The older boy reveled in his new power as head of the household and had already hit him twice, once for being slow to get to the table and once simply because he could.

All around it was a terrible meal. Though Matt had taken on the roll that Miss Feanor had played in the house, he hadn't sat in her chair at the table or even removed it. It sat empty and each of them worked very hard not to look its way, going to exaggerated lengths to pass their eyes well above it if their heads happened to swivel in its direction. Except of course the mouse who seemed unable to mentally process the loss of Miss Feanor. Her eyes spun in the direction of the empty chair and her lips whispered half-heard words to it.

"Why? Why? Why would you do that?" she said with very painful repetition.

It was grating and not just to Curt, whose guilt could not be any heavier within his chest. The others were bothered as well and looked at her with growing concern while they edged further and further away over the course of the meal. The mouse didn't seem to notice. She went right on whispering despite the escalating anxiety in the air.

There was a great deal of tension in the house. Its harsh mood had never fully calmed after the meeting in Amber's room and an aura of uncertainty and dangerous unpredictability seemed to follow them about. That capriciousness became apparent just as Curt's spoon scraped the bottom of his bowl.

A movement away from the table caught all of their attention at once. The mudroom door swung easily and silently open, and there immediately beyond it, the basement door stood open as well. From his side of the table, Curt could see partially into the basement. It was utterly devoid of light and the blackness seemed thick and tangible.

Something moved within it.

The children bolted as one. Silent screams spread across their faces as they raced out of the kitchen and down the long hall. In his panic, Curt easily outdistanced the others and gained the stairs quickly. He tore up them blindly, allowing his body to worry where to place his feet to avoid the worst of the creaks and groans in the wood and it was only when he spied the door to his bedroom and knew the false promise of security that his bed afforded was only just there, that he was able to think at all.

Amber!

He stopped abruptly on the main stair, dancing to the side to let Paul zoom by. Amber was still coming up the hall. She was moving slower than the rest mainly because her head was cranked all the way around so that she was looking backwards and running into things as she moved.

Curt wanted to scream at her to just run and not look back, but of course, he couldn't. Finally getting to the stairs, the first thing she did was to trip on the initial step, falling on her hands; still she wouldn't watch where she was going. She scrambled to her feet and stumbled up the stairs like a drunk, intoxicated with the terror of being left behind.

She seemed to be moving in slow motion and his heart quaked in fear. He very nearly left her, and he would have too, but when his hands gripped the railings he could tell something wasn't right. When the mouse ran by next, he let go of one of the railings and hugged the wall to let her pass and now he could sense the same feeling beneath his cheek and hand.

The mood of the house hadn't changed. It felt the same as it had when they were eating—nasty and evil, angry as well, but not in proportions that suggested the house was angry enough to send out the creature. Not only that, he could discern the thing, deep in the tombs it had dug for itself and its victims beneath the house. It lay unmoving.

But his mind had no time to come to terms with this, because in a blink Amber was upon him clawing past him like a drowning girl fighting for the surface. In her frenzy, she fell again and then once again a second later. Battling his own mixed emotions, chief of which was the great panic in his chest, he forced himself not to run and instead stooped to help her up. Grabbing her around her thin midsection, he hauled her bodily up and once steady on her feet, they raced hand in hand for the top of the stairs. There he propelled her vigorously towards her room, pausing only long enough to look back down the stairs.

They were blessedly empty.

He didn't wait to see if anything was going to come along and stepped lightly into his room and slipped under his covers. There he went completely still while his ears strained for the slightest sound of the telltale Crreik, that would mark the coming of the creature—yet no sound came. He waited, but for what exactly he wasn't sure. As far as he knew there had been no reason for the creature to come up, or for the basement door to open on its own either.

It made no sense. He tried to puzzle this out, but the sheets were reassuringly soft; the warmth and the dark familiar, and weary as he was after the terrible night, he was soon asleep.

2

Later he came awake, feeling disoriented, wondering what time it was and what, if anything had happened. The warmth and smoothness of the sheets had disappeared, they were now damp with sweat, and the stale air beneath them suddenly became suffocating. He had to get up, and so Curt, very slowly reached out a cautious hand and felt the floor. The house seemed content and the creature slumbered.

Curt pulled back the covers looking around; the sunlight slanting through his shutters had changed considerably and he judged the time to be late afternoon. Climbing out of bed, he walked with the light feet of a cat to the hall and paused again, this time to note the air in the house. It had never before seemed this still.

Feeling like the only visitor in a terrifically odd museum, or a boy walking through a moment frozen in time, he went from room to room and saw the other teenagers lying huddled beneath their covers.

They all seemed so small, even Matt.

They were like children. Curt lingered in Amber's room and stared the longest at her slim form. She was closest to him in size and it was easy to imagine himself under those covers, thinking he was safe by virtue of a single sheet and a thin blanket. The idea was ludicrous. He went cold picturing the creature coming into his room at night standing over him just as he stood over Amber.

There was no safety under those covers. The creature got off on the fear it caused and in his mind's eye, he pictured Mr. Havacheck as he looked in his photo, standing over his victims. The children would've been even smaller than they were and probably more terrified. How long did he keep them alive? How long was he content to watch them crying miserably, their little bodies shivering with fright beneath their covers, before his perverted need would drive him into a frenzy?

Feeling a little sick, Curt left the room, heading for the stairs. There was something down in the kitchen that had to be done.

The basement door had to be closed. It wasn't just that he wanted it closed; Curt needed it closed on a very basic level. Every second or so since he got out of bed, he pictured the utter blackness of the basement he'd seen through the mudroom door. The creature lurked down there in that blackness and Curt feared greatly that the thing would wander up at anytime, attracted by the light. With all his heart, he felt that the door had to be closed and soon.

He just wished that he didn't have to do it alone. As he ghosted from room to room, he wanted desperately to wake the other children and have them come with him to shut the basement door, but an insidious voice had stopped him.

"I say we tie him up and throw him into the basement," the voice, one that sounded like Paul's whispered in his mind. A mental picture came with the voice as well. One in which the other children, driven by anger over what he had done to Miss Feanor, attacked him in the mudroom just as he was about to shut the door and threw him into the basement. He had to fight his imagination to stop the vision from going further; he knew that if he didn't, there'd be no way he could go on.

And so, slowly and warily he made his way to the kitchen...alone, stopping frequently to gauge the mood of the house. His steps were measured, delicate even and the realization that he was now practically as quiet as Matt came to him.

The thought gave him a little boost of courage and it couldn't have come at a better time, because just then he stepped into the main hall and looking down its length saw the mudroom door still standing open. Though he had expected exactly this, the sight nevertheless jarred him.

For a long moment, he considered scampering up to his room to hide once again like the others. However, a quick touch of the wall reassured him that the house was not stirred in any great way and steeling himself, he pressed forward to the kitchen with a heavily beating heart.

Without Miss Feanor, sitting in her customary chair, the room seemed lonely. The cookbooks sat lined perfectly, but unread. The appliances gleamed, yet were essentially unused. Only the kitchen table appeared to have fulfilled its purpose. The plastic bowls with the hardened remains of oatmeal coating their insides lay exactly as they had left them, marking the places where each child sat. The chairs were scattered, pushed back from the table at odd angles, denoting the wild panic in which their occupants had fled the room hours before.

After a quick glance, Curt didn't give any of this a second look.

His attention fixed entirely on the mudroom door and the yawning black depths of the basement just beyond it. It became everything to him, holding him mesmerized. Nothing had ever seemed so impenetrably black and he wondered if the movement he had seen was all in his head.

He turned sideways sidling up to the door, ready to sprint away at the first sign of movement. His feet were like leaves in an autumn wind, skipping about, each barely touching the floor before it was up again. Lighter and lighter they seemed as he moved closer to the door. His feet wanted to run. They wanted to tear out of there. They knew only fear.

But Curt, his face screwed up as if in pain, forced his feet onward. As he passed the counter, he snatched up one of the cookbooks. It was the very one that he'd picked up on his first day in the house and as he held it, it fell open in his palm to the recipe for Goulash, just as it had before.

This registered on his mind only distantly; he was too focused on the black of the basement and absently he closed the book, hefting it in his hand. It would do.

A few steps later, he was in the doorway of the mudroom. Now he started to breathe heavier and faster. His body wanted to hyperventilate and it was a struggle to keep his knees from knocking together. The basement door stood open only four feet away and it should've been nothing to step over and shut it, but he could see fully the darkness coming from the basement.

Though he knew little of physics, Curt knew that the light from behind him should've been able to illuminate at least some of the basement, but three steps and a bit of the wall was all that he could see. The rest was only reeking blackness. He noticed the smell on the air just then. It streamed out of the basement and filled the mudroom with the stench of rotting flesh and the dank of long wet mildew. It was a horror to breathe and Curt choked on it. Gagging and coughing lightly, he caught another scent that at first he welcomed and clung onto. It was the rich smell of freshly turned earth.

But the odor brought with it a fully formed mental picture of a newly dug trench. He saw it clearly in his mind; deep in a rough-hewn tunnel beneath the basement, he pictured a shallow grave that fit him perfectly; it sat nestled amongst the low humps of older graves but just next to it were three recently filled ones.

As he stood there in the doorway to the mudroom, Curt's imagination brought forth horrible details that could never have been seen in the thick blackness beneath the basement; a swath of long thin silky brown hair flowing from under the dirt; part of a pale white face, its mouth wide open but filled with wet brown earth; and from the grave closest to his, a hand and part of an arm were partially exposed. The hand twitched suddenly, coming alive, slowly clawing at the dirt, unearthing a hideous face. It was Miss Feanor.

A gasp escaped his throat just then and Curt nearly ran from the room, but his logical mind asserted itself. Miss Feanor wasn't in the basement, he told himself, she was in the attic with her children...dead. This thought made him look up to the ceiling and for a few moments guilt overrode his terror.

The guilt allowed him to cast aside the horrible images filling his mind and he stooped and placed the cookbook in the doorway, hoping it would be enough to stop the door from shutting if the house looked to trap him in the mudroom. Taking a deep breath, he took two slow cautious steps and grabbed the doorknob of the basement door and made to close it.

But abruptly the air coming from the cellar changed, turning cold and damp, like sea air in a winter fog; it stopped his hand and it fell to his side useless, as if his muscles were no longer his to control. With wide eyes, he peered into the deeper darkness below him. Almost it seemed a figure began to take shape in the pitch and though his mind screamed for him to slam the door and run, he stood as if shackled to the floor, hypnotized by what he was seeing. Seconds clicked by and the form became more substantial, more clearly feminine and the air more dreadfully foul.

The cold air stopped his breath, stiffened his joints, and held him in placed as the figure coalesced before him. It now formed eyes within a horrid ebony face. Terrible eyes that held accusations and anger and blazed with bitter hatred. He feared completely those eyes and if it were possible, he felt even more spellbound than before and thus it was a shock to see in his lower periphery, his own trembling hand come up from his side. It reached out on its own volition and simply shut the door in Curt's now startled face. The hand then fell back limply to his side.

For a moment, he did nothing but stare uncomprehendingly at the door, feeling his warm sweat compete with the cold mist that covered his body. Eventually he backed away from the basement door, slowly, cautiously as if sudden movement would cause it to fly open with a wall-rattling bang. His eyes never wavered from the door, even as he stooped to retrieve the cookbook.

Only when the mudroom door shut with a tiny "Click" did Curt relax in any way, though in truth he didn't so much relax as he collapsed without strength into the nearest chair. There his entire body shook with pent up fright and unused adrenaline, even his breath came in sharp panting waves, shooting out from between his chattering teeth. He knew that it would be smart to go up to bed and hide there, but he felt too weak and his legs wobbled alarmingly on his first attempt to stand.

Sitting back fatigued, he began to understand that it really wouldn't make much difference whether he laid in bed or sat at the table. He lived solely at the whim of the house. It could call the creature at any moment it wished, and no amount of pretending it was his bed that made any sort of difference would help him. If the house wished him dead, then he'd die, and die horribly.

Chapter 27

Matt in Charge

1

Depression settled over Curt and it mixed with his grief and his guilt and his exhaustion. It became so bad, that his head lolled at the table and he nearly fell into a stuporous sleep, but with a huge effort of will, the boy rallied his remaining strength and set to work.

That the house could kill him at any time didn't mean there weren't still odds to play and angles to shoot for. Curt decided if he were to die, he wouldn't be the first of the children to, and with that in mind, he began to clean his areas of responsibility. He quickly saw how Miss Feanor had sought to sabotage him the night before. All of the stupid girlish nick-knacks that he was forced to dust on a daily basis were piled in a jumble on the floor of the powder room.

Seeing them there made the guilt that he carried around within him lighter and as he worked, dragging his weary and aching limbs through the monotonous labor, he thought about Miss Feanor. Though he felt bad for the terrible predicament that she faced, he decided grimly that she got what she deserved. There'd been no reason to turn the creature loose on him. None whatsoever. And worse than that, she had sentenced Amber, Paul, Matt, and some girl named Beth, whom he felt as if he had never really met, to death.

That thought sent a flame of anger burning in him and for a while, it lent him energy. Curt fed on the emotion and used it to get through his chores, though he would've been the first to describe his work as mediocre. Still it was better than the other children's areas except for maybe Amber's which he worked on next.

Lastly, with great caution, Curt went back to the kitchen and cleaned up the bowls as best as he could. Even Matt's. He stared at the older boy's dirty bowl for the longest time and the greatest part of him wanted to leave it untouched. But in the end, he felt it too hypocritical of him to leave it as the only bowl left out.

When he was done, Curt saw the light fading from the sky and feeling heavy with exhaustion, he dragged his tired feet to his lonely bed. In truth, he felt anxious to be with someone, Amber in particular, yet just then, he would have settled even for the mouse. But with night coming Curt was fearful of being out of bed at the wrong time. And it was no longer just the creature he feared; he was frightened of the house itself in a manner he hadn't before.

The black apparition in the cellar had proved Miss Feanor correct; it was far worse than the creature in a way that was difficult for Curt with his limited vocabulary and youth to comprehend. The creature's desires though a horrible perversion was at least a perversion of a human mental illness. The black figure on the other hand had simply been beyond understanding, except that Curt knew it to be wholly unnatural and utterly evil.

The thought of the evil spirit of Mrs. Havacheck had Curt lying under his covers dreading the coming night. With the last of the light slipping from the sky, he put a hand out to check the feel of the house. Volatile was the word Curt would've used to describe the house, if he had known it. Instead, the best he came up with was unstable.

The house's emotions were precariously balanced and Curt worried that he had done something terribly wrong by having the temerity to shut the basement door. Almost immediately upon pulling his hand back under the covers, he heard the first movement downstairs. The creature in its unbridled eagerness had come stalking out of the basement earlier than it ever had before.

It was loud as well. Not only were the CRREIKS on the stairs almost exaggerated, it swaggered carelessly about the house, knocking into the walls and bumping the furniture. These weren't accidents. It wanted its presence known; it wanted the children to tremble under their blankets.

Three times, it went slowly through the bedrooms and each time it became louder and Curt could almost feel its horrible desire building. On the third, he wept silently in the greatest fear, his tears poured from his face in twin rivers. The creature had become even bolder, going so far as to run its black scab covered hands over the very covers under which Curt shook and shivered out his overpowering fear.

He tried to remain perfectly still. But it was an impossibility. He remembered looking down at the other children just that afternoon and he knew that even the slightest movement would be seen. When the hand came down on him, his muscled jumped involuntarily and this seemed to excite the creature. Another hand touched him and this time he could feel the things long nails bite through the thin covers.

Curt held himself rigidly in a little ball and though he tried not to think about what was coming, he couldn't help it. He imagined that the face that would form out of the grey ghost like aura of the creature would be that of Miss Feanor and she'd bite out her revenge with endless cruelty. This image had him so petrified with fear that when the creature next touched him, gripping his arm with what felt like the talons of a monstrous eagle, Curt didn't budge. His muscles thrummed as if he was lying on an electric wire, but he didn't budge.

This might have been what saved him that night, for seconds later the creature left his room and didn't return.

A few minutes later, a scream rang out: "It wasn't me! I didn't do it! I didn't do it!"

2

Matt's first screams were terrifying in their fear, but Curt only wilted into his damp sheets, relieved at not having been chosen.

The night had already been very long and the day had been stressful, and despite the tortured cries of the older boy running along the polished wood and fineries of the beautiful house, Curt fell asleep.

It was a deep refreshing sleep. Of course, he had no idea of its length, but he felt good when hands shook him roughly awake. Despite his head feeling still half-asleep, he knew the hands were human and so he popped his head from the covers without fear. However, he recoiled at the sight before him and his woolly thinking disappeared in a blink.

It was Matt who awakened him and he looked grotesque.

The bite marks were deep and fresh. They covered his face, overlapping in spots and in many places the teeth had bitten through the skin. Black scabs lined with harsh red swelling, seeped a pink fluid. His turtleneck was already discolored at the collar. It seemed that the creature had concentrated on the boy's face. When Matt turned slightly, Curt saw that the tip of one of his ears had been bitten clean off. There were even bite marks in Matt's hairline and he could see where a chunk of his scalp had been torn away.

Matt didn't even look like himself and Curt only recognized him from his brown hair and the hate behind his eyes. The hate made Curt flinch back further in his bed.

'Eat,' Matt motioned sharply and turned away; he swayed slightly as he walked from the room.

The sight of those bite marks, momentarily checked Curt's hunger. He didn't like the look of them, and not simply because of how painful they appeared but rather the evil they heralded. Curt reached up and gingerly touched his own slowly healing wounds. It was true that he had been bitten on the face as well, however not only had he had been out of bed at the time, he'd also fought back, something he was sure Matt hadn't done.

And still he had only been bitten on the face in one place. It looked as though Matt had *only* been bitten on the face. This worried Curt greatly. The creature it seemed was no longer being held in check by the house and it was now doing as it pleased. In Curt's mind, it was clear that it was only a matter of time before the thing began to kill them off, biting them to death and burying them in the basement.

Shivers ran down his skin uncontrollably at the thought.

Thinking to gauge the feel of the house, he put his hand out to the wall, only to yank it away in an instant. The house churned with uncertainty and suspicion at his touch. It made him want to slip back under the covers, but he had spent so much time in bed in the last few days that he got up to eat.

Only Amber and Matt were at the table when he came down. They were eating slowly, watching the mudroom door with great trepidation. Amber gave him a tired red-eyed smile when he came in and then went back to eyeing the door, studiously avoiding looking at Matt. Curt followed her lead. His injuries were simply too disturbing to look at and Curt amazed himself as he began to feel sorry for him.

The mouse came down a minute later, her spinning eyes stared without reservation at the older boy's miserable face. Paul came down next, he too stared at Matt. He tried to eat one handed so that he could hold back the twitch from one of his eyes, but it was no use—he was becoming effectively blind from the spasms.

"Do you see that?" Paul whispered unexpectedly. His head was cocked to the side and he had pulled back on the skin of one of his eyes and was looking just behind Amber.

"I know. Shut up!" Paul hissed, he clamped a hand over his own mouth.

The words seemed to stimulate the mouse, who began whispering loudly, "Do you see that? Do you see that? Do you see that?"

Paul tried to hush her, but soon he fled the kitchen, whispering heated words of revenge upon all of them.

When he left, the mouse went on speaking very low between bites of food, but her words changed, "I didn't do it. It wasn't me."

Now it was Matt's turn to stare at the mouse, as he did he slowly went green beneath his injuries. He left as well. With just the three of them Curt worried that the mouse would begin repeating Miss Feanor's last words, but Amber cut in, stopping it before it could happen.

"Shhhhh," she hushed the crazy eyed mouse.

"Shhhhh," whispered the mouse right back. Relieved Curt smiled at the blonde girl and for the rest of the meal they took turns whispering this to the mouse. It turned out to be a nice breakfast after all. And a filling one.

Eventually the mouse finished eating and dutifully or perhaps habitually, she proffered her empty bowl towards Curt for inspection. He nodded feeling very much like an imposter and she scooted away. Now Curt finished also, but being famished as a wolf, he shared Paul's untouched bowl with Amber and then ate the remainder of Matt's breakfast as well. The food wasn't particularly good, though it was better than the day before, still he felt full for the first time since they ate McDonald's on the day the caseworker had died.

As he ate, he noticed Amber giving him a shrewd look and as soon as he finished she pulled him up, tugging him to his bedroom.

'What's your plan to escape?' She gestured the second they walked through his door. *Escape* came out run away, but he understood. He gave her a little shrug. Even with the knowledge of certain doom hanging over their heads, he was reluctant to mention his idea. It was such heinous scheme.

'No. You have a plan to escape. I know you. Now don't lie to me.' They sat on his bed with their knees touching. She eyed him very closely. When he started to shrug a second time, she pinched him hard on the leg.

'Ok, ok!' he motioned with a hint of anger clouding his face. Slowly, he told her his plan, mostly through gesturing but also with mouthed words and a whispered one here and there as needed. As he explained his corrupt idea, he pictured the black of the basement and the hideous form of Mrs. Havacheck within it. He imagined the great fear erupting in the mouse's eyes as the thing materialized in front of her. It made him queasy, the oatmeal shifting like a heavy weight in his stomach.

Amber's face had darkened as he went on and he felt sure that she would look upon him as if he were more of a murderer than he already was, but when he finished she grimaced and then nodded.

'It's a smart plan. It might work,' she gestured.

Curt shook his head and explained precisely why it wouldn't work, but she was quick to respond. 'Even after last night? I think that the monster will start to kill soon. Matt has to see that,' her hands said.

'Matt no hear plan from me,' Curt motioned.

'I could say that the plan was my idea,' she replied, her hands moving excitedly.

Frustrated with his poor sign language, Curt whispered, "Will he believe you?" Her face fell, which was answer enough.

'Maybe you could tell Paul and get him to understand that it's important that Matt thinks the plan comes from him and not you.' Her hands were such a blur that he had to have her repeat it a second time before he understood.

'Me?' he asked mouthing the word. 'What about you?'

Amber shook her head. 'No it has to be you. Paul thinks that I'm...stupid.'

'You no stupid...' he began to motion, but she cut across him by grabbing his hands.

'It has to be you. I'll show you the proper way we talk with our hands before you try.'

3

For the next few hours, she drilled into his head the correct movements to explain his plan. Curt agreed with the necessity of doing it right the first time since Paul could slip in and out of sanity very quickly.

The plan nearly ended before it began. As Curt slid up the blonde boy's bedroom door, he heard a very light whispering. Cautiously he poked his head through the slightly opened door.

"My name is Paul. I am Paul. My name is Paul. I am Paul."

The boy sat upon his bed rocking back and forth whispering the words to himself over and over again. Both of his thin hands held his face in a sad attempt to end the twitching, which alone would've driven Curt crazy. The spectacle stopped Curt in his tracks and for a long miserable time he could only stare at Paul, feeling his heart peeling away, exposing his soul to the boy's pain. It hurt to see this and tears of sympathy clouded Curt's eyes. Eventually he sniffed, somewhat loudly.

Paul reacted with a start and turned toward Curt with deep-rooted fear in the black pits of his eyes. The boy mumbled something that Curt didn't catch, then went back to rocking, casting suspicious glances in the direction of the doorway every few seconds.

"Paul?" Curt whispered gently.

"We're busy...go away," was hissed in his direction.

Curt almost did, too. His plan depended on Paul just as much as it did Matt, only it depended on a sane Paul. A lucid Paul, who was capable of listening to instruction and following orders without having to consult with all the voices in his head first.

But Curt felt the situation dire enough to make the attempt. Walking very near to the blonde boy, he whispered, "I have a plan to escape, and I need your help."

Now this caught Paul's attention, his eyes went wide despite the muscle spasms. Paul hopped out of bed and slid quietly to his door where upon he made a series of jerky movements, bobbing his head about to look up and down the hallway. It was an odd motion as if the boy looked not only for people lurking about, but perhaps mice as well. He then darted around his room, eyeing the baseboards and the floor of his closet, again looking for mice or so it seemed.

Finally, he moved back to Curt's side and holding his face with one hand, he asked, 'What is the plan? What is the plan?' with the other hand.

Curt began his series of gestures though he went far slower than he had practiced. Paul's twitch slowly became a horrendous thing to look upon and by the time Curt finished, it took the poor boy two hands to hold even a single eye open.

"Beth?" Paul asked sadly. "Really?"

Paul's words had been loud and Curt gave him a small yet gentle, "Shhhh." He nodded his head, sad as well. 'Yes, Beth. It has to be her. Do you understand why?'

Paul nodded slowly, but then spoke savagely in whisper, "We can't trust him. It's a trap. You know it's a trap. I know it's a trap...everyone knows."

Curt stepped back alarmed at the quick change that had come over the boy. 'It no trap,' Curt tried to gesture, but Paul had turned away, sliding along the floor to his bed. There he commenced to rock back and forth again, and worse he kept up the running argument with himself, which was becoming quite heated.

This wouldn't do. If Curt didn't act, the creature would come. Though it would be Paul on the receiving end of a punishment and not Curt, it still meant a further weakening of the group and perhaps an end to a sane Paul

Therefore, Curt jumped full upon Paul. Now Paul was a good five inches taller than he, but so skinny was the boy that they were roughly the same weight and what's more, the move was a complete surprise. In a blink, Curt had the boy gripped from behind and he slapped a hand over Paul's mouth.

"Shhhh," he warned in the boy's ear. Paul tried to twist away, but Curt wrapped his legs around his slim waist and held tight. "Stop it or the creature will be here in seconds. Is that what you want?"

Paul shook his head under Curt's grip and went limp, defeated. They sat this way for nearly a half hour as the house slowly, very slowly began to settle down.

When he thought it safe, Curt whispered, "Did you feel that? The house is very angry..."

"It's your fault," Paul hissed the accusation. Now it was Curt's turn to feel defeat and he let go of Paul fully and climbed off the bed.

'I know it is,' he motioned. 'That's why we have to leave. Can you talk to Matt?'

Paul nodded glumly, 'Yes. He will be very angry with me.' Curt nodded and Paul went on, 'But will the plan work?' Curt nodded again as if he knew for certain that it would. In truth, he had no idea.

"You know we can't trust him," Paul suddenly said, dashing Curt's hopes. "Don't call me a turd. No you are..."

Curt watched for a few seconds before he turned and walked away.

Chapter 28

Hide and Seek...Games Children Play

1

Curt pointed in the direction of Paul's room and waggled a finger around his ear, shaking his head sadly. 'It didn't work. Paul's too crazy.'

Amber nodded her understanding and looked glum, but also pensive and distracted. It was the feel of the house. Paul's argument with himself had really stirred it up and it was difficult to think past the fact that at any moment the creature could come up from its dirt tombs. Curt understood completely and gave her a quick kiss before giving her a little shove toward her room.

She would go hide there beneath her covers. All day long if she had to, despite the fact that she'd spent the greater portion of the last day and a half there. Curt couldn't do that. He was too impatient and his muscles hadn't yet atrophied and still bounded with unused energy. Instead, once he was alone, he sat on the floor and began to stretch.

As he pressed his body lower, feeling the pull of his muscles, he could sense the anger in the house easily through the wood. Forcing himself to ignore it, he worked his body harder, realizing that he missed exercising. It felt good.

That Paul had ceased arguing with himself was evident simply by the fact that the creature never came charging up the stairs and eventually, after a very long, but unknowable time, the house grew more settled. Amber came back to his room in the late afternoon, which was a good thing because Curt had begun to feel terribly lonely. The hours spent by himself were like a punishment and rather than just sit there, he had ghosted through the house as he had the day before only to see the other children lying under their blankets.

The sight made him melancholy and he began to blame himself once more for their predicament. When Amber came in, her face showed she was clearly afraid of the coming night and with good reason.

The creature was sure to attack again; he could feel it in his bones. Now it was the thing about Curt to be naturally contrarian and so when he saw her growing sad, he suddenly felt the need to pep her up. First, he tried a big smile, which failed. Then, he pulled a series of silly faces, but perhaps due to his still bruised face, she just looked a little repulsed.

Finally, he moved in closer and gave her face a great wet lick. She giggled and tried to pull away which only made him want to lick her all the more. At last, he pulled back from her glistening face and smiled at her in a genuine way.

'How do I taste?' she asked with her hands, while a big smile played about her lips. 'I haven't showered in a few days.'

Curt pretended to get sick and she swatted him playfully on the rear. Now that she had mentioned not showering, he realized he hadn't bathed in a while himself and he gave his own armpit a tentative sniff and immediately wished he hadn't.

'I stink!' he told her. 'I bathe in sink. Wait here.'

She waved him away while holding one hand over her nose and it was her turn to pretend to get sick.

Curt washed in the sink; he would freely admit to being simply too afraid to use the shower—he could picture finishing up and pulling back the curtains only to see the creature there waiting for him. The thought was too much for him. The sink would do just fine either way; he had bathed in sinks for most of his life and had never given it a second thought.

However, he gave it a second thought that day and bathed with the door cracked open, while keeping a finely tuned ear turned toward the hall. It was a good thing that he did too, for just as he was finishing up he heard the light swish of footsteps in the hall. They were moving away from him toward the backstairs and quick as a wink, Curt had his shirt back on and slid noiselessly after.

When he peeked around into the hall, he saw it was Paul. The older boy was moving with a jerking fashion rather than the nice slide step that kept them all relatively quiet. Even going down the stairs he was loud, hitting those spots that were guaranteed to produce a crreik. All of this worried Curt and he slunk after, stopping just shy of the kitchen on the back stairs.

From the room, he heard a tiny whispering but it was too low to make out anything. Knowing that movement attracted the eye, Curt, with great patience, inched his head very slowly around the corner.

'What?' Matt mouthed to Paul. The eldest boy's brows furrowed in irritation beneath the swelling and discoloration, he appeared frazzled, and Curt could see a spill of rice on the counter and floor. It made him realize that it was indeed dinnertime, in fact likely well past the time. Paul couldn't have picked a worse moment to make the attempt at explaining the plan, if indeed that was what he was doing.

Paul, sweating in fear, started gesticulating quickly, while he mouthed words at rapid pace. Even Curt, who knew the plan, became swiftly lost with all the movement and Matt didn't seem to be following along much better. But something he did catch was the word *escape*.

'Are you talking about trying to run away?' his hand motions were hard and fast. Tension pulled the muscles of his face back and he looked so fearsome with his swollen and bruised skin that Paul stopped his hand movements in a wink.

'No.' Unbelievably Paul began to deny he had ever mentioned anything. 'No...I just wanted to know when dinner was so I could run down here.'

Matt moved with viper swiftness and pinned Paul to the wall, 'Stop lying. You said you had a plan to escape.' He was able to convey this one handed, while the other twisted into Paul's turtleneck.

'No...I...' Paul could think of nothing else to say and now his twitch took over his face completely, effectively blinding him. Because of this, he missed the next series of motions from Matt, who was forced to speak.

"You were planning to escape! And you were going to throw Beth down into the basement?" Matt hissed into the boy's ear, causing Paul to cringe. "What kind of bastard are you? Is this really your idea?"

Gallantly the blonde boy nodded. "It can work. We can get out of here for good."

"Smashing in one of the windows? You tried that once before and you didn't even scratch it." Now Matt leaned in very close, but despite that, he still whispered loud enough for Curt to hear him, "I said there'd be no escape, and here you are trying to do just that. You're going to be punished and I think it's fitting to do to you, what you were planning on doing to Beth."

"No..." Paul whined miserably, like a wretch.

"Yes," Matt said. "And I think we should do it tonight. Right at bedtime, you'll go into the basement."

Paul went wild with fear, but being blind, it was easy for the larger boy to hold him down, and he ended up cringing on the ground. "It wasn't my idea! It was Curt's. He made me tell you it was my idea. He made up the whole plan. He said we could finally escape. Please not the basement. Don't do that to me."

"That's what I thought," Matt replied slowly. "Where is he?"

Curt watched in astonishment as Paul, though completely blinded by the muscles holding his face twisted as a Halloween mask, pointed right at him.

2

Curt leaned away out of sight of the doorway, and in his fright he leaned too far and fell back onto his rump. He tried to scramble up but his limbs seemed to be moving, not only independently from each other, but at cross-purposes as well and after a few seconds he hadn't moved even three stairs. Now Matt would be on him for certain and an odd sort of depression sprung upon him so that Curt sagged weakly.

It was useless, he couldn't fight the older boy. This he knew for a fact and that knowledge sent the last of his hope flitting away from his soul leaving him feeling empty inside. With nowhere to run, Curt gave up and lay there on the stairs awaiting the inevitable, but the inevitable seemed to take longer than he thought it would.

A minute passed and Curt was just beginning to wonder where Matt had got to when he heard Amber hiss, "No! You can't."

Curt spun around in an instant, shooting up the stairs on all fours, quiet and quick as a leopard. With his breath still light he paused at the top of the stairs, but due to the way the hall jotted at each door he couldn't see the length of it. So he stepped into the hall using the angles to keep from being seen. Moving with utter silence along the hall, he darted his head around the last doorway and saw Matt standing not fifteen feet from him.

Just in front of Paul's bedroom Matt stood, his eyes draped over with a black anger. Yet worse than the boy's eyes was the jagged, foot long shard of wood that he held in his right hand. For a moment, Curt thought it was the very stake that had been used to tear open Amber's face and he stared, flummoxed at how Matt could have gotten a hold of it. As far as he knew the chunk of wood was still up in the attic, keeping company with three decomposing corpses. Then Matt turned slightly to look into Paul's room and Curt saw that the wood of the stake was a pale white, unblemished by the stain of blood.

The sight of it held him perfectly mesmerized and he took in every detail. The point looked wickedly sharp as if it had been made for murder while the edge where it had been split from a larger piece of wood seemed so keen as to appear knife-like. Curt was so taken with the stake that he stood quite openly in the center of the hall and all Matt had to do was simply turn to his left to see him.

Fortunately for Curt, the older boy stepped into Paul's room instead. Now Curt was instantly on the move, he rushed down the backstairs feeling the air cool the sweat that soaked his shirt. As he moved he came up with a brilliant plan: Don't get stabbed with the stake.

Not only was it brilliant, it was a simple plan as well.

His mind strove to come up with something different, but the house was only so big and the hiding places were very few. Therefore, with no other ideas coming to him, he embarked on a hopeless game of cat and mouse. The outcome of which was foreordained. He could not hope to keep out of the reach of Matt and his stake indefinitely, and in fact he wondered whether it would be better just to give up rather than add frustration to Matt's already huge anger.

If Matt was going to force him into the basement, he didn't want to go in bleeding fresh wet blood. The thought caused him to picture a feeding frenzy in the dark and it was all he could do, not to cry.

Now the game, if it could be called such, lasted far longer than he had expected. For over twenty minutes he eluded the larger boy, moving with a silence that could only have been exceeded by the very person stalking him. Using every trick he could think of, doubling back, leaving false trails, hiding when it was smart to run, running when it was smart to hide, he was able to keep Matt second guessing himself. But it couldn't last—Curt became mentally worn down with the stress and began to make mistakes. At one point, he doubled back in his tracks and for whatever reason doubled again so that inadvertently he headed straight for Matt, who was coming down the backstairs. Standing in the kitchen, he spun to glide-run out of there and just as he did he saw the mudroom door open menacingly.

Still moving, his huge blue eyes were pinned to the doorway and, *thunk*, he walked square into a cabinet, stunning himself. Suddenly he heard the light patter of footsteps on the backstairs, which marked Matt running at full speed. Aghast at his stupidity, Curt just had the presence of mind to step around the corner into the dining room.

There he was trapped.

It was one way in and one way out, and the only hiding spots were under the table or flattening himself against the wall beside the china cabinet. He didn't bother with an attempt at hiding, instead he stood on the balls of his feet straining to hear either the telltale swish of Matt's feet, or the fast heavy tread of the creature charging up the basement stairs.

Neither came to him, which was a surprise and after half a minute, he slowly peeked around the corner into the kitchen. There he saw Matt walking toward the mudroom sideways, crablike, just as Curt had the day before. His body was tense and looked ready to book it out of there at the first sign of danger.

As Matt moved toward the mudroom, Curt kept a close watch, thinking if Matt went in, he'd make a run for it. Yet just as the older boy went to step in he glanced down the hall and it was all Curt could do to dance back to remain unseen. By the time he dared to peek back around the corner again, he saw Matt stepping once more into the kitchen, his face an ash grey color. Curt ground his teeth, frustrated that he wasn't catching any breaks.

The thought gave him a flash of inspiration. If he wasn't catching any breaks, he would make one instead. On the runner that went down the length of the dining room table were a number of frolicking porcelain kittens. Acting quickly without pausing for needless worry, he snatched up the nearest one and not looking back toward Matt, sent the thing skimming along the polished wood toward the front door.

As soon as the kitten had left his hand he pulled his arm back and listened: a second later a gratifying, *thunk* came from the end of the hall. A moment after this he heard the near silent swish of Matt's feet, racing in the direction of the front door. Curt ducked behind the china cabinet. The ruse worked better than he had expected. When he glanced down the hall, Curt saw Matt disappearing at a sprint up the stairs.

Feeling enormously pleased with himself, Curt made to follow along after the larger boy, but hadn't gone far when he spied Matt's feet coming back down the stairs. Cursing silently, Curt turned and zipped toward the kitchen and saw that Matt had closed the mudroom door, he felt a second of relief—his anxiety was just too great for it to last any longer. After taking the right into the kitchen, he started going up the backstairs, and just then a shadow bobbed against Matt's door. It was low down on the door, which meant whoever it was hadn't progressed far down the hall but was definitely heading his way.

Unsure of himself, Curt paused not knowing if Matt doubled back again or if it was one of the other children. He didn't know what to do. Still he couldn't just stand there waiting to find out and yet he couldn't go back for fear of running into Matt if this were in fact one of the other children. Seconds ticked away and as the shadow moved slowly forward, Curt made the decision to go back into the kitchen.

Nobody in their right mind would be out of bed just then. All during the long chase about the house, Curt had noticed the other children hiding beneath their covers, awaiting the outcome. And now he felt relatively certain that it was Matt coming toward the backstairs, therefore he coasted along heading for the main stairs. But just as he came up to them, he saw Matt's feet at the top of the stairs moving down.

Matt had doubled back again! Curt felt his sanity fraying at the edges, and his mind took a bigger hit as he fled into the kitchen only to see the mudroom door swing open once more. It stopped his feet cold and he stared as the door opened toward him. Had they been too noisy running around the house?

He didn't know. Curt had been so engrossed on evading Matt, that he hadn't checked the walls once and he was perfectly petrified that the creature would be standing right there when the door finally opened all the way. A second later his shoulders slumped with the tiniest relief and he found he could breathe again; the basement door was still closed.

But he was only allowed that one breath, because as he stood and watched, the basement door opened as well. Curt's breath stopped a second time, expecting to see the creature or perhaps the ghost of Miss Feanor, or worst of all, the black entity that lived within the walls of the house. Yet when it finally came open, again there was nothing.

This time relief didn't flow over him. He was just too frazzled to go on. Matt was so silent and so slick that he could be anywhere and now Curt felt his mind becoming slow to react, and thinking was becoming a chore. All he knew for certain was that it was only a matter of time before he was caught and then...Curt looked into the basement.

He could go down there—into the horrid black— bleeding, perhaps kicking, and screaming or he could just go and get it over with.

Fatalistically he started walking toward the doom that awaited him. Stepping into the mudroom, the black of the basement seemed to reach out for him, and a wet stench billowed up from the depths, coating him, so that he felt slick and oily. There were eyes down there, staring up at him from deep in the blackness. A horde of eyes. They were hungry for him, for his warmth.

Those eyes stopped him for a moment, and an urge to run gripped him, but then behind him the mudroom door swung shut on silent hinges. He was trapped now and a part of him again screamed and pleaded for him to run, only he was done-in mentally. Physically he was beaten and exhausted. Spiritually he was empty.

There was nothing he could do to stop Matt, or the creature, or the house for that matter. They all had power over him and could hurt him whenever they wished to. Drained of any will to live, Curt went to the gaping maw of the basement.

Chapter 29

The Thief in the Basement

1

Cold and black; the basement was just like his mind.

He stopped, poised at the precipice overlooking the deep gluttonous chasm. Behind him, the light from the mudroom should have shown deeper into the basement than it did, but the darkness seemed to be substantial and seven or eight stairs was all that Curt could see and even that was shadowed, the walls were black and crusted looking. Though he had meant only a pause to see down into the gloom, the pause stretched out as a spike of fear cut through his apathy.

Something was down there, waiting with quickly eroding patience. Yet it would not wait forever and he guessed that if he stood there much longer, teasing it with his presence it would come for him. The thought built a great terror in him and his subconscious mind screamed for him to get the hell out of there before it was too late.

That desperate scream wasn't enough.

For days there had just been too much desperation surrounding him. Curt would go down, but for Amber's sake he'd shut the door behind him. He didn't want her to hear his screams. Curt reached for the brass knob and that was when his mind was slapped back to its normal state.

The brass in his hand was cold beyond belief— shockingly, painfully cold. And what's more it and held all the enmity for life that the spirit of the house possessed, only it was blunt or muted as if the house was trying to camouflage its true nature. It was too late for that: Curt knew the evil that existed down there.

Finally coming fully awake to the dangerous position he'd put himself in, he shut the door and held it closed with his slim form.

For a moment, he feared that the thing would come up from the black and try to push its way into the mudroom, but seconds passed and there was nothing, no sounds, no movement. He began to shake all over, feeling like a suicide saved by circumstance.

His right hand stung from the cold of the knob and he messaged it with his left as his mind started to come slowly back around and as it did, he realized he still didn't know what to do. No direction seemed likely to get him out of his current predicament and the only thing he knew with any certainty was that he didn't want to go into the basement anytime soon. That he would go down there eventually, hopefully dragged in unconscious, he no longer doubted, but there was no cause to head there just yet. Something could still happen. They could even be rescued.

That thought brought a rueful smile to his lips and he even chuckled weakly. The sad truth was they'd all be long dead before anyone would think to come by.

Still he was safe at the moment. And perhaps he could be safer for a while longer. Curt decided he would use the mudroom to lay low in, hoping that hiding in the very jaws of the lion might shake Matt off his trail. He needed the break, badly. His hands still shook and he felt a weakness clear to his bones.

With his knees threatening to buckle beneath him he sat down, his back to the basement door, and the entrance to the kitchen a few feet to his right. For a long while he lacked the energy to do nothing more that stare at the white, white walls, but gradually his brain started to function again and the first thing that got past his tired fuzzy thinking was the question of why Miss Feanor called this a mudroom.

Like the rest of the house, it was perfectly clean, without a speck of mud anywhere in evidence. It didn't make sense. Personally, he'd have called it a laundry room since a gleaming washer/dryer set sat only a few feet from him. Curt would've put money down that if he pulled out the lint trap of the dryer it would be as clean and lint free as the day it had been put into the house.

Now the only other thing about the mudroom that drew his attention was the garage door. Its ornate knob was merely a long-armed stretch away and it seemed to beckon to him to touch it. He dared not. Like the front door, it just looked too easy and besides, there was no reason to go into the garage either way. It was as impossible to escape from as the rest of the house...or was it?

Curt suddenly sat up straighter. Something nagged at the back of his mind and he strived to recall all he could about the garage. There wasn't much to remember. Its walls had been bare; no shelves, no tools, no bikes, no nothing.

Literally, it contained only the car, the door that lead to the backyard and the main door. Out of the blue, Curt pictured a garage door rattling upwards and his heart began to thump heavily. The garage door opener!

The key to getting out of the house had been there all along; he was even certain that the car itself was unlocked. It had been unlocked on that first day when Miss Feanor told him the rules to the house, and as people were creatures of habit, he was reasonably sure that she hadn't locked it the day Darla the social worker had been killed either.

If he wanted to, he could leave right then! And by the time the house had roused the creature, Curt could be halfway to the nearest police station. With growing excitement he reached for the shiny knob, he could see his hand reflected in its surface as closer and closer it went. His hand looked disfigured or perhaps warped in the curved brass and he stopped it only an inch from the metal.

Don't be a fool, he chided himself. Again, this just seemed too easy. In the fourteen years that Miss Feanor lived in the home doing foster care someone surely would have thought of this before now. And if they had, why didn't they escape? What stopped them?

The solution was obvious: the house stopped them of course. But how? Curt pictured the garage door once again and the answer popped out at him quick enough, the garage door operated using an electric motor and the electricity for that motor came from the house.

"Damn," he whispered, barely loud enough for his own ears to hear.

The day he had tried to use the phone, the house had proved that it could control the flow of electricity within it without a problem. Curt sagged back down and ran his fingers through the mass of curly hair weaving about his head.

His spirits sank very low and gloominess laid a hold of him so great that he just sat there without moving, without caring. Curt came to the sad conclusion that he would die in the house. He had tried everything he could think of. He had been in every room and had seen everything there was to see, except the horrors of the basement that is. And surely, there could be no escape down there.

His gut told him that the garage was the way out, but his own mind mocked him for the coward he was.

'Your *gut* told you to kill those two people in the attic as well,' a voice within him spoke up suddenly. It was a snide voice, but it was also an accurate voice and he wondered if he wanted the garage to be the way out simply because it was easier than facing the terrors in the unknown basement.

He again smiled at himself but this time in contempt.

That was certainly it. The garage held nothing for him. Even if he had the keys to the car, he couldn't get it out of the garage....

Suddenly Curt sat bolt upright. The car! The car was the key! Forget smashing down an anchored, inch thick window with a chair, he would drive that car right through the garage door. In his excitement, he spun around and laid himself on the pure white linoleum. Barely he could see under the crack of the door and there in the garage was a faint glimmer of shining metal.

This could work.

That he could smash through the garage door, he was pretty certain. He'd heard of these sorts of things happening before and always it had been a mistake, an accident on the part of the homeowner. So he felt his prospects were good that if he were to purposely ram the door it couldn't hold against him.

His problem lay in starting the car.

Thankfully, there were indeed keys, since his plan would have been doomed if the house controlled the car as it did everything else. Unfortunately he was very certain that they were now in the attic. Likely in the pocket of a dead woman.

Here lay another problem—getting to the keys seemed an impossibility as well. Without any metal he had no way to pick the lock to the attic, and the door was so sturdy that it would be easier to smash his way through one of the windows than to attempt to break it down.

He blew out noisily in frustration. Again, he wished that he were more of a thief. Since it was only a matter of exposing the correct wires and connecting them, he was relatively certain that he could actually hot wire the car. It was the time involved that would doom him. He had seen the mass of wires running from a steering column before and it had thoroughly intimidated him then. Even with the mouse as a human sacrifice, he'd have maybe three minutes to go through all the wiring and strip off the rubber coating of the correct ones, using nothing but a plastic fork.

Even if he knew which were the right wires—which he did not—it was flat out impossible.

With a heavy sigh, he let his head rest on the floor. It was then that he felt an icy draft on the back of his neck.

2

The house had become whimsical again.

He turned his head quickly and sure enough, the basement door was in the process of swinging open, revealing its black depths, spilling out its noxious fumes. It made his heart thunder in his chest to feel the eyes upon him and Curt gave the basement only a quick terrified look to satisfy himself that nothing untoward lurked just there and then he hopped up to shut the door.

As he did, he wondered why the house had begun to act in this manner. Was it simply trying to scare him? Was there a psychological hiccup in its evil mind? He didn't know. Then he considered the possibility that the house had always done this and that Miss Feanor had sat in the kitchen every day simply to counter act it; he hoped that was the case.

These thoughts ran quickly through his mind and he had just begun to shut the basement door when quite unexpectedly, the mudroom door came silently open and there in the kitchen was Matt. He was not more that fifteen feet away, standing near to the cabinet where the small amount of excess food was kept. In his hand, he held the long sharp stake. He gripped it tight, dagger like.

Fortunately for Curt the older boy had his back turned to him. Only that was little consolation, for Curt was stuck, trapped in the very worst possible place. His logical choices to proceed from there seemed to have dwindled down to just two: make a mad dash for the hallway and hope to outrun the larger boy, or fight. The latter idea was simply plain crazy, while the former looked impossible as Matt stood a mere seven or eight feet from the only path Curt could take.

With running out of the question and fighting amounting to near suicide, Curt was left to abandon logic. The first illogical option was to just stand there and hope that Matt wouldn't feel the dread cold roiling about his ankles, or sense the uptick of fear that was fast permeating the room, or that he would simply fail to see the door standing wide open. Illogical and stupid.

His second option was not only illogical and stupid, it was fantastically dangerous as well, and that was to go into the basement on his own as he had planned earlier.

Now this thought process occurred in a blink of an eye and just then, Matt began to turn. With no time left to consider any more ramifications, Curt stepped lightly onto the first step heading down into the basement—down toward where the feral creature dwelled in its freshly dug grave—and with his breath caught up in his throat, Curt shut the door behind him.

All was black.

And at first, Curt could see nothing as the damp frigid air closed in on him and the smell of rotted death grew thick in his nostrils. His throat undulated convulsively and he gagged in silent spasms at the smell. Somehow, he was able to hold back the vomit that threatened to erupt and he clung to the ice-cold doorknob as if it were his salvation.

In a way it was. For Curt's world began at that doorknob. If he were to let go of it for any reason, he felt certain that in that deep black he would never find it again and he'd simply fall away into the horrid nothingness. Until perhaps he would land upon the dirt floor of the cellar, where he'd be lost amongst a maze of crypts and graves and low mounds under which countless bodies lay entombed forever.

His mind, now bordering on the edge of insanity, pictured what the blackness would never reveal and try as he might, he couldn't shake the vision. It clung stubbornly, but suddenly something happened that tore his mind from petty imagining, the doorknob moved beneath his hand.

3

The doorknob moved, turning, however not as if someone looked to open the door. Rather just the opposite.

It may have been a tremendously foolish thing for Curt to go into the basement alone, but that didn't mean that he went in as a fool. When he had shut the door on the light and the world above, he had very purposely kept his hand heavy on the knob and held it hard over, keeping the simple latch from engaging. He feared the house too much to trust that he would be able to walk out of the basement as simply as he walked in.

And he had been right. The doorknob strained to the left, gently at first but the pressure against his palm soon grew strong enough that Curt had to fight it from turning with both hands. He felt his skin peeling back, making his face twist into a grimace of pain, still he held tight, fighting perhaps not just for his life, but for his sanity as well. Tenaciously he held onto the freezing knob, and began counting just under his breath. His goal was to hold on for thirty seconds at which point he would throw his weight against the door and escape. He could only hope that Matt would've left the kitchen by then.

He made it to the count of eighteen when unexpectedly the knob went slack against his efforts. Was this a trick to get him to drop his guard? Curt didn't know, but he wasn't going to take the chance.

Panting from his effort, he sagged against the door, yet still he didn't relax, though he took one hand off at a time to wipe sweat onto jeans. When he put his hand back to the knob, he noted the anger of the house. It was plain beneath his palm, it swelled in its ferocity and with the foul smelling darkness clinging to him, it turned his pant of labor into a pant of fear.

Suddenly he felt the air change behind him and he cranked his head around searching into the blackness with giant eyes. It didn't seem possible, but his fear grew in proportion to the depth of the darkness that enclosed him and as a symptom of his increasing terror, his breath blew out of his lungs fast and hard. But then, unbelievably, he felt a return breath on his face. Putrid and fetid, it smote his senses and was enough to stop his panting cold. Whatever it was that breathed upon him must have been large indeed, since the odor came from below him, perhaps only a few steps down but still it struck him like an ill wind.

His body went instantly numb and only his eyes could move, straining into the darkness, which, for the first time, he realized was not complete. Light from the mudroom slipped under the door and showed him that something seemed to be moving. It swirled and eddied, feet from him, black upon black. It wasn't the creature, it was the horror that he had seen before and no longer was it bothering to hide its evil nature. Perhaps it no longer could as it solidified into an actual being.

A blacken burnt looking arm reached out of the eternal night of the basement. It reached for Curt.

Feeling a fright beyond normal human awareness, and without a single thought or care as to where Matt was, he turned to run screaming from the basement, but though the knob was cranked all the way over, the door wouldn't budge. He hammered at it with his shoulder, raging against it in a frenzy of fear but to no avail. With a frantic desperate cry, he turned around in the darkness not wanting his back exposed to the thing and just then his hand struck something upon the wall.

He fingered it softly, categorizing the shape quickly. It was the wall plate for a light switch. His mind toyed with the idea of flicking it on, but then his imagination took over and he snatched his hand back away from it. Whatever was in the basement; he didn't want to see it fully. Though it would likely kill him, he couldn't bring himself to see it in the light and letting out a little spastic gurgle of fear, he pressed himself against the basement door and clamped his eyes shut tight.

A second later, a long scream of anguish rent the air, coursing through the wooden bones of the house.

Chapter 30

The Thief's Worst Punishment

1

The scream was more of a desperate shriek than anything else.

"Nooooooo!" The sound was harsh as if vocal cords had been ripped or torn lengthways like delicate ribbons. It came from upstairs, all the way from the second floor and Curt instantly recognized the voice; it was Amber's. She was in trouble, and he knew exactly what sort of trouble. He should have seen this coming. Undoubtedly, Matt was threatening her to get to Curt.

Now the scream had an interesting effect on both the cowering little boy and the angry black entity forming in the dark. One second, the deep ebony figure of a woman, exuding a terrible unnatural feel grew before him and the next, the thing seemed to dissipate like smoke in the wind. For his part, Curt forgot completely his fear for himself. He pictured only Amber's face contorted in misery and with his heart in his throat, he pulled himself up and made to dash his scrawny shoulder against the door once again.

Yet it came open without the need. The evil spirit in the house, as Curt knew, couldn't concentrate on more than one area at a time and it had evidently sent its focus to the room from where the scream had originated. Now, the air in the mudroom felt hot, wonderfully so and for just a second it made him light-headed and he could only teeter slightly still holding onto the basement door. However his fear for Amber forced his worn body onwards. At first he staggered from exhaustion and a lack of strength, hitting the table, then bouncing off a wall, but quickly he felt his mind clearing and he began to run.

Perhaps it was the scream or the fact that Curt had escaped the basement so easily, but whichever it was, the anger of the house grew steadily as he raced, fleetly, yet quietly on practiced feet. First down the hall and then up the stairs, he sped, paying the anger little attention. That there would be a punishment soon he did not doubt in the least.

At the top of the stairs, he paused and sent a fast look into his own bedroom, but it was empty, just what he had expected. He would find Matt and Amber in her room and two seconds later, he did.

The older boy had Amber in the corner and straddled her, pinning her beneath the weight of his body. In his hand, he held the stake and with it poised above Amber's eye, it looked very large, capable of doing a great deal of damage to her beautiful face. But then Curt saw that it already had.

Its wicked point was bright red and dripping.

Amber had been stabbed a number of times already. Blood bubbled up from four different wounds on her face and neck. Curt's mind had trouble understanding what was happening. He hadn't expected to see Matt up here attacking the girl, but only threatening her, and it made him stop in the doorway in indecision.

"Curt, no. Run!" Amber cried out to him the second he came panting up. Now he understood. Amber was being stabbed for not crying out to him. She had only let loose with the one scream despite her jagged brutal looking wounds. It touched him deeply to see her sacrifice herself for him.

"No, if you run anymore, *she* will be the one going into the basement," Matt said in a long practiced whisper. The sound was calculated to reach his ears and no further. "And if you don't do exactly what I say, she'll lose this eye first and I'm not messing around now."

The point of the stake came closer to the girl's eye and she tried to turn her head, but he gripped her hair viciously and pulled it around. Matt's battered and bitten face looked fiendishly cruel and set in determination. Curt had no doubt whatsoever that he would carry out his threat

"I won't run...but...I think you should listen to me," Curt pleaded quietly. "No one's coming to rescue us. I've..."

"Shut the hell up!" Matt's voice rose louder than he expected and the air became as charged as Curt had ever felt it. Matt didn't seem to care. "This is all your fault. Look at my face! Look at my face! This is all because you thought you could escape, but you can't. No one can. We have all tried and no one has ever gotten even close. You can't beat the house, Curt. There's no winning here, there's only surviving, and until you learn that lesson, you are going into the basement every day."

"I just came from the basement," Curt said blandly as if it had been no big thing.

Matt's face contorted. "You lie!"

"No I'm not. Why do you think you couldn't find me?"

A thousand thoughts seemed to explode at once in Matt's mind and for a few moments, he did nothing but look strangely about, his eyes blinking in odd confusion. "That doesn't change anything. You still need to be punished and you're still going down there," he said eventually.

Curt shrugged noncommittally.

That simple movement was the best lie he had ever told. The basement and that terrible black thing scared him more than he could ever put into words and even as he lifted his shoulders, he had to fight his bladder from letting go.

But Matt bought into the lie.

"Ok, then the monster can come up here and you two can flip a coin to see which one it attacks." Matt no longer bothered to whisper and he had an evil light behind his eyes, "Call it," he said to Curt and raised the stake.

Amber tried to shake her head to tell Curt not to, but Matt held her hair with his fingers enmeshed and tangled.

"It's ok, Amber, it won't be so bad," Curt lied. Defeat weighed heavily upon his shoulders, making him droop almost as if it were an emotion in itself. That he felt fear, there was no question. It was a cold lump in his chest, and as he glanced to the window and saw the light fading in the sky that lump expanded, making it difficult to breath, but it was defeat that he was having trouble dealing with.

Or perhaps more likely it was the absence of hope. He'd tried everything that his fertile mind could think of, yet he had been stopped at every turn and now there seemed nothing else to do, but to call the creature. Pausing only for a second to collect himself, still unsure of the exact manner in which to call the thing, he took a large breath.

"Hey!" Curt shouted, and then waited. The air practically roiled to the point that he could feel it moving gently against his skin. Matt's eyes darted about and then his brows furrowed deeper as nothing more happened.

"Come on, damn it!" Curt screamed at the top of his lungs. It felt good to scream, to use his lungs to their full capacity. But that good feeling lasted only a moment.

Then came the rushing noise of the creature pounding up the stairs of the basement and any good feeling within him fled before the sound. The creature's eagerness to cause pain could not have been more obvious, and instinctively Curt turned to run, but had only taken a few steps, stopping in the doorway, when he realized that if he ran, Amber would likely be punished instead of him and with a great force of will he flung his hands out and gripped the frame.

A millisecond later, Matt crashed full into him, sending him sprawling to the floor. Dimly, he felt feet treading upon his back and arms as the older boy dashed for his room. Curt struggled up, not knowing what to do. He could not bear for Amber to be punished, yet he felt stark terror at the notion of meeting the creature again in the hall and every fiber of his being called for him to run.

At that moment an idea struck him.

He'd fly to his room and call the creature again. In that way Amber would be safe and his own punishment would occur in his bed, where supposedly it'd be less severe. The sound of the creature barreling down the main floor hall meant he had bare seconds left, but he used one of those seconds and turned to look into Amber's room, fearful that he would see her in one of the catatonic states that gripped her under the extremes of stress.

She was fine. He saw her climbing into bed, wearing a hard look, a look that showed angry determination. The look made him hesitate for the briefest time, just a fraction of a second; it was so unexpected. But then their eyes met, her pale blue eyes held his and he knew she'd be all right and with that tiny amount of relief feeding him, he turned and ran.

"I love you, Curt," she called softly after him.

2

He loved her too, but he was in no position to reply, though later he wished with all his heart that he had. Just as he heard the words, he neared the end of the hall from which his bed lay only a few feet away, and it was then that he heard the great thumping of the creature's heavy footfalls upon the stairs; he had been too slow.

His fortitude crumbled at the sound. Instead of running across that little bit of open hall to his bed, exposing himself to the creature and making himself a target, he backed away. He backed around the corner of the hall toward where Matt and the mouse had their rooms and felt like a miserable coward doing so. Now the creature came to the top of the stairs and paused, building the tension and fear within the breasts of the children, purposely. With it so close, Curt's throat locked up, almost choking him and with his fear turning to panic, he glanced back and saw the stairs leading to the kitchen only a dozen feet away. But the door to Matt's room was just a few steps beyond that.

A new plan wormed its way past his fear.

He would scream right there in the hall, calling the creature to him and then make a run for Matt's room. The words *"... and you two can flip a coin to see which one it attacks,"* that Matt had said with such nastiness were now an inspiration. Perhaps the creature would only attack Curt, but there was a chance that it would also go for Matt, especially with Curt struggling to use the older boy as a shield. A grim smile spread across his boyish features at the image and at the knowledge that the older boy would never see this coming.

He had just made up his mind to call the creature, when someone else beat him to it.

"Hey! Over here, you p-p-piece of c-c-c-crap!" Amber called out.

Her voice, barely loud enough to be considered conversational, shook, warbling up and down in the extremes of her fear. The sound stunned Curt. The notion that Amber would do this was so completely unexpected that for a few seconds he doubted his own ears. Even as he heard the creature streaking down the hall towards her, his mind refused to accept what was happening.

Then his bewilderment came to an end.

Amber screamed a heart-rending shriek of fear. It went right to Curt's soul and tattooed itself there; marking him forever, and always afterwards he could hear that scream. He would recall it in perfect detail and each time goose bumps would flare at the memory.

Amber screamed again. Long and piercing. This one bespoke of fantastic pain. It carried throughout the house and the house took it in with relish, Curt could feel its nasty voyeuristic enjoyment through the wall under his hand. It made him sick with anger, and he started forward not exactly sure what he was going to do when he got to her room, but only sure that he would stop her from being hurt. If he could.

However, he had only taken two steps before a hand reached out and spun him around and he found himself staring up into Matt's eyes. The hall light hadn't been turned on and in the dim, the older boy's brown eyes were black. Deep black. Black with anger and remorseless hate. Startled and more than a little bit fearful, Curt flinched back, striking the wall behind him.

There was a flash of movement to his left and instinctively Curt put up a protective arm, but he was too slow. Matt struck him in the side of the head with the back end of his stake, toppling him to the floor.

3

The ceiling of the hall was at first a spinning nightmare, he couldn't make sense of it, nor could he understand the screams that drifted in distantly to his ears. Lying on his back, his world was a great confusion.

Eventually Curt focused enough to see a very tall figure towering above him. The person, gaunt with a dark, almost purple face, seemed to be on a teeter-totter, waving up and down. Curt couldn't recognize who it was. Not until the figure knelt down, squatting heavily upon Curt's chest. It was Matt.

Matt brought the stake close to Curt's face, very near to his blue eye, however that close, Curt lost focus on it and it seemed to disappear altogether. Instead, he looked at what he could see, and noticed Matt speaking. He couldn't hear the words, there was simply too much noise.

In his head a great rushing sound filled him, and the only thing he could hear beyond that were screams. They came from all around him; even coming up from the wood of the floor, or so it seemed and he wondered if it was he himself who cried out with such pain. It couldn't have been Curt decided, since he barely felt any pain at all. He barely felt anything, and was only dimly aware of his limbs.

"Hey!" Matt shook him, roughly. At first Curt's eyes swam even more out of focus, but then they sharpened until he could see the stake clearly. The thing held no fear for him whatsoever. His eyes might have focused, but his brain was far from it.

"Huh?" he asked looking past the browned tip of the stick.

Matt's eyes, very dark and angry, peered into his. "Do you hear that?"

Curt could hear the screaming more clearly all of a sudden. The huge rushing in his ears became less with every second. "Who is that?" Curt asked. It seemed suddenly very important that he knew.

"That's Amber, and you did that to her. You! You did that to her," Matt hissed. "That should be you being punished. What a coward you are, letting a little girl get punished for you."

"Amber?" Curt began to remember. Bit and pieces, flashes of images, of running throughout the house, of standing in the basement, feeling the wet air covering his skin, of watching the black thing becoming solid in the darkness and finally of seeing Matt straddling Amber with the stake poised above her eye.

"No...that was you. You did this to her," Curt said feebly. Now the stake grew in importance to him and from where he lay, the thing suddenly looked like a spike or part of a long spear. It gave him a twinge seeing how readily it could puncture the delicate orb of his eye.

"Wrong, this is all your..." Matt started to say, however a new sort of scream came from Amber's room. It seemed impossible, but the pain in her voice doubled and now they could hear a frantic beating of something upon the floor, vibrating through the wood. The sounds clearly unnerved Matt and he pulled back quickly, looking ready to run.

"That's going to be you, tomorrow," Matt whispered, very low. The older boy heaved himself off of Curt's chest and a moment later, he glided silent as a breeze toward his room.

The scream had unnerved Curt as well and with a feeling of growing panic that he would be too late to help Amber, he tried to get up. Three times, he attempted to pull himself up, yet each time his head spun so much that he collapsed. On the fourth attempt, he clawed at the wall and managed to get to his hand and knees, and he swayed there, red spots blooming in his vision, but then he saw dark red spots appearing on the wood as well. These were different. They didn't fade in and out as the others had and feeling vaguely upset, he swiped at them with one of his hands.

They were wet and left a red smear upon the wood. He was bleeding. Somewhere on his head, he was bleeding. He didn't care too much. The only thing that held any sort of attention for him was Amber. She screamed and sobbed frantically, yet it was all Curt could do to kneel on his hands and knees. His head felt huge and now pain started to wash over him.

"Uhhhh," he let out a slight moan and fought to stand up, only to collapse to his knees again. Not knowing about the cumulative effect of concussions, he couldn't understand how being hit in the head with the end of the stake could be as bad as being hit with the baseball bat. His vision went in and out, while the hallway seemed to spin, but he needed to get to Amber.

Stifling more groans and a growing need to vomit, he crawled slowly along, and as he did, he noted that Amber's screams had become sporadic, with more loud sobbing between the cries. Her punishment was coming to an end. At the moment, time was impossible for him to fully grasp, so it seemed that her torture had been relatively quick, and naively, he felt relief for her.

For a few seconds more he doggedly crawled on toward her room before it dawned on his injured mind that it would be better to get back to bed before the creature finished with Amber and caught him in the hall. Slowly he crawled the eight feet to his room and pulled himself into his bed, where he meant to wait out the end of her punishment before going to see how she was. However, his head injury was too great and he passed out almost as soon as the blankets covered him.

4

It was full dark when he came awake with a pounding head.

"Uhhhh," a moan escaped him involuntarily. He pulled back the covers. Gingerly he touched his scalp where Matt had struck him. Beneath a great mat of dried blood he could feel the wound swollen and oddly lumpy. Another small moan escaped him, and just then he heard a soft child like whimper. It came from the hall.

Amber!

He climbed out of bed, and had to hold fast to the door for a few seconds as his knees threatened to send him crashing to the floor. When the feeling passed, he went out into the dark of the hall. A small figure lay upon the floor, halfway down it and Curt rushed over, uncaring that he was breaking the most important rule of the house.

The person on the floor was indeed Amber and despite the night, Curt could see that she was covered in blood; it was dark against her white skin. More blood trailed out behind her, leading back to her bedroom, the sight of which caused Curt to gasp, horrified. There was a lot of blood.

Amber was only semi-conscious and slippery with fresh blood so it took every bit of Curt's strength to pull her into the bathroom. Breathing heavily, he snapped on the overhead lights and his wind caught in his throat as he saw the atrocious wounds covering her. That she had fought back was clear by the number of defensive wounds she bore. Her arms were no longer clean limbed and smooth. They had been bitten dreadfully and in some places, the bites had gone clear to the bone. These still bled profusely and Curt took hand towels and bound them tightly.

The creature had ripped away her shirt, leaving just rags and there were more bite marks on the length of her torso, but thankfully none of these were very deep and only a few still bled. He cleaned them as best as he could and then inspected her face. She had fought to save her face and for the most part, she had succeeded, though her left eyebrow was partially torn away. There was also a series of ugly bruises and fresh teeth marks high up on her forehead, but all in all, her face looked much better than Matt's did.

She came awake more fully as he washed the wounds on her face and began to cry in pain, clutching her hands to her chest.

"I'm sorry, Amber," Curt said softly. "I tried to come and save you, but Matt attacked me. I'm so sorry."

"M-m-m my hands," she whimpered through her tears.

"Your hands?" he asked, confused. Her hands had been clenched into fists and covered with blood, he had assumed it was blood from her other injuries. "Let me see them," he demanded quietly.

She held them out and they shook, dripping.

"Uh...." Curt was at a loss for words. On her left hand, most of her pinky was gone and a tiny bone stuck up out of the raw looking wound. Her ring finger of the same hand had been chewed down to the second knuckle. Both fingers bled freely, making her hand glisten bright red. Her right hand wasn't so horrible to look upon. The fingers were all intact, but a huge chunk of meat from her palm below her pinky had been torn away. This wound bled a great deal as well.

"I'm going to bleed to death, aren't I?" Amber said in a fear-quivered voice. She couldn't seem to stop staring at her hands, her head turning from one to the other, repeatedly.

"No. You won't bleed to death, you'll be ok," Curt replied, not knowing at all if that were true. He got up and rushed to the closet that held the extra sheets and rummaged through them.

"Don't leave me!" Amber cried out to him.

The words had been very loud and Curt's heart skipped a beat, he grabbed the first sheet his hand fell upon and dashed back.

"Amber, please. I know it hurts, but it's still night out. You can't scream like that...it might come again," Curt whispered. Her head snapped to the window and her eyes went big with the realization that he was right.

"Don't leave me," she blubbered this time more quietly. "Don't let me die here."

Curt found a weak spot on the sheet and began tearing it in long strips and as he worked, he reassured her, "You won't die here. I'll tie up these wounds and this should...this *will* stop the bleeding. Ok?" She nodded to him, trusting him. He was relatively sure that he could stop the bleeding. After all, he had never heard of someone bleeding to death from being bitten like this.

It was infection, however that scared him.

His whole life, he had scoffed at the specter of infection. Like all boys, he had been cut and scraped a thousand times over and never once gave these minor injuries a second thought, unless it was to brag about or to hope for a cool looking scar. However, Amber's wounds were far worse than anything he had ever had to contend with and that bone sticking up made him anxious.

He tried his best to clean the pinky, hoping the bone would simply wash away, but it didn't and what's more, it hurt her so badly that it was all he could do just to run water over it. It looked sort of hollow and again the thought of infection came to mind, chilling him.

She stifled her cries as best she could as he bound up her fingers and though the pillowcase soon turned a deep red-brown color, the bleeding looked to eventually stop. Her head wound was another matter altogether. That bled continuously. Not in great gushing waves, but in a trickle that wouldn't end. Not until he held a strip of cloth there for nearly a half hour, pressing it hard to her skull did it eventually cease.

While they sat there waiting, he asked in a very quiet tone, "Why did you call out to the creature? I would've taken the punishment for you. In fact, I tried but Matt smashed me in the head and knocked me out...for a while, see?" He turned so that she could see the mat of blood, tangled in his hair. What she'd done, being tortured in his stead, had been very brave and he felt the need not to look like a coward in her eyes.

Her face went from misery to anger. "I hate him so much. I would kill him if I could." Her voice had a hard bitter quality, "If I was a boy I would k-k-k-kill him for sure."

Curt looked away briefly in shame. He was after all a boy, yet he didn't think he could kill Matt; in fact, he was afraid to even try. Matt was just too big, too devious and what's more he was evil, lacking any scruples whatsoever.

Amber didn't seem to notice his look and proceeded in a low whisper, "He's the reason I called out to the monster. He kept talking about putting you in the basement. He even said he was going to feed you to the monster." Curt swallowed hard at that, feeling his stomach do a slow barrel roll. She went on, "And I knew you were the only one who could stop Matt and save us from the monster. So I...so I..." she trailed off, not needing to explain the rest.

Now Curt was at a loss at what to say. He didn't think he could do either of the things she had mentioned and it must have shown on his face.

"You have a new plan right? You have to have one. Please tell me you have one?" Panicky fear made her voice tremble, "The monster is getting worse, way worse. It's going to start eating us for real. I could tell when it was chewing on me, it got so excited that its *thing*..." she stopped talking abruptly and only cried in quiet misery.

Curt felt like crying too. He wanted to cry for her pain and what she went through for him. He wanted to cry in fear of what tomorrow would bring and he wanted to cry in frustration. He had no way to get the keys to the car from the attic and no way to get the rest of the doors open. And he couldn't count on any help from the other children. Paul was a schizo and practically blind, the mouse was too insane even to make toast, Matt was his mortal enemy and would rather die a horrible death than to help Curt, and now Amber, with her hands torn up as they were, was practically a cripple, in other words, she was useless.

In essence he had nothing; no help, no hope, no plan and no way, short of a miracle, would he be able to come up with one by the next morning.

Curt could find nothing to say and eventually Amber looked at him through her tears. He saw her faith in him fading from her face and she began shaking her head, and whether she meant it or not, there was accusation in her eyes. It made him feel small that he was letting her down and with a feeling of desperation he fell back upon what he knew best.

"Don't worry, I have a plan," he lied. So smooth was the lie that despite the horror that she had gone through for him, a smile lit up the pallor of her face and her blue eyes shown bright with renewed hope.

Chapter 31

A Plan to Lie

1

He put her to bed and kissed away her tears. Her hands, in their red-brown wrappings shook almost nonstop. They had to hurt terribly and she made great measures not to let them touch anything, so that he even pulled the covers over her head for her.

"Is that ok?" he asked. "Can I get you anything?"

There was nothing in the house that he could get for her, but he felt that he should ask nonetheless.

"No...th-th-thank you," her breath hitched in her chest, making him feel even more miserable. Her pain was his fault. She had gone through hell for nothing. "I l-love y-y-you," she whispered.

"I love you too." Another lie. Inside, he felt dead.

He went back to his bed, thinking that he'd spend the rest of the night coming up with a plan, one that would be foolproof. Instead, he fretted and worried, sweating through his pajamas.

"That's going to be you, tomorrow," Matt had whispered to him. The screams of Amber's had been horrendous. Their memory stayed with him all night long, making it impossible to think beyond them. The worst screams, the one that had been accompanied by the thrumming of her heels upon the floor, must've been when the creature had bitten off her fingers. Each time he pictured it, he felt a nasty sickness and at one point when he envisioned what would happen the next day and saw his own fingers being bitten off, he laughed aloud, feeling a mania come over him. To think he had been worried about infection! The creature's attacks were escalating in severity and he felt it in his bones that death was right around the corner.

And if one of them were to die, the others were going to follow suit very quickly; infection would be the least of their worries.

At some point, he fell into a nightmare-plagued sleep. In the dream, Curt spent hours running and hiding from Matt and always the boy stayed just behind him. As he ran through the rooms, he saw the other children beneath their sheets but they were no longer hiding. The sheets above them were all stained through, bright red and without looking under them, Curt knew that the others were all dead.

Eventually, Curt became trapped in Paul's room and in desperation, he ducked under the sheet, hiding with a mutilated corpse. It looked as though it had been feasted upon by a horde of sharks, great chunks of flesh had been ripped from the boy, and the many teeth marks in his body were quite evident. They were so obvious and so perfectly preserved that it seemed that Paul's flesh might have been made from cheese.

Despite the horror of the corpse, Curt forced himself to snuggle close to it, until Matt had moved away into a different room. At that point, he was up and running, breathing in great gasps to clear his lungs of a rotten smell that lingered there. He made it to the kitchen only to be trapped again. Matt seemed to be coming from two directions at once and suddenly, the basement door came open and Curt could see the stairs heading down; they were draped in shadows.

In dream slow motion, he backed up as greater fear settled onto him, just then a shadow passed across the doorway and danced there and with the shadow came a deep cold that set him immediately shivering. Curt continued to back away until he reached the counter and then all in the basement and mudroom was a midnight black, but still a shadow played in it.

As was usual with dreams, he was without reason, and he found himself hiding within the cabinet where the extra food was stored. Unlike reality, it was filled with food. Lots of pink spam were stacked all about him and seeing it all, suddenly made his stomach growl and before he knew it, he had one opened. Now the meat looked as it always did, pink and slightly gelatinous, but when he dug his fork down into it, blood welled up around the tines. In disgust, he threw the can from him and it landed on its side so that the meat slid out, pink and bleeding, looking suddenly like processed human flesh. He gaped at it, feeling sick, and he wanted to flee from his hiding place in the cabinet, certain that all the spam would hold the same revulsion, but just then, Matt came in to the kitchen carrying somebody covered by a red stained sheet.

Somehow, from his hiding place in the cabinet, Curt was able to see that the person Matt laid upon the table was Amber. The older boy stared for a moment at the girl's disfigured body, before he stepped away out of Curt's vision. When he returned to the table, he carried a cookbook in one hand and a large knife in the other.

Curt wanted to run. Above all else, he wanted to run and not look back. Only in the dream, he seemed frozen in place and couldn't turn his head even as the cookbook came open to the page marked Goulash.

Matt brought the knife up.

2

Curt awoke with jarring suddenness, but he had been in the house long enough not to jump, or even twitch. Only his eyes moved, and though he wanted to take in great gulps of air, he didn't and forced himself to breathe just as he had been.

The ambient light slipping through the blanket told him it was only minutes after sunrise, and with care, Curt pulled back the covers. He quickly noted that it was actually later than that and heading to the window; he saw that stern grey clouds hid the sun. A ray of hope struck him and he prayed for rain, in fact, he begged God for rain.

But it didn't rain as he stood there peering up through the heavy shutters and after a while he decided he needed to check on Amber. She wasn't doing well. Her wrappings had come loose and the wounds had bled throughout the night, staining her covers a red and brown, the sight was horrible and he held back an audible gasp, but just barely.

"It h-h-hurts so b-b-bad," she said between trembling lips.

"Which one?" he asked, though he knew the hand with the missing fingers would hurt the worst and indeed, it was just that one that she held up. "Would you like me to wrap it tighter?" To this, she nodded while tears splashed down her face. She looked so much like a little kid then that it hurt his soul and he wanted so bad to fix her, to keep her from any pain, but there was little he could do.

When Curt turned to get more sheets, he saw Matt standing in the door and jumped back in alarm.

"You don't have to worry, Curt," Matt said casually. In his belt, the stake was thrust downward like a play sword. Curt knew better. That hunk of wood could kill him readily enough. "I have never slept better in my whole life than I did last night. And for that reason, you won't be punished until this evening, right before bedtime. Just think you won't have to do any chores."

"But it might rain," Curt whined, desperate to avoid his fate.

"So?" Matt whispered quietly.

"So...it might rain," Curt repeated. He felt a weird need to cry and before he knew it, he had to blink back the tears, but it was no use and they soon spilled out of him. Ashamed, he kept his back to Amber.

"I tell you what," Matt responded with a smirk on his face. "If a tornado comes along and rips down the front door, you can skip your punishment. How's that for a plan?" Matt started to leave but turned back. "Oh yeah, I've made breakfast."

After he left, Curt didn't turn about. He kept looking at the empty doorway for a while longer until he felt that he could speak without his voice breaking, "I'll get those sheets."

He was glad that Amber didn't say anything, but at the same time, he felt her eyes drilling into him. He knew she was going to ask about the plan when he got back. And she did.

"Tell me of your plan," she whispered.

In order to forestall her further he chose that moment to pull off her bandage in the quickest manner. "Oh! Uh...uh...uh." She groaned deep in her throat and tears bloomed in her eyes. For a long time he couldn't think past her poor hand. It bled freely as soon as the bandages had been removed and he was forced to pull her along to the bathroom so as not to make a bigger mess.

"Don't look," he commanded her. He wished he didn't have to look. Her hand had become swollen to twice its previous size and he didn't know what to do other than bandage it up again and this he did with as much force as he could without making her cry...too much. It still bled and he decided to hold on to it with all the pressure that she could bear. It took a long time to stop the bleeding.

During that time, she asked again about the plan. "I can't tell you...if Matt knew, or even suspected that you knew he would force the details from you and then..." He left off with purposeful vagueness.

"Please tell me that you'll do it today, ok."

"I can't tell you that either...the timing has to be perfect or we'll lose this chance forever and I don't think we'll get another opportunity." 'Can you eat?' he decided to switch over to their version of sign language. The mood of the house was very hard to judge since the death of Miss Feanor, and he felt it better to be safe than sorry.

"No. Not with Matt at the table. You're going to kill him, right? That's part of your plan?" She couldn't sign with her hands bandaged as they were.

He nodded and hoped that his eyes didn't give away the fear that he felt sinking into the pit of his stomach at the very idea.

3

'I will bring food up here,' he signed. She shook her head looking sick to her stomach. 'You need food! Remember, you tell me that?' he urged her.

To this she nodded, but with heavy reluctance. After giving her a very light kiss, he went to the kitchen, moving with great caution. He didn't trust Matt. Though Curt figured he knew how the attack would occur; even armed with his stake, Matt was a bit of a chicken and would likely find Amber and use her to get to Curt. It had worked well enough twice already and if Matt tried it again, Curt knew he'd end up calling the creature a third time.

Only Matt and Paul still sat at the table eating and Curt was outraged to see that they were eating his and Amber's food. After having only a single meal the day before, Curt wasn't in the mood to be picky and his need for food gave him courage. Looking as if he were going to start to whine about the injustice in front of him, Curt startled the two boys by grabbing the bowls with lightning quick moves and ran.

He ran without worrying about noise and thus was far up the stairs before Matt had made it to the first step. Curt slowed only enough to move quieter, but made it to the bathroom in plenty of time to lock the door in Matt's face. Thankfully Amber hadn't moved.

She didn't look like she had either the energy or the will to move, or to eat for that matter. She was so lethargic that it took him the better part of two hours to get all the food into her; in truth, the loss of time wasn't a big deal. He had nowhere to go and actually hoped that Matt waited out there for him. It would only dull his senses. When Amber finally finished, he waited a good long time to make sure it wouldn't come hurling up again and then decided to put her to bed. She looked terrible. How a girl as white as her could look any more pale was a mystery, but somehow she managed to pull it off. There were great dark blue circles beneath her eyes and her lips looked a very light shade of pink.

Curt worried for her—a thousand worries.

Matt wasn't lurking outside the bathroom, which was a good thing since Curt still had no clue how he was going to deal with the older boy, especially with Amber on his arm. She moved listlessly, and tottered enough that he had to hold her up, barely making it to her bed before she collapsed with a groan. The next six hours he spent in more worry. Amber slept and he worried.

He prayed for rain, but the clouds and the gods refused. His hands began to shake and his insides felt filled with a swarm of antsy butterflies. Even in his lungs, they swirled about keeping him from taking deep breaths. After a few hours, his legs began to jiggle. First one, then the other, back and forth uncontrollably. There would be no stopping this coming punishment, he decided. Hiding in the basement wouldn't work since he was sure that Matt could get Amber to scream her head off, what with her hands the way they were. Fighting the older boy seemed insane...

An idea popped into his head, what if Curt had a stake as well? A bigger one, perhaps the size of a small spear? The concept shot energy into him and Curt ducked beneath Amber's bed. It was dark, darker than he expected and Curt pulled his head from beneath the bed to look to the window. The sun was setting behind the clouds, there wouldn't be much time.

He crawled beneath the bed and began fighting the wood, first with his hands and when that didn't work then with his sock covered feet. However, the planks were thick and he couldn't budge them. Next, he slithered out and zipped quietly to his own room and dove beneath his own bed. This was where the original stake had come from and surely he could break off the rest of it. And likely he would've been right, if the plank was still there.

It was gone.

Just then, he felt something sharp jab him in the foot. Spinning under the bed he saw the sock covered feet of Matt, and there gently tapping on the wood with a tiny thunk, thunk, thunk, was a part of the frame of his bed. Curt crawled out from beneath his bed, well away from Matt, as if it would've mattered. In the older boy's hands was a long, sharp hunk of wood and on his face was a deadly smile.

"Dinner time."

4

Curt backed to the wall with his hands out. Cold dread smote him and suddenly he felt his throat tighten and amazingly, he was worried that he wouldn't even be able to call the monster. But after swallowing hard, he managed to breathe just enough to squeak out a few words.

"It's too early...please." The whine in his voice would have appalled him had he been thinking straight. However, he was in near panic mode and it was all he could do keep his bladder in check.

Matt laughed quietly, in fact so quietly that it was more just a moving smile than a laugh. "No, it's not the monster's dinner time yet, that'll be in about one hour. It's your dinner time and don't even think of being late...I'm awful hungry." With a sneer that might have been a smile, he left.

Amber was up by this time and moving down the hall, sluggishly. Curt came to greet her, she looked terrible, but he was in such a state of fear for himself that he barely noticed. Together they moved toward the kitchen, pathetically slow and solemn, like an old couple on the way to a funeral. The only consolation that Curt found to her wretched state was that she didn't ask him about his plan. He could no longer lie to her.

They got to kitchen only to find that half their dinners had been eaten already. Neither Curt nor Amber cared all that much, since neither had an appetite for more than a grain of rice, but they sat down at the table, perhaps out of habit. Curt was thirsty at least, and drank deeply from his water glass.

Through his twitch, Paul looked shocked to the core at Amber's injuries and with a sheepish cast to his face at having taken the food he slid over the plate that he had been feeding off of. Curt gave him a tiny smile and Paul smiled back.

This was his *Paul* that Curt looked upon. His friend whom he hadn't seen in days. It gave him a tiny glimmer, a feeling of life to see Paul again, whole and sane.

Sane, at least for the moment, yet that moment might last a little while since the pressure—the fear of the creature was squarely on Curt's shoulders. Paul left a minute later and gave Curt another small sad smile on his way out, it wasn't much, but it was something and it gave him another little boost. This feeling allowed him to eat and to feed Amber, who had become more and more listless. Curt only took a few bites and gave the rest to the girl, hoping to invigorate her, but it was not until she had drank off three tall glasses of water that any life came into to her. She used the energy to sneer at Matt. He sneered right back, fingering the edge of his new spear.

The opposing sneers did nothing to help Curt who was quickly losing the brief amount of energy he had left in him. A minute later and thirty minutes before his dinner date with the creature, Amber refused the last bite of spam. Still hungry, Curt had just put it in his mouth when he happened to glance over and saw the cookbooks lined up neat as you please on the counter. His dream came back to him suddenly, as he saw that the first cookbook was still marked in that one place, the recipe for Goulash.

Just then, the spam in his mouth took on the consistency of human flesh and feeling his gorge rising, he uncaringly spat it out onto the floor at Matt's feet. In his periphery, he saw the older boy coming alive in anger, but Curt had only eyes for the cookbook, while his mind recalled the dream in all of its intricate gory details: the pink spam that bled; hiding under Paul's sheets and snuggling next to his corpse; Amber's dead body on the table, but most of all, that damn cookbook. The same one that opened every time to the same disgusting recipe, Goulash.

Without warning, his body began to heave up his dinner, but Curt, knowing he needed the nutrients fought it, covering his mouth. Now his stomach started to hitch, and Amber moved closer, while Matt backed away and Curt angrily realized it was no use. He would lose his small dinner, possibly the only good part of his day, all because somebody decided to mark the most useless recipe imaginable. It was stew! Who needed a recipe for stew?

The first of his dinner came to his throat and he fought it back, but only barely. He tried to breathe deeply, hoping that would relax his churning stomach. This did nothing and he slowly felt the need to vomit rising even greater. His anger increased.

And why would you need to mark the page? He thought bitterly. If you've made stew once, would you ever need to go back to that one page to refresh your memory? Curt envisioned the page, just as it had fallen open that first day he arrived in the home and then he saw it again in his mind as it fell open only two days before when he had used the book to block the mudroom door.

His dinner rose once more, but he was so enthralled with the image coming to him that he found that he could ignore the need to vomit.

That page in the cookbook had been marked with a paperclip.

Chapter 32

Evening of the Morningstar

1

A paperclip. Just one, sat nestled in the book. Almost in disbelief, his eyes held fast to the barely visible rounded top edge of it, and he felt his mind turn slowly and clumsily, like a kangaroo walking, moving from anger and fear to something that seemed more like actual thinking.

And amazingly, between the great heavings of his stomach, a rudimentary plan came to him like a bolt of lightning. The pieces had been there all along, he just needed them to come together, and oddly, he had found them bound by a single paper clip. Yet it was a weak plan with gaping holes, and had he been in a comfortable position, in another foster home, he would've cast it aside in a second.

Unfortunately, his choices had dwindled to just this:

1) Incapacitate Matt, use him to distract the creature, 2) during that time, use the one paperclip to unlock the attic door, grab the keys from Miss Feanor's pocket, 3) use the car to smash down the garage door.

What could be easier? The thought almost made him smile.

He forced himself to grimace instead. The setting sun would be his greatest obstacle and he worried that each step in his plan would take far longer than he had time for, and now more than ever he wished there was a working clock in the house. He turned his head and covered his mouth as if his nausea were becoming too much, but in truth he took a long look at the window in the kitchen. The clouds had tricked him. First, they had held out the false hope of rain and now they hid the sunset. Already daylight was fast fading from the grey sky and he knew it was going to be dark sooner than he had first realized.

The creature would be coming up those stairs in fifteen minutes whether he called it or not. It was now or never.

Curt retched loudly, purposely, "Huuuagh!" and then he staggered up, toward Matt. The older boy retreated, holding the length of stick out in front of him, but Curt turned aside going to the counter instead and leaned there, trying his best to look sick, while his mind worked at a feverish pace. Breathing heavily, he placed his head on the counter as if the cool granite helped to control his heaving stomach, but in truth, he was trying to buy time.

He needed only a few seconds, perhaps just two.

The cookbook with the paperclip sat inches from his hand, unfortunately, Matt stood all too close and Curt dared not grab it with the boy right there. He hoped that Amber would distract the older boy in some way, but she didn't know anything about the plan yet and only stood as spectator at a show, wearing a look of disgust that was the equal to Matt's.

Seconds ticked by and still Matt just stood there. Curt swore to himself. He could only feign sickness for so long before Matt would suspect the ruse, so after a moment where nobody moved, he made one more attempt in Matt's direction.

"Huuuagh!"

This time he actually felt a small chunk of something come up, still it didn't matter. The larger boy stepped aside, but the wrong way, further into the kitchen. With his little act, Curt's momentum was toward the main hall and because it would seem odd to turn around, he continued on in that direction, holding his mouth. At the main stairs, he paused, bent over, and gave a bleary eye back. Thankfully, there was no sign Matt and what's more, he saw Amber slowly making her way toward him.

Excitement flooded through him and frantically he gestured to her. 'Hurry to the bathroom,' he motioned. She nodded tiredly.

Now instead of going up himself, he paused as his mind raced. He needed a weapon desperately. Something heavy...a chair? Too heavy and cumbersome. A table leg...good, but it'd make too much noise breaking off and besides he needed it right then, right that moment. It would have to be a makeshift weapon, like something you would find in prison...this thought led directly to another and suddenly his mind hit on something an ex-con had bragged to him once about.

Curt turned and went into the family room. What he wanted there were the two large brass kitten shaped bookends that sat on one of the shelves. They were heavy and once he placed them in a pillowcase, they would make a weapon of sorts. A terribly pathetic weapon, but he had no other choice.

He walked into the room expecting it to be empty, but instead he found both Paul and the mouse there. Paul was cleaning, hurriedly casting looks toward the window every few seconds, while the mouse appeared to be standing guard over the puzzle box again. Her back was to Curt as he entered and she seemed at first not to notice his presence and only reached up to caress the box gently. Paul saw him a second later and his face filled with alarm.

Curt gave him a quick smile, and acting as if he had every right to them, he headed for the brass bookends and picked them up, one in each hand.

'Hey!' Paul shook his head angrily; he was worried about being punished for not having his areas of responsibility in proper order.

Curt now faced another challenge to his ragged plan. By his own admission, Paul couldn't be trusted, yet Curt needed the boy's help badly. What he wanted, more than anything, was Paul's help with fighting Matt; together they could beat the older boy. However just seeing the boy's twitch begin to escalate, simply over the bookends made him realize that fighting was out of the question.

Paul began to gesture to him, but Curt didn't bother trying to translate. He was in a zone; his mind was far away, thinking in a blaze. Ideas came to him three, four at a time and each he discarded, seeing flaw after flaw. Seconds passed. Precious seconds that he would never be able to get back and now Paul stopped his futile motions.

"Hey?" Paul whispered with sudden concern and then touched Curt on the arm. Curt looked up, but not at the blonde boy, but past him. Paul's fingers had been cold on his arm. They had reminded Curt of his nightmare and how cold Paul's dead body had been under the covers. This triggered a new idea.

"We're escaping...tonight," Curt whispered. "If you want to come, get up the bathroom now."

"What?" Paul's face was heavy with indecision.

"We'll all be dead in a week..." Curt started to say, but the mouse cut him off.

"We're escaping...tonight," she whispered in his ear and he jumped in fright, as did Paul. The girl had slipped up close while his attention had been diverted and her whisper had sent a jolt of electricity straight through him. With his heart hammering in his thin chest, Curt turned to look at the girl.

"We're escaping...tonight," she whispered again. Her eyes started to spin about the room. "We're escaping...tonight," she repeated a third time.

Curt gave her an intense look, wondering how much of this she understood. Normally, he would've thought she comprehended only a little of what she had heard, but in her hands, she held her cat puzzle box. That alone gave him pause.

"We're escaping...tonight," she whispered to him. Now Curt began to feel a touch of panic sliding over the constant thrum of fear within him. She couldn't go around saying that, it would make Matt even more difficult to handle.

"Curt is in the bathroom," he whispered to her. "Curt is in the bathroom. Curt is in the bathroom." Her head pointed toward the ceiling as if she could look through the intervening walls and see him there. "Curt is in the bathroom," he said a last time and then gave her a little shove toward the doorway and like a robot she headed off in that direction and as soon as she did, Curt grabbed Paul's hands.

"If you want to come with us, get to the bathroom quick."

Time seemed to be slipping away and Curt couldn't wait any longer for a decision from Paul. Taking the brass kittens, he scootched past a bewildered looking mouse and headed up the stairs hoping not to run into Matt. Thankfully, the upstairs hall was deserted and even better, Amber had made it to the bathroom. She sat on the white tiled floor looking miserable.

She rocked gently, holding her wrapped hands to her chest and as Curt neared, he saw tears coming down her cheeks. When she saw him sliding into the room her tears became more intense.

"My hands...they hurt so much," she said in obvious misery.

Wishing he had more than a second to console her, he bent down and kissed her head. "I know. I'm so sorry, but Matt could be up here any second."

She nodded in understanding, and then her eyes widened, Curt knew that someone was behind him and turned with a heavy heart. It was only Paul and he sighed in relief at the blonde boy.

"Get in here," Curt whispered urgently and when Paul had entered, Curt shut the door. "Your part of the plan is very simple," he said to them. "Stay in here, lock the door and whatever you do, don't talk to Matt. He's going to say anything to get you to open the door, but whatever you do, don't open it and don't say anything. Just sit tight."

"What about..." Paul started to say, and Curt cut him off fast.

"He could be here any second!" Curt snapped. "Now either sit in here and be quiet or go hide in your bed and pray the creature doesn't come for you next."

Paul took a step back. "I'm sorry...I'll stay here. I want to escape too. Ok? Please, take me with you." His voice shook with fear at the thought of being left behind.

"Then lock the door behind me and keep quiet," Curt whispered and stepped out into the hallway, avoiding the first two floorboards, which had small but obvious squeaks to them. In his right hand, he hefted one of the brass bookends, ready to throw it if Matt happened to be there. But the older boy was nowhere in sight and for just a moment, Curt wondered if Matt was coming at all. Perhaps he had a change of heart, he mused, feeling a bit of hope.

Despite the tension that ran through his slim young body, Curt smiled at his own foolish thought. Matt would show up all right. He would never take the chance of being punished so soon after his last. And that there'd be a punishment that night, there was no doubt in Curt's mind. Even if Matt had a change of heart and the house was in perfect shape, spotless and beautiful, the creature would come. Whenever Curt touched the wall, he could feel the beast down in the pits it had dug for itself beneath the basement. It had become accustomed to the taste of flesh and it wanted more.

Oddly, upon thinking these morbid thoughts, Curt had another queer thrill run through him. It was as if he stood alone against the unnatural power of the house, against the terrifying desires of the creature and against the unrelenting cruelty of a young man. The odds were terrible, but he was at least doing *something* and it put a charge into him and he smirked, suddenly sure that he would find away to prevail, but then a little voice within him spoke up.

'What about Mr. Gallarti? What about the day you came here? Weren't you feeling the same way?' the voice asked.

That was true enough, he had been feeling very confident that day, even when he'd been caught by the janitor, he had been quite certain he would get away. But that was the way it was supposed to be. A thief had to be cocky and confident and in control of his fear, not the other way around. For too long in the house, he had let his fear control him. Not to the extent that it controlled the others in the home, but still far too much.

However, he decided, that way of thinking was ending...starting now. With that thought, Curt made a quick dash across the hall to Paul's room and before entering it, he cast a glance down toward Matt's room and the backstairs. There was no one about.

He climbed into the bed, covering himself over. Under the sheets, he worked quickly, stripping off the pillowcase and putting the two heavy brass kittens in place of the pillow. He then began twisting the pillowcase tighter, to keep the bookends from moving about and clanking together.

But he stopped halfway through when he heard a small sound. Freezing in place, he strained to catch the noise again and sure enough, it grew louder. The mouse, perhaps due to her mental state, was not very quiet when she moved and what's more, she whispered as she walked.

"We're escaping...tonight," she murmured as she came up the stairs. He could hear her then go the bathroom door. "We're escaping...tonight," she said to it.

Amazingly, she then went to Paul's door and repeated the words before moving off down the hall out of earshot. Curt had to stifle a scream of anger. Even if Matt wasn't nearby to hear the girl, the house certainly did and the word *escape* always got its attention and not in a good way.

After a moment, he went limp, feeling frazzled, wondering if he would have the energy to fight Matt. It turned out it was a good thing that he went limp because a second later: Wwhhhhhh.

Paul's door came open and Matt entered the room.

2

When Matt slid in, he seemed to bring with him a malignant presence, a foul air.

It made Curt's skin crawl, but by long practice, he remained limp under the blankets. Matt moved about the room hurriedly making more noise than usual and Curt heard a little grunt as he looked under the bed. He left a moment later. The search had been perfunctory at best and it made Curt smile. Matt was seeing what he had expected to see...what Curt wanted him to see.

Curt waited, listening. Shockingly, he actually heard Matt dashing from room to room. Clearly, the older boy had realized that he had misjudged the time as well and was cutting it very close.

Finally, Curt heard Matt at the bathroom door.

"You don't think hiding in there is going to save you from the monster?" he asked in a loud whisper.

Silence greeted this. Excellent, thought Curt and gently pulled back the covers. Fear smote him like an arrow in his stomach, the light trickling in from the outside was markedly less than it had been only a few minutes before. He was fast running out of time.

"Come on out, Amber," Matt drawled in what he considered a nice voice. "There's no need for you getting punished two nights in a row."

As Matt spoke, Curt used the sound of his voice to cover any noise that he might make as he slipped out of bed and made his way to the door. He would have one chance now. The next time Matt spoke, Curt would have to make his move, there was simply no more time left.

"Really? The silent treatment?" Matt said with an air of superiority as if he were talking to a couple of six year olds. "Amber, please. He's only using you so he won't..."

The thief slipped around the door and charged at Matt. Curt moved in complete silence, yet despite that, he moved very fast and saw that he had a chance to hit the older boy nearly from behind. Matt leaned against the door as if without a care, but at the last moment, he caught sight of the motion coming toward him.

He spun with astonishing swiftness, bringing the homemade spear to bear on Curt's chest. In a tenth of a second, the tables had turned on Curt. No longer did he have the upper hand with surprise, and now he faced a foe who was not only bigger, stronger, and faster, but one who had beaten him at every turn and in every way. In everything that Curt excelled at, Matt was simply better.

Even in his choice of weapons. The plank of wood that he carried, had a large split at the top that formed a very sharp point, but it was also capable as a defensive weapon as well. It was easy to handle, while Curt's was a clumsy weapon at best.

The weighted pillowcase could only be used offensively and worse, within the narrow confines of the hallway it could only be used one way. He would have to bring it up and back, before swinging it from over the top of his head. That was it. There was no other way to attack with it.

But despite all of his shortcoming and his weapon's inadequacies, Curt attacked. He had no other choice.

He brought the slow, unwieldy weapon up, feeling that his entire midsection was open to attack from Matt's spear—and indeed it was. Matt could have danced forward and sunk the sharp edge deep into him, before the smaller boy was half way through getting his weapon around, but for a single reason he didn't.

The reason was clear on his face, which was lit with a dreadful glee; Matt wanted to play with his food before he ate it. With all the confidence in the world and with the speed of a viper, Matt brought the flat of his spear up to block the blow that he had seen coming a mile away.

But Matt, as good as he was compared to Curt, was not trained to fight against someone wielding a makeshift Morningstar. His very quickness proved his undoing, as he didn't reckon with the slight lag in time, as Curt's hands, at the light end, sped faster than the rest of the ungainly weapon. The pillowcase struck the spear midline, and folded over it easily, which sent the brass kittens at the end of the pillowcase, hurtling even faster into Matt's face. Matt was down before he had a chance to be surprised.

For a moment, Curt stood there in shock, disbelieving that he had actually knocked the older boy out. But the moment was quite short lived. The air in the hallway became instantly charged with the anger of the house and Curt had the disquieting feeling that the house knew what was going on.

Stepping to the bathroom, he hissed, "Open the door!" But no sound came from the other side. His face quickly went red. "It's me, Curt. Open the door before the damn creature comes!"

Now the door swung open, revealing a frightened looking Paul. It seemed that Paul had regressed in age over the last few minutes, he looked younger, almost a child.

"Look what he did." There was awe in his voice. Curt was just about to begin issuing orders when Paul spoke again, "I know. I think we should get back to bed quick...it's getting close to sundown... I know I feel it too."

Curt felt his head spin. In his fear and stress, Paul had slipped beneath his many personalities; it couldn't have come at a worse time. Curt looked at Amber and all she could do was shrug.

"He was coming apart in here," she whispered. "I thought for sure Matt heard him, he kept whispering to himself and was getting louder and louder."

Curt grabbed his hair in frustration. He needed someone to throw Matt into the basement, before he came awake again and before the creature ventured forth, either of which could happen at any moment.

"Paul!" Curt decided to give the insane boy at least one shot. "Drag Matt down to the basement door. I need you to tie him up before you roll him..."

"We're not going down there," Paul said with a tone of nastiness. Curt had no time for this. In fact, none of them had time. He knelt down and picked up the spear.

"Move the body to the basement. I'm not going to ask again." Curt's face had become hard with resolution and he advanced slowly on Paul, keeping the spear dead set on the boy's throat.

"Ok...ok," Paul squeaked and then reached down and began pulling the larger boy along.

Turning to Amber, Curt ordered, "Grab some sheets, make him do his best to tie him up and put a pillowcase over Matt's face. It's not right that he sees what's down there."

Amber turned a light green at her orders but went to the bathroom and began grabbing sheets with her teeth and laying them over her better hand, the right one. For a second, Curt wanted to help her, but regrettably his next task needed every second they had left to them and probably even more than that.

Heedless of the noise he made, Curt ran down the main stairs and then to the kitchen. The mudroom door began opening, but he paid it no mind. Instead, he went to the cookbooks and snatched up the one with the recipe for Goulash and like magic, it laid itself open right to the correct page. Grabbing the paperclip he then dashed to the basement door, which had opened as well. It billowed wet disgusting air coating him in a second. Without bothering to look into the black depths, he calmly shut the door and then went to the mudroom door and did the same thing. He turned on his heel and dashed to the backstairs and there was Paul, huffing and puffing, pulling the limp form of Matt along.

"Paul," Curt whispered, "Throw some water on his face before you roll him down there, I think him being awake might buy us some more time."

Paul blanched at his orders, but Curt couldn't wait longer and ran for the main stairs, bending at the paper clip as he did. This was to be the trickiest part of the operation. It had taken him over thirty minutes to pick the lock to the attic the last time, now he'd be lucky if he had five.

Chapter 33

The Thief, The Runaways, and The Dead

1

Curt worked the paperclip, bending it back and forth as quickly as he could. His goal was to snap off a third of it, and this he would then re-bend, using it as the lever to turn the lock assembly. It broke off in seconds and Curt didn't know whether to be happy or worried over this. He decided to worry. The paperclip was likely old and brittle with age. Not a good thing.

While he worried, he first bent the small piece into a U shape and then began to work on the larger one. This he tried to fashion into a series of V shaped waves ending in a very stiff U, which would act as the handle of his 'key'. He worked quickly, but a minute passed, and still he had only made two waves in the metal.

Time seemed to be flying and after another minute, with sweat running into his eyes, he heard the first scream, it was as if it shook the very floor upon which he knelt. It was Amber.

His hands went numb at the sound and he stopped working on the paperclip. His heart seemed to break inside his chest. For a few seconds his emotions became scrambled and his mind was all confusion. A part of him wanted to run to her, to battle the creature if need be, yet to do so would mean to give up on their one chance at escape.

He was completely torn at what to do, but then he realized there hadn't been a second scream. Either she had died or had been incapacitated in the time it took to draw a breath, or she had screamed at the sight of something. Something horrible. Curt guessed at what she screamed at and it sent a long wave of shivers coursing just below his flesh. She would have to deal with the sight of the ghost of Mrs. Havacheck on her own.

With a quick swipe of his sleeve along his eyes, he gave up on bending the paperclip and began working it into the lock. Back and forth, up and down he sent his makeshift pick against the pins. With each attempt, he gave the U shaped piece a little tug to the right, but by the time Matt came alive, shrieking in the greatest pain, Curt still hadn't made any headway.

It sounded like Matt was being eaten alive.

It was a horrifying to hear and soon Curt wept as he worked the pick back and forth.

Something was wrong, or more likely he wasn't doing something right. He tried to recall what he had done that first time, only the memory wasn't clear. Certainly, he had the U shape in right...

Just then, he heard feet running up the stairs. With a terrified glance over his shoulder, he saw it was Amber.

"Hurry! I don't think Matt will last much longer!" she screamed. "The house knows! It knows!"

"What? What does it know?"

"That we are trying to run away!" she wailed at him. Her face shone brightly with tears and he could feel his own coming even more freely now as well, dribbling off his chin.

"Get back down there! Put stuff in front of the basement door!" he screamed at her and bent to his lock.

With a deep breath, he tried his best to calm himself, and was surprised that he felt suddenly a slight bit better. His hands however had not yet got the message and they shook as he brought them up to the lock.

"The pins are old," he murmured to the lock. "As are the little springs beneath them. By now they want to be done with this fiddling." Curt put the pick and driver into the lock. The U shaped driver, he kept turned to the right, while the pick, he began to work back and forth, raking it over the pins in a sawing motion. "You are getting tired of this up and down. You just..."

The lock turned.

Just as when he had defeated Matt, for a second he couldn't believe what he had done.

But again, that was for only a second, and with a surge of strength he yanked open the door and charged up the stairs into the attic.

He was halfway up, when the house realized where he was going and perhaps what he was up to, and then the lights went out. Curt stopped as fear and uncertainty held him. A second later, the door behind him slammed shut, enclosing his world in complete darkness.

2

Now absolute terror washed over him. He tried to panic and run, but his mind was in such a state that he didn't know quite where up or down was. So instead of running, he gripped the rails as if his life depended on it. At first, he could hear nothing except the pounding of his heart and his own ragged breathing, but gradually, he came to hear the faint cries of Matt.

For some odd reason they calmed him a little, perhaps because they added context to the darkness and allowed him to orient on the sound so that he had an idea where he was, but after only a few moments, the cries grew quieter and as they did, Curt felt his panic rising once again.

"Hurry! I don't think Matt will last much longer!"
Amber's words of a minute or two previous came back to
him, as an echo in his mind. How much time had elapsed
since Matt went into the basement? Four minutes? Five, six?

There was really no way to know. But it sure wasn't very
long.

He had to move. Wearing an invisible grimace, he forced
himself upwards, but ran out of stairs quickly and now it was
only a matter of finding his way through a maze of junk in
complete darkness. But Curt had an impressive mind, and
recalled minute details of the layout of the attic.

His left hand found the partially destroyed upright
piano... now he felt the dresser that had no drawers, and
within half a minute, he discovered the beds of his two
murder victims. His hand coming down unpleasantly on an
arm or a leg; he snatched it back in an instant, feeling
revulsion. Unfortunately, that little movement caused him to
become disoriented in the dark and he couldn't recall which
way it was that he faced. He had to put his hands out once
more and in a second, he found the bed and the body part
again.

"Uhhhg," he groaned aloud.

Moving around the bed, toward where he hoped Miss
Feanor's body lay he came aware that the house was once
more silent as the dead littering the attic. No longer could he
hear even a sniffle coming from Matt, three floors below him
and he suddenly realized that he was too late. The creature
would be coming very soon.

He hurried forward, his hands running along half remembered hunks of furniture and suddenly his right foot struck something. It wobbled slightly and he pulled back. Why he did this he had no idea, but it was at this moment, he decided to sniff the air. It wasn't that bad. Curt had half expected the attic to smell similar to the terrible stench coming from the basement, and that he would inhale the rotting smell of spoiled meat, but the air up there was more stale than anything else.

Knowing that he was out of time, he knelt quickly and found the legs of Miss Feanor in the dark. They seemed much bigger under his touch than he had remembered, as if she had swelled since her death. He tried and failed not to picture her face, bloated huge and green, and for that second, he felt glad that it was pitch black in the attic. His hands traced their way up her legs until he found her pockets, but unfortunately, she lay face down and the keys weren't in either of the back ones.

He rolled her over.

"Huuuuahh..."

The noise came from the body and Curt jumped back in alarm, smashing his head against something hard behind him. The body was rotting from the inside out and the smell was bad, as well as, indescribable. It was atrocious and he had to fight a great nausea building in him just to crawl forward to get the keys. Holding his breath, his wildly shaking hands went first to one pocket and with a growing alarm, to the other, but the keys weren't in either.

Panic threaten to overrun his mind and he fought back with a single idea: *Check again*. Her pants were tight over her bloated thighs and he forced his small hands deeper into her pockets and was rewarded a moment later by the feel of metal, but it was a nightmare of a struggle to squirm his hand out again.

As he pulled his hand free, the dead body spoke once more in its horrible, ghastly language, "Ehhhhh..."

Vomit came up this time, right to the top of his throat.

"Oh God!" he groaned, desperately trying not to lose his dinner as he groped in the dark. With one hand covering his mouth, he staggered into the maze and just as he blundered against the roll top desk that marked which way he needed to go, pandemonium broke out down stairs.

Layered screams of panic tore through the air, and then came a rumbling that at first confused him, until he realized, what he was hearing were the other children running for their lives.

The creature was loose.

It dawned on him then just how trapped he was up in the attic and with growing terror he sped through the maze, only to find that he was lost. Nothing seemed to conform itself to a shape that he recognized. Every box felt the same and each piece of furniture was so much like the last so that he wondered if he was going in little circles.

The mayhem below seemed to disperse and grow faint except for a single set of footsteps that grew clearer and clearer as the seconds hurried by. They were particularly heavy and they raced steadily toward the attic.

Curt tried to hurry, to make it to the stairs before the creature could, however he was completely turned around and just then, he realized with certainty there was no way he would make it out of the attic alive. Without warning, he began to blubber. He was so afraid.

A second later, there came an odd scrambling sound as if claws on wood and then the attic door burst open. Immediately light from the second floor hallway flowed up to greet Curt and in a flash, he saw exactly where he was. But it would do him little good since the creature was between him and the one exit out.

Curt ducked down, sliding along the floor to a better position, well to the right of the main part of the maze. He didn't know if the creature could see or hear or even smell, but it was instinctual for the little thief to hide and it was one thing that he was very good at. The creature came up the stairs and paused at the top and from where he crouched, Curt could see part of the grey of its shifting mass. It turned in his direction gliding around an old bed frame. A lead ball of fear suddenly dropped into Curt's stomach.

In this corner of the attic, there were few choices to move, but Curt decided not to move just yet. Instead, his hand closed upon a shard of wood, a small chunk that had broken away from some long forgotten piece of furniture. He threw it further into the attic, toward where the corpses lay, and like a dog, the creature turned at the sound and in a heartbeat began racing in that direction. As soon as it did, Curt was off, keeping low, sliding along on his knees heading for the stairs, but just as he came up to them he stopped and shied back.

The thing from the basement had come out and was now floating at the top of the stairs.

3

It was a horror far beyond that of the creature, yet in some ways they resembled each other. It was nearly fully formed and Curt could see that it had that same blackened, scabbed over skin as the creature, but though it had far more of a body, it appeared as if it were still in the process of decaying. Even as he looked upon it, a great slough of skin and hair slid from its head, dropping to the floor with a sick wet splatter.

But nothing could compare to its eyes. They were the eyes of a demon. There was simply no humanity left in them and they were black. Deep, deep black, as if they went on into its skull forever. Curt couldn't look into those eyes for more than a second before he turned away. Those eyes were unreal, and shook the foundation of his thinking so much that he literally ran his hands over the skin of his arms just to prove that he still existed.

That was what this thing ultimately wanted, not only for him to die, but for him to cease to exist on a much more basic level. It wanted his soul.

Behind him, Curt heard a sudden movement and he knew without having to turn that the creature was now alerted to his presence. He was trapped. In front of him was the thing, the demon thing. Behind was the creature, which began running at him, twisting through the maze at a great speed.

Somehow, perhaps as a way to save his soul, the thief in him took over. There was only one-way out and that was the stairs, and so that was the direction he would take, demon or no demon. In a flash, Curt charged at the thing, knowing that it would be slow to move. He had seen it before and each time it had moved almost leisurely. This was no different.

He saw an old chair near to the stairs and jumping on it in midstride he leapt to the side of the ghost of Mrs. Havacheck. Missing it by inches, he came down on the stairs awkwardly, fell, rolled down six or seven and then was up again, leaping the last few, heedless of any pain. The door to the second floor began to shut in front of him and instead of trying to force it open, he slid to his left, clearing it just as it closed.

"Everyone! Run to the garage!" He screamed at the top of his lungs as he raced down the hallway toward the backstairs. Behind him, he heard again that weird clawing and he could picture the creature at the attic door trying to force its way out. Curt didn't look back.

This was a good thing too or he would have run full into the mouse who stepped out of her room just ahead of him.

"Come on! Run!" He grabbed her hand without breaking stride, dragging her along. In a second however, he wished that he could let her go. She pulled against him, slowing him down. But he couldn't let go, to do so would be the same as murder, and unlike Matt, who was guilty as sin, she was innocent.

However as they reached the stairs, she took matters into her own hand, literally. With a force he didn't know she had in her, she yanked her hand out of his, almost toppling them both. She turned and ran back, heading toward the great thumping footsteps of the creature charging down the hall.

"Beth! Come back!" He called after her. But he didn't wait to see if she would, waiting was now a luxury that would cost him lives and pain. Instead, he spun about and jumped down the stairs like a gazelle, five at a time. When he gained the kitchen, the first thing he saw was Amber and Paul fighting against the door to the garage as if a large invisible man stood on the other side and was slowly closing it upon them.

Curt took only a single step forward when a scream shredded the air behind him. Beth! He froze for a moment, not in indecision, but in guilt.

"Hurry!" Paul grunted, his skinny arms quivering with the effort to hold the door open.

Curt's head snapped back to the boy and without the need for further encouragement, he raced to the door, and threw himself against it, straining with all his might. It barely budged, and it was not until he got his legs under him and drove with his thighs that he was able to help push it open enough to get through.

"Go, Amber," he cried out. She wasn't much help in keeping the door open. Both of the bandages on her hands were soaked through with blood and her arms were shining bright red. She darted through the crack and ran for the car.

Now Curt turned to yell to Paul, but his eyes caught a sight that held him. The basement door stood open and the light was on. It was a cheery warm white light and it cast a nostalgic glow upon the remains of Matt. From where Curt stood, only a few feet from the basement door, he could look down the stairs and see Matt's body, littering the steps. Bitten through and dismembered; it was torn apart as if by pack of wild dogs.

His blood, fresh and wet looking coated the walls of the basement. It ran down them in sheets and in rivers and also little trickles—an impossible amount of blood, or so it seemed to Curt. The walls that this fresh bright red blood dripped down were an awful brown/black. It was the color of old blood. There were layers and layer of this old coagulated blood, and Curt knew in his heart that the blood went deep into the wood, right to the core of the house.

At the sight, his legs wobbled a moment and then gave out. He half fell, half slid into the garage.

"Wait, what about Beth?" Paul gasped as the door closed upon him with relentless force.

Picking himself up, Curt hurried to the driver's side door, yelling over his shoulder, "Leave her! She wouldn't come. I tried, but she ran." It was all the explanation he had time for.

Jumping into the car, he noticed as if they were someone else's that his hands shook to the point they were almost beyond control. Taking the key to the car in both of them, he fed it into the ignition, and with his foot heavy on the pedal, roared the engine to life.

Paul was still at the door, and Curt noticed just then that the blonde boy bled from a large wound on one side of his face, it was gaping, and torn looking, but it didn't hold Curt's attention for a fraction of a second. But what did, was that Curt also noticed what a handsome brave looking boy Paul was. His awful tic had completely disappeared and what's more, for the first time, Paul's face was unblemished by the haunting of fear.

Just that little thing caused Curt to lose a second, but it was worth it to him. To see Paul as he was truly meant to be, striking, perhaps even beautiful and courageous to the point of being heroic, was well worth the loss of that second.

But Curt could lose no more.

With shaking hands, he yanked the transmission into reverse and gunned the car backwards.

"Oh God!" Amber screamed just before they struck the garage door. The door buckled and the two kids were thrown back and forth. Amber shrieked in pain, but Curtis barely heard. He looked around and could see that he had crumpled the door, but that it still held. He threw the car into drive, and it leapt forward out of his control, too late did his foot find the brake.

They slammed into the wall, sending them banging hard into the front console. Amber cried out in misery again. There was no time for anything gentle now.

"Forget her, Paul!" Curt screamed at the top of his lungs for he saw that Paul still struggled against the door. The blonde boy, gritting his teeth with effort, shook his head resolutely.

"Damn it!" Curt worked the transmission angrily, and sent the car flying backwards a second time. They crashed with what sounded like a great shriek of metal and the door bent well over, practically in half and Curt knew that it would take only one more good shot to bring it down.

Not wanting to crash going forward again, Curt found the brake before he moved the transmission to drive and as an added precaution, he saw the little sun symbol on the dash and pulled the knob toward him.

There in the sudden glare of the headlights, Curt saw that the creature had given up on whatever it was doing to the mouse and had come full into the garage and now it had a hold of Paul. Out of the grey mist of the thing, huge scabbed over arms, which ended with great-clawed fingers held Paul by the face and chest. Curt watched in horror as the creature pulled Paul's head back. A moment later, a tremendous mouth, lined with razor sharp teeth formed in the mist and before Curt could think, the creature sunk his teeth into the side of Paul's neck.

"Paul!" Curt screamed in agony for his friend.

At the sound, the creature tore its head up and an immense gout of blood shot up from the wound in Paul's neck. Somehow still alive, the boy staggered away from the creature. He took a few steps into the narrow garage and stopped directly between Curt's headlights.

"No, no, no." Next to him in the car, Amber wept and pleaded.

Now Curt was at an impasse. He couldn't go forward with Paul only eight or nine feet in front of him and he couldn't go back, the garage door was still too much of an obstacle. And he most definitely couldn't stay where he was. He felt trapped once again.

But sadly, the creature helped Curt. Its bloodlust was too strong to be ignored and it jumped forward and latched itself once more to Paul, its long teeth tearing open the boy's shoulder. With one great twist of its newly formed neck it practically tore off the boy's arm.

Curt saw that Paul would die right there in front of him, only a few feet from freedom and Curt knew that his soul would go to the house. Deliberately, he pulled his foot off the brake and stamped it with all his force onto the gas. The car shot forward and took both Paul and the creature in the midsection. Curt drove straight and hard for the wall in front of him, and with the greatest crunch yet, slammed into it.

With a loud sob, he yanked the transmission into reverse and sent the car careening backwards. The garage door seemed to explode with the impact—pieces of it flew everywhere, but in a moment, the car was clear of the house and continued to drive backwards until it hit a large bush.

In front of him, the headlights picked out the creature. It looked as though the weight and velocity of the car had sent it partially into the wall. Its scabbed over arms waved feebly, for a few moments and then it seemed to dissolve into its mist and was sucked back into the house. Of Paul, there was no sign.

For a few seconds, Curt sat breathing hard, letting his tears come unchecked, while his hands continued to shake. He couldn't understand what happened to Paul. Next to him Amber wept, and bled. Her face ran freely with blood in a number of places. She looked at him in confusion. Against his better judgment, he hopped out of the car.

"Where are you going?" Amber asked with pitiful fear in her still very quiet voice.

He didn't answer, but instead went to the front of the car not expecting the shock that awaited him. Paul's body was there. It seemed to have been fused to the front of the car.

"Oh God!" Curt rushed to the boy and gently pulled him back away from the car. Paul's eyes stared up at the night, but were blank and unseeing. "Oh God," Curt said a second time and began to cry hard. He put his head to Paul's chest and held him tight and there beneath his ear, Curt heard a heartbeat.

It was very faint, yet still definitely a beat. Curt laid the boy down and again listened, however as he did, Paul's heart gave only a few more weak thumps and then ceased all together. He was dead. But he didn't die in the house. And he didn't die being torn apart and eaten by the creature.

That was something. It wasn't much, but Curt held onto it. The house hadn't taken Paul.

"Curt!" Amber screamed his name in horror.

His head snapped up and fear shot through him at Amber's cry. In the garage something moved. A shadowy figure stepped from the kitchen door and walked brazenly forward. Curt jumped up and began backing to the car door, but stopped when he saw who it was.

It was the mouse. In her hands, she held her cat puzzle box, it was stained with blood and flesh drops rained down upon it from a nasty would high up on her left arm. She didn't seem to notice it and Curt could only stare at her completely bewildered.

"We're escaping...tonight," she whispered as she came up to him. Ignoring the body of Paul, she calmly got into the back seat of the car and buckled her seat belt.

Curt shook his head again in amazement and then went to Paul. It took some effort, but finally he got the boy's body into the car and then with more care than he had shown previously, he drove away.

"We're escaping...tonight," the mouse whispered.

Epilogue-22 Days later

The Return of The Thief

"This isn't how you said it would be," Dale Norby whined. The boy sitting next to Dale with the wild tangle of curly brown hair simply looked at him with steady blue eyes. "You said we was only going to take the truck," Dale continued, for some reason he felt unnerved by the boy.

"You need to listen closer next time," the boy answered in his usual quiet manner. "I told you that I would pay you to move the truck and to park it where and when I said to. This is where I want it parked; now if you are going to hit one of the walls, make sure it is the one on the left, closest to the house."

Dale looked in his rear view mirror at the fine suburban house. The truck would most definitely hit one of the walls and the ceiling as well.

"No! No, I won't! This thing will blow up, if I hit anything." The smell of gasoline in the cab of the truck was very strong; it was making him quite nervous.

"First off, the fuel truck is full and so it probably won't explode," the boy replied. "It's when they're empty, you gotta watch out. It's because there's a buildup of gasses in the chamber and any spark could set it off...I looked into this. However, that being said, it will burn. I'll admit that." Smiling grimly at this the boy continued, "Now secondly, and I think you better put on your good listening ears for this...my friends won't be too happy with you, if you consider backing out."

The boy nodded, indicating one of three cars that had accompanied them. The other two were stationed further up the road, their occupants acting as lookouts.

Dale's guts churned at this.

Peter Meredith

When the boy had come to him with the job offer two days previous, he hadn't mentioned any friends coming along, nor had he mentioned that it was a fuel truck they were going to steal, and he certainly hadn't said anything about crashing it into a home.

"I...I don't know...I'm still on parole," Dale's voice sounded shrill even to himself, while the boy spoke with the quiet authority of a man.

"I know. That's why we agreed on a thousand dollars and not a hundred." The boy slipped a large wad of cash from his pocket; many of the bills looked crumpled as if he had just pulled them from a piggy bank. "Now, I took all the risk getting the keys, and you've done half your job, but in order to get paid you'll need to finish. All you have to do is back it up good and hard. And if you don't mind getting on with it, I've got people waiting on me."

Dale looked a long time at the money. He had needs.

Ten minutes later the flames were a hundred of feet in the air and the pall of black smoke, invisible in the night sky, was far higher. Dale watched as they drove away, unable to take his eyes from the spectacle, but the boy...he refused to look back.

The end.

*

Author's note:

Thank you for reading, The Punished. Just a small note; my wife and I were foster care parents and over the years, a total of 56 children came through our doors. None were eaten and very few bitten. If you enjoyed this book, please consider leaving a kind review on Amazon and perhaps on your Facebook page. The review is the most practical and inexpensive form of advertisement an independent author has available in order to get his work known. Thanks in advance,

Peter Meredith

For more spine tingling chills may I suggest The Trilogy of The Void:

The first book in the series, *The Horror of the Sha*de was inspired by one of the paranormal events that I've been connected with. Quite simply it was a two second ghost sighting, witnessed by me and two of my brothers. So how is that extrapolated into a trilogy? Step one: Remove me and my two brothers. Step two: Change the ghost to a demon, add a hot, but diabolical witch. Throw in a hunky seventeen-year old and his hell-powered schizophrenic sister and you're in business. Oh, I forgot to mention there will also be: Gypsies, exorcisms, blood, bullets, a nice sprinkling of sex, sin, murder, and a couple of trips into the wonderful vacation spot known as Hell...and did I mention sex? Right, check that off the list. Step three: Churn these all up into non-stop action, until you realize what you have is nothing more than a family in dire peril. What is this story about? What every story is about: people. People in love, people in danger, people fighting for their very souls.

Peter Meredith

Fictional works by Peter Meredith:

A Perfect America
The Sacrificial Daughter
The Horror of the Shade Trilogy of the Void 1
An Illusion of Hell Trilogy of the Void 2
Hell Blade Trilogy of the Void 3
The Punished
Sprite
The Feylands: A Hidden Lands Novel
The Sun King: A Hidden Lands Novel
The Sun Queen: A Hidden Lands Novel
The Apocalypse: The Undead World Novel 1
The Apocalypse Survivors: The Undead World Novel 2
The Apocalypse Outcasts: The Undead World Novel 3
The Apocalypse Fugitives: The Undead World Novel 4
Pen(Novella)
A Sliver of Perfection (Novella)
The Haunting At Red Feathers(Short Story)
The Haunting On Colonel's Row(Short Story)
The Drawer(Short Story)
The Eyes in the Storm(Short Story)